BAYONETS ALONG

THE BORDER

JOHN WILCOX

Allison & Busby Limited
12 Fitzroy Mews
London W1T 6DW
www.allisonandbusby.com

First published in Great Britain by Allison & Busby in 2014.
This paperback edition published by Allison & Busby in 2014.

A CIP catalogue record for this book is available from
the British Library.

10 9 8 7 6 5 4 3 2 1

ISBN 978-0-7490-1697-5

Typeset in 10.5/15.5 pt Sabon by
Allison & Busby Ltd.

The paper used for this Allison & Busby publication
has been produced from trees that have been legally sourced
from well-managed and credibly certified forests.

Printed and bound by
CPI Group (UK) Ltd, Croydon, CR0 4YY

For Betty, again

CHAPTER ONE

On the road to Marden, North-West Frontier, India.
July 1897

They could see from the way that Jenkins sat his horse, up ahead, that he was disconcerted. His head kept swivelling to scrutinise the barren jumble of scree, rocks and large boulders that climbed relentlessly on either side of the narrow track and he kept easing himself in the saddle and occasionally wiping, with a dirty handkerchief, the black moustache that spread across his face as though some great rat had died under his nose. It was hot – nearing a hundred degrees – and it was clear that the Welshman was less than comfortable. A verbal explosion was close at hand.

Eventually he twisted round and addressed Simon Fonthill and his wife, Alice, riding together on the seat of the wagon behind the two mules. 'I 'ave to say, look you,' cried Jenkins, 'that this is the most miserable country on the face of God's earth. It matches the bloody Sudan – savin' your presence,

7

Miss Alice – for bleedin' misery – sorry again, miss. There's been not a drop of shade and nothin' but rocks for miles now. 'Ow much further, then, do you reckon, bach sir?'

Fonthill nodded. 'I knew you'd enjoy the trip. Maybe another ten miles, I'd say. Don't break into a lumbering trot, now, or you'll exhaust yourself.'

Alice waved her sun umbrella. 'If you see a bit of green growing, 352, stop and pluck it and I'll pop it into a bottle and save it as a curiosity.'

'Humph.' Jenkins turned back and urged his plodding horse onwards. Then, half to himself, but loud enough to be heard: 'Just don't know why we 'ad to come all this way back to these bleedin' 'ills. Nearly got our throats slit last time we was 'ere. Barmy, if you ask me. An' not a beer to be 'ad for miles, see. A bloke could die o' thirst if these Parteens don't get 'im first. Just plain barmy . . .'

Alice leant towards her husband. 'Dear old Jenkins has a point, darling,' she murmured, low enough not to be heard by their servant and old comrade. 'This must be one of the most desolate places on earth in which to hold a party. Too late now, I know, but perhaps we should have thought a bit more about it before coming out, don't you think?'

Fonthill frowned and used his whip to flick the flies away from the muzzles of the mules. 'Now, Alice, you know as well as I do that we were bored to tears in green, wet, flat, old Norfolk. I'd been patiently farming without a word of complaint ever since we got back from nearly getting killed with Rhodes in Matabeland – which I see he's now named after himself, the arrogant bastard. So the invitation was a blessed excuse to take a break for a while.'

8

He gestured with the whip to where a distant snow-capped mountain could just be seen poking its tip above the grey tumble of rocks stretching ahead. 'Look, my love. The beginning of the Hindu Kush. That's wonderful country, leading on to the Himalayas and providing some of the best climbing in the world. We're not exactly young but we're fit enough. Probably our last chance to get up high while we can and witness some of the world's best scenery. Think on't, lass.'

Alice gave him an affectionate smile. They made a good-looking couple, sitting close together, one arm linked through that of the other. Both forty-two years of age, they seemed younger. Fonthill carried little weight but he was broad-shouldered and although not exactly tall at 5ft 9in, his body – toughened by years of campaigning far from home and then farming back in Norfolk – was obviously hard. His hair, flecked at the temples now with grey, remained thick and his face was well formed, only marred by a nose broken years before by a Pathan musket so that it now seemed hooked, giving him a hawk-like expression like that of a hunter. Yet the eyes, brown and soft, seemed unusually diffident for those of a man, born in the upper class in the middle of Queen Victoria's century, who had spent much of adult life fighting in her wars throughout the Empire. In addition, his cheeks and jaw remained clean-shaven, marking him as a man who did not march with fashion.

His wife, too, had retained her figure and her hair carried very few strands of grey. With high cheekbones, cool grey eyes and a smooth skin – touched a comely brown by the sun (not for her the anaemic, chalk-faced appearance of most British memsahibs in India) – she would have been flawlessly beautiful if it were not for the firm, almost masculine set of a jaw that revealed the determination that had earned her a reputation as one of the best war correspondents in London's Fleet Street, irrespective of gender.

Now she grinned at her husband and nodded towards Jenkins. 'I don't see him climbing many mountains, my love, do you?'

Fonthill returned her smile. Jenkins – his Christian name long forgotten and always known as 352, the last three numerals of his army number, originally to distinguish him from the many other Jenkinses in that most Welsh of Regiments, the 24th of Foot – had the heart of a lion, could ride a horse like a dragoon, and was as accurate a shot as any Pathan. At 5ft 4in, he was almost as broad as tall, and although four years older than Fonthill, he remained immensely powerful. Years of fighting in bars, barrack rooms and on battlefields around the world had given him formidable skills as a fighter, with fists, knife, bayonet or rifle. Simon had seen him crack the neck of a Hindee thug almost twice his size. Yet he retained a lifelong fear of heights and water and had absolutely no sense of direction. The two had met when Fonthill was a young subaltern in the 24th and Jenkins had recently been released from 'The Glasshouse', the feared and newly opened army correction centre, where, in addition to losing his two stripes, he had served two years' detention for striking a colour sergeant. He had become Simon's batman and then inseparable comrade as the two had carved out unique careers and no little fame as army scouts and very irregular soldiers throughout the Empire. Now the Welshman, though nominally a servant, was an integral part of the small (Simon and Alice had been denied children) Fonthill family.

'Agreed.' Simon nodded. 'But we couldn't leave him behind. I had already had to work hard to get him off two charges of being drunk and disorderly in Norfolk.' Suddenly a shadow fell upon them and Fonthill looked up. High in the sky, an eagle had flown across the face of the sun. He frowned. Wherever he looked, the terrain presented the same grim face: jagged rocks, crumbling scree and jumbled, broken ground stretching up above them for hundreds of feet, the prevailing colour gunmetal grey.

The North-West Frontier was, without a doubt, harsh, unforgiving country. The indigenous Pathans who bestrode it called it Yaghistan, 'The Land of the Untamed'. Their folklore maintained that when Allah created the world there were many stones and rocks left over and he scattered them along this border between the Punjab and Afghanistan. The trio had got to know it well eighteen years before during the Second Afghan War. It was then that Simon and Jenkins had begun to earn their reputations as army irregulars, operating on the fringe of the armies high in the hills, and Alice, well before her marriage, had earned her spurs as a fearless – towards British generals, as well as the enemy – war correspondent. It was then, also, that Fonthill had received his broken nose and sustained other, more frightening wounds at the hands of the Pathans. And it was then that he had first become part of The Queen's

Own Corps of Guides, one of the Frontier's most famous regiments in the Indian army.

Holding temporary postings as, respectively, captain and sergeant in the Corps, Fonthill and Jenkins had lived and fought in these unforgiving hills, before cementing their fame – and a touch of notoriety among the British army's senior ranks – over the next couple of decades in South Africa, Egypt, the Sudan and Matabeland. It was still a surprise, however, when, in the tranquillity of Norfolk, Simon had received a letter from the Colonel-in-Chief of the Guides, inviting the trio to be the guests of the Corps at its headquarters in Marden on the occasion of the delayed celebrations of the fiftieth anniversary of its establishment.

'Come and get some mountain air, do a bit of shooting and climbing,' the Colonel had written. 'It would be an honour to have you and show you a little of how the Corps works to keep the peace here now. Get here by 27th July before the champagne runs out. And belated congratulations on your appointment as C.B. after the Gordon business in the Sudan.'

So, free from financial cares after the inheritance of two estates, following the deaths of both Simon and Alice's parents (they were the only issue of both families), the trio had taken a steamer through the Mediterranean, down the Suez Canal and then on to Bombay, marvelling again at the colour and vibrancy of that place, vying as it did with Calcutta to be the largest city east of Suez until Tokyo and the second city in the Empire after London. The sea voyage had been refreshing, which is more than could be said for the hot and long train journey which had eventually taken them to Peshawar, the capital of the Border territory. Now, they were on the last stage of their tortuous perigrination.

Fonthill had been sceptical at first about riding without escort on the thirty-three-mile last lap from Peshawar, where the rail ended, to Marden. The North-West Frontier of India had been in a more or less constant state of unrest since the British had subjugated the Sikh nation and taken the Punjab into the Empire half a century ago. The Pathans who straddled that border and looked down upon it from their mountain fastnesses were not a homogenous race. They were made up of at least sixty different tribes who were in a constant state of warfare among themselves and, particularly, with the army of British India.

They never accepted formally the suzerainty of the British and they made a national sport of raiding army outposts, killing sentries and stealing rifles, which became a form of currency for them. They shared the ability to stalk a man with the stealth and cunning of a panther and, when making a night attack, they would discard baggy pantaloons to avoid rustling against the undergrowth and would carry twigs to act as funnels and so reduce noise when they had to relieve themselves during a long wait before they sprang. Their morals were oxymoronic. They had a tradition of unquestioningly extending hospitality to strangers who arrived unannounced in their villages but would unhesitatingly slit their throats once they were outside the village boundary. Their word for cousin, *tarbur*, was synonymous with 'enemy'. Fierce warriors and splendid marksmen with their old *jezail* (musket) or stolen British Martini-Henry, they were casual homosexuals and quoted a saying in Pushtu: 'across the river lives a boy with a bottom like a peach, but alas I cannot swim . . .'

It was rare that the Frontier was quiet. But in Peshawar Simon was assured there had been no major outbreaks of hostility along the 200-mile Border for at least two years – a most remarkable period of tranquillity. There would be no interference with travellers journeying the road to Marden, particularly with the fearsome Guides in residence in that town.

And yet. And yet . . .

They had camped the previous evening at a rare shady spot by a trickling stream, feeling safe enough and wrapped well in their sleeping bags. Indeed, Fonthill thought it unnecessary to take it in turns to keep watch. The new day seemed to bring no threat and they had made tea over a low fire, watching without concern the smoke rise languidly above them. It was only then that Simon had realised that, on this allegedly busy highway, they had met no fellow travellers. It seemed strange, although not particularly alarming. Nevertheless, before resuming the journey, he had quietly removed from the back of the wagon the two Lee-Metford army rifles he had purchased at Peshawar and slipped into them the magazines, each containing ten .303 cartridges. He had also taken out from their luggage the three Webley revolvers he had also bought in town from the resident army quartermaster. He left them lying within reach on top of their bags but took the precaution of shortening the leading reins on which his and Alice's horses were tethered behind the cart. Jenkins and Alice had noticed what he was doing, although his wife made no comment. Also without speaking, Jenkins picked up his rifle and rode now with it balanced across his saddle.

They remained the only riders on the dusty track as the sun climbed in the sky and the intense heat, the dryness of the air at their high altitude and the monotony of the landscape seemed their only enemies as they plodded along. Their only company were three vultures which circled, seemingly disinterestedly, high above them.

The first shots, when they came, then, startled them. The bullets clipped into a boulder on the right above their heads and the crack of the rifles – certainly not old *jezails* – echoed along the pass, rebounding from the rocks in dull booms.

'Can you see 'em?' shouted Simon to Jenkins. 'Can we outrun them, d'yer think?'

The answer came with two more shots, from the same direction. The first whistled harmlessly above their heads, but the second thudded into one of the mules, sending it slowly to the ground, sighing and still in its harness. With only one mule, there was no way they could ride out of trouble.

'I can see these two buggers,' shouted Jenkins and, standing in his stirrups, he levelled his rifle and loosed a round into the rocks on the other side of the track, slightly above them. It seemed to have no effect.

Fonthill leapt out of the cart and lifted his arms to receive Alice as she leapt down to him. 'Quick,' he cried, 'take this revolver and get behind that large rock just there.' She nodded mutely and scrambled away up the scree.

'352.'

'Bach sir.'

'Give me some covering fire as I try to bring the horses over here behind the wagon. With the baggage, it might provide enough cover for them. We can sacrifice the mules but we mustn't lose the horses. We shall be lost in this godforsaken country if we did.'

'Very good, sir.'

Jenkins slipped from the saddle like a jockey, wrapped the reins around his wrists and then, kneeling, let off a series of rounds to where drifts of gunsmoke could now be seen rising above two large rocks opposite them. It was done almost with one movement, it seemed to Fonthill, as he desperately tried to unknot the lead reins of his and Alice's mounts. As he did so, he heard the lighter crack of his wife's revolver. At least this would show their attackers that they weren't to be taken easily.

The horses were trembling but not rearing as he led them behind the fragile cover of the wagon. He tied their heads close to the side boarding and heard two more bullets thud into their baggage as Jenkins brought in his horse.

'What are they after, then, bach sir?'

'Our rifles, without a doubt. They will be worth a small fortune in these hills.' Fonthill levelled his own rifle over the edge of the buckboard. 'Ah, I can see where they are now. Alice,' he called. 'Keep your head down and keep behind cover. I think we can handle these two if there are no more.'

'Balls, darling. I'm as good a shot as you. I nearly winged one, then, I think.' She fired again.

Simon fired and clipped the edge of one of the boulders. 'Damn!' He called across to Jenkins. 'They've probably

16

found new cover. Take a good look, old chap. See if you can see 'em move. And particularly, if there are any more of the bastards.'

'Can't see 'em. P'raps we've scared 'em off.'

But that was not so. Four separate rifles sounded now, still from the other side of the track and about a hundred feet above them. The bullets pinged off the rocks behind them, giving Simon the small satisfaction that these Pathans weren't quite living up to there reputation as marksmen – at least so far. Yet the original two had moved so quickly and seemingly imperceptibly among the rocks. And now, it seemed, there were four of them.

Both Fonthill and Jenkins were now sheltering behind the wagon but, despite the cover provided by their baggage, it was clear that it was giving inadequate protection, for bullets were now thudding through the bags and woodwork, narrowly missing them.

'Better get back among the rocks,' grunted Simon. 'Spread out a bit. You go first and I will cover you. Then you do the same for me.'

Jenkins nodded. He let off a round and then sprinted behind up the hill as Simon delivered three rounds of rapid fire at where he could see the faint smoke trails of the Pathans' gun barrels. Of the men themselves, though, there seemed no sign. It was like shooting at wraiths.

'Right,' shouted Jenkins. Simon reached forward from the baggage and grabbed the box of cartridges he had placed on the top, tucked it under his arm and then turned and scrambled, slipping and sliding, up the shale as he heard Jenkins and Alice firing to cover him. Puffing, he flung himself behind a large rock, roughly level with where his wife was crouching.

'Are you all right, darling?' he called.

'Yes, thank you. How the hell are we going to get out of here?'

'God knows.' Fonthill turned his head and looked up behind them. 'We shall be in real trouble if they get behind us to shoot down on us. And we shall be in even worse trouble if we are still here after nightfall. They will creep up, rush us and then we would have little chance of stopping them, I'm afraid.'

'Hmmm.' Alice's voice was cool. 'Do you think that the Guides might send out a patrol and hear the gunfire?'

'It's a possibility.' He ducked his head as a bullet clipped the rock near his cheek and went pinging its way up the hillside. 'Damn. They're getting better at this. I doubt if the Guides would be actively patrolling around here. It's supposed to be quiet, if you remember.'

'Yes.' Four more shots rang out, bouncing and echoing away from hilltop to hilltop. 'I've noticed how quiet it is.'

'Quite. As long as there are only four of them, we have a chance.' He lifted his head. '352.'

'Yes, bach sir.'

'If I were these bastards, I would try to get behind us, on this side of the track. So I think one or two might make a dash for it across the road to get up the hill on this side. Be alert and see if you can pick them off if they try it. They'll be in the open and it's our best chance.'

'Good idea. Let's 'ope they try it.'

And they did. Three more shots rang out from the

Pathans, and immediately a figure appeared some hundred yards up the track, broke from cover and, head down and rifle at the trail, sprinted across the road. Quick as he was, Jenkins was quicker. Swivelling from the hips as he knelt, the Welshman fired one shot and then, working the bolt smoothly, another. The first brought the man down, his rifle skittering away from him in the dust and blood spurting from his thigh. He tried to crawl to safety, but Jenkins's second shot took him in the head, sending his turban spiralling away like a Catherine wheel. Then he lay still, as the echoes faded away.

Fonthill blew out his cheeks. 'Well done, 352. Bloody good shot. Couldn't have done better myself.'

Alice let out a quiet snort of derision. 'Do you think this might scare the others off?' she asked.

'Maybe. We'll have to wait and see. Jenkins.'

'Bach sir?'

'I don't intend to hang about here and wait while they pick us off.'

'What, ride for it, d'yer think?'

'No. They *would* pick us off as we fumbled about untying the horses, mounting and riding off in full view of them.'

'An' you'd fall off if we 'ad to gallop, of course.'

'Certainly not. I'm much better now. No. I've got a better idea . . . Listen. I estimate that we are only about eight miles or so from the Guides' cantonment at Marden up the road here—'

Interrupting, Jenkins's voice now had an underlying note of terror. 'Ah, no. Not me. You know I can't find me way anywhere, unless there's a pub at the end of it. I'd get lost in these bloody 'ills, so I would. You go, bach sir. I'll stay and look after Miss Alice.'

'No. It must be you. You will have to ride like the wind in this heat and you're a much better horseman than me. You can't possibly get lost because this road leads straight into the garrison. You just follow your nose and bring back a troop of the Guides as quickly as possible.' He looked up at the blue, unforgiving sky. 'It's midsummer. I reckon we've got a good eight hours before nightfall. You can do it, I know you can.'

'Oh, very good, bach sir. Give me some cover while I mount. Ah . . . er . . . which way would it be, then, like?'

'Oh, for God's sake. The way we were heading. Straight up there.' He indicated to the right. 'I reckon with only three of them, Alice and I can keep their heads down while you get away. And keep them out until you get back. Throw me your rifle and take this revolver. It will be easier for you to handle from the saddle if you have to. Don't stop for anything till you get there.'

'Very good.' The rifle and the Webley were exchanged in mid-air. Simon threw the Lee-Metford sliding across the scree to Alice. 'Do you think you can handle this, darling? It will be more effective than that popgun you've got.'

'Yes, I think so.' She picked up the heavy weapon but she now wore a frown. 'How many rounds left in this magazine?'

'Work the bolt and you will see. But Jenkins has fired quite a few so you will need these.' He pulled out three more magazines from the ammunition box and threw them to her. 'Now, 352, are you ready to go?'

'Oh, aye. I'm looking forward to it, look you. Fire off a few rounds while I scramble down. Give me 'alf a minute to free the 'orse and get on it and then blaze away while I ride off.'

'Very well. Ready, Alice?'

She nodded.

'Right. Fire!'

The two rifles barked as one and then again. But they did not prevent two guns blazing back from the other side of the track. The bullets, however, hit the scree just behind Jenkins as he leapt and skidded down to the dubious protection of the wagon.

'I can see where those two are now, Alice, can you?' called Fonthill.

'I think so. But this bloody thing is a bit heavy for me. Never mind. I'll fire away and hope for the best.'

'Good. Don't expose yourself unduly, darling. Are you ready, 352?'

'Got one foot in the stirrup. Right. Let the buggers 'ave it and good luck to you both!'

Jenkins swung himself into the saddle and dug his heels into the flanks of his mount and with a whoop was off, his back lying parallel to that of his horse and his head alongside its neck as Simon and Alice began firing as fast as they could, Fonthill inevitably emptying his magazine before Alice had let off three rounds. Nevertheless, the modest fusillade was heavy enough to provide the precious cover that the Welshman needed and horse and rider rounded the bend to their right and disappeared out of sight, leaving a cloud of dust dancing in the rays of the sun.

'Thank God for that!' Fonthill flattened himself behind his rock and cast an anxious glance at his wife, five feet away from him. 'All right, darling?'

Alice put down her rifle and dashed the perspiration from her brow. 'I think so, Captain.' Then she cast an anxious glance at her husband. 'I'm not sure, though, Simon, that I'm going to be good enough with this damned rifle to support you in keeping these three at bay. It's a bit heavy for me in this heat.'

'Don't worry. Go back to the revolver if you are more comfortable with that, but I think you'd better keep most of your ammunition for the handgun until they get close, because it won't be too effective at long range. In the meantime I'll do my best and they will have to cross the open road to get to us. That's when we can bring them down. But keep behind cover most of the time – and go to the other side of the boulder to keep them guessing.'

'Do you think there are any of them behind us?'

'No. They would have revealed their hand by now. Keep under cover and leave the fine marksmanship to this Bisley champion.'

They exchanged grins and Fonthill marvelled once again at the great good fortune that God had bestowed on him in allowing him to find and then marry this magnificent woman: so cool in a crisis and as brave as a guardsman. Their one joint regret over the years of their marriage had been the failure of the pregnancy incurred in the Sudan, after a heavily disguised Alice had found her way over the barren desert sands and then through the lines of the Mahdi's camp outside Khartoum to rescue him and Jenkins from imprisonment, torture and slave labour there. The miscarriage – it had been a boy – had damaged Alice's ability to conceive again. But they remained close, each one's love of adventure and challenge matching the other's – and that of Jenkins.

Simon licked his lips, which were now beginning to blister from the heat and the cordite. This would be one of the closest scrapes that they had ever endured. The question was: could they keep these three Pathans at bay long enough for Jenkins – a Jenkins who notoriously couldn't find his way from A to B if it was lit for him by blazing torches – to bring relief? And would the Welshman meet any further Pathans on the road, waiting to bring him down? On that score, however, he felt more at ease. Jenkins could fight his way out of the tightest corner. He shook his head. Just as well, for he was their only hope!

He stole a glance around the rock, which immediately brought a shot crashing into the stone. This wouldn't do. If he didn't keep constant watch, they could creep up on them. And if he continually exposed himself to do so, then he would provide an easy target to men whose shooting was now beginning to match their reputation. What to do?

Fonthill nodded reassuringly to Alice and gestured to her to stay covered. Then he seized a sizeable stone and, keeping low behind the outline of the boulder, tossed it as far as he could to the right. It fell with a crash amongst the scree and immediately produced three shots from across the track, which slammed into the rocks where his stone had landed.

Simon had realised some time ago that the Pathans

were firing with old single-shot Martini-Henry British rifles not the rapid-firing Lee-Metford. So he immediately took advantage of their clumsy reloading to scramble high up the hill and seek the shelter of another large rock – there were plenty of them about. This gave him a slight height advantage and he levelled his rifle and took careful aim – Jenkins's oft-repeated mantra of 'squeeze gently now and don't jerk' ringing in his ears – at the scrap of fabric he could see protruding around a rock opposite. He swore happily as he heard the soft thud of the bullet hitting flesh not stone and saw a rifle fall from behind the rock and slither down the slope.

'Think I've got one of the varmints,' he called down to Alice, who looked up and nodded wearily. He realised now that it was like being in a blast furnace, crouching on this hillside among the rocks that were reflecting the heat. It was obviously getting too much for Alice. She had removed her pith helmet the better to fire around the side of the boulder and he became aware that she was in imminent danger of suffering from sunstroke.

'Pour water over your head from your carrier,' he shouted. 'Do it quickly, otherwise you could lose consciousness. Then put your helmet back on. I will keep firing, don't worry.'

She nodded and complied. Fonthill pulled out the tail of his cotton shirt and tore it off. Dousing it with water from his own bottle he tied it around his head and, poking his rifle around the rock, fired at a quick flash of movement he caught from near the road. Ah, they were inching nearer! He must never relax. Keep watching and firing!

Reaching out, he scraped together a pile of medium-sized stones and made a low rampart. Then, sprawling on his stomach, he crawled out behind it, rested his rifle in a 'V' between two large stones and realised that he had a much better protected and viable firing position, giving him cover and a stable platform. Sighting to where he had noticed the movement earlier he waited patiently. Ah, another flash of colour from higher up! Instinctively, he fired, without any obvious result. But it was clear that they were trying to get nearer, using cover as only skilled mountaineers like the Pathans could, slipping between the rocks like eels in a stream. How long, dear God, before Jenkins arrived?

The three Pathans, of course, had the advantage of numbers, demanding that Fonthill deter each of them from crawling closer. However, now that he was better able to take aim, Simon realised that they also faced his own problem – how to fire without revealing themselves and, additionally in their case, how to move from cover to cover without drawing down fire. The answer, of course, lay in each of them moving at the same time. Would they think of it?

They would and they did. Almost immediately, there was a flurry of movement and Fonthill gained a quick impression of three figures, dressed in dun-coloured long garments and wearing high turbans, wound like dirty washing on top of their heads, breaking cover and sliding down the scree to a last line of rocks near the edge of the track. He fired five shots, working the bolt of the Lee Metford as hard as he could but he was not a good enough shot to hit, although he glimpsed one of the three wearing a bloodstained bandage around his forearm, where his previous bullet had found a home.

He shook his head. Damn! Any hope of them being deterred by his and Alice's resistance had obviously disappeared. They had invested time and loss – one killed, one wounded – in attempting to kill these infidels and they were not going to waste that effort. They must know that Jenkins had ridden for help and that they had little time left. Or . . . a disconcerting alternative thought struck him. Perhaps they knew that there was plenty of time because there were more of their clan waiting up the track to cut Jenkins off! He gulped.

Squirming, he pulled out his pocket watch. It was now well past 1 p.m. How long had Jenkins been gone? Less than an hour. Not long enough for him to have reached Marden and get back on the road. He flicked a bead of sweat from his brow. He and Alice would have to fight their own way out of this.

He called down. 'Alice.'

'Yes.' Her voice had lost some of its strength. But she cleared her throat and then called back, more firmly this time. 'Yes. Don't worry. I'm all right.'

'Good girl. Now listen. They are now close enough perhaps to try and rush us. This means that, as they run – and they've got about a hundred yards to cover – they can't fire. So when I shout to you, get to your feet, aim carefully across the top of your rock and shoot to kill. Take your time and make sure you hit. You will have time to get at least one of them. I will get the other two.'

'Well, my love,' her voice had recovered its strength and

that familiar note of irony had entered it, 'I only hope you do. I have no wish to be ravaged by some smelly Pathan.'

'I promise I shall not let that happen. Bad for the family tree. Now. Be on your guard.' He inserted another magazine into the rifle and looked down at his wife, some six yards below him. If they failed to pick off all the Pathans as they rushed, then he reckoned he had about five seconds to scramble down to her aid . . . with what? He had no bayonet. He shrugged. He had better aim carefully, that's all. Oh, to have Jenkins here now, with his steady hand and eye!

Suddenly, he heard a yell and saw the three assailants spring to their feet, their rifles thrown aside and the famous curved Pathan sword, the *tulwar*, in their hands and reflecting the rays of the sun as they were waved.

'Here they come, Alice,' he screamed, and steeled himself to aim carefully. Mercifully, his first shot took the leading Pathan in the breast as he reached the centre of the track and he fell back without a sound. He heard Alice's pistol crack twice but the two other men disappeared from sight behind a boulder fringing the near side of the track and he could not release another round. Scrambling to his feet and desperately working the bolt of his rifle to insert another cartridge as he did so, he half bounded, half slipped down the hill towards Alice.

He reached her just as the second Pathan rounded the rock, his *tulwar* raised. For a split second they looked into each other's eyes. Those of the hillman were black, blazing with intent and set above an equally black beard and high cheekbones. Fonthill's brain inconsequentially recorded the fact that the Pathan was remarkably handsome before he pulled the trigger in a reflex action. The bullet took the man in the chest, springing a flash of crimson from his cotton *angarka* smock and, at this short range, exploding him backwards down the hill.

There was one man to go and, with no time to insert another round, Simon spun round towards Alice. She was standing, her back to the rock, the back of one hand to her mouth and her pistol dangling at her side from the other. She tried to speak but, for a moment, could find no words. Then, 'It's all right,' she half whispered, half mouthed. 'I got the other one.' And she gestured over the rock with her head.

Simon worked the bolt, inserted another cartridge and carefully put his head round the boulder. Down at the bottom of the slope, the first man he had killed lay face downwards, his mouth open but his body quite inert. Near to him and half buried in the scree he had brought with him as he had tumbled down the hill, lay the second, equally dead. The third lay very close to the rock that had protected Alice, two bullets in his chest from which blood was oozing, finding its way down the slope in a little rivulet through the shingle.

His breast heaving, Fonthill took his wife in his arms and stroked her sodden hair. 'Well done, my love,' he whispered eventually. 'Messy and sad, I know, but they were savage creatures and we had done them no harm. It was them or us. We had no choice.'

Eventually, she withdrew her head. 'I know, I know. But it's a long time since I have been so frightened or seen such barbarism at such close range – and even longer since I have killed anyone.' She forced a smile. 'This is a far cry from playing bridge with Mrs Hill-Dawson and Miss Brackley in Norfolk, you know. I thought we were just going to do some gentle climbing, that's all.'

'I know. I'm sorry. Now sit down for a moment. I'm just going to make absolutely certain that there aren't any more of these chaps about in these rocks.'

But there was no need. As he straightened to look about them, he heard, in the distance, the sound of a bugle, sounding clear in that mountain air and as refreshing as a douche of spring water.

'Thank God,' he exclaimed. The bugle sounded again and then was complemented with the distant drumming of horses galloping. 'Jenkins is arriving with the whole of the Indian cavalry by the sound of it.' He looked at his watch. 'He must have met a troop on the way. Well,' he grinned at his wife, 'better late than never. At least the dear old devil found the way.'

'That's because there weren't any pubs on the way.' Alice returned the grin but perspiration was now pouring down her face and her chest was heaving.

Within two minutes a troop of khaki-clad horsemen of the Corps of Guides rounded the bend, fronting a curtain of dust. At its head, tall in the saddle, rode a *daffadar*, or Indian sergeant, carrying a lance bearing a coloured pennant, closely followed by an English subaltern and the figure of Jenkins, now almost unrecognisable because of the thick coating of dust covering him.

Reining in, the subaltern shouted a stream of orders.

Immediately, in a smooth sequence of actions, single troopers ran forward, each taking the bridles of three horses; others broke into two sections, each of which selected a side of the track and began climbing fast up the scree, carbines at the ready. A weary Jenkins scrambled up towards where Alice and Simon were standing.

He embraced them both roughly and then stepped back with a sheepish grin. 'Ah, sorry about the dust, beggin' your pardon, but I felt we'd be too late, see. I was worried sick. But . . .' he nodded down the hill, 'I might 'ave known you'd both be able to look after yerselves.'

Fonthill and Alice each grabbed a hand of the Welshman. 'Well, we nearly needed you, old chap,' smiled Simon. 'You could have been in on the final act if you hadn't wandered off the track looking for an alehouse. But you virtually made it in time, so thank you. Well done.'

They turned to welcome the young subaltern – the only white man in the sixty-man troop – who now joined them. He extended a hand. 'Freddie Buckingham, Second Lieutenant, Royal Corps of Guides,' he said. 'I am so sorry, sir – madam – that you've had this welcome to our party. Damned bad thing to happen, doncher know. Apologies from the Corps. I know the colonel will be most upset.'

'Thank you, Freddie,' said Simon. 'This is my wife, Alice, and, of course, you have already met 352 Jenkins – late sergeant in the Corps, I may say.'

The formalities over, the officer turned and shouted something in what sounded to Simon like Pushtu to the tall *daffadar* who was high on the other side of the track. The soldier responded with a negative wave of the hand.

'I don't think there are any more of these Pathans about,' said Simon, 'otherwise they would have been down on us like a swarm of locusts. We could only just handle four, as it was. So I think you can recall your men.'

The eyebrows under Buckingham's helmet rose and his pink cheeks seemed to glisten in the sun. 'Ah, you understood the order, so you speak Pushtu, Captain. Splendid. By the way, everybody calls me Duke. Inevitable with a surname like mine, dash it, but I'm no relation, more's the pity . . .'

Fonthill smiled. 'Duke it is, then. As to Pushtu, I learnt a bit of the language when I was here in the Second Afghan War but I am not fluent, alas.'

The young man's face opened up again. 'Yes, I heard how you and your remarkable chap here blacked up as natives and disappeared up into the hills for weeks on end before reporting back to General Roberts and then warning him of the Afghans' depositions at Kandahar. Oh, yes. You're quite famous around here, sir, I will have you know. It's a pleasure to have you with us on our anniversary – and your famous wife, too, if I may say so.'

Alice gave a small curtsey. 'Oh, you may say so, Lieutenant. Now, tell me. You must have met Jenkins while you were out on patrol, no doubt?'

'No, ma'am. We had come looking for you. Colonel had learnt that you had arrived in Peshawar and sent a wire to say not to start out until we had sent an escort but we were told you had left. So I was sent off hotfoot to rescue you.' He looked ruefully down the hill. 'Though it looks to me, Captain, as though you and Mrs Fonthill are well able to look after yourselves.'

Fonthill and Alice exchanged glances. 'I wouldn't exactly say that,' said Simon. 'It was touch and go. But we were told that the Border was quiet and that this road was safe.'

Buckingham pulled a face. 'And so it was. But things have stirred up almost over night. Now, we'd better get back to Marden.' He shouted another order to his troops then nodded down to the bodies of the Pathans. 'These chaps are not exactly locals. They look to me as though they're from the Wazir tribe from near the Khyber. Big troublemakers when they want to be and as fierce as hell. We can't bury them in this terrain, but we'll just cover them with rocks – and, of course, take their rifles. Come along, let's get your wagon back on the road. I'm afraid that, with one mule dead, you will have to ride your horses, but it's not all that far.'

All this was said with a fluent air of knowledge and self-confidence and Fonthill was reminded again of how amazed he had always been at the skill of these young men who, looking as though they had just left the sixth form of their schools, were leading men into action with the sangfroid of veterans. It was, he reflected, the Empire at its best.

Buckingham turned as he picked his way down the shale. 'Oh, by the way,' he called back. 'There's someone in my troop who is most anxious to meet you. Come on. As soon as we're safely on the road, I'll introduce you.'

CHAPTER TWO

The troopers, who had ranged over the hills on both sides of the track remarkably quickly, now trudged down again and quickly re-formed on the road. Intrigued by the reference to someone who wanted to meet him, Fonthill regarded the men with interest.

They were smartly turned out in collarless khaki tunics atop riding breeches with tightly bound puttees and black boots. (Simon recalled that, at their formation in 1846, at a time when every British soldier wore scarlet, they were the first troops to adopt khaki – an Urdu word of Persian origin meaning dusty or dust-coloured.) Polished leather cross belts gave prominence to their chests and red cummerbunds circled their waists. Their turbans were tightly bound and featured contrasting colours. They carried Martini-Henry carbines and cavalry sabres dangled from their saddles.

They were all Pathans, natives of the Frontier, with the high cheekbones, prominent, sharp noses and ferocious black beards indigenous to these peoples, and they were, without a doubt, a handsome bunch.

Returning their grins now, Fonthill remembered that they had been recruited originally as an irregular force whose purpose it was to gather intelligence of tribal movements and act as guide to troops in the field. Shortly after their formation, they had won acclaim in the Mutiny by marching in record time across the north of India, from the Border to Delhi, to support the loyal troops besieging the city. From that moment, although they had retained their nomenclature as Guides, they had been subsumed into the India army as fighting men – and specialists in mountain warfare. Although recruited from the Border tribes, the Guides never suffered any defections or mutinous revolts. They were regarded as one of the most trusted units in the British Raj.

With snorts from the horses and a jingle of harness, the troops mounted and Simon, Alice and Jenkins trotted forward to join Buckingham at their head.

'Now, Captain,' said the lieutenant, 'I promised you that there was someone in particular who was most anxious to meet you.'

'So you did.' Fonthill looked into the dark faces behind them. 'I must confess I can't quite think who it would be.'

'Ah.' The young man chuckled. It was clear he was happy to be playing some sort of game. 'Well,' he said, 'I will give you a clue. You've met him before, although a long time ago.'

Simon looked again around the troop. All of the men were grinning at him again, their teeth cutting slashes of white in their black countenances. All, that is, except the *daffadar*, who sat ramrod-straight in the saddle holding the pennanted lance and frowning straight ahead of him. He was clearly much taller than the rest of the troop and, although bearded and dark-skinned like the others in this Pathan unit, Simon realised that he was a Sikh. But his appearance rang no bells with him. He exchanged puzzled glances with Alice and Jenkins, who shook their heads negatively.

'Very well.' Buckingham raised his voice. '*Daffadar!*'

'Sahib.' The Sikh gently heeled his horse forward, so that it was level with the quartet.

'Captain Fonthill, Mrs Fonthill, Mr Jenkins,' said Buckingham formally, 'may I introduce you to just about the best soldier in the Queen's Own Corps of Guides. This is Inderjit Singh, *daffadar* in my troop.'

The tall Sikh immediately gave an impeccable salute and, for the first time, allowed himself to engage in eye contact with Simon. His handsome face slowly relaxed into a warm smile.

'So glad to see you again, sahib, memsahib, sahib,' he said to each in turn, in impeccable English, with only the trace of the Indian lilt to show that he was not some public schoolboy from Winchester or Harrow.

Fonthill frowned and stared at him. 'I am sorry,' he began haltingly. 'We have met before, have we?'

'Oh yes, sahib, but only when I was a little boy. I am grateful to you, for you paid for my education at Amritsar.

My mother, who is dead now, wanted to write to you to tell you I had joined the Guides but she did not know where to write. Now, when Buckingham Sahib tell me that you were coming, I was delighted and wondered if I could meet—'

'Wait a minute.' Fonthill's frowned deepened. 'You say *I* paid for your education?'

'Yes, sahib. You see I am the son of my father, Inderjit Singh, once of the Guides. You knew him, I think, as W. G. Grace.'

'What! You are the son of W.G.?'

'Good Lord,' cried Alice.

'Bloody 'ell,' crowed Jenkins.

'Oh yes, sir.' Singh was clearly delighted at the impression his father's name had created. 'His name is well known in the Guides – almost as famous as yours and Jenkins sahib, I think.'

Buckingham intervened. 'So glad you've resumed acquaintance,' he said, 'but I think we had better get moving.' He nodded to his *daffadar* and spoke to him in Pushtu. Immediately, the Sikh lifted his arm, pointed ahead and fell back as the troop began to walk forward, three scouts thrown out far ahead, two at the rear and, in the middle, the wagon, with one trooper squatting on its seat, urging the mule forward.

'Now,' said the lieutenant, 'I've heard a bit about the elder Inderjit Singh, but do tell me about your involvement with him.'

But first Simon reached back and grasped the hand of the Sikh, who then, rather self-consciously, shook hands with Alice and Jenkins, before falling back again to take his place at the head of the troop. Then, Fonthill, with many an interjection from the other two, told of how Singh's cricket-loving father – such an aficionado of the game that he had changed his name to that of the famous English batsman of the time – had guided the disguised Simon and Jenkins to Kabul and then up in the hills to gain information about the massing of the hill tribes in the Second Afghan War, eighteen years before. The trio – later joined by Alice after she had been refused permission by the authorities to report at first-hand on the conflict – had survived many a clash with the Afghans before reaching Kandahar in time to warn General Sir Frederick Roberts of the Afghan placements at that battle which had ended the war. The Sikh had died in a skirmish just before the battle and Fonthill, had, indeed, made provision for his son before leaving Afghanistan.

'Do you know I had forgotten that,' Simon confided at the end of his story. 'And he's turned out to be a good soldier?'

'Remarkably so,' said Buckingham. 'Born to the job, so to speak. He's very young to be a *daffadar* but everyone respects him and he rose through the ranks quickly. He's a splendid horseman, a good shot and as brave as a lion.'

'Just like 'is da, then,' interjected Jenkins. 'Wonderful bloke, old Gracey, look you. Miss 'im still.'

'Well,' said Fonthill, 'he must have been only about four when I saw him for the only time, so no wonder I didn't recognise him. I look forward to reminiscing with him about his father. Thank you for bringing him along.'

'Humph.' The young man snorted. 'Wouldn't dream of

going out into the hills without him. Come along. I could do with a drink.'

'What a splendid idea, bach,' rejoined Jenkins.

They rode into Marden some three hours later and Simon and his two companions looked around them with interest. It was hardly a town, or even much of a village in its own right, for it was dominated by the Guides' cantonment on its edge. Nestling between towering mountains on a small plain through which a small, gin-clear stream trickled, the garrison was similar to many that Fonthill had seen in India: barracks, bungalows, a church, a club and, inevitably, a cemetery, all surrounded by a low wall. The buildings were all of red brick and seemed, amidst the grandeur of their surroundings, to possess an air almost of melancholy, something perhaps that had leached out from the nearby graveyard, with its many stained and leaning headstones telling their sad stories of deaths in action and from cholera. Attempts to enliven the club and the bungalows had been made with the planting of shrubs and flowers, but Simon could not help but feel that this outpost of Empire was rather a sorrowful place.

The welcome, however, was warm enough. A short, khaki-clad full colonel, his Sam Browne belt trying but failing to restrain his corpulence, bustled out to greet them. His red face boasted a clipped, salt-and-pepper moustache and a wide smile.

'Nigel Fortescue,' he cried, pumping each of their hands in turn. 'You are all most welcome . . .' Then his voice trailed away as he took in the dust still engrained on Jenkins's figure and his trained eye observed the traces of cordite on Fonthill's cheek. 'Ah,' he said. 'You've had trouble. Damnit. Those idiots at Peshawar shouldn't have let you come on your own. Tell me about it.'

Simon related the story of the attack on them and of the deaths of the Pathans.

'Wazirs by the sound of it,' said the Colonel. He turned up to Buckingham. 'Eh? What, Duke? Wazies, eh?'

'Yes, Colonel. But, by George, the captain and Mrs Fonthill here knocked 'em off – all four of 'em – before we were able to get there. Remarkable stuff.'

'Well,' interjected Simon, 'Jenkins here got one before we were forced to send him for help.'

'Not surprised, from what I've heard about you all. Now, enough of all this. You must be in urgent need of a bath, all of you – ah . . . er . . . particularly you, Mr Jenkins, eh?'

'Very true, Colonel bach. And p'raps a drink of somethin' cold d' yer think?'

'Most certainly. All in good time.' He turned back to Simon. 'The bad news is, I'm afraid, that you've missed our main celebrations by just a couple of days, don't you know. Our fault. Should have given you a notification that we had had to bring it forward to accommodate our colonel-in-chief and, indeed, Lord Roberts, C-in-C India. Yes, both of them were here. Great honour. But they've had to leave for Simla. Bit of trouble about, as you have already probably heard. Oh, by the way, Lord Roberts sends his warmest regards to all three of you. Most insistent that I should pass them on. He's sorry he's missed you.'

Simon and Alice exchanged wry smiles. The relationship between them and the fiery little general had rarely been warm, despite Fonthill and Jenkins's good intelligence work in the campaign, and Roberts had not taken kindly to Simon's curt refusal to accept a permanent commission and higher rank in the Indian army offered to him. It looked now as though all had been forgiven. Another mark, he noted, of his now seemingly warm acceptance by the British army after his work in the Sudan and his appointment as a Commander of the Bath.

'That's very kind of them, sir. Yes. We would certainly welcome a tub.'

'Right. I'll get the adjutant to show you to your quarters and allocate your boys to you. The fact that you have arrived safely – oh, and by the way, have you met *Daffadar* Iinderjit Singh?'

'Yes, we have. Very rewarding to see how well he has grown up – and so like his father.'

'Yes. Good. Now. Your safe arrival has given us the excuse to have another damned good party in the mess tonight. And madam, you shall be our main guest of honour and you, Jenkins, Sergeant or whatever you are or were – got the DCM after Khartoum, I hear, eh? – shall be our honoured guest as well. No need to dress up. You've been travelling. Just put the best on that you have with you. Shall we say 6.30? Good. That should give you time to relax after your exertions. Welcome again.'

'Thank you, Colonel.'

Willing hands unloaded their bags and took away their horses and they were escorted to their quarters in the club.

These were spartan enough – all for single visitors so there was no double room for Alice and Simon – but the great luxury awaited, a little further along the wooden corridor, of three separate bath houses where *bhistis* were already boiling water for them. Within fifteen minutes Fonthill was lying with only toes and chin breaking the surface of the steam as he listened to the voice of Alice softly singing from the cubicle next door.

As he relaxed, his mind turned to the colonel's phrase 'bit of trouble about'. Well, they had already met that and there was obviously more unrest in these hills. He knew what Alice's view of that would be. Why, she had always argued, did we expect native people to take sanguinely the British occupation of their countries? Would *we* accept the French moving into Surrey and Norfolk and imposing their rule and culture on *us*? It was no use pointing out that Indians and Pathans were primitive races who benefited from the examples we set with our higher economic, social and political values. These peoples, she maintained, should have been left to have found their own levels in their own way and in their own time.

Simon wrinkled his brow. And wasn't she right? The lives that Jenkins, Alice and he had taken that day had been forced on them, of course. They were acts of self-defence. Yet the root cause of all that violence – he saw again the blood oozing down the scree, the hatred in the eyes of the man he had killed at point-blank range, the overweening barbarity of it all – didn't it all spring from the British invasion of their country?

He splashed the water gently with his hand to generate

more heat. As he closed his eyes at the luxury, he recalled the famous message that the British General Sir Charles Napier had relayed back to the British army HQ at London's Horse Guards after he had occupied the Indian province of Sind by force for the British East India Company in 1843. It consisted of the single Latin word, '*Pecavvi*' – 'I have sinned'. Such smirking arrogance! Such a pompous, self-regarding display of superiority! How very British!

Simon's thoughts turned back to his wife. He had undoubtedly pushed her rather in persuading her to come on this trip. Fresh air and gentle climbing indeed! If his instincts were right, they could be about to become immersed in a tribal uprising that might well involve them in more violence, more killing. He stirred in the warm water. Well, perhaps they might be able to escape to the tranquillity of Kashmir and the lower reaches of the Hindu Kush, further to the east, before the trouble escalated. He must seek the advice of the colonel. They would do their duty to their hosts, take part in the final cordialities of their anniversary and then be on their way. Yes. He felt better at the thought. He had no right to put Alice in the way of further danger. They would be off as soon as possible.

The Guides' mess that night was warm and inviting. Low, candled chandeliers had been lit and their yellow light was reflected in the wooden panelling of the room, with its many trophies of the hunt – heads of tigers, buffalo and large-horned mountain goats – studding the walls. The Guides had not yet accumulated the mass of silverware possessed by the older, great British regiments of the Line, but there were sufficient examples lining the centre of the long table to lend a kind of baronial magnificence to the gathering.

Simon, who had consistently rejected attempts over the last two decades to lure him back into the warmth of regimental life, remembering the stupidity of the British officer class displayed at Isandlwana in Zululand and at Majuba Hill in Natal, felt an unfamiliar sense of collegiate belonging engulf him. Damnit, he and Jenkins had once been part of this strange, irregular unit many years before! He saw a sparkle in Alice's eyes, too. She *was* a brigadier's daughter, after all. It was difficult to ignore the sense of tradition and past sacrifices and glory that imbued the gathering in this remote corner of a very savage land. He raised his glass happily, then, and joined the others in toasting the Queen and the Regiment.

At dinner, he sat on the left of the colonel, with Alice on the CO's right, and both of them, albeit with an anxious eye on Jenkins, who was growing increasingly garrulous further down the long table, began a gentle cross-questioning of Fortescue about the state of the hill tribes along the Border.

The colonel frowned. 'It's been strangely quiet for some time, yer see. Perhaps the pot had to boil over sooner or later, given the temperament of these chaps. But what has just happened,' he lowered his voice, 'was quite strange and very unsettling, doncher know. Just a few days ago, Lieutenant Colonel Bunny of the 1st Sikhs, part of the Punjab Frontier Force, as are we – delightful chap, by the way, an excellent, experienced officer – led just over a hundred of his troops to a small village called Maizar in the Tochi Valley, not so far from here, as an escort to the local political officer. It was a fairly low-key little outing, so to speak, so that the PO could settle some dispute with the locals about the non-payment of a fine.'

Fortescue wiped his moustache with his napkin but his eyes were sad. 'Everything was peaceful, with women and children millin' about as usual and the local Waziri headman suggested that the ideal resting place for the troops would be under some trees, with running water nearby. He also proposed that a meal, then being prepared, might be acceptable to the Muslim sepoys of the escort while the business was done. Dear old Bunny accepted this, of course – it was all part of the ancient Pathan tradition of offering hospitality to guests, their word for it is *pakhtunwali*.'

The whole table had now fallen silent as the colonel continued. 'The troops were squatting about, trying to find shade, and Bunny, being the sort of chap he was, ordered his bagpipers to give the villagers a tune, which they did. The PO went off to a nearby village to do the business, which was about getting reparations for the murder of a Hindu clerk, and returned with it all sorted happily. The Muslim sepoys were in the middle of the meal, the Sikhs were eating their rations under the trees and the bagpipers were playing again, by popular request, when suddenly, on a nearby rooftop a Pathan appeared waving a sword.

'At this,' Fortescue's voice suddenly hardened, 'the villagers suddenly scattered and two shots were fired, hitting one of Bunny's lieutenants in the thigh. More shots followed and suddenly the whole unit was under fire. Bunny himself took a bullet in the stomach and, although in great pain, managed to rally his chaps and retreat with them. The trouble was that the opening salvoes from the tribesmen had been directed at the six British officers. They were all hit and eventually unable to give orders, so it was left to the native officers to take command.

'They did a capital job – as you would expect from the Sikhs, of course. They led a fighting retreat for about three miles, pressured all the way. The sepoys carried their wounded officers until some sort of defensive position was established and that's where dear old Bunny died from his wounds. Somehow, word was got back to Datta Khel nine miles away, and a relief force managed to get to Bunny's men just before dark when they were down to five rounds of ammunition per man.'

The colonel shook his head. 'A miserable business all round. The Sikhs lost three officers and twenty-four men killed and twenty-eight wounded. It seems that they were attacked by more than a thousand tribesmen. You will see, then, that this was not yer usual sniping or a stealthy hit-and-run attack on sentries to steal rifles. It was quite an affair – and the worst thing about it was the treacherous nature of the ambush: the defiling of the Pathan code of hospitality and all that. What's more,' Fortescue's voice had now risen in indignation, 'it was found later that not only had the dead Sikhs' bodies been mutilated – which was to be expected, of course – but so had those of the Muslim sepoys. Unheard of, damnit. Absolutely unheard of!'

Fonthill nodded his head slowly. This was not what he had wanted to hear. 'So perhaps the attack on us today was some sort of fallout from this business?'

'Oh, I wouldn't be sure of that. Wazirs in both cases, of

course, but this is a huge tribe, containing many different clans. And Maizar is in a different sector, yer see.'

'I presume that some sort of punitive action will be taken against these Pathans?' asked Simon.

'Oh, indeed. It is being mounted now. A field force, no less, given the strength of the uprising.'

The colonel took a reflective draught from his claret glass and the gathering gradually began to buzz again as down-table conversation resumed. Alice leant forward.

'But what do you think caused this sizeable attack?' she asked. 'Would it be part of a growing unrest at the establishment of the Durand Line?'

Fortescue shot her an appraising glance. 'Ah, I see you've been doing some homework, dear lady. Yes, I would think it extremely likely and it is worrying me.'

'Alice knows more about this than I do,' said Fonthill. 'I know a little, but do tell us more.'

Fortescue sipped his wine again and then dabbed at his mouth with his napkin. 'It's fairly straightforward,' he began, 'but I'm afraid that it reflects badly again on our politicians in Delhi. Didn't think the damned thing through. Here's what happened.

'The border between India and Afghanistan had never been exactly defined – awfully difficult to do, anyway, in this rough, tangled country of mountain passes and difficult slopes. The whole business of trying to improve the defences of India by extending roads and railways and so on had caused friction between Kabul and Delhi and the question of who was responsible for which Border tribe had never really been resolved. So . . .' The colonel drew out the word, as a good storyteller should. 'So,' he repeated, 'some sort of agreement was reached between the Amir in Kabul and the British Indian government. It was supposed to have been amicable but it seems clear that the Amir was not completely in agreement with the line that was established, but went along with it.'

'So there was an actual line?' asked Alice.

'Yes. Well, not exactly on the ground but pillars being knocked in to mark it – much to the local tribesmen's disgust. From 1894, it formally extended the area of British responsibility into Afghanistan and as a result the lands of Chitral, Bajaur, Swat, Buner, Dir, the Khyber, Kurram and Waziristan all became under British protection, although not, it should be said, under as close a control as in India. No, a more loose arrangement, whereby these places became tribal territories, supervised – not governed, you understand – by British agents who would become close to the tribes and wean them away from violence by a mixture of inducements and threat of punishment.'

'Hmmm.' Alice, predictably, was frowning. 'It sounds as though the Amir of Afghanistan lost out in this.'

'Not really. He was given a slice of land in the north, next to the Russian frontier. To be honest, the word is that he didn't really want it because he knew that we were really looking for him to administer it as a kind of neutral buffer zone between us and the Ruskies. And he didn't really lose much, except on paper, with the transfer of the Border tribal regions. The tribes didn't really ever formally acknowledge their fealty to him, though they would always side with him against the British if it came to a fight.'

'And Durand,' asked Fonthill. 'Who was he?'

'Indian government's foreign secretary at the time. He's the chap, supposed to be on the spot, who didn't think it through, damnit.'

'Why not?'

'Well, d'yer see, in theory we extended our defences and area of influence into the Border territories. Pushed out the famous North-West Frontier, if yer like. But in practice, these territories are virtually ungovernable. The tribes won't swear allegiance to anyone – well, they might swear it to get some rupees out of us, which they do, but they will never really toe the line.'

'But, Colonel.' Alice was frowning again. 'Why should they? Just because they are not one conventional, integrally knit nation, why should they allow their lands to be carved up between two larger powers?'

Fortescue smiled, not without pleasure. 'Ah, dear lady, that is a perfectly logical and acceptable question you pose. And encapsulates, if I may say so, the Liberal Party's position on this back home. I suppose the answer to it is our acceptance of some sort of lofty responsibility for trying to teach these undoubtedly warlike and, by our standards, immoral people – witness their quite unprovoked attacks on you this afternoon – a better way of life.'

Alice drew in her breath to respond, but a warning frown and raised forefinger from Simon behind the colonel's head made her keep her silence, allowing him to move in. 'You mentioned, Colonel,' he said, 'the problems that came from not thinking this policy through. What has ensued, then, as a result of the establishment of the Line?'

'For the first couple of years, nothing but trouble. Attacks all the way along the Frontier on the working parties putting in the damned poles. We had to send in three brigades to put down the Mahsud country. Then, far to the north, at Chitral, the political agent and a small force were penned in to the fort there for two months by armed tribesmen, while two army columns, from the east and south, had to fight their way through hugely difficult country to relieve them. As a result we had to establish a new garrison at the Malakand Pass, near here, and forts along the Khyber. We've got a new Pathan regiment, raised locally, like the Guides, to man 'em and keep the peace along the Pass. They're called the Khyber Rifles.'

Simon noticed that Alice was now discreetly scribbling notes on a pad on her lap. 'What about these new political agents?' he asked. 'Were they effective?'

'Yes and no. I believe that they were just beginning to work – particularly along the Khyber Pass, which, as you know, is the main route through into Afghanistan and Kabul. There, the Afridis and our friends the Waziris are among the most warlike tribes but the agent there, Colonel Robert Warburton – the son, by the way, of a British officer and an Afghan mother – has done a remarkable job in winning their respect. He's reaching the end of his career, alas, and in fact, I think he's just gone on final leave, so I don't know what will happen when he's gone for good.

'But it seemed as though things had definitely quietened down over the last two years, as I said. Now, though, we've this nasty business in the Tochi Valley, with an uprising that ain't exactly small in size, Fonthill. So I have to confess that I have a bit of an itchy feeling in me breeches, if you'll pardon the expression, ma'am. That's why I sent young Buckingham out to bring you in.'

He raised his glass again and took a healthy mouthful then turned and addressed Alice and Simon on either side of him. 'But, look here,' he chortled. 'I am being very miserable. This is an old warhorse speaking, who is quite possibly wrong in sniffing from his stable a gallop that is not on the cards. Let us enjoy ourselves while we can. Not a bad drop of Bordeaux, eh? What do you think, Mrs Fonthill?'

Alice hid the pencil in the folds of her dress and raised her glass. 'Delicious, Colonel,' she said. 'It's like finding pure spring water in the Sudanese desert.' She sipped. 'No. Better than that. It's elixir!'

The three raised their glasses and, from down table, a beaming Jenkins, his face glowing like that of a well-scrubbed schoolboy, raised his too and another silent toast was drunk to the company, to the great British Empire and to its dumpy, widowed sovereign so far away.

So the dinner wound on its amiable way, with the voices of the young subalterns at the lower end of the table increasing in volume as the excellent claret was consumed from a line of silver jugs. White-jacketed Pathan servants, red sashes looped diagonally across their chests, brought a succession of scrumptious local dishes: curried lamb and what appeared to be goat with its skin crisply roasted; rice containing eggs and chillies; chapattis; a selection of green vegetables, no doubt raised with care from the allotments surrounding the bungalows; and fresh fruit that caused

Simon to wonder how these barren lands could produce such fine fare.

He gently introduced to the colonel the question of when they might be able safely to leave the haven of the cantonment in the valley; to amble on, so to speak, to enable them to view the beautiful lakes of Kashmir and attempt a little climbing on the lower slopes of the Kush. They did not wish, he emphasised, to make demands on the escorting duties of the Guides, who might well have much more important things to do shortly.

Happily, Fortescue was not offended. 'My dear fellow,' he said, 'let me get some further information along the telegraph line to see how things are going further north and east. Should be better in that direction, I should have thought. You are most welcome to stay here for a day or two to get your breath back, so to speak, and then . . .' He was interrupted as a khaki-clad orderly bent deferentially, whispered in his ear and presented a telegram to him.

The colonel adjusted his spectacles, read the contents quickly and reread it more slowly. He sat back in his chair for a moment, staring straight before him. Then he turned to Alice. 'Excuse me, madam.' Speaking across her to the major who was his second in command and seated on her right, he spoke crisply. 'George, pray have both units – the cavalry and the infantry – ready to leave camp within three hours. Seventy-five rounds per man and rations for two days. Full water bottles, of course. One company of infantry to stay defending the camp. See to it now.'

'Very good, sir.'

Then the colonel banged the table lightly and stood. A

hush fell on the room. 'Madam and gentlemen,' he said. 'I am afraid we must end our dinner immediately. I have just received a telegraph from Malakand. The garrison there is expected to be under attack within the hour from a force of tribesmen approaching them and rumoured to number some ten thousand. We are the nearest post to them and we must hasten to their aid, so we shall ride and march through the night, leaving as soon as we are ready. The whole command will be involved. The cavalry will ride ahead and the infantry will follow. Major Darwin will give you your orders. See to your men. That will be all.'

Fortescue turned to his guests. 'I am so sorry, but I doubt whether you will be able to get away now. The Malakand Pass is some thirty-six miles away and is a vital link in the road to the north and we must not let it fall.' He sighed. 'It seems that I was right and that the whole Frontier will soon be ablaze. This uprising is more than a little local affair and the way to the north is closed. You should be safe, of course, within the camp, so do make yourselves as comfortable as possible and please do finish this bottle of claret. Now you must excuse me.'

Fonthill became aware that Jenkins had materialised by his side. He exchanged glances with his wife. 'If you will allow, sir,' he said to the colonel, 'Jenkins and I will come with you. Even an extra couple of rifles may be of some help to you.'

'And I will come, too,' said Alice immediately, rising from her chair.

'Certainly not, Alice,' Simon spoke firmly. 'I will not allow it. You must see that you must stay here.'

'On the contrary, I don't see that at all—'

Fortescue interjected. 'I am afraid, my dear, that your husband is right.' He smiled. 'From what I have heard, particularly today, you shoot as well as any trooper.' Then his tone hardened. 'But I fear I must request – no, order – you to stay. Having a woman with us would impose an extra burden on me as commander. I am sure you will understand.'

He turned to Fonthill. 'But glad to have you and your man, Fonthill. Please both of you ride with me with the cavalry. We leave within three hours – earlier if Darwin can get us provisioned in time.' He gave a curt bow to Alice and then strode away.

Alice face was white. 'Damn and blast this masculine superiority,' she stormed. 'I was fighting as well as . . . as well as Jenkins this morning, but all that is forgotten now. I'm just a frail little woman who must be protected. Well, I think that is just nonsense. There is a damned good story in this for the *Morning Post* and I must write it and I can't write it if I don't observe it at first-hand.'

Simon sighed. 'Well, my love, this may be male chauvinism but we must respect the colonel's wishes. We must not add to his problems. Having to worry about keeping a woman safe when he is about to deploy his small force in the face of ten thousand warriors would be asking too much of him. You must see that.'

'Well, I don't—'

Another, more effective argument struck Simon and he interrupted her. 'Look, you have an exclusive – what do the Americans call it . . . ? A scoop, yes. A scoop. By staying here you have the chance to write a story about the fact that Malakand is about to be attacked, set against the background of the general uprising, and get it on the telegraph to Peshawar and via the cable there to London before anyone else has heard about it. I saw you scribbling away while the colonel spoke. Get writin', my love!'

He grinned and brought a rueful smile to his wife's face. 'Very well, Simon. But you and Jenkins must not go on this ridiculous ride. You are both too old to go soldiering again, really you are. Please don't go. I shall be so worried about you both. Stay here and protect this poor fragile woman.'

'No. You will have a whole company of the Guides doing that, by the sound of it. And I know the colonel could do with an extra couple of guns. He jumped at it, in fact. Sorry, darling, but I must go – if only to look after Jenkins. You know what an old frump he is.'

He leant forward and kissed his wife, who, knowing when she was beaten, nodded and glumly returned his embrace. Then she turned to Jenkins. 'Look after him, 352. If you both get killed I shall hold you personally responsible.'

'Very good, Miss Alice. I shall wrap 'im in cotton wool. Come on, bach sir. We've got to get packin'. We can't keep the whole of the Indian army waitin', now, can we?'

CHAPTER THREE

It was, of course, quite dark as Fonthill and Jenkins lined up on the parade ground with the rest of the cavalry and, behind them, the serried ranks of the infantry. The heat of the day had diminished but it was still hot, with the dry air clinging to them all like the breath of a furnace. The densely indigo cover of the Indian night hung over them, with the stars pricking through it like sequins and the emergent moon lighting the scene as though it was day.

As Simon looked at the horsemen, sitting erect with their eyes bright in their dark faces, he could not help but feel exhilarated at being part of such an impressive gathering. He was about to ride with arguably the best regiment in the Indian army. He stole a glance at Jenkins and sensed that the Welshman shared the exaltation. They exchanged grins.

Fonthill looked over his shoulder but there was no sign

of Alice. She had helped him prepare for the ride – although there was little to take: his rifle, freshly oiled; a revolver in its holster; a bandolier of ammunition; one change of shirt, socks and underpants; a *poshteen* sheepskin coat tightly wrapped in a groundsheet, to serve as a sleeping bag and for warmth in case they had to fight in the high passes; his water bottle; and slices of lamb wrapped in chappatis. They had said their goodbyes in his room. She was dry-eyed but she clung to him for at least ten seconds before he was allowed to go.

A bugle sounded and four mounted pickets galloped out to range widely ahead of the main column. A second call was sounded, the colonel raised an arm, pointed forward and the cavalry moved out from the cantonment at the walk, four abreast.

Fortescue beckoned for Fonthill and Jenkins to join him and Major Darwin at the head of the column. 'It's goin' to be a hard ride, this, Fonthill,' he growled, adjusting the chinstrap of his helmet. 'We are going to have to climb 2,000 feet up to the Malakand Pass right at the end, when we shall be feeling damned tired. And despite the altitude, it will remain hot, damned hot, with plenty of dust.'

'Do you think you will be attacked on the way?'

'Wouldn't be surprised. But not until we get near Malakand, I would think. The tribesmen from here will be massed there. I just hope we will be in time.'

'Will we arrive before dawn?'

'Good Lord, no. Not a chance. It's just a trail really, not a proper road, and very rough underfoot. Trouble is, we must keep goin'. Can't afford to take proper stops for rest. Our chaps on foot will have the worst of it, of course, and they will arrive long after us. Still, can't be helped. Just got to grin and bear it and then . . .' he turned and grinned mirthlessly . . . 'with a bloody great fight at the end. What could be better, eh?'

Fonthill gulped but returned the grin.

So began one of the most arduous nights and rides of Simon Fonthill's life. Most of the time, the colonel restricted the pace of the riders to a walk, but he interspersed spells of trotting and cantering on the level ground to maintain their progress. Simon had no idea how many men were defending the fort and post at Malakand, but it was clear that the colonel knew that they would be facing overwhelming odds and it was vital to arrive in time before the defenders were overrun.

At one point, as they dismounted and walked their horses to rest them for a brief spell, Fonthill asked the colonel about the insurgents. Did they have one overall leader on the Frontier?

The CO wiped his brow with a soiled handkerchief and shook his head. 'They will never be that organised,' he confided. 'What I estimate is happening is that this is a jihad – a holy war – and it is being whipped up all along the Border by a series of holy men, preachers – they call 'em mullahs. It like a series of bush fires, yer see, with the flames leapin' over the passes and running down the valleys from mullah to mullah as though blown by the wind.'

'The preachers – we know of the one in the Malakand area and we call him the Mad Mullah – will be promising their followers that this is the chance to rid the hills of the infidels once and for all. They will tell 'em that anyone who is killed will go straight to Paradise and be welcomed

57

by houris and lustin' virgins. So they'll have absolutely nothing to lose by hurling themselves at our guns. Oh, yes.' His mouth was set in a grim line. 'It's going to be a tough one, this.'

Fonthill drew in a deep breath. The colonel was only a couple of years younger, if that, and certainly seemed stouter and in less good condition. Yet the little man was riding as though he was a subaltern.

'What about reinforcements?' asked Simon.

'Well, I have telegraphed down the line to Peshawar and told my commanding officer there that we were on the way and that we would need help. He is organising a larger column, of course, to follow us but it will take time to get it together, so we shall be on our own for a fair bit.' He grinned again. 'Wouldn't have it any other way, mind you. Chance for glory and promotion, eh what, Fonthill?'

'Of course, sir. I wish you luck.'

'Thank you. Wish this bloody moon would go in, though. Makes us exposed. Feel as though I am walkin' through these hills in me pyjamas.'

So they continued this gruelling ride, pushing mounts and men as far as they could, short of exhaustion. The darkness brought little relief from the heat, despite the altitude, and the troopers in the rear of the column suffered excessively from the dust kicked up by the horses in front of them. Fortescue, the thoughtful commander that he was, changed the line of march so that the lead squadrons changed places for those in the rear from time to time to alleviate this problem. In the centre of the column rode ten mules, carrying two dismantled mountain guns, or, as they were known, 'screw guns', so called because they could be screwed together. With well-trained crews, these could be assembled within minutes to fire a 2.5 inch, 7lb explosive or shrapnel shell over a maximum range of 4,000 yards and they were much feared by the tribesmen.

Fonthill noticed, however, that, despite the high reputation that the Guides enjoyed within the Indian army, they, like the rest of the native troops, were issued only with the out-of-date, single-shot Martini-Henry rifles, as used by the British army nearly two decades before in the Zulu War. Only the British regiments serving in India carried the new, quick-firing, ten-shot Lee-Metfords. He reflected ruefully that, with memories of the Mutiny still fresh after forty years, the Raj still did not *quite* trust its native sepoys.

Dawn broke while they were still some seven miles or so from their objective, all riding now, slouched in the saddle, with dry throats and lips and half blinded by the dust that still accompanied them. Simon hoped to God that the outriders remained watchful, for the main column would find it hard to resist a sudden attack. He looked back at the long, weary trail stretching behind him. As far as he could see or hear, there had been not one single rider who had fallen out of the column through the night. Now the sun's rays were burning through the dust to increase their discomfort.

He exchanged glances with Jenkins, riding at his side. Unlike most everyone else in the column, the Welshman still rode impeccably erect in the saddle, but his eyes were red-rimmed and weary. He wiped his moustache to rid it of the dust. 'I could do with a beer,' he muttered. 'Should 'ave put some o' that Indian light ale in me canteen before we set off. This water's fair boilin'.'

Too tired to speak, Fonthill nodded.

'When we get there,' continued Jenkins. 'What d'yer think? Are we just goin' to charge them ten thousand black fellers? Wavin' our swords an' that – though, mind you, we ain't got any, now, 'ave we?'

Simon shook his head. 'Don't try to use your rifle,' he croaked. 'These rifle buckets are meant for Martini-Henry carbines. Our rifles are too long for them and they'll jolt out if we gallop. So tie 'em to the saddle. And, if we do charge, use your revolver only.'

'Ah, very good, bach sir. An' you remember, if we do charge, grip tightly with yer knees an' stay low. I'll be at your side.'

'I know. As always.'

Fonthill allowed his horse to slip back until he was able to fall in with Lieutenant Buckingham, leading his troop with Inderjit Singh by his side. The subaltern touched his helmet in a weary salute. 'Tough going, eh, sir?'

Simon nodded. 'Not exactly a hack down Rotten Row. How are your men?'

The young man grinned through the dust coating his face. 'Oh, they're topping. D'yer agree, *daffadar*?'

The Sikh returned the grin. 'Oh yes, Sahib. Just a jolly little ride through the hills. With a nice charge and gallop to finish, yes?'

'Good Lord,' said Simon. 'You sound just like your father. Tell me Inderjit, do you remember him well?'

'Oh yes, sir. I can see him now telling me to keep my

left elbow up when I try to play with straight bat. "Keep it up", he would cry, "then the ball go straight back past bally bowler for four".'

Fonthill nodded slowly. 'Do you know,' he said, 'I can hear him now, too.' All three fell silent for a moment. Then Simon asked of Buckingham: 'Have you ever been in a cavalry charge before, Duke? I mean – one in anger, not just in training?'

For a moment, the young man dropped his eyes and licked his lips. 'Not exactly, sir,' he said. Then, looking up, 'But I'm looking forward to it. Must be exciting, I would think.'

'Oh, very. I must remember not to fall off.' Simon touched his once white pith helmet, now stained a very deep khaki by the dust. 'Well, good luck to you two. I hope to see you later.'

As the morning wore on, Fonthill pulled out his pocket watch. It was seven-forty-five. They must be near now, for the road was getting steeper and climbing towards the Pass. And, indeed, within minutes a faint sound from up ahead – distant firing.

'Thank God for that,' cried Fortescue, reining in. 'They're still there and defending the place by the sound of it.' A palpable sense of relief ran through the leading squadrons. 'Bugler,' called the colonel. 'Sound officers to the front.' He turned to his second in command. 'George, the pickets need relieving so that they can breakfast, but I want to brief the reliefs before they go out. Have them report to me. Quickly now, we may not have much time. Fonthill, stay close to me with your chap.'

Within seconds, it seemed all of the officers had cantered to the head of the column and gathered round the colonel.

'Right, gentlemen,' he said. 'I hope and trust there have been no dropouts while in column. Report please.'

Each troop commander reported negatively.

'Splendid. As was to be expected. Now, listen carefully.' The little man eased himself forward in the saddle. 'We will break here for breakfast and to feed the horses. No more than thirty minutes, but we shall need that after our long ride. Then we shall move up towards the pass at Malakand. There was a brigade in there defending the post and the road to the north but God knows how many are left now. The geography there is this.'

He cleared his throat of dust. 'Commanding the Pass itself is a fort, on a spur to the left of the road looking north. From this spur the road runs down to a kind of bowl, some six hundred yards in diameter, called the "Crater", if I remember rightly. Originally there were about two hundred men manning the fort – it's not much of a place I'm afraid – but the camps of the 24th Punjabs and 45th Sikhs, with some sappers, miners stores and so on are, or were, in the Crater, surrounded by a line of protective *abattis* and a bit of wire.

'The rest of the brigade – the 31st Punjabis, a cavalry squadron, a mountain battery and the transport – are, or were, camped about thirteen hundred yards away up the north-west road, protected by a low *abattis* and breastworks. In short, the whole place is a bit of a defensive mess, spread out in three places. Things will have changed now, I suspect, with some integration. But we shall have to see.

'Now. We will probably have to cut our way through, so

we will go in at the walk, then, at the order, canter and then, at the order, *daffadars* will lower lances and other ranks draw their sabres and charge. We will make for the fort as the nearest point, if, of course, it has not yet been taken. If the defenders are still there, they will hear our bugles and open their gates to us. Once inside, handlers take the horses and the rest disperse to the walls. I may need to change these orders in the light of circumstances. Now see to your men and horses and good luck, gentlemen.'

The relieving pickets had been waiting until the colonel had finished and he now turned to them. 'You heard all of that,' he said. 'I want you to ride ahead now and spy out the disposition of the enemy. I may have to change my plan of attack in the light of what you tell me. *Daffadar*, when you have seen where the defenders are and how the enemy is placed, ride back and report to me. The rest of you stay on picket to ensure we are not attacked. Had your breakfasts?'

'Yes, Colonel sahib.'

'Good. Off you go.'

Fonthill and Jenkins, on the periphery of all this, exchanged glances and Simon nodded in appreciation. Colonel Fortescue undoubtedly knew what he was doing – and he cared for his men. The best type of British senior officer and typical, Simon was beginning to feel, of the Queen's Royal Corps of Guides.

As anticipated, the 2,000ft climb up to the Malakand Pass proved to be the most demanding sector of the whole march, for horses and men were tired, caked in dust and thirsty. In addition, the climb was now steep and, towards the end, Fortescue felt it necessary to dismount and lead the horses, leaving the column at a great disadvantage should a flank attack be mounted. But none came and the Pass was reached just as the *daffadar* in charge of the forward picket came riding in.

He reported tersely to the colonel and Fortescue immediately ordered his officers forward – by gesture this time, for he did not wish to signal his presence yet by bugle call.

'Change of orders, gentlemen,' he announced, speaking quickly. 'The good news is that the garrison has held out throughout the night. But the bad is that, while the fort and the Crater have withstood what looks like continuous attacks, the forward camp, up the North-West Road, has had to be abandoned, by the look of it. At the moment, it looks as though the attackers have retired but are massing for a further attack. Our pickets can see a considerable number of tribesmen approaching from the north. There remains considerable sniping, so we must ride through that.

'Once over the summit, we will now pass the fort and instead canter down to the Crater and reinforce our people there. Now mount and draw sabres.'

Fonthill drew out his watch again. It showed 8.30 a.m. They had been on the road for just over ten hours. Now they must fight. He nodded to Jenkins and they removed their long rifles from their saddle buckets and strapped them to the saddle pommels. They both checked their revolvers to ensure that the magazines were full and then, exchanging nervous grins, they dug their heels into their mounts and gently moved forward behind the colonel and Major Darwin.

As they crested the brow of the Pass a compelling vista met their gaze. The Malakand Valley unfolded beneath them in a series of broken-topped, undulating hills towards a purple and mountainous horizon. The road fell steeply down, past the small, primitive fort on its left, from where, down the hill, it forked left and right just before the tents, shacks and surrounding wired perimeter that was the Crater. Beyond that, in the mid distance, were the remains of the forward camp, through which tiny, white-clad figures could be seen swarming, setting fire to buildings and tents. It looked as though the fort itself had not suffered attack – surprisingly, because the Pass looked down on it. The Crater itself was crowded with defenders.

It was clear, however, from where the attacks had come, for the low hills to the north, east and west of the Crater and surrounding it were alive with figures – brought into focus through field glasses as turbaned, rifle-carrying and sword-bearing Pathans – all swarming now towards the defenders of the Crater. Fonthill brought his binoculars to bear further up the road to the north-east and saw an indistinct mass of men moving towards the action.

'God!' he whispered to Jenkins. 'There must be thousands of them coming in—'

He was interrupted by the colonel, who raised his sabre and turned his head back. 'Bugler, sound the advance. To the front, cantaaah!'

Then, in columns of fours, the regiment rode down towards the Crater, receiving a thin cheer from the defenders of the fort as they passed. The canter seemed to Fonthill to be a rather stately advance, with the horses moving in an unhurried rhythm as though on parade and their riders sitting erect, with their sabres raised vertically aligned to their bodies, as though ready to salute their sovereign at a presentation of their colours at the Horse Guards in London.

Then things changed.

From the foothills to the right, tribesmen began breaking cover and pouring towards the protecting *abattis* surrounding the Crater. Fonthill, riding directly behind the colonel, could feel the joy in the little man's posture as he noted this and then turned and pointed forward with his sabre, his face agleam, and shouted 'Bugler, sound the . . . Chaaaaarge!'

Immediately, there was a whoop from the troopers as the notes sounded out and the horses, as one beast, gathered themselves and launched into the charge. Fonthill drew in a great gulp of hot air, lowered his head and dug his heels into the side of his mount. He had little need to have done so for the beast flared her nostrils and thundered forward with the rest. As the column charged, so its leaders slightly fanned out so that a broader front could be presented to the enemy to the front.

Fonthill hardly had time to see where the charge was leading them until he was suddenly in the middle of a mass of scattering figures in white-and-dun-coloured clothing, some who were kneeling and firing their rifles, others who were standing defiantly, sword in hand, to meet the charge and more who were now simply attempting to flee.

Bending low and desperately gripping with his knees, he rode down one man, which nearly unhorsed him, but the beast recovered and bounded forward and he just had time to fire with his revolver into the breast of a Pathan who had his sword raised. He felt himself slipping from the impact but a firm hand from the right pressed him back into the saddle and he became aware of Jenkins riding close beside him. Then they parted in the melee and Fonthill was bending low and firing at a succession of figures who tried to bring him down and desperately urging his horse on until, blessedly, he was through the attackers and into open space on the other side.

He reined his horse around and found Jenkins, bleeding from a sword wound in his thigh, galloping towards him, grinning and waving his revolver. As he watched, others emerged from the fray and, there was the colonel, Major Darwin at his side, blood oozing from his calf, waving his sword and ordering the bugler to sound the re-form.

Somehow, the regiment began to make a coherent formation again and Fonthill realised, with relief, that there were very few riderless horses among them. The pace and force of the charge had taken the tribesmen on their flank and carried the cavalry straight through them, leaving scores of lifeless figures on the plain behind them.

A cheer sounded from behind the low wall of the Crater and it was immediately answered by the tribal cry of the Pathans – the Pathans, that is, who formed the Guides' cavalry, who were now waving their sabres at their colonel and forming up into some kind of formation.

Wiping his brow, Fonthill realised that, for the first time in his life, he had taken part in a cavalry charge in earnest – and he had survived. What's more, so had Jenkins. He took out his watch. The whole thing, from the moment they had cantered down from the brow of the Pass until now, had taken just three minutes! He realised that he was trembling.

'You're hurt,' he called to Jenkins.

'It's nothing. The tip of the bugger's sword just caught me before I got 'im. 'Ardly worth patchin'. But blimey – what a ride, eh!'

'352. Thank you for pushing me back. I think I would have regained the saddle, so it was not necessary to nursemaid me, you know. But thank you, anyway. Damnit, you're always there, aren't you?'

The Welshman, perspiration trickling down into his wide moustache, had the grace to look embarrassed. 'Ah, bach sir. I don't mean to be pissin' in your pocket, so to speak. But it's me job, look you. What else would I be doin', now?'

A sudden crackle of musketry from the hills to their right caused the colonel to raise his sword and shout, 'Back to the Crater now, at the gallop!' As he led, so the whole column, now strung out less than tidily, followed until they were all safely through the wooden gate that was swung back for them.

Safely inside, Fortescue was warmly welcomed by the officer commanding the post, a fiercely moustached Colonel Meiklejohn, of the 20th Punjabis, who shook hands all around. It was clear that he was vastly relieved to have reinforcements.

'Are your infantry on their way as well, Fortescue?' he asked anxiously.

'Right behind us – though I don't expect them to arrive for about another nine hours or so, poor blighters. It was bad enough for us but it will have been worse for them. But they will get here, don't you worry. Here, come and meet someone interesting.'

He walked Meiklejohn over to where Fonthill was attempting to bandage Jenkins's thigh. 'This is Fonthill – you may have heard of him. You were at Kandahar with Roberts, I know. Fonthill was there too, and he's the chap, with his man here, Jenkins, who got through to Gordon in Khartoum and then was nabbed by the Mahdi as he tried to get back. They've already shown they're damned good fighters, as if we didn't know already.'

'Good Lord, yes.' Meiklejohn held out his hand. 'Heard of both of you and I'm delighted to meet you at last.' He gave a wan smile. 'Don't quite know what you're doing here charging around with this superannuated cavalryman here, but you are most welcome. Welcome then, from the frying pan to the fire.'

Everyone smiled and Fortescue briefly related Fonthill and Jenkins's reasons for visiting Marden.

'You must have had a tough time of it through the night, Colonel,' observed Simon.

'Yes. They just kept coming at us, throwing themselves forward almost onto our bayonets, so to speak. We have made some bayonet charges straight back at 'em in counter-attacks through the dark hours and that's shaken 'em a bit. But they have still kept coming in the darkness and there has been a lot of hand-to-hand stuff.'

He turned back to Fortescue. 'I have deployed men to extend our defences out behind stone sangars along the ridge up to the fort on our right. The Pathans haven't shown much interest in the fort, so I've taken some of the two hundred 24th Punjabis defending it to man our perimeters.' He gave a weary smile. 'We've taken a fair number of casualties through the night, including some of my officers, but now that you're here I'm sure we can hold out. I doubt they will attack us during the heat of the day, but they are showing no sign of retreating.'

Fonthill nodded. 'Who are they? I mean, what tribe?'

'They're Swats, from directly north of here. We are just about in their territory.' He gestured up the road. 'But there are new fellers arriving in considerable numbers, as you can see. They're the chaps dressed in brown coming from the hills to the left. They're Bunerwals from the west. We've not had trouble with them since 1863, but obviously the word has got out that there is rich pickings to be had and the vultures are gathering for the feast.'

He lowered his voice. 'Trouble is . . . see that little mud-walled building beyond our defences on the road that forks to the north-east?'

The three men nodded. 'That was our *serai*, where we held our ammunition reserves. There was no time to evacuate it with the ammunition, so it was held by one of our *subedars* and a handful of sepoys for six hours during the night. Most of them were killed but the *subedar* and five men were just able to get away in the final onslaught. Wonderful chaps but they couldn't bring the ammo with them. So I'm afraid we are running low. What have you brought, Fortescue?'

'Enough to share with you, and the infantry will have reserves.'

'Splendid. Now, the attacks have eased since you have come, so get some rest and perhaps we can talk about deploying your men. Are you happy, old chap, to put yourself under my command?'

'Of course. It's your show.'

The two men walked away in deep conversation and Fonthill and Jenkins exchanged glances.

'I'd say, two of the old school, bach sir,' observed Jenkins.

'Yes. Better than at Isandlewana. Just as brave but with more sense, it seems to me.'

'Well, I do 'ope so. It all sounds a bit Rorke's Drift to me, look you – though you were there and I wasn't.'

'No. Not as bad as the Drift. We've got the best part of a brigade here. There, we had only a company of half invalids, although the Zulus only had a handful of rifles, of course. This lot seem to have a veritable arsenal supplying them. Ah well, never mind.' He tightened the bandage. 'Now, how's that? Too tight? It's stopped bleeding, anyway. Do you want to see the doctor?'

'Gawd no, thank you kindly. I am now once again a splendid example of a Welsh fightin' machine. Though a bit tired, look you.'

'Let's see if we can find a bit of shade and curl up somewhere. I can hardly keep my eyes open.'

They found a patch of shade behind one of the huts in the centre of the Crater, unravelled their *poshteens* and were soon blissfully asleep, in spite of the sporadic rattle of rifle fire from the low hills around them.

They woke, some three hours later, to eat what was left of their sandwiches and drink water from their canteens.

Some of the Guides were now manning the perimeter wall of the Crater and Simon could see others lining the stone sangars up the ridge to the right. Fonthill unslung his field glasses and focused them up the roads that wound down and round to the right and left after they split just down below the Crater. He frowned. The narrow gaps in the hills from both directions were filled by masses of tribesmen, advancing towards the defences of Malakand. He put down the glasses and shook his head. How could this badly mauled post hold out against such numbers?

He beckoned to Jenkins. 'See if the horses are all right. Then find the colonel – either one will do – and ask where they would like us. Oh, and see if you can find a couple of bayonets from somewhere. I would feel much happier with lungers on the end of the Lee-Metfords.'

'Blimey, so would I.'

Inevitably, Jenkins – the indomitable forager – returned within the half-hour carrying two bayonets, two mugs of hot tea and a fistful of chapattis, concealing something hot and spicy. Then the two took up their positions with the native troops manning the east side of the *abattis*. These were just hastily positioned poles of wood fixed at just below shoulder height and topped by strands of barbed wire.

There they crouched through most of the afternoon, ducking their heads as an occasional bullet thudded into the *abattis* or pinged overhead.

Towards late afternoon a bugle sounded from high on the Pass and a cheer went up from the fort, then echoed by the defenders in the Crater, as a line of khaki-clad figures could be seen cresting the *kotal*. There they paused and the sunlight glinted off steel as bayonets were fixed. The Guides' infantry had arrived!

The line of troops manning the stone sangars up to the fort set up covering fire to protect the infantry and no attempt was made by the Pathans to attack as they marched wearily but solidly down to the Crater. There they were dispersed inside the defences to get some rest before the inevitable night attack, for they had marched for nearly eighteen hours, with only brief breaks, and they were exhausted.

As the sun set, however, drums began beating from the hills and the cries of the tribesmen began to rise to a crescendo that made the defenders manning the *abattis* feel that they were caught in the centre of some kind of crazily discordant orchestra, conducted by the devil himself.

'What they tryin' to do, burst our bleedin' eardrums?' shouted Jenkins.

'Save your breath,' grunted Fonthill. 'They're creeping nearer and, as soon as the sun goes down, they'll be at us over this bit of open ground in their thousands. We'll need to fire as fast as we can, so lay out your spare magazines.'

So it proved. No sooner had the last rays of the sun flickered away over the jagged hilltop then the cries changed to screams and the earth shook as thousands of sandals thudded across the beaten ground. As Fonthill and Jenkins levelled their rifles and squinted down the barrels a solid mass of figures, waving swords, emerged from the gloom, startlingly close.

Immediately, the wall of the *abattis* was lit by the flashes of the rifles. There was no need for the defenders to aim. So massed were the attackers and so short the range that it was impossible to miss. The complete front rank of the charging tribesmen fell, bringing down with them those immediately in the rear. But the following lines jumped over the bodies and ran on . . . into the wall of death produced by the line of Martini-Henrys, firing and being reloaded as fast as brown fingers could ram the cartridges into the breeches.

Despite the speed with which the sepoys could fire and reload their single-shot rifles, the ten-shot magazines of the Lee-Metfords at the shoulders of Fonthill and Jenkins could more than treble the firepower of the older rifles and, working the breech bolts feverishly, they were able to cut a noticeable swathe in the phalanx of attackers immediately in front of them. Nevertheless, it was more than ten minutes before the tribesmen, now seriously hindered by the bodies at their feet, paused and then – as was their custom – began retrieving their wounded and the corpses that littered the earth before retreating.

'No firing,' shouted Meiklejohn. 'Save your ammunition. Let them collect their dead.'

'Blimey!' Jenkins wiped his mouth and moustache with the back of his hand, spreading the smudge of cordite across his cheek. 'I thought they'd never stop comin'. They've got guts, I'll give 'em that.'

Fonthill slumped down, his back to the barricade. 'They think that if we kill 'em, they'll go straight to Paradise.' He grunted. 'The pearly gates are going to be a bit crowded by the time this night is over.' He looked up. 'You all right, 352?'

'Just about, thank you. 'Ow long will they keep chargin', d'yer think?'

74

'Well, there are certainly enough of them out there to keep attacking all through this night and then the next. How's your thigh?'

'Ah, stopped bleedin' ages ago. It was just a scratch.'

'Good, but you will have lost a bit of blood, at least. Close your eyes for a minute. I'll keep watch.'

'Thank you, bach sir. Best keep lookin'. They come out of the darkness so quick, bless you, that they're 'ere before you'd know it, see.'

Further down the line, the *abattis* had been breached after intensive hand-to-hand fighting and a handful of Pathans had broken through. The small reserve that Meiklejohn had stationed in the middle of the Crater, however, rushed forward and the intruders were killed within seconds, after which anxious hands restored the barrier.

The respite after the first charge lasted only long enough for the tribesmen to clear away their dead and wounded, before more beating of drums announced a fresh wave of attacks. Once again, the Pathans rushed forward in a maniacal desire to get to close quarters where their swords and knives could take effect. And once again, the crashing volleys brought them down in untidy lines, like piles of seaweed left high on a beach to mark the highest of the tide.

So it went on through the night until dawn brought succour to the exhausted defenders. Immediately, the officers began checking the casualties.

Fonthill wandered over to where Meiklejohn and Fortescue were crouched, sipping from tin mugs of coffee.

'Thank you, Fonthill,' said the former, raising his mug. 'I watched you. You and your chap have done sterling work through the night. Sorry we can't put you in charge somewhere but, to be honest, your sharp shooting with those Lee-Metfords are more valuable to us than having you charging around waving a sword.'

'Of course he's useful,' grunted Fortescue. 'He's a Guide – even if only an honorary one.'

'Have some coffee, my dear chap,' offered Meiklejohn, 'you've earned it.'

'Ah, thank you, Colonel.' Simon accepted the mug. 'It seemed touch and go through the night. Tell me, have we suffered many casualties?'

Meiklejohn extracted a scrap of paper from his pocket and consulted it. 'Bad enough. Forty-two casualties in all. Not as bad as the night before, though. We lost three officers killed then and three wounded. Of the men, there were twenty-one killed and thirty-one wounded. If these losses continue we shall be in trouble. One good thing, though – just before daybreak I was able to get parties out on both sides of the Crater with bayonets and screw guns to clear the foothills. They had trouble at first but we managed to beat back the devils near to us, so the sniping during the day should be less dangerous.

'Now.' He threw away the dregs of his coffee. 'You must excuse me. There is much to do.'

Indeed there was. As before, there were no direct attacks during the day and the sorties just before dawn had cleared the close foothills of snipers, although spasmodic firing continued through the day at long range. The tired defenders were put to work repairing the defences. Trees were cut down to thicken up the *abattis*, the breastworks were strengthened and the barbed wire entanglements renewed. The wounded were tended and then, when the perimeter was judged to be suitably improved, the men were marked off in sections to gain sleep in preparation for another night of attacks.

Once again, at dusk, the bugles sounded the stand-to and, as the light faded, the drums increased their tempi and now the voices of the mullahs could be heard urging their men forward, promising everlasting life for every infidel they killed. And, once again, as the darkness descended, the tribesmen attacked, screaming derision and waving their swords, banners and long daggers.

The Pathans' tactics never changed during the long hours of darkness. Broken only by spells during which they carried back their dead and wounded, the tribesmen kept hurling themselves forward, supported by their riflemen firing from the positions they had been forced to evacuate during the day.

For Fonthill and Jenkins this second night descended into a cauldron of robot-like firing, reloading, cooling their rifles with precious water whenever there was a lull, and – on two heart-in-mouth occasions – thrusting with their long bayonets at the wide-eyed figures who had managed to approach the *abattis* and were hacking at them with their long swords. The Guides' troopers on either side of the pair lacked bayonets, which could not be fitted to their shorter carbines, so they had to resort to slashing with their sabres, sword on sword, taking the conflict back, in Simon's heightened imagination, to the days of the Crusades.

So the weary defenders survived another night of

continuous attacks. Yet ammunition was now running low and orders were given that there should be no replying to the sniping during daylight hours. The hours of darkness were the threat and, just before dusk, parties rushed from the safety of the *abattis* protected by a ring of bayonets and lit bonfires at intervals round the camp.

If the defenders' disciplined musketry had wreaked havoc in the ranks of the Swats and Bunerwals – as surely it must have done – then it seemed to have had no effect on their fanaticism because on they came once again in massed ranks, hurling themselves into the gunfire. They were clearly being reinforced by the arrival of yet more tribesmen, fresh to the battle, and this was marked by the increased number of groups who were able to leap over the barricades and the rifles to enter the inner arena.

For Fonthill, the nadir of this night took place at approximately 3.30 a.m. when, fumbling in his pouch for another magazine, his rifle barrel was knocked aside by a Pathan who had reached the barrier. The man swung his sword horizontally and Simon was able to duck underneath it, withdraw his rifle barrel and, using the last vestige of his strength, plunge the long bayonet into his assailant's chest.

As he was attempting to twist his bayonet and free it, he was only dimly aware of a giant warrior who had leapt onto the top of the *abattis*, his bare feet ignoring the barbed wire that studded it, and swung his sword vertically down. The blade was met, with a clang of steel, just above Simon's head, by the bayonet of Jenkins. The Welshman, a covering of perspiration, cordite and grime giving his face the appearance of some devilish gargoyle in the light of the bonfires, twisted the bayonet round, pushing the sword blade upwards. Immediately, he rammed the butt of his rifle onto the warrior's bare instep, forcing it onto the barb of the wire. The man howled and staggered and Jenkins's bayonet took him in the groin, hurling him back over the barrier.

'Thanks, 352,' gasped Simon. 'I thought he had me then.'

'Not while I'm 'ere, bach. Look to your front now. They're still comin', see.'

And so they did, all through that fiendish night – although the numbers who were able to break through the perimeter were all quickly dealt with by the bayonets of the reserve companies, who remained through the night, watching for such breakthroughs.

Dawn brought relief at last again and with it, the news of fewer casualties this time: only fifteen. More important, however, was another bugle call from the heights of the Pass. It heralded the arrival of a squadron of the 11th Bengal Lancers, with supplies of provisions and ammunition, and the welcome news that the 35th Sikhs and 38th Dogras, plus more ammunition, were on their way up from the south. It had been another forced march and they were forced to stop ten miles from Malakand, for it was reported that they had lost twenty-one men on the way from heatstroke. Colonel Meiklejohn, confident that he could hold for at least another night, sent a message back that they should stay and rest.

Throughout that next day, eager binoculars from the Crater scanned the hills to see if there were signs of the tribesmen withdrawing, at last. But they were not forthcoming. Indeed, fresh warriors were seen to be still trickling down the passes. Attention, then, was turned to employing more sophisticated techniques to strengthen the perimeter of the Crater.

During the day, the remains of the native bazaar near to the destroyed *serai* were cleared to improve the field of fire to the front of the camp and the remnants of the *serai* itself were mined so that explosive charges could be exploded by the pulling of lightly buried wires.

It was just as well, for the ferocity of the attacks that night seemed to be greater than before. The east side of the *abattis,* where Fonthill and Jenkins were stationed, had taken the brunt of the fighting so far and Meiklejohn directed that the Guides who had manned the perimeter there, including the two white men, should change their positions and, hopefully, gain some succour by joining the 24th Punjabis on the less pressed west side. It proved to be what Jenkins described, during the night, as 'an Irishman's gift', for the buried explosives were so effective that they diverted the attackers to the west perimeter, putting the Punjabis, who had now been manning the barricades for five nights in succession, as well as the Guides on that side, under great pressure, particularly for a hectic hour from 2.15 when wave upon wave of tribesmen hurled themselves forward.

There was one incident, however, that occurred that brought smiles even to the haggard features of Fonthill and Jenkins. The Afridis who formed the 24th Punjabis were distant kinsmen, it seemed, to some of the Swats who were attacking them. During a lull in the fighting, the Swats called to the Afridis and suggested that these fellow Pathans and Muslims should lay down their arms and allow the attackers to walk over and jump the *abattis*. Their reward would be to share in the plunder that Malakand would provide. The conversation was relayed simultaneously to a curious – and anxious – Simon by an English-speaking Afridi. The Punjabis immediately agreed and, trustingly, the Swats rose to their feet and walked towards the defences only to be mown down by the grinning Punjabis.

Fonthill and Jenkins observed all this with open mouths. 'Ah, sahib,' explained the friendly Afridi, 'we never like the Swats, you see . . .'

Once again, the defenders survived the attacks, this time most of them asleep on their feet by the morning. But a rumour spread that the Mad Mullah himself had taken part in the attack on the west side – so explaining the intensity of the fighting in the middle of the night – and been wounded and had to withdraw, so disproving his claim to be personally invincible. It was also said that another mullah had been killed outright. This raised spirits as did the defenders' casualty count: only one man killed during the night and nineteen wounded.

During that day, it seemed clear that the Swats and Bunerwals had shot their bolt. Long-range sniping continued but the tribesmen confined their activities to taking away their dead and wounded. One seemingly last attack was mounted later that evening after dark but it was easily beaten off. More frenetic was the very last assault launched later in the middle of a dust storm against the 45th Sikhs. Heated while it lasted, the bayonets of the Sikhs took their toll and the last of the assailants on Malakand limped away.

The next day the 35th Sikhs and 38th Dogras were cheered in on their arrival from Dargai from the south. The siege of Malakand was over at last.

Fonthill and Jenkins slept where they sat that morning, with their backs against the west *abattis*. They were woken by Inderjit Singh, with two steaming cups of coffee and sandwiches containing very old mutton.

'I watch you during the nights,' said the Sikh shyly, 'and if I may say it, you are wonderful fighters, as I remember my father telling me. I am glad you are of the Guides.'

'Well,' said Jenkins struggling to his feet, 'I'm glad we are too. Let's shake 'ands on it, shall we?'

And they did so, exchanging handshakes and grins, although Simon was too tired to stand.

'Right,' said Jenkins stretching his arms above his head and gently shaking his bandaged leg. 'What's next, bach-wonderful-fighter-sir – a bit of a gallop up these bleedin' 'ills and then another charge, eh?'

Fonthill nodded. 'Something like that.' Then he took a bite of his sandwich and fell immediately asleep again.

CHAPTER FOUR

The fighting, however, was not quite over. About ten miles up the road to the north, some two hundred men of the 45th Sikhs and 11th Bengal Lancers were garrisoning a small fort overlooking a bridge at Chakdara. It was from this direction that the Mad Mullah had led his hordes and there was considerable anxiety among the defenders of Malakand about the safety of this small outpost. Just two words had been received from them – 'Help us' – via the heliograph. Meiklejohn had immediately despatched a captain and forty men of the 11th Bengal Lancers to reinforce the post, but nothing had been heard since.

Now that Malakand was safe the relief of Chakdara became an urgent priority and Meiklejohn immediately organised an additional force of Lancers and Guides' Cavalry to ride to Chakdara. Colonel Fortescue bustled over to Fonthill to inform him of the plans.

'No need for you two chaps to go,' he said. 'You have done more than enough here and I am sure that you will want to get back to your wife and make plans for the rest of your . . . er . . . holiday.' He gave a wan smile. 'Fine start you have had to it, that's for sure.'

Simon returned the smile. 'Thank you, Colonel,' he said. 'Yes, I think we will sit out this next bit, thank you. I am becoming just a little concerned about Alice because she will be worried about us, of course. So we will return to Marden, thank you.'

'Good. Now, I hear that a pretty large body of troops – a field force, no less – is on its way here to teach these Swats and Bunerwals a lesson they will remember, so you should be safe on the way back. Nevertheless, I will send Buckingham and his troop back with you as an escort . . .'

'Oh, thank you, but it sounds as though that won't be necessary, sir.'

'No. I would rather. We can spare them now and I would hate to have some random Pathan sniper pick you off on the way back after all you've been through these last five days. I will detail them now and you leave as soon as you wish. The ride should be easier than when we came.'

He held out his hand. 'You must forgive me if I go now. I have much to do. Thank you, Fonthill – and please thank Jenkins on my behalf. You two made a most valuable contribution to the defence of Malakand and it has been a pleasure to serve with you. I am only sorry we have ruined the start of your holiday.'

The two shook hands and Simon went off to find

Jenkins and prepare for the journey back to Marden. He was not sorry that they were not expected to continue fighting. His shoulder was bruised from the constant recoiling of the Lee-Metford through the four nights at the *abattis* and his eyes were red-rimmed from lack of sleep. Was he too old for adventuring now? He sighed. Yes – well, perhaps too old for intensive soldiering at this level, anyway. And it would be good, so good to see his wife again.

It was a very relieved Alice who threw her arms around him and embraced a rather embarrassed Jenkins similarly as they dismounted after riding into the compound at Marden two and a half days leisurely days later. News of the successful defence of Malakand – and the later successful relief of Chakdara – had already reached her so her anxiety had been virtually dissipated.

'Nevertheless,' she said, 'I didn't know whether you would have volunteered for some other ludicrous expedition. We were supposed to be doing a bit of gentle climbing, remember? Now, let me get my notebook. I want to know all about the defence of Malakand. The *Morning Post* wants me to send a full follow-up story, giving all the details. You see, I took your advice. I am a working girl again.'

So Simon gave her a blow-by-blow account of the battle at Malakand – Alice particularly enjoying the juicy tit-bit about the Afridis in the Punjabis pretending to join their Swat kinsmen on the other side of the *abattis* – and she then began writing a long colour piece that she knew would delight her editor back home, for it would be exclusive.

Nevertheless, Fonthill was uneasy about the excitement and self-satisfaction she was clearly enjoying as a result of her return to active journalism. If these insurrections along the North-West Frontier grew to be of serious proportions, would she insist on staying in the Border territories to report on them?

That first evening, she gave an intimation that this could be so.

'Do you know,' she said, 'the government back home is taking all this very seriously. They have sent out a senior man, a really hardened old sweat, to take charge of three brigades which are making up this Malakand Field Force. He's the delightfully named General Sir Bindon Blood. Do you remember him? He was at all the places we were: Zululand, Afghanistan and Egypt.'

Simon nodded. 'Yes. Quite a character. Didn't one of his ancestors, Colonel Blood, try to steal the crown jewels in Charles the Second's time?'

'Well, I wouldn't know that, but he is supposed to be on his way to Malakand already, ahead of his army.' Alice sniffed and put down her knife and fork. 'What's more, I've heard from London that somebody called Winston Churchill – he's the son of the old Tory Chancellor, Sir Randolph, and he's been home on leave from his regiment in the Indian army – has pulled strings and is on his way out here to join the field force and report on the campaign for the *Daily Express* and also the Indian paper, *The Pioneer*, Kipling's old rag.'

She looked down at her plate. 'So there's going to be a bit of competition around in terms of reporting on this little war.'

Simon drew in a breath to ask her what her own intentions were, but then thought better of it. He certainly did not wish her to resume her former career, which, knowing her, would certainly put her in harm's way. Better to let the matter lie for the moment and defer the inevitable argument that would ensue until it had to be faced.

In the meantime, they all relaxed within the cantonment and continued to enjoy the hospitality of the Guides. The three of them went riding with Buckingham and Inderjit Singh, exploring the valley and the foothills that surrounded it. It was pleasant to deepen the friendship that had already sprung up between them all and Alice and Simon in particular admired the unusually close relationship that obviously existed between young subaltern and his *daffadar,* two men of roughly the same age but from very different backgrounds. It was quite uncommon for such a bridge to be built across the race divide that existed in the Indian army.

It was a tranquil few days that was shattered by a telegram that arrived for Simon. He read it with a frown and looked up to Alice.

'It's from someone called Elgin in Simla,' he said, 'asking me to report immediately to Peshawar where a long letter awaits me. Who the hell . . . wait a minute. He's the Viceroy, isn't he?'

'He certainly is, my darling. He's *Lord* Elgin, in fact. He is going to want you to do something extremely stupid. I can feel it in my bones. Let me implore you now – whatever they ask, don't do it!'

'Well, I certainly have no great desire to get caught up

in what is obviously turning into a great mess along the Frontier.' He frowned. 'But equally I am rather intrigued at what they want of me. I had better ride back into Peshawar right away. It all sounds rather urgent and one can't keep the Viceroy waiting, can one? After all, he represents the Queen here, you know.'

'Yes, I did know that, my dear. And there is no question of you riding back to that miserable place on your own. Jenkins and I will come with you – and the Duke of Buckingham and his merry men, too, if they can be spared.'

The young subaltern immediately insisted on escorting them back to the provincial capital. 'My orders were to look after you, sir, so of course we shall come with you.'

In fact, the thirty-odd miles of riding back the way they had so uncomfortably journeyed some two weeks before were quite uneventful, except for the sun that beat down on them, the rays of which seemed to increase in intensity as they bounced back from the rocks that towered above them on either side of the track. Simon envied the apparent disregard of the heat exercised by the Guides as they jingled alongside their charges.

In Peshawar the trio booked into the little hotel where they had stayed on their recent arrival and Fonthill immediately washed, changed his shirt, brushed his hair and set off for the headquarters of the Punjab Frontier Force, of which the Guides formed part, situated in the heart of the town. He declined the offers of Alice and Jenkins to accompany him. 'It would be like taking my mother and father to see the headmaster on arriving for the first day at a new prep school,' he explained. On reflection, however, he did invite Buckingham to join him. The presence of the young officer, he felt, might give him just a touch of military respectability. He had suffered before at the hands of the British Raj's bureaucracy.

In fact, he need not have worried. He was met at the Guard Room by Commissioner Udny who apologised for the absence of the general commanding the PFF, who was away upcountry with General Blood. 'There's a hell of a lot goin' on at the present, Fonthill,' said Udny. 'We have the letter waiting for you – in fact, there are two. Come into my office, both of you. It's slightly cooler there, though not much. My punkah wallah has been working overtime.'

The punkah wallah was a small Indian who sat on the floor with his back to the wall of the colonel's office, with a long cord attached to his big toe which he languidly twitched to rotate the blades of the fan set in the ceiling. If he was working overtime, reflected Simon, then it would be interesting to see his normal work rate, for the fan did little more than stir the air which hung like swamp fever in the little room.

'Excuse me now if I leave you to it,' said the commissioner. He handed Fonthill a paperknife and then left the room.

Buckingham stood. 'Would you like me to . . . ?'

'No. Stay where you are. This chap in the corner might be a Pathan mullah in disguise. I shall need you to protect me because I'm too bloody fagged in this heat to raise a finger. In fact, I might have difficulty in opening this letter.'

He disregarded that which was addressed to him and looked with interest instead at the second envelope, which was addressed in an ornate script to 'His Highness, the Amir Abdur Rahman, The Royal Palace, Kabul, Afghanistan.' In the bottom corner had been inscribed, 'By Hand of Special Bearer,' and the envelope had been closed on the reverse with the heavily embossed red seal of the Viceroy of India.

'Ah,' muttered Fonthill. 'It looks as though I am being asked to play postman.'

'Good Lord,' exclaimed Buckingham, 'what a strange request.'

'Indeed.' Simon tore open the similarly sealed envelope addressed to him and began to read:

My Dear Fonthill,

We have not met and this alone gives me cause for unease in writing to you in this fashion. I was anxious to invite you to Simla, for I have long admired your distinguished career in various parts of the Empire.

Alas, recent events – of which you will have had cognisance – have prevented me from issuing this invitation, and in this context I must congratulate you on your recent splendid work in helping with the defence of Malakand.

It was my old friend Field Marshal Viscount Wolseley, the Commander-in-Chief of the British army, writing to me from the Horse Guards, London, who informed me of the invitation that had been sent to you by Colonel Fortescue.

In doing so, he said that if ever the need should arise for someone outside the ranks of the army or Diplomatic Corps to give special service to British India during your time here, then he could think of no one more suitable than yourself to undertake this work.

I think that you will already realise that that need has arisen and I am taking advantage of Lord Wolseley's advice in seeking your assistance now.

You will be very much aware that the uprising along the North-West Frontier between the Punjab and Afghanistan looks already likely to become the most dangerous conflagration in India since the Mutiny. We are despatching considerable forces to contain this revolt of the Pathans but I am most anxious that this business should not escalate into a third Afghan War.

To this end, I wish to exert every effort to persuade the Amir in Kabul not to assist the Pathans across his border, either by sending troops to their aid or by giving stimulus or succour in any way to the tribes who are revolting.

I have therefore written him a letter beseeching him to stay neutral in every way in this affair. I am unhappy to despatch this letter to him through the usual channels for two main reasons.

Firstly, the normal methods of communication cannot be relied upon during this time of great

Border unrest and I do not wish the letter to fall into the wrong hands, where its publication could give the Border tribes every reason to think that their activities are causing us distress. Secondly, I wish the bearer of the letter to be a person of some distinction and ability – not merely a senior army officer or political officer – so that he can answer any questions that the Amir may direct to him.

It is important that the bearer has some knowledge of Afghanistan and the wit to be persuasive in argument in terms of whatever points the Amir may put to him. I well remember Viscount Wolseley telling me that you served a similar purpose for General Colley in the Anglo-Boer War when he sent you to deliver an appeal to the President of the Orange Free State, asking him to stay neutral in that conflict. You were successful in that mission. I pray that you will agree to my request to travel to Kabul now, with a similar intention.

I can imagine that, despite the qualifications for this task that I have outlined above, you may well still ask: 'Why me? Is there no one already in India who could fulfil this duty?' The answer is yes – one man, perhaps, Sir Robert Warburton, Political Officer of Khyber, who is respected by the Pathans of the Border. Alas, he is now quite elderly, near the end of his career and anyway is away on leave. I cannot delay the sending of this letter and therefore turn to you with every confidence.

My letter to the Amir, of course, must remain

sealed but it is important that you know the contents and the arguments I use in it. I therefore enclose a copy herewith.

You must be escorted in your journey, of course, and I have therefore telegraphed Fortescue asking him to send a squadron of Guards Cavalry to serve this purpose. Anything larger would savour of some sort of invasion force and anything smaller would be inadequate for your safety and your rank.

In summation, my dear Fonthill, I earnestly hope that you will accept this mission. I must confess that the Amir is elderly and frail but is ruthless and as slippery as an eel. There are rumours that he has published a pamphlet describing himself as 'King of Islam' and is surreptitiously urging a jihad against the British.

He has denied this and I cannot therefore charge him with these acts in my letter. However, if your negotiations become difficult it would do no harm to say that evidence has emerged proving his involvement and see how he reacts.

The main thing, however, is to explain to the Amir – as discreetly as possible, without playing the bully – that if he throws in his lot with the Pathan rebels across the Border then our governments both in India and at home would have no hesitation whatever in invading Afghanistan.

If necessary, you have my permission to point out that at the time of the Mutiny we had only 16 Queen's Line infantry battalions based in India. By the time of the Second Afghan War, in which you were involved, there were not that very many more. Now, however, we have a total of 51 such battalions, out of 141 in the Indian army as a whole. We can, therefore, deploy considerable and highly skilled resources, if we need to.

To repeat, we do not wish to threaten. But it is vital that the Amir does not deploy some of his trained troops over the Border to give the rebels backbone. His restraint in this matter would long be remembered by the British government.

If, as I hope, you are able to accede to my request, then please take every care with your journeys to Kabul and back. You will be travelling through very dangerous territory, I fear. It goes without saying that, should you be in imminent danger of capture, then you must destroy both my letter to the Amir and please destroy this one as soon as you have digested its contents.

Please telegraph your answer to me as soon as possible.

Remember, Fonthill, your Queen-Empress and country need you at this juncture!

With warmest regards,

Yours sincerely,

Elgin

Fonthill sighed and rubbed his forehead.

'Not bad news, I trust, sir?' enquired Buckingham.

'No. not exactly.' He gave a wry grin. 'Well, probably, I

suppose. But you must excuse me, Duke, for I have another letter to read.'

'Of course, sir. I shall retire. Call me when you need me.'

Simon unfolded the copy of the letter to the Amir and began to read. It opened with a brief description of the bearer, emphasising that he was a man with a wide experience of warfare and diplomacy (Fonthill raised an eyebrow at this latter reference) throughout the Empire and held the order of the Companionship of the Bath – a high honour bestowed by the Queen-Empress on him for his services to the realm. He had been entrusted with delivering the letter to the Amir because of the importance of its contents. The Viceroy then expanded a well-modulated argument, outlining the treacherous nature of the uprisings that had taken place at Chitral, in the Tochi Valley and at Malakand and of the role of the mullahs in fermenting jihad in the valleys.

The British army in India, he continued, was well capable of putting down the rebellion but it trusted its good friend, the Amir, not to give aid of any sort to the Pathans occupied in fighting the British Raj across the Amir's border. Such aid could extend the conflict unduly and would, of course, bring the Afghanistan government into a state of open warfare with Great Britain, so undoing the years of amicable friendship that both sides had worked so hard to create.

It ended – to Simon's surprise – with a reminder that the previous Viceroy had only recently supplied the Amir's agent in Peshawar with a gift of 5,000 Lee-Enfield rifles as a 'mark of his confidence in Your Highness'. The present

Viceroy had every trust that that faith would be maintained in these 'more trying times'.

Fonthill put down the letter with a sigh. With trouble imminent – witness the attack on Chitral two years before – why on earth would the then British Viceroy give 5,000 *of the latest* British rifles to a potential enemy? If bribery was needed, why not offer rupees, less instantly convertible into weapons of aggression?

He folded his letter and its enclosure and carefully placed them inside his jacket, called Buckingham and, with a non-commital handshake of thanks to the Commissioner, the two walked back to the hotel. On the way, Simon kept his own counsel and let the young subaltern restrain his obvious curiosity. He had some hard thinking to do.

Alice, of course, had no doubts about how he should reply.

'For God's sake, Simon,' she snorted. 'It's ridiculous to expect someone whose knowledge of India and Afghanistan is nearly two decades out of date to undertake this task. You must refuse, of course. Plead old age, influenza, curry stomach or whatever. But you can't go. Apart from anything else, it will be terribly dangerous. You will be putting your head into the lion's – or rather the tiger's – mouth. Surely you must see that?'

Fonthill thought for a moment. 'Dangerous?' he repeated eventually. 'Well, it looks as though anywhere along the Border just now is likely to be dangerous, although things seem comparatively quiet in the south – and, particularly along the Khyber Pass, which is the route we would have to take to Kabul. As I understand it, the Waziris, whose lands line the Pass, possess reasonably good farmland which they wouldn't want to risk and many of them are ex-sepoys who equally wouldn't wish to risk their pensions. As for the Amir, I doubt if he would lift a finger, either openly or surreptitiously, against an envoy of the Viceroy. So I think we ought to be safe enough.'

Jenkins had joined them and had sat listening intently.

Simon turned to him. 'What do you think, 352?'

The Welshman sniffed. 'It's up to you, bach sir. You know that. But if it's a peaceful postin' I wouldn't object. Me shoulder's still achin' from firin' that Lee-Metford, so I wouldn't be too anxious to go chasin' a Victoria Cross again just yet awhile. But, either way, if you go, then I go with you.'

'And so do I,' said Alice, with conviction.

'Ah.' Simon shook his head. 'Now, that would be out of the question, my love, and you know it.'

'And why, pray, should it be out of the question? Is this the "feeble woman" argument again? That is tosh and you know that.'

'I can't think of a less appropriate description for you, Alice. No. There are two strong points against you accompanying us. The first is that you know how Muslims consider women to be second-class citizens – no, don't object. Hear me out. For me to bring my wife with me on this mission would be to portray myself either as a rather weak object who could not bear to travel without his spouse or as someone who has seriously misunderstood the purpose of the journey, making it a sort of social occasion.'

Alice opened her mouth to interrupt but Simon held up his hand and continued. 'The second reason is more important. You are now a working journalist, known to be reporting on the situation out here for one of Britain's leading newspapers. To take you with me would seriously compromise my position as the Viceroy's envoy on a confidential mission for him.'

A silence fell on the gathering.

Alice sniffed again. 'So,' she said eventually, 'you mean to go?'

Simon shrugged. 'I don't see how I can refuse, to be honest. That *cri de coeur* at the end of his letter – "your country and Queen-Empress need you" – is a bit emotional and penny dreadful, I suppose. The bloody man is blackmailing me, of course. But, to be equally sentimental, I must answer the call.' He put an imaginary bugle to his lips and blew a 'tataa-ta-taa.'

They all smiled.

Alice's face now set in firm lines. 'Very well, my love,' she said. 'I will do a deal with you.'

Fonthill frowned. 'What sort of deal? Now don't be frivolous, Alice. This is serious.'

'And so am I. I won't insist on coming with you to Kabul. But I wish to come part of the way.'

Simon's frown deepened. 'What do you mean, "part of the way"?'

'You said yourself that the route to Kabul is through the famous Khyber Pass. You also said that the Pass is quiet . . .'

'For the moment.'

'Very well. But there are three fairly new-built forts that have been erected along the Pass to protect travellers and that are, by the sound of it, formidable constructions – much more capable of being defended than that sprawl of an encampment at Malakand that, despite the presence of you two, resisted the attack of thousands of Pathans.'

Simon ignored the jibe. 'Yes. Sooo?' He drew out the word suspiciously.

'Sooo. I will come with you to the furthest point of the Pass where the largest of the forts is situated – it's called Landi Kotal. You can leave me there and I should be completely safe within those great walls. I fancy the idea of writing a feature for the *Post* on what life is like garrisoning a fort on the very periphery of the Empire. Dull, perhaps, but not the way I would write it.' She grinned. 'And then you could pick me up on your return from Kabul and we could all go climbing in the Hindu Kush.'

The two ignored a groan from Jenkins.

Fonthill levelled a grim stare at his wife. 'And you would promise that you would not do anything stupid like trying to follow me to Kabul?'

'Cross my heart and hope to die.'

Simon looked across to Jenkins who grinned and shrugged his shoulders. 'Very well. But don't you dare go looking for trouble.'

'And I could well say the same to you, my love. Now. When do we leave? I really must wash my hair.'

'Well, Fortescue must send us his squadron, I suppose, first. Our way will not take us past Marden. And I would like to telegraph the colonel and ask that Buckingham and his troop are included in the escort. They might fancy a break.'

'Ah, what a good idea. And Inderjit too, of course?'

'Of course. He is the troop's *daffadar*.'

Fonthill cabled his acceptance of the Viceroy's request to Simla, keeping the message simple but giving no details of the request, to ensure confidentiality: 'Honoured to be asked. Answer is yes, of course.' Then, after consulting Buckingham, he telegraphed to Fortescue asking that the subaltern's troop should be included in the escort and set about preparing for his journey.

The travelling and holiday garments that had been suitable for the long voyage out and serviceable in the mess at Marden and even at the Malakand *abbatis* would not do, he felt, for the demands of an Amir's court, so he set about finding something in Peshawar more suitable for an envoy of the Viceroy. He settled for a formal dark-blue dress coat and narrow trousers, with the Maltese Cross depicting the order of the Companionship of the Bath, normally worn on a ribbon round the neck, fixed firmly to the jacket. It would, he felt, look a touch more viceregal there. A smart red sash completed the look of a diplomat who would stand no nonsense.

They found a facsimile of the Distinguished Conduct Medal to be worn by Jenkins (he had long since lost the original) on a smart warrant officer's dress tunic. Fonthill felt that, as a representative of the Viceroy of India, he had every right to promote Jenkins on the spot – while pointing out to him that, alas, a regimental sergeant major's pay did not come with the jacket. He persuaded, for 100 rupees (roughly £6.10s.), the armourer at the army barracks to clean and grease his and Jenkins's rifles and revolvers and also replenish the ammunition they had expended so lavishly at Malakand. A cavalry officer's sword was added to Fonthill's kit, to give his mounted presence more military authority.

A pair of trustworthy and beautifully groomed army mounts provided by Commissioner Udny at Peshawar completed the more substantial elements of the provisions for the journey as the eighty-two men of the second troop of Guides sent from the Guides' depot at Marden arrived, to complete Fonthill's escort of a squadron, one hundred and sixty-four men in all.

Buckingham was standing with Fonthill as this second troop arrived. His face fell noticeably as the smartly attired men jingled towards them.

'What's the matter, Duke?' asked Simon.

'Ah, er, nothing important, sir.'

'Come along. I couldn't help noticing. You seem disappointed to see your lot arrive. I was told a full squadron was needed, you know.'

'Yes, of course. It's just . . . well . . . I really shouldn't say this, sir, but as you are not actually in the army and we've, er, got along so well so far, if I may say so, I might perhaps confide in you. I'm afraid I don't get along frightfully well with the chap who will command the squadron.' He nodded discreetly to where a tall, heavily moustached officer was dismounting. 'Captain Appleby-Smith, sir. Not quite my cup of tea, I'm afraid. Forgive me if I say nothing more.'

He sprang to attention and saluted smartly as Appleby-Smith approached. The salute was returned casually to acknowledge Buckingham and then the captain gave a half-deferential nod of the head to Fonthill.

'Good day, Mr Fonthill. Appleby-Smith, sir. Good to see you again. I have the honour of commanding your escort to Kabul.'

Simon extended a hand and examined the captain carefully. The man was, of course, older than Buckingham by perhaps ten years and slimly built, with the cavalry man's rather bowed legs. His countenance was the walnut-brown of an old Indian hand but rather more ruddy than most. And red veins coursed down the nose which hung over the great moustache. Fonthill had met him, of course, in the Guides' Officer's mess at the depot, but they had spoken little, for Appleby-Smith had remained rather out of the circle of officers who had cheerfully mingled with Simon, Jenkins and Alice, during their time at Marden. Almost, Simon remembered, as though he resented their presence.

The two men shook hands and the captain gestured towards a Guides' subaltern who strode smartly towards them.

'This is Lieutenant Dawson,' he said. 'He will be second in command of the squadron.'

Handshakes were exchanged again with Dawson, a rather plump young man, with a pleasant, open countenance, some two years older than Buckingham.

Fonthill turned and introduced Jenkins, who had been standing deferentially to one side.

'Ah yes,' drawled Appleby-Smith, '367, or something like that, isn't it?'

Jenkins favoured them both with his face-breaking grin. 'Ah, bless you bach, no. Good try, though. It's 352, as a matter of fact.'

There was a faint intake of breath by the captain at being addressed so informally but he and his second in command exchanged handshakes with Jenkins cordially enough.

'Delighted to have you escort me,' said Fonthill. 'Have you been to Kabul before, Captain?'

'No. Can't say that I have. Bit of a dump, I should imagine.'

Simon shook his head. 'Well, no. It's a long time since I was there but I remember it as being rather unusually beautiful. Nestling beside the river with lots of flowers and fruit orchards in the outskirts.' He turned to Jenkins, anxious to demonstrate both his comrade's status and their joint experience. 'Wouldn't you say, so, 352?'

'Ah, yes indeed, bach sir. Almost as pretty as Rhyl, look you.'

Appleby-Smith lifted an eyebrow. 'Really?' he responded faintly. 'How interesting.'

Fonthill decided to introduce business quickly. 'When will you be ready to leave, Captain?' he asked. 'I presume you will need perhaps a day to prepare for the journey?'

'Two days, I should think, Mr Fonthill. We have to provision ourselves adequately for the ride.'

'Ah yes.' Simon allowed a faint frown to cross his face. 'Very well. May I suggest that we leave, then, shortly after dawn on the day after tomorrow?'

'Very good . . . er . . . sir. We shall parade shortly after 5 a.m.' He turned to Buckingham. 'I presume you are ready to ride, Buckingham?'

'Yes, of course, sir.'

'Good,' affirmed Fonthill. 'By the way, my wife will accompany us for part—'

'What?' Appleby-Smith's tone was peremptory, his astonishment and disapproval quite clear.

'Yes.' Simon replied quietly but firmly. 'We will go via the Khyber, of course, and we will leave her at the fort at Landi Kotal. She has work to do there. And then, of course, we will pick her up there on our return.' His tone hardened. 'I presume you have no objections?'

'What? Oh no. Of course not.'

'Good. Now. I hate to stand on formality. My name is Simon and I would prefer it if you would call me that. May I enquire . . . what is yours?'

It was clear that Appleby-Smith did *not*, in fact, welcome informality. He cleared his throat. 'It is Clarence,' he said, distantly.

'Thank you, Clarence. Now, tell me. Do you have any news about any possible trouble we might meet with on this journey? Are the Afridis along the Khyber reasonably quiet?'

'Yes, I believe so, er . . . Si . . . Yes, I believe so. But, of course, we shall be prepared to repel boarders at any time, so to speak.'

'That is good news. So we will leave at 5 a.m., then, the day after tomorrow.' Fonthill allowed himself a smile. 'Oh, I am fairly sure that the road to Kabul is straightforward and I hope that I can remember it, anyway. But I understand that Buckingham's *daffadar,* Inderjit Singh, is familiar with this part of Afghanistan so we should not get lost.'

Both of Appleby-Smith's eyebrows rose this time. 'Who? Oh, the Sikh. Yes. But I doubt if we shall need his help. Good day to you, sir. Buckingham. Come with me.'

As the three officers strode away, Fonthill and Jenkins exchanged glances.

''E's not exactly a chuckle-face, now, is 'e, bach sir?' commented Jenkins.

'Now, don't be disrespectful to a holder of the Queen's commission. Come along now. Let's go and see if Alice has found a hairdresser yet.'

CHAPTER FIVE

The sun was painting the mountain tops to the east a promising magenta when the little force assembled on the parade ground at Peshawar. Captain Appleby-Smith gave Simon and Alice what could only be interpreted as a reluctant salute and bade them good morning.

'All present and correct, Mr Fonthill, Mrs…ah…Fonthill. Shall we proceed?'

'Good morning, Clarence. Yes. Let's get off and put as many miles as possible under our feet before this blasted sun gets intolerable.'

Orders were issued and the column set off onto the Kabul road. Outriders were despatched to front and rear, sufficiently distanced from the main body to give effective warning of an attack, and the squadron split into two, with Appleby-Smith in the van with Dawson and his men and, perhaps predictably, Buckingham and his troop in the rear. Fonthill, Alice and Jenkins rode, a touch self-consciously, between the two troops, with troopers carrying pennants riding on either side of them.

Alice, serviceably dressed in jodhpurs, riding boots and a simple, long-sleeved blouse, settled a wide-brimmed, soft hat on her head and tugged it down.

'I don't much like riding like this in the middle,' she confided to Simon. 'I feel like our dear beloved Queen riding out to inspect the troops at the Horse Guards.'

'Just as well you managed to get your hair done, then. At least we're not kicking up too much dust at the moment. This could be a problem when we get out of Peshawar proper.'

So it proved. The road was not metalled, of course, and they met plenty of traffic as they wound their way out towards the little town of Jamrud, which marked the end of the railway and virtually the point where the old administrative area of the Punjab ended. Despite the unsettled state of the Border it was pleasing to Fonthill to note the number of trading caravans that were heading towards Peshawar, for the Pass, of course, marked the main route between Kabul and British India.

'So where is this damned Durand Line?' asked Alice, when they stopped to breakfast just outside Jamrud. 'Shall we feel a bump as we cross it?'

'From what I remember, it is about five miles straight ahead. We should see the marking posts on either side of the road as we cross it.' He looked up at the hills which now climbed on either side of the road, preventing

Appleby-Smith from posting mounted pickets abreast of the column. 'Forgive me if I leave you for a minute and stroll along and say good morning to Buckingham and Inderjit Singh. I would hate them to think that I am ignoring them now that they are outranked.'

Jenkins was already perched on a rock talking to the two men as he joined them.

'I trust Appleby-Smith will give your troop a spell at the head of the column to save you from the dust at the rear,' Simon said.

'Thank you, sir. A kind thought. But I doubt it.'

Fonthill noted the reply but thought better of pursuing the subject and turned to the *daffadar*. 'When did you come this way last, Inderjit?' he enquired.

'Oh, I have patrolled this way into Afghanistan many times, sahib. It is not a difficult way into the Afghan state, for we just have to . . . ah . . . what is the saying – follow our chins?'

'Follow our noses, or in the case of 352, our moustaches.'

A grunt from Jenkins greeted this. 'Better than the last time we came this way goin'. . . er . . . east, is it?'

Simon shook his head. 'No. Almost due west.'

'Yes. That's what I thought. West.' Jenkins turned to the Sikh. 'We rode this way with your father, old W.G. We was pretendin' to be carpet salesmen from, where was it, bach sir – Burma?'

'No. Persia. Nearly right.'

'Ah yes. That's what I thought. Persia. Fat lot of good that pretendin' did us. We nearly got shot for our trouble an' we had to move out smartly, leavin' be'ind our very expensive samples.'

Inderjit Singh's eyes lit up. 'Ah yes. I never had chance to talk to my father about that. You must tell me what happened.'

'Another time,' said Fonthill. 'I think we are ready to move again.' He stood and spoke, almost to himself. 'I must have a word with the captain.'

As the column moved off, he pulled his horse out of line and urged it forward, causing minor consternation to his two lance-bearing attendants, who immediately dug in their heels so that they quickly fell into station on either side of him.

'Clarence,' said Simon as he motioned one of his escorts away and drew alongside Appleby-Smith. 'I would be grateful if Alice, Jenkins and I could ride in the van with you, at least for a while. The dust in the middle of the column is getting rather beastly, I'm afraid.'

'What?' The captain glared at Fonthill as though he had suggested a game of billiards. 'I am sorry, but I could not allow that. Your position in the middle of the column is where we can best protect you if we are attacked. You are my responsibility, you see.'

Fonthill smiled. 'Thank you for your care. I really must insist that we move, though, otherwise your very precious charges, Captain, will die of suffocation before we get into Afghanistan. And, while we are at it, I do suggest that the two troopers riding alongside us with their pennants should be removed. If we *are* going to be attacked, they make us obvious targets, I would have thought. What do you think?'

'What?' Simon reflected that this word seemed to be the man's initial response to any request. 'I am not sure that that is a good—'

'Oh, I think it is,' replied Fonthill. 'See to it, please. I don't wish to interfere with your procedure en route, but I presume that you will be rotating the troops in the line, perhaps by sections, to relieve those in the rear from suffering from the dust all the time? I understand that that is the Guides' procedure – or at least that is what Colonel Fortescue certainly did when we rode to Malakand. But these details, of course, I leave to you, Clarence. I will fetch Alice and Jenkins now, if I may.'

He touched the brim of his cloth-covered army helmet, pulled out of line and rejoined his wife and Jenkins.

'What was all that about, darling?' asked Alice.

'Oh, I was just giving a little advice on good army manners to what I am afraid is a prig of our escort commander.'

Jenkins nodded sagely. 'Therefore aliechasin'. . . alianantin . . .'

'Alienating?' offered Alice.

'That's what I said,' sniffed Jenkins. 'Alienatin' our best 'ope of survival on this postin'. Oh dear, oh dear. Oh dearie me. I fear the worst, I really do.'

Simon led his wife and Jenkins forward but no change was made in the order of march for the rest of the column until it had reached the beginning of the Pass, some five miles after Simon had pointed out some white-painted posts set in the hillside on either side of the road, marking the Durand Line. Then, although Buckingham himself was left in the rear, roughly half of his troop was moved into the van. The delay in effecting the manoeuvre, Fonthill noted, was, of course, Appleby-Smith preserving his dignity as formal commander of the column. At the same point, the two troopers protecting Simon were ordered to remove their pennanted lances, although the men themselves remained in position.

The Khyber Pass had already established itself in Border folklore as the main invasion route into India from the rest of Asia. Although there were other passes between Afghanistan and the Punjab, they were of high altitude and often impassable in winter. To the north and east the great ranges of the Hindu Kush and the Himalayas presented an impassable barrier. As a result, the Khyber had offered the easiest way into the subcontinent since Alexander of Macedon had approached it some fifteen hundred years before and led his 120,000 men towards where the mist rose from the valley of the Indus behind the mountains, luring them on. Then, the Pathans had opposed the young conqueror, just as they had stood in the path of every invader from the north for centuries before and since. Alexander, with all the arrogance gained from his twenty-five years and recent defeat of the Persians, had led a small, elite force himself over the Kunar Valley in the north into Swat, swinging down to meet up with his main force as it swept aside the Pathans in the Khyber and pushed on down towards the Indus and the invasion of India proper.

Fonthill, then, looked at the Khyber again with renewed interest. In many places the Pass itself was little more than a defile cut through the Zakka Khel mountain range by the

Kabul River, although now the road wound its way some ten miles to the south of the river. At first, at the Peshawar end, it was flanked by green fields set in the valley, but then, as the travellers made their way to the west, the hills ranged formidably and occasionally almost vertically on either side of the road, a mass of brown-grey stone offering virtually no traces of foliage at all. The road twisted round the many projections of the range, disappearing in a series of narrow zigzags into the blue, serrated horizon.

'Strewth.' Jenkins sucked in his chinstrap. 'Ain't there a level bit of land in this awful bloody country?'

It seemed to Simon that the Khyber itself would present no danger to them, for as Alice had pointed out, the British had recently established three forts along the Pass. These were formidable buildings of brick and stone, built on spurs alongside the road and increasing in size until the last of them, the Landi Kotal, towered at the Afghanistan end of the Khyber. It was here that Alice, of course, had to part company with the column.

Reaching it, Fonthill looked up at the high walls of the fort and the craggy mass of rocks looking down on it and shook his head.

'Look here, Alice,' he said. 'I don't think that this is a good idea at all. Things may seem peaceful here at the moment, but God knows what will happen if this revolt spreads to the Khyber. This fort looks safe enough, but Buckingham tells me that the troops manning it, the Khyber Rifles, are all Afridis and a comparatively new unit only recently raised and with nothing like the background and tradition of the Guides behind them. It's not too late to send you back to Peshawar with Duke and a section of his men. It makes sense—'

'No.' Alice interrupted him firmly. 'If you won't let me come with you, I shall wait for you here.' She gestured to the walls, towering some fifteen feet above them. 'It seems to me that this is more secure than the Tower of London, and besides, the commander here is expecting me. It would upset him now if I turn back at his very gate.' She grinned. 'He would think he'd offended me. Don't worry, my love. I will be fine.'

Then her grin disappeared to be replaced by a frown. 'It's you who will be in the most danger.' She turned to Jenkins. 'Look after him, 352. I am holding you responsible. And don't let him fall off his horse.'

'Ah,' Jenkins returned the smile. 'That could be the difficult bit, Miss Alice. But I'll try.'

The massive gates were opened to them and the party was welcomed by the commander of the fort, Captain Barton, once of the Guides Cavalry, who combined the duties of assistant political officer at Landi Kotal with command of the Khyber Rifles. He was delighted to see Alice and confirmed that, since the outbreaks further north, he had strengthened his garrison, arranging for stockpiles of fourteen days' water and supplies and building up an ammunition reserve of 50,000 rounds.

'Your wife will be perfectly safe with us here,' he assured Fonthill.

Simon decided that they would not linger at Landi Kotal and so, the goodbyes made, the column rode on through what remained of the Pass and crossed the invisible border into Afghanistan. The road now led upwards and they passed many tribesmen tending goats and small cattle. The men looked at the column with interest but were unarmed and certainly not threatening.

Fonthill called Inderjit Singh forward. 'I am told,' he said, 'that you speak several languages. Is this true?'

The tall Sikh nodded. 'Yes, sahib. I speak Urdu and English, of course, and both dialects of Pushtu – the soft, Pashtu, and the hard, Paktu. I know the Persian, Parsi, but I am not so fluent in that. Sorry, sahib.'

'Don't be sorry. It sounds a pretty formidable list to me. It's the Pushtu in both dialects, I seem to remember, which is the main language spoken around here. Is that true?'

'Very true, sir. Although cultured Afghans will speak Parsi as well.'

'Good. Well, I suggest, Clarence,' he turned to Appleby-Smith, who was riding within hearing a little way to the right, 'that we make the *daffadar* our interpreter on this mission. Do you agree?'

'I have no objections, sir.'

'Good. Consider yourself so appointed. I shall apply to Colonel Fortescue on our return for an appropriate addition to your wage to reflect the additional responsibility.'

'The sahib is kind. Thank you, sir.'

The air was now becoming markedly less warm, although the sun continued to beat down, as they climbed a little before beginning the descent to the Logar and Kabul valleys. Dusk was beginning to turn the mountains a deep purple so Appleby-Smith ordered that camp should be made for the night.

Guards were set but the hours of darkness passed without incident, except that everyone felt the cold after the heat of the Khyber. Shortly after the fires were lit for breakfast, a party of some fifty or so Afghans appeared, riding ponies and aggressively armed, with rifles – Lee-Enfields, Simon noted – slung across their backs, swathes of bandoliers bristling with cartridges across their breasts and curved swords thrust through their cummerbunds. They wore turbans piled high on their heads, so unlike the tightly wound headgear of the Guides.

They paused just outside the lines of fires and shouted what seemed like a greeting, although their bearded faces expressed nothing but animosity. Inderjit Singh was summoned and, as Fonthill stood by, engaged the leader of the party in conversation.

'He says,' interpreted Inderjit, 'that he wants to know who is entering the Amir's land so armed and looking like an invading force.'

'Tell him,' said Simon, looking directly into the dark eyes of the Afghan, 'that we bring the blessings of Allah upon him, his children and his children's children. But that it is wrong to speak of invasion and warfare and against the renowned tradition of Afghan hospitality. We expected welcome, not talk of invasion.'

The Sikh gave a brief nod and a half smile at the fluency of Fonthill's response and so translated.

'But, why,' related Inderjit, 'do you come with troops if your purpose is peaceful?'

'These troopers,' replied Simon, 'are members of the Queen's Own Royal Guides and are with me purely as an escort to mark my rank as the envoy of the Viceroy of India, the Queen-Empress's representative in all of Asia.'

'He says where do you go and what do you want?'

'I go to His Highness the Amir's palace in Kabul for I carry a message to His Highness from the Viceroy which is of the utmost importance.'

At this, the Afghan turned his head and consulted with a trio of his followers arranged behind him. Then, he growled at the Sikh again.

'He says, give the message to him and he will take it to the Amir. Infidels are not welcome in Afghanistan at this time.'

Immediately, Fonthill raised his voice. 'Tell him he is impertinent to speak thus to the Viceroy's envoy. My message is for the Amir's eyes alone and I shall deliver it to him personally. If this man – or anyone else – interferes with my mission it could lead to very adverse consequences for him. The Amir is expecting the message and he will undoubtedly be angry if its delivery is delayed to him.'

Fonthill turned and shouted to Appleby-Smith. 'Captain, have the guard turned out behind me, immediately, with their carbines presented to these ruffians.'

'Very good, sir. Guard – at the double – line up in two ranks behind Mr Fonthill. NOW! PRESENT ARMS!!'

The effect was immediate. The ponies of the Afghans involuntarily took a half pace backwards and a murmur rose from the ranks of the tribesmen. Some immediately unslung their rifles but a command from their leader led to them being lowered. He spoke again to Inderjit.

'He say he do not wish to give offence. You go in peace

with your message, but we may meet again.'

With that, the Afghan raised his hand and wheeled the head of his pony around and led the group away at the trot until they had disappeared around a bend in the road leading upwards towards the high pass.

'Blimey!' Fonthill became aware that Jenkins, rifle in hand, was at his side. 'You certainly spoke a bit sharply to that feller, bach sir. You was quite shirty, in fact.'

Fonthill let his face relax. 'I am glad we met him. Now the neighbourhood will know who we are and that we are not to be threatened or interfered with. Come on, let's have breakfast.' He turned to Appleby-Smith. 'Thank you, Clarence. That was done very smartly. You may stand down the guard but we must be very vigilant from now on. It looks as though the truculence of the Pathans has crossed the Border.'

The camp was broken and the column, with outriders now doubled at front, rear and on either flank, road on up towards the Shutargarden. At last, they reached the summit, with the horses' breath rising like steam from their nostrils. Fonthill was half expecting to find his way blocked by hostile Afghans but the view that met their gaze was reassuringly pastoral and peaceful. The road fell away less steeply than their path to the summit for they had now reached the central plateau of the Amir's kingdom and a fertile valley lay before them, with the little town of Kushi glittering at them in the distance.

They met few people as they wound their way down towards the town, reaching it within the hour. Fonthill had no desire to stop there and they picked their way through the dirty, unpaved streets, this time attracting lines of bystanders, watching them sullenly as the cavalcade passed through.

'Ah, I think the word has got out,' murmured Fonthill to Jenkins. 'That is good, for it will reach Kabul quicker than we can, so the Amir will be expecting us.'

Jenkins turned a puzzled face towards him. 'But I thought you said that he was expectin' the letter, like?'

'Did I? Well, he will be now.'

Now the going was much easier and they followed the Logar River and camped that night above the settlement of Zahidabad, some fifteen miles from Kushi. Guards were posted but the night was uneventful. They passed through a pretty little village called Charasia, which nestled in orchards and gardens, and then approached the gorge of Sang-i-Nawishta, through which the Logar gurgled and jumped. Here the river had carved its own passage through the low range of hills which overlooked Charasia and blocked the passage to Kabul, creating a narrow defile only a hundred yards in length, before opening out again into the plain beyond. Fonthill remembered this as a perfect place for an ambush but none came and they passed through it with some relief.

They then rode through pleasant countryside, seeing a scattering of Afghans tending the fields and skirting a dozen villages that told them that they were nearing Kabul. It was a fertile area and behind stone walls they could see a profusion of fruits and recognised mulberries, peaches, plums, apricots, apples, quinces, pomegranates and even vines.

Fonthill caught Appleby-Smith's eye and called, 'Almost like Kent, eh, Clarence?' but received only a surly nod in reply.

That night they camped by the Kabul River, wide and fast flowing, running over and between hundreds of rocks that caused the water to swirl and foam. Up early the next morning, the walls of Kabul itself came into view, looking down forbiddingly onto the river.

Fonthill looked behind him and waved forward Inderjit Singh.

'Do you remember where the Amir's palace is?' he asked.

'Yes, sahib. We must go through the main gate, which is straight ahead. The streets are narrow and crowded so we must take care, for it would be easy to stop us there. We continue past a fortress place called the Bala Hissar . . .'

Simon nodded. 'Ah, I remember that place. It overlooked the old Residency.'

'Yes, sahib. The palace is very near there. I can find it.'

'Good. Lead the way, then.'

The column passed through a high, narrow gate in the wall – so narrow that the Guides, now riding eight abreast with Fonthill and Jenkins in their midst – had to squeeze together to ride through it. Immediately they were into streets that were only slightly wider and which were lined with houses made of mud, interspersed, here and there, with stone-walled gardens in which grew a variety of flowers and fruits. It was clear that Kabul was a city of colour and fragrance, despite its grim exterior.

It was also a city with a large population, and crowds lined the streets and gazed askance at the Guides, with their coloured turbans, smart khaki uniforms, gleaming brown belts and prancing horses. Before leaving camp that morning, Simon and Jenkins had changed their clothing and now were wearing their own uniforms with their decorations. Few troops of the British Raj had been seen in the streets of Kabul since General Roberts had led his army from the Afghan capital after his victory at Khandahar some sixteen years before. Now the Guards were regarded as though they were creatures from another planet, evoking gasps and the occasional shout of derision.

Looking about him, Fonthill could not help but think that this was what London, perhaps, might have looked like in Tudor times, with narrow streets, crowded thoroughfares and the top storeys of the houses almost meeting overhead. Except that, of course, there were few signs of timber being used in construction, only mud and, here and there, some stone and brickwork.

The palace itself, when they reached it, showed little attempt at architectural pretension. Made of stone, it was set back in a street round the corner from the square where the old British Residency had been destroyed by the mob in 1879 and its occupants killed, so leading to the British invasion of Aghanistan and the Second Afghan War.

The column was led through an archway into a small courtyard, where Fonthill, Jenkins and the officers dismounted. From there, Simon, with Inderjit Khan's help, sent through a flowery message to the Amir, asking the ruler's permission to call on him, at the Amir's convenience, to deliver a personal letter from the Viceroy at Simla.

A message came back with commendable promptitude –

confirming Simon's suspicions that the column's progress had been reported back to Kabul regularly – explaining that the Amir was momentarily indisposed but would receive him 11 a.m. the next morning and requesting that the letter should be left so that His Highness could study it. In the meantime, Fonthill and fellow Britons were invited to stay as guests of the Amir in a house within the courtyard. (Simon remembered that there had been no permanent British representative at Kabul since the end of the war in 1881, this being part of the settlement of the conflict, so there was no British embassy or consulate.) The royal stables would accommodate the horses and the men of the escort.

Fonthill was reluctant to release the document from his possession but could see no alternative and it was therefore passed over to someone who appeared to be a senior member of the Amir's household, who also conducted them to their accommodation.

Their rooms were cell-like and spartan but perfectly adequate and, having deposited his bag in the room, Fonthill immediately walked to the stables to ensure that the men of the escort were comfortably housed. He did not like the sound of them being deposited in stables. In fact, he met Buckingham on the same mission – although there was no sign of Appleby-Smith – and found the men grooming their horses. They had been allocated a long, communal room above the stables, with mattresses on the floor and a large washroom on the same level. The men would be cramped but comfortable enough.

He took Buckingham and Inderjit Singh on one side. 'I

need to know as much as I can about the role that the Amir is playing in this game,' he said. 'I doubt if you, Duke, as an Englishman in this town, can find out much. But you, Inderjit, might be able to. Do you have mufti – civilian clothes – with you?'

'Only a loose gown and slippers, sahib, but I could borrow more. You want me to fit into the town here – be like the people?'

'Exactly.' Simon dug into his pocket and handed the Sikh a handful of rupees. 'I don't expect you to pass off as an Afghan exactly, but there must be Sikhs here in Kabul, I would have thought?'

'Oh, I am sure. Yes. Particularly horse-traders, I think. My people are good at that.'

'Good. Take these coins and go into the bazaars. Drink tea with the locals and pick up the gossip. See if you can find out if the word is that the Amir is backing the Pathan rebels across the Border – if not with troops, then in some other way. Perhaps with sending mullahs across to foment *jihads* in the hills and villages. Anything you can find might be useful.'

'Very good, sahib. I go as soon as horses are settled.'

'Good.' He drew Buckingham to one side. 'Now, Duke. Do you know where the captain is?'

'In his room, I presume.'

'Has he not been to the stable to see if the men are all right?'

'No. I'm afraid he is well known for not doing that sort of thing.'

'Is this why you dislike him?'

The subaltern immediately became uneasy and looked away. 'I spoke out of turn that day, sir. And I am sorry. I do not wish to criticise my superior officer.'

Fonthill nodded. 'I understand and that does you credit. Whatever you say will stay between us. But, listen. We are far from home here and I am not at all sure that the return back to the Punjab will be as easy as it was coming here. I will need to rely on the officer commanding the escort to take us through. If he has any faults – no, damnit, we *all* have faults – any *inefficiencies* in the way he carries out his duty, then I would like to know so that I can watch out for them and, if necessary, prepare for them.'

Buckingham gulped. 'Very well. I consider the captain to be . . . to be . . .' he paused and then spoke hurriedly, as though in relief 'unfit to command in action, sir.'

'Do you have evidence of this?

'Yes. Two examples of this.'

'Tell me.'

'I was out on patrol with him as squadron commander six months ago, when we came under fire from Pathans hidden behind rocks up a defile north of Malakand.'

'Go on.'

'Instead of ordering the squadron to dismount, with handlers taking the horses at the double behind cover – Pathans don't usually fire at horses because they are worth money, if captured.'

'Yes, quite so.'

'Then, of course, we should have taken cover with men moving quickly on either wing to scramble up the hillside to outflank the riflemen, while a central section kept firing at them, to pin them down and to prevent them from slipping away.'

'So, what happened?'

'Appleby-Smith panicked. He drew his sword and screamed "recall, recall" and led the way back we had come at the gallop. It was some time before Dawson – he is senior to me, you know – was able to overtake him and calm him down.'

'Hmmm. And the second instance?'

'A similar thing. We were approaching a Pathan village that we suspected housed tribesmen who had killed a sentry of ours three nights before and stolen his rifle. Instead of leading the patrol into the village, which anyone in command, of course, should have done, he sent me in with my troop and stayed outside "covering us", as he said. But he deployed his men too far away to be of any use to us in the village if we had been attacked. Luckily, we were not.'

'I see.'

'And you have seen, sir, that, in my view, he does not look after the troopers well. He does not rotate the men on the march to alleviate the nuisance caused by dust and, as you have seen, he has not been down here to make sure that the horses and the men are comfortable.'

Fonthill frowned. 'But I know Colonel Fortescue to be a splendid officer. Has he not noticed this?'

'No, sir. The problem is that the colonel, who, as you say, is much respected by everyone, seems to have a blinkered view of the captain. He has always, well, rather nurtured him, since he joined the Guides a year ago. I am afraid that this is well known. You see, sir, Appleby-Smith is the colonel's brother-in-law.'

'Oh Lord. Very well, Duke. This will go no further, but to be warned is to be prepared. Thank you. I presume we will all meet at dinner this evening.'

The meal was a rather miserable affair. Native food, of course, had been provided for them in a tiny room leading off their washroom. Fonthill himself was introspective, digesting the information supplied to him by Buckingham; the latter seemed disturbed by breaking one of the rules of the service and remained silent throughout; Appleby-Smith was monosyllabic as usual in the presence of Jenkins, clearly disapproving at having to mess with a ranker; and only the Welshman and Dawson chattered away, the subaltern happily recalling holidays he had spent in North Wales as a child.

Eventually, Appleby-Smith spoke to ask Fonthill when they were expected to return.

'Well,' responded Simon, 'I am not exactly sure, to be honest. I have no wish to stay here longer than is absolutely necessary but when the Amir gives me his response to the Viceroy's message, we can be gone. By the way, 'I have asked Inderjit Singh, Buckingham's *daffadar*, to mingle in the bazaars to see if he can pick up any intelligence about the Amir that might be useful. Obviously, we mustn't leave without him.'

'What?' Appleby-Smith lowered the mutton bone on which he had been munching. 'You sent one of my men to carry out intelligence work, without informing me?'

'Yes, well. I was going to mention it to you, as, indeed, I have. But you have no objection, surely?'

'I have every objection. You are a civilian, as I understand it, and you have no right to give orders to my men. And,' his voice now took on a higher pitch, 'if he is discovered doing this . . . this . . . *spying* it could go badly with us, here in the Amir's capital.'

Fonthill frowned. 'Now, look here, Captain. I am in charge of this mission – in *complete charge*. On military matters, concerned with escorting me, then of course I shall defer to you. But in every other way, I am in command here, as the Viceroy's emissary. It is important to find out as much as I can about the Amir and his attitude towards the rebellion across his Border. Asking the *daffadar*, who speaks the local language fluently and is a most intelligent man, to carry out this work is quite within my remit. My apologies if I was a little slow to inform you of what I had done but, frankly, I did not think it that important.'

An awkward silence fell on the gathering. Then Appleby-Smith, his face flushed, muttered: 'My apologies, Mr Fonthill. I spoke out of turn.'

'Very well. We will say no more of it.'

The next day was spent relaxing in their lodgings. Jenkins, reverting to his original role as officer's servant, had somehow found a hot iron and had pressed Simon's trousers and tunic, had rubbed the Maltese Cross that proclaimed that he was a member of the Companionship of the Bath until it glittered on the dark blue of his jacket and had given his riding boots the shine of a guardsman. Fonthill, then, felt as debonair as an ambassador as he presented himself the next morning. The official of the household who had met him the day before led the way into the interior of the palace, with two turbaned and sashed Afghans, carrying large curved swords, falling into place on either side of Simon, making him feel that he was being escorted towards, if not formal execution, at least facing a charge of being drunk and disorderly – or, more likely, improperly dressed.

After winding down a dark corridor, he was ushered into a spacious room through which the sunlight filtered only dimly through wooden screens, carved delicately. On the stone walls, he could make out colourful tapestries hanging and, at the far end, a small, frail man sitting on a large, wooden seat, more than a chair but rather less than a throne, set on a stone dais. On either side of him sat an elderly Afghan, each adorned with a long white beard and wearing robes of an undoubted richness.

Fonthill realised, of course, that he was in the presence of the Amir Abdur Rahman, who rose from his chair and waved a thin, bony hand to him in welcome. Simon regarded him intently as he approached.

He knew that the man was only about fifty years of age, yet he looked much, much older. A member of the ruling family in Afghanistan, he had spent his younger years in exile, under Russian patronage, in Samarkand before the events of the second Anglo-Afghan War had brought him to the throne, supported by the British. There he had remained for nearly two decades, proving to be a strong and ruthless leader, reputedly throwing those who opposed him down a well and leaving them to rot on top of the other bodies lying there. Nevertheless, he had maintained good relations with the British Raj, despite his successful determination to exclude all foreign influences from his country. Now, however, the word came that he was growing increasingly frail and suffering from gout. His beard was as white as those of his secretaries, but it was thin and his skin seemed stretched almost to bursting point over his high cheekbones. His eyes, however, shone brightly, like black precious stones in his chalk-white face. Simon remembered the Viceroy's phrase 'ruthless and as slippery as an eel'.

The old man stepped gingerly down from the dais and waited, with outstretched hand, for Fonthill to approach him. Simon did so and took the hand carefully, bowing low over it. The Amir barked a command and two chairs were brought forward and then a small table was placed between them. He gestured for Simon to sit.

'I am honoured,' he said, in excellent but accented English, 'that His Excellency the Viceroy should entrust his letter to such a distinguished bearer of it.' The old man gently lowered himself into the other chair. 'Even I, separated in this humble country from the rest of the world by these mountains, had heard of the Sahib Fonthill who slipped through the armies of the Mahdi to reach your General Gordon in the Sudan.'

Simon lowered his head again, this time in genuine admiration. The Viceroy's letter had contained no details of his experiences in the Sudan. 'I am flattered that Your Highness should know of these unimportant things,' he said in reply.

'Ah yes. You see I have made it my business, as best I could over the years, to keep myself informed of the happenings in your Empire. After all,' he gave a thin smile, 'we are neighbours, you know.'

He clapped his hands and gave an order to a servant who rushed forward. 'I have ordered tea,' he said. Then he leant forward, as though in intimacy. 'Is it not strange that two races so different from each other as the Afghans and the British should each place such a dependency on this strange drink? Personally, I do not think I could live without it. But I do hope you like it with mint. Is that to your taste?'

'That would be perfect, Your Highness.'

'Good.' The Amir turned and snapped his finger to one of his secretaries, who stepped forward and gave him a letter, heavily sealed.

'Now, Mr Fonthill, here is my reply to the Viceroy.' He gave his mirthless smile again and handed the letter to Simon. 'It is much shorter than his to me. I have merely said that there is no question of me sending troops to help my former subjects across the Border. I have given him my word on that.'

Fonthill nodded slowly. 'I know that the Viceroy will be very glad to hear that, Your Highness.' He paused for a moment. 'Your former subjects . . . ?'

'Ah, Lord Elgin will take and understand the reference. It is the result of that Allah-cursed Durand Line. You know, Mr Fonthill, I never wanted this relocation of the boundary between my country and the Punjab. I was . . . what is the phrase? I think it is "leant upon". Yes, I was leant upon to accept it.'

'I am sorry to hear that, sir. I understood that there were

compensatory allocations of territory to you.'

'Oh yes.' For a moment the black eyes in the depths of their hollows narrowed and flashed, and Fonthill glimpsed something of the ruthlessness and cruelty that lay beneath the Amir's urbanity. The 'well that gives no water' suddenly became a reality rather than a rumour. 'I was given what was known as the Wakhan Corridor, a strip of land in the far north next to the Russian territories. Useless to me but, of course, I was now expected to oversee it as a kind of buffer state between these two great European powers. Difficult to do, for there is no thanks in that role and there is a real chance of upsetting either one of these huge empires if things go wrong.'

The smile came again but it did not reach the old man's eyes. 'But what did I lose in return for gaining this precious piece of barren ground? My dear Mr Fonthill, I lost,' and he began slapping one finger after another into his palm, 'the lands of Chitral, Bajaur, Swat, Buner, Dir, the Khyber, Kurram and Waziristan. Those were all my people. Now they are yours. Ah, tea.'

Simon was not sorry for the interruption. The Viceroy had asked him to supplement his letter in any way demanded by the Amir. But did this extend to debating with him the politics of the Border? If so, he was not sure he was up to it.

He sipped his tea. 'You put your point well, Your Highness,' he said, 'as I am sure you did to the present Viceroy's predecessor. But allow me to ask you one question. Were the people of these lands your filial and devoted servants?'

The Amir waved an exasperated hand. 'Of course not. They are tribesmen of the hills, who pay no formal loyalty to me or anyone else. They are as independent and as free as the wind that blows the clouds from the mountain tops. But they have been people of my religion and nationality for centuries and they have known me and my family for years.

'Listen. When I was forced to acknowledge the presence of this accursed line three years ago, I wrote to the Viceroy warning him that these people would never be of any use to him. I said that he would always be engaged in fighting or other trouble with them and that they would always go on plundering. As long as your government is strong and in peace, you will be able to keep them more or less quiet by a strong hand, but if at any time an enemy appears on the border of India, these frontier tribes will be your worst enemy. Now, they are rising in rebellion and I can do nothing to help you. Because by taking these people away from me you have injured my prestige in the eyes of my subjects and made me weak – and my weakness is injurious to your government.'

He took another sip of his green tea. 'And you must realise, my dear Mr Fonthill, that the white man has never been exactly loved by the Pathans. In fact, they have a saying.' A faint smile stole over his face. 'It goes: "first comes one Englishman for *shikar* – that means hunting; then come two Englishmen to draw a map; then comes an army to take your land. It is best to kill the first Englishman."'

Simon could think of nothing to say, so smiled in

appreciation of the joke. Then he remembered, from years before, a saying that Inderjit's father had related to him. Why not? Why should the Devil have the best tunes? 'And that, sir,' he responded, 'reminds me of a saying that the Sikhs had about the Pathans. I think it goes: "Trust a Brahmin before a snake, and a snake before a harlot and a harlot before a Pathan".' Then he leant forward. 'But to be serious, Your Highness, there does not appear to be an enemy approaching the border of India at the present. Our relationship with Russia now seems placid. Why should the tribes revolt?'

For the moment, it seemed that he had scored a debating point, because the eyes of the Amir closed for a second. Then, he said, 'I do not know. This is for you to find out and deal with. But, as I have said to the Viceroy, I will give no assistance to my ex-subjects.'

Simon thought again. How far could he push this clever old man?

'Your Highness,' he said, 'there does not appear to be any obviously national interest from outside the borders of the British Raj stirring the tribes, but they seem to be showing unusual signs of unity. They have rarely come together in this way before. We have some evidence that strange mullahs from outside the Border territories are going from valley to valley demanding a jihad against the government. Do you know of this?'

The Amir's face remained implacable. 'I have heard of something similar, but I have no details.'

'But – and forgive me pressing Your Highness on this point – we understand that most, if not all, of these religious fanatics come from Afghanistan in answer to your pamphlet recently stating that you were "the King of Islam".'

The Amir shook his head. 'That was misunderstood. I merely pointed out that I was the senior representative of the Muslim religion in this part of Asia. Which is perfectly true. Now . . .' He put down his teacup and rose unsteadily to his feet. 'I know that you will wish to set out on your return journey as soon as possible, so I must give you Allah's blessing for your journey.'

It was dismissal and Fonthill had to accept it without further argument. There was no chance to gently threaten the Amir with the greatly enhanced size of the British army in India. He rose to his feet, bowed from the waist and, clutching the letter, said, 'I will take this back to the Viceroy with all despatch. I thank Your Highness for his courtesy and hospitality.'

The thin hand was extended again. 'Good day to you, Mr Fonthill. Have a safe journey back. I shall pray for you.'

'Thank you, sir.'

Back in his room, Simon found Jenkins waiting for him. 'Old Gracey's son is anxious to see you,' he said. 'He may 'ave some word, I think, from the bazaars. Pity they don't drink proper stuff around 'ere. I could 'ave gone with 'im.'

'Yes, well, please have Inderjit report to me at once. Oh, and please find the captain. Present my compliments and say that I would be grateful if he could arrange for us to begin the return journey tomorrow.'

'Very good, bach sir.'

The Sikh came in almost immediately. 'I have news, I think, from the bazaars, sahib.'

'Good. Report.'

'Well, all the old men say that the Amir has definitely not ordered any of his army to move towards the Border and the talk is that he will not, because he does not want the British to invade.'

'Good.'

'But there is something else, sahib.'

'Go on.'

'Everyone knows that Amir has been calling for many mullahs – that is religious preachers, sahib.'

'Yes, I know what they are. Go on, do.'

'He has been telling them to go across Border and preach jihad, that means . . .'

'Oh, I know what it means. Do go on.'

'Sorry, sahib. They go across in many numbers to start holy war against British. One mullah, very strong man, very good preacher, they say, has recently left to raise tribes that have not so far fought against British.'

'Ah, interesting. Well, the sooner we leave and get back to the Punjab the better. Thank you, Inderjit. What you have found confirms the Viceroy's fears. We leave tomorrow.'

They were interrupted by the arrival of a trooper, who spoke in dialect to the *daffadar* and handed a letter to him. Inderjit passed it on to Simon. 'From the Amir, sahib,' he said. 'It just arrive this minute.'

'Strange. I only left him half an hour ago.' He broke the seal and read the following, written in a strong, forward-sloping hand and signed by the Amir:

News has just reached me since you leave. I hear that Mullah Sayyid Akbar, very powerful preacher, is in Khyber region raising ten thousand Afridis against forts there. I did not send him. But could be dangerous for you if you take that route back. Go different way. May Allah go with you.

Abdur Rahman

Fonthill crushed the letter in his hand, clenched his fist and put it to his mouth. Ten thousand men against the Khyber Pass forts – and Alice was in the first of them! He turned to Inderjit Singh. 'Please find Captain Appleby-Smith and ask him to report to me immediately. Tell him it is urgent.'

'Very good, sahib.'

Simon straightened out the letter and read it again. The Amir must have known about the planned attack on the forts all along but had written this letter as an afterthought after pondering Fonthill's implications that he was linked to the mullahs' activities. His warning obviously was an attempt to curry favour with the Viceroy. The old devil! *Ten thousand warriors!* Would the forts – particularly the Landi Kotal, the first they would reach if the Afridis came from the west end of the Pass – be able to hold out? He bit his lip.

Appleby-Smith came bustling in, his face very red and the veins in his nose standing out sharply. Had he been drinking or merely sleeping?

'Clarence,' he said, 'I have ended my business with the Amir and have just received news that an attack is about to be launched on the Khyber Pass forts in great force. We must hurry there. We must leave this afternoon.'

Frowning, the captain shook his head. 'Oh, that would be very difficult, I fear. I gave the *daffadars* permission to let the men go into the bazaars today, reporting back this evening. I thought that—'

'Damnit, man. Never mind what you thought. That was a stupid thing to do. This is hostile country. Individually, our men will be vulnerable to attack in the crowded bazaars. Can you recall them immediately?'

'Well, I am not sure, I—'

'Get them back. Send out the *daffadars* to round them up and bring them back. At least they won't have been drinking. I want us on the road by 3 p.m. at the latest.'

'What? That would be diff—'

'DO IT! Lives are at stake. Go man. NOW!'

CHAPTER SIX

Once inside the fort, Alice followed Captain Barton up steep stairs to the little room that had been allocated to her. Thanking him, she threw her bag onto the trestle bed, waited for him to leave, then hurried out onto the battlements to catch one last glimpse of the column as it wound its way to the west. She was just able to see Simon, a small and distant figure, sitting upright in the saddle in the midst of the troopers, before a bend in the road took them out of sight.

She rested her chin on the stone rampart, closed her eyes and let her troubled thoughts run free. Why, oh why, did she and her beloved husband keep putting themselves in harm's way? What were they doing in this strange, barren and brutal country, anyway? And why couldn't she have stopped him from undertaking this ridiculous mission – not so much putting his head into the tiger's mouth as pulling it shut on his neck?

Turning her face to the hot sun and leaning back, Alice speculated on how much she loved Simon Fonthill. If only they could have had a child, if only the good Lord had allowed that single pregnancy of so many years ago to reach fulfilment, then their son would be now – what? She calculated quickly: twelve years old. A big, strong lad with a taste for rugby football and maybe hunting and Jenkins would have taught him how to catch trout by tickling them with his fingers . . .

If he had lived, their lives would have been so different. The boy would have made demands on them, of course, he would have had to receive a good education, like his father, and there would surely have been other children. Events would have taken such a different course – no adventuring with Cecil Rhodes, no rushing to respond to this silly invitation to a birthday party on the edge of nowhere. Just a conventional acceptance of their responsibilities as parents in this age of Victorian family fealty.

Or would they? She smiled, letting her head fall back in the gap of the castellated wall and allowing herself the rare luxury of taking in the hot sun on her skin for a little longer. No. They could never have settled for that sort of prosaic life, children or not. They had adventure in their blood, both of them, and the call had to be answered. The Empire, this strange accumulation of foreign lands by people from a small island off the coast of mainland Europe, was the place to answer it.

Her lip curled. The Empire. The *British* Empire! So

beloved by the jingo press and the Tory party and usually portrayed by cartoonists as some mystic combination of a lion and a bluff old John Bull. But what was it? No more than a collection of other people's countries invaded by the British army over the last three hundreds years, serviced by the British navy in that time and exploited by British merchants at the expense of their indigenous inhabitants. Oh, how she hated it!

And now it could be about to break up her precious marriage.

She twisted and looked back up the Khyber Pass towards where Afghanistan lay somewhere over those mountains. They – she and Simon and, of course, Jenkins – had tempted fate for so long that sooner or later she knew that it would catch up with them. Had the time come now?

Alice pushed herself upright and sucked in the hot air. Stupid to think of that just because she and Simon had been parted again. He could look after himself, and where he might fail there was always Jenkins. Better, much better, to get on with her work. It's time she looked round Fort Landi Kotal. She prided herself on the wealth of detail in her reports. Now, she must make notes.

It was, indeed, an impressive bastion. It completely commanded the road, so that it could halt invaders coming from the west and provide safety to travellers along it. The trouble was that it was overlooked by the hills climbing up behind it. But then, she shrugged, it would have been impossible to have found a cleared, flat piece of land at this end of the Khyber. And it was strongly built, with castellated ramparts and a huge, single, iron-studded door that it would take heavy artillery to break down. Yes, Fort Landi Kotal seemed quite impregnable.

So Captain Barton confirmed that evening over dinner, a delicious stew, whose provenance Alice had trouble in defining but which was of no importance, so flavoursome was it. She found to her surprise that he was the only European officer in the fort and that he messed with the *subedars*, the Indian officers; four of them, a cheerful, handsome bunch, all bearded and with flashing teeth. Although respectful, they were not above engaging in mild flirtation with her and Alice enjoyed that.

What, she asked of Barton, were the tribal affiliations of the soldiers of the Khyber Rifles?

'Oh, they are all locals, all Afridis, from along the Khyber,' he said. 'All raised by Sir Robert Warburton, the political officer here, who, alas, is now on retirement leave. We shall miss him.' He looked along the table at the grinning faces, 'Particularly these chaps and, indeed, all the men of the regiment, for they all respected him.'

'Indeed,' Alice spoke quietly now. 'But I remember that the Afridis from this area were a great problem for General Roberts in the Second Afghan War. They harried his troops at every stage, if I remember aright.'

Barton nodded. 'So I believe. But Sir Robert has been able to keep them quiet for the last sixteen years or so. No trouble at all with them. And, of course, they make perfect soldiers, you know. Cheerful, hard-working, good with weapons and brave, very brave. Of course, it helps that the Afridis of the Pass have been given an annual subsidy of goodness knows how many rupees to keep the road open.

It has certainly paid off, but Warburton has been the key. He is almost an honorary Afridi, you know.'

'Really.' Alice made a note on her ever-present writing pad. 'As you know, we met some trouble in the north – Malakand and all that – which seemed to have been inspired by some kind of mullah, who preached fire and brimstone along the valleys and persuaded so many of the tribesmen that they would reach Paradise if they attacked the British troops. You've had no sign of that sort of trouble along here?'

'No.' He paused for a moment and his face took on a slight frown. 'However, it is true that my spies tell me that a new mullah has, it seems, arrived in the hills further west and is attempting to spread the same gospel. But I hear that General Blood has cleared up things beyond Malakand and I should be very much surprised if rebellion takes hold in this area. The Afridis along the Pass are too used to having their annual pension handed down to them. And there is the influence of Warburton, too, of course, although he has gone now.

'However, as I explained to you and your husband, I have taken precautions in the form of replenishing our supplies and ammunition. We could withstand quite a siege here, if we had to, don't worry. We are in a far better position than the forts along the Pass towards the Punjab end. At Masjid they have no proper water supply and Maude is overlooked, even more than we are here. But we are all interdependent to some extent and reinforcements would soon come our way if we are seriously attacked.'

Alice scribbled away. 'And I presume you send out patrols?'

'Oh yes. There is no way we could be taken by surprise.'

Putting down her pencil, Alice directed at Barton one of her most winning smiles. 'It would be fascinating, Captain, for me to go on one of those patrols. You know – to pick up the atmosphere, a sense of the discipline and routine and so on. Would you be kind enough to arrange this?'

Barton smiled back. 'Alas no, madam. I really could not allow that. You would not only be in danger but you could impair the safety of the patrol. In these troubled times, these chaps have enough to do to look after themselves, let alone a white lady of some distinction. I am sorry.'

'Ah well,' Alice let her beguiling smile slip into a comradely grin. 'It was worth a try. Although I am not all that distinguished, I must say.'

'Oh, but you are. I remember reading your reports about the Second Afghan War in the *Morning Post* when I was a cadet at Sandhurst. It's an honour to have you here.'

Alice nodded at the compliment. 'You are far too kind, Captain – but not in reminding me of my age. *Really*, a lady must have her secrets, you know.'

Barton blushed. 'Oh, I say. I didn't mean to—'

'Don't apologise. I was just joking. Now,' her pencil reappeared 'do tell me how many men you have here.'

The next two days presented more cloudless skies and hot sun. Alice strode around the fort and studied the soldiers' routines and found one or two who could speak English – particularly one, rather elderly *havildar* (sergeant), who came from a nearby village and was proud that his son was serving with the regiment and in the garrison. She also took note of the firing sight lines from the surrounding hills and was a touch depressed to see how overlooked the fort was.

At the end of the third day, she had written a colourful, pen picture of life in this fort on the far corner of the Raj – and then wondered how she was going to fill the rest of her time until Simon returned. It would be terribly dull, she reflected that evening, sitting on her favourite spot on the firing step on the ramparts, if she was not allowed to step outside Fort Landi Kotal to go into the hills. It was, of course, oppressively hot still. Was it the heat, she reflected, as she studied the guards on duty, or was there an air of unease amongst the men? They seemed, somehow, restless and even sullen – an unusual trait among the Afridis she had met so far. Perhaps the men, too, had now become rather bored, like herself. She shrugged. The sun, of course, and the monotony of garrison life.

The next day just before noon, Captain Barton knocked on the door of her room. He took off his helmet and perched on the little chair by her dressing table as she sat on the bed.

'Bit of bad news, I'm afraid,' he said.

She sat upright. 'Not about Simon?'

'No, no. And it might be rubbish. But one of my spies has just come in from the surrounding villages. It seems that the people around here are agog with the news that a mullah from Afghanistan – the one I mentioned to you the other night, his name is Sayyid Akbar, a real troublemaker by the sound of it . . .'

Alice grabbed her pencil and wrote down the name. 'What about him?'

'Allegedly he is raising the tribes all along the valleys up

143

the Khyber and he is on his way here with a force numbering more than ten thousand men to attack the forts along the Pass. We, of course, could be the first one to be hit.'

'How reliable is this information, do you think?'

Barton wiped his brow with his handkerchief. 'Oh, pretty reliable, I think. This man has never got things wrong before.'

'What will you do?'

'I have telegraphed the news to Peshawar to my commanding officer there and have requested that he send me reinforcements, particularly mountain guns. The Pathans hate these.'

Alice scribbled away and looked up. 'Well, Captain,' she said with a level smile, 'I was just becoming a teeny bit bored. It looks as though there will be no fear of that.'

He gave an answering grin. 'No. They will undoubtedly have a go at us. But they will bounce off the walls of this fort, I can tell you that.'

'And you can trust your men, of course – if the neighbouring people join in, they sound as though they will be fighting their own people.'

'Yes, but it has always been thus. My chaps won't break and run. I can assure you of that.'

'Well, that's good to hear. Please keep me informed. May I use the telegraph to cable a story back to Peshawar?'

'I'm afraid not. If and when these chaps arrive the line will undoubtedly be cut and I must keep it open until then for military purposes, you understand.'

'Of course.'

That afternoon, Alice scribbled a story in cablese ready

for despatch as soon as the line became clear. Then, as an afterthought, she rummaged among her belongings and extracted the Webley revolver that Simon had left with her. She cleaned it with a piece of rag and made sure that it was loaded, with six cartridges. Then she placed a small box of ammunition nearby.

She looked out of her small window at the hills and gulped. It had been a long time since she had been in danger without Simon by her side. Ah well. She put the revolver down on the dressing table. If she *would* wander down places like the Khyber Pass to the very edge of the Empire . . !

Early the next morning, Barton knocked on her door again. 'I am most sorry,' he said. 'But my CO has ordered me to ride immediately back to Jamrud to report. It is only about twenty miles back up the Pass and if I push hard I should be back in a couple of days. Now, do come with me, if you wish, but I warn you that it will be a hard – a very hard – ride, so I would prefer it if you stayed here because I must set a fast pace and you would almost certainly be safer here. There is no sign of the Pathans approaching us yet and I should be back with reinforcements before they do.'

'Ah.' Alice put a hand to her mouth and immediately regretted this sign of weakness. 'Of course I shall stay. I must be here when Simon returns. Who will be in command while you are away?'

'The senior *subedar, Subedar Major* Marshal Akbar Khan. He's a first-class man. You can rely on him. But I must ask you, ma'am, to follow his instructions if we do come under attack. However, I am sure that won't happen before I get back. Now, you must excuse me please, for I must leave.'

'Of course. Good luck, Mr Barton.'

'Thank you, ma'am.'

Alice climbed back up to the battlements to watch the captain and his escort of three men, gallop away to the east. She looked down on the inside working of the fort: guards mounted high on either side of the open gate, pacing back and forwards, almost nonchalantly; a cook coming out of the cookhouse, as though to smell the air; a small group of off-duty riflemen, sitting in vests playing cards. Everything seemed quiet and in order. And yet . . . she sensed that she was sitting on some sort of powder keg. Why was that man on the other side of the battlements, hardly moving, but staring intently to the west? Why was the fort, housing all these men, so strangely silent? Why had she let herself be left here, the only woman among 370 Afridis?

She tossed her head. It must be the heat getting her down. Barton said that she would be safe and the fort, he had insisted, was impregnable. She had no need to worry. Alice opened her window wide to catch what she could of the almost imperceptible breeze and lay down on the bed and directed her thoughts towards Simon.

That evening, not quite liking to embarrass the *jemadars* with her presence in the mess, she remained in her room with a bowl of rice and retired early, although sleep eluded her in that hot little room. Eventually, she walked out onto the battlements, wrapping a shawl around her and exchanging nods and smiles with the sentry patrolling there.

She sat staring up at the blue bowl of stars – was there anywhere but here, far away from street lights and other urban illuminations, where they shone so brightly? The hills, coloured indigo now in the semi-darkness, loomed everywhere. It was not cold but she found herself shivering and crawled back onto her bed, managing to find sleep just before dawn.

She spent the next day, rewriting her copy and staying in her room. She emerged disgracefully late the next morning and decided not to draw attention to her tardiness by asking for something from the cookhouse. She was not hungry anyway. Later she sought out *Subedar Major* Khan, a tall man with a face as black as soot and a few threads of silver beginning to appear in his equally black beard. He, in particular, had been cordial to her, in an avuncular way, in the mess.

'Congratulations, General,' she greeted him. 'I hear that you are now in command.'

The Afridis teeth flashed amidst the blackness. 'Ah, yes, memsahib. Soon I shall be Viceroy, you know.'

'I am sure it won't be long.' Then Alice allowed the smile to leave her face. 'I hear that we might have visitors before long. Do you think that these men will be here soon?'

Before the question could be answered, a patrol of riflemen appeared trotting down the hill towards the great gate. Then, in the distance, Alice's ear picked up a faint thumping sound that, as she strained, grew gradually louder. It was the sound of hundreds of drums being beaten.

The *subedar major* inclined his head towards the west.

'There you have your answer, memsahib. They will be here within one quarter of an hour, I would say,' he gave a sad smile. 'At least my family will be reunited.'

'What do you mean?'

'Ah, memsahib, you will find this strange. You see, I have one son who is serving in the garrison here and two more,' he pointed up the Pass to the west, 'with those tribesmen coming here. We fight each other.' He shrugged. 'It is the way of our people.'

'Good gracious.' Alice drew in her breath to question him further, but the tall soldier leant over the parapet and barked an order. The gate swung open to allow the patrol to enter, then it was locked and a bar of timber lowered across it to secure it. Then, at a further command, a bugler sprang to attention in the square below and the alarm was sounded.

Subedar Major Khan turned back to Alice. 'That patrol will tell me that we are about to be attacked by many men, madam,' he announced gravely. 'We shall be fired upon down from those hills,' he indicated with his head. 'It would be better, then, if you would go to your room and stay there, memsahib. You will be safe there.'

'Of course, *Subedar*. But is there any news of Captain Barton? He hoped to be here with reinforcements by at least today, I understood.'

'No, madam and the telegraph line to the other forts and to Peshawar has been cut. Now, if you will excuse me.'

She bowed her head and retreated to her room. There, for a moment, she reflected on the strange ways of the Pathans. If brother was fighting brother here and sons fighting their father, could the slender allegiances to the Queen Empress created by the British be relied upon? She shook her head. God knows. Then, she thrust her loaded revolver through the sash at her waist, grabbed her notepad and pencil, wound a scarf around her head as protection against the sun and crept back to the embrasures.

As she watched, she saw the garrison, all dressed in their field service uniforms of sand-coloured khaki and with tightly wound turbans of the same colour on their heads, trot out and fall into line in the square within the walls. They all carried Martini-Henry rifles and had long sword bayonets swinging from their belts. Alice felt reassured as the men fell into impeccable lines, as straight as those of guardsmen, and then, on the commands of their *havildars*, deployed and quietly climbed to man the ramparts.

Alice retreated to her room quickly and then reappeared carrying the field glasses that Simon had left with her. She levelled them up the Pass towards the west and focused them. The road was empty, so she swung the glasses up to the right and higher, refocussing them to gain more distance onto the mountain slopes that swept down to the road. She caught her breath as she saw them now: hordes of tribesmen dressed in a variety of colours, swarming over the landscape, looking like ants at that range as they undulated over the swelling hillside. She tightened the focus and she could see that they all seemed to be carrying rifles and many were bearing flags and banners of green and black. The drums were now louder and the noise boomed back down from the hills.

She drew in her breath again. *There were so many of*

them! How could the fort withstand attacks from such a host – particularly if they could fire down onto the interior of the fort from the hills? She looked upwards around her. The sides of the hills, of course, did not rise vertically and she estimated that the nearest firing positions commanding the interior would be at a range of some three hundred yards, so it was true that this fort was better sited than Fort Maude. The distance, at least, would demand expert marksmanship to kill at that range. Yet the Pathans were supposed to be splendid shots!

Turning the binoculars back to the road, she saw the vanguard of the attackers now appearing around the bend and swelling out from behind so that they completely occupied the Pass. So many, again! She pulled out her small dress watch. It was exactly twelve noon. How long could the fort hold out against such a host?

The bugle rang out again and the defenders were now lining the walls, with enough men, it seemed to Alice, for each embrasure to be occupied. She took up position just outside her room, behind the kindly old *havildar* to whom she had spoken earlier. He turned his head to her and gave her a warm smile. She forced herself to smile back reassuringly. It wouldn't do for a memsahib, even less a *havildar*, to display concern.

Orders were now shouted and the men rested their rifles on the stonework, some kneeling, some standing, according to the varying levels of the firing step. None of the men yet aimed their rifles for the Pathans were not within range. Alice looked keenly to see any sign of anxiety among the riflemen. But there seemed none. They merely settled down, waiting, comfortably it seemed, not even adjusting the sights on their rifles, for no range orders had yet been given.

Alice was immediately reassured at the cool discipline exhibited by these Khyber Riflemen. It could have been soldiers of a foremost British regiment of the line that she was observing. Despite the sun, now at its highest, they seemed to be as cool as guardsmen.

Picking up the glasses again, Alice saw that the Pathans were now climbing higher up the hills and spreading out, obviously to gain better vantage points for sniping. Clearly, they were not just a rabble. Someone was directing the attack. Someone was in command.

The defenders still held their fire and Alice noted the *subedars* and the *havildars* were now walking carefully, fully erect, behind the riflemen. She caught the eye of *Subedar Major* Khan, who brusquely waved her back from the firing positions and to her room. Chastened, she crept back inside.

She opened the box of cartridges and took handfuls and deposited them in the pockets of her riding breeches, so that they exaggerated the curve outwards of the jodhpurs. She looked again at the Webley. She had no idea of its range but, obviously, it would be useless at long range, so having no effect on the snipers. It was a close-quarters weapon. Useful only if the fort was overcome and the Pathans swarmed up the stairway to her room . . . She gulped. Well, that wouldn't happen, she had been assured of that.

Sitting on her bed disconsolately, Alice heard an order barked outside and then repeated around the walls. To hell with this! She was not going to stay in this stuffy little room waiting for her door to be knocked down by some knife-carrying tribesman! She crept outside again and realised that some shots were now being fired on the fort from the surrounding hillside. Nothing, however, seemed to be having any effect on the defenders, who were now all studiously adjusting the rear-sights on their rifles in response to the orders given.

Alice crouched next to the old *havildar*, who had now taken up his position at one of the embrasures. He turned, with a frown, and she grinned and put her finger to her lips, indicating her revolver. His frown disappeared and was replaced by a grin. 'Be careful, memsahib,' he grunted. 'These men are good shots.' He pointed towards the lines of tribesmen, now gradually approaching the walls.

Whatever she was about to say in reply was drowned by an outburst of firing from the hills and the road below. It evoked no response from the defenders for the firing was badly directed and still at long range and the officers were showing no sign of giving orders to return the fire. They were clearly biding their time – in for the long haul.

Then there was a huge shout from without the walls and, looking over the *havildar*'s shoulder, Alice saw that the mob was now rushing towards the walls. An order was shouted by *Major Subedar* Khan, to be repeated by the other *subedars* commanding the firing positions. Immediately, all the riflemen at the embrasures nestled their rifle butts to their cheeks and sighted down the long barrels of the Martini-Henrys. But still they waited. Then a second command was shrieked and repeated and the embrasures came to life in a volley of flame.

Through the smoke, Alice glimpsed men on the hillsides throwing up their arms and falling. Yet many more still came on. As one man, all the sepoys inserted another cartridge in their magazines and then fired again. They continued to do so until the battlements were wreathed in smoke and Alice fell back, the sour taste of cordite on her lips, her cheeks blackened by gunpowder and half deafened by the sound of gunfire.

As the order to cease firing rang out, she took another look over the embrasure. The defenders' disciplined firing had taken its toll. Bodies, looking like children's rag dolls in their variously coloured cotton clothing, lay scattered along the side of the hills and across the road. The Pathans were retreating and finding cover. Then, a bullet thudded into the stonework by her head and another glanced off and pinged away. The snipers were finding the range now and the *havildar* at her side ducked his head and waved her away.

Alice crawled back into the open doorway of her room and wondered if the *subedar major*'s sons were deliberately firing at him. Perhaps it was a family feud that had caused a rift – or just some silly and deadly game these strange people were playing? She shook her head in bewilderment again.

For perhaps ten minutes there was comparative quiet around the fort, except for the exchange of shots between the snipers and the defenders at the embrasures, consistently from the attackers and desultory from the soldiers. Alice realised that they had obviously been told to conserve their ammunition and wait for the tribesmen to leave their cover. Then she heard the drums – so ever-present, so threatening! –

increase their beat and the screaming and shouting began again, to mark the beginning of another attack.

Once again, the *subedars* screamed orders – obviously telling the defenders to hold their fire – and then, at the commands, the volleys began again, their crashing sound mingling with the drums and bouncing the echoes back from the mountainsides until Alice, crouching just away from her open doorway, thought that her eardrums would burst with the noise. Then, again, the orders to cease fire and the beginning again of the individual rifle duels.

So it continued throughout the afternoon, as the sun blazed down. During a momentary pause, Alice realised that she must make some contribution to the defence, for clearly her revolver was of little use. She looked around her room and ripped off the bed the cotton sheets, which she tore into strips, then cut some of them into squares with her nail scissors, to use as pads. Thrusting the pads into her pockets, she threw the strips over her shoulder, poured water from her jug into her washing bowl and picked up the bowl and, crouching as best she could, carried her load onto the platform behind the embrasures and then, awkwardly, down the steps into the square below. Immediately, bullets thudded into the ground around her and she realised that she was a target for the snipers looking down from the hills. Perspiring, she scurried into the cookhouse.

Immediately, she saw *Subedar Major* Khan sitting on a table while a sepoy was trying to cut away his tunic to reach a wound in his upper arm. 'Go back to your room, memsahib,' he shouted to make himself heard above the din. 'Dangerous here.'

'It's dangerous everywhere, *Subedar Major*,' she shouted back. 'I must help. Here, let me do that.'

She thrust the sepoy aside, and sawed away at the tunic with her scissors. The bullet seemed to have passed straight through the arm, chipping the bone, so that she did not have to probe for it, thank goodness, although it was bleeding profusely. Using one of her pads, she bathed and cleaned the wound, and bound the bandage onto it tightly, to restrict the bleeding.

'Well done, memsahib,' grunted the *subedar major* through clenched teeth. He pushed himself off the table and gestured around.

Alice realised that the kitchen was being used as a rough-and-ready medical centre and that several wounded men were lying groaning on the tables.

'You can help here, miss,' said Khan. 'These men not good nurses and we have no doctor here. I must get back to the walls.' He rapped out an order. 'Thank you, memsahib. I tell them to do what you say. You good woman – and brave too.' Then he ducked through the doorway and sprinted across the open ground, holding his wounded arm, to reach the partial cover of the stone stairway set in the wall.

Alice sucked in her breath as she looked around her. Two sepoys, who had obviously been acting as medical orderlies, were looking at her expectantly. Their faces and hands were filthy and they were using dirty strips of kitchen waste as bandages. At least seven wounded men were lying on the tables.

Alice's heart sank. She had never received any medical training and retained only the most fundamental notion of first aid. She gulped. What had been Nurse Nightingale's mantra in the Crimea? Ah yes. Cleanliness, that was it. At least they could clean and bind the wounds and, hopefully, prevent too much loss of blood.

'Do you speak English?' she asked.

The two men shook their heads.

'Oh,' sighed Alice, 'now that's just splendid.' She gestured to the cooking bowls and to the primitive cold-water tap that stood in one corner. She ran across and filled one bowl. Then picked up a coarse piece of soap and went through the motions of washing and indicated that the sepoys should do the same. Then, while they washed, she laid out her bandages and pads and began inspecting the wounds.

It was miserable work. There was no morphine or other drugs to staunch the pain and all that she could do was to wash the wounds and apply the pads and bandages. She gestured to the orderlies to watch her and then do the same for some of the others. But they were able to do little to help three of the wounded who had serious gunshot wounds, in the chest or head, from having been exposed to the snipers on the ramparts.

The four of them worked hard through the day as more wounded were brought in and Alice hardly noticed when dusk fell, except that suddenly there was an influx of hurt men from the walls. The darkness meant that they could limp across the square – sometimes helped by their fellows – without fear of being hit, and make it to the cookhouse door.

Getting some of the fit men to lift the corpses and lay them outside, Alice indicated that the newly wounded should take their places on the tables and she carried on with her work of washing and bandaging, although now she began to feel a sense of hopelessness, realising that, so often, something more radical was needed if the wounded men were to survive.

She had hoped that the end of daylight would mean some diminution in the wave of attacks. But the noise of the shouting, the beating of the drums and the awful cacophony of the firing continued through the night. Exhausted, at about 3 a.m., Alice gestured to her orderlies to stop their work and to find something to eat, while she brewed tea. For a precious few minutes, the three of them squatted on the floor of beaten earth, sipped their tea and ate chapattis, smeared with strawberry jam, amidst the groans of the wounded.

Alice eventually realised that there was now little more they could do in their crowded makeshift hospital, for they had no more bandages or pads left and the numbers of wounded demanding attention – those that had been able to reach the dubious safety of the cookhouse, that is – were increasing, so that many were forced to sit outside the open doorway. She must seek help, so, as dawn was breaking, she dipped her hands in the red water in the bloodstained bowl, wiped them on her jodhpurs and ventured outside to find the *subedar major*, while she was still able to cross the square.

She grabbed the arm of a sepoy. '*Subedar Major* Khan?' she asked, pointing up at the firing step running behind the battlements.

The man shook his head. 'Dead,' he said.

Alice put her fist to her mouth. 'Oh, God,' she exclaimed. For a brief moment, she wondered if the bullet that had killed him had been fired by one of his sons. She hung on to the sepoy's arm as he tried to pull away. 'The other *subedars?*' she demanded, whirling her arm around to emphasise the question.

'Dead. Fort finished.'

Then the man slipped away. Alice looked around her in growing anxiety. She realised, then, that the firing step above her was littered with inert bodies and that very few sepoys were still lining the embrasures and firing. There was a furious banging on the outside of the great gates. How had the attackers been allowed to get that close to the entrance?

She ran up the steps to the battlements and, picking her way over the dead and wounded, found the embrasure outside her room where the old *havildar* had been. He was now half hanging, head down, through the gap in the stonework, the top of his scalp torn away. Then she stole a glance over his body. The base of the wall was now a mass of tribesmen, all jostling to get towards the gate of the fort. She looked along the firing step. No one – not one single sepoy – was left manning the embrasures. Those that were left were now trotting down the steps towards the inside of the gate.

She realised with horror: *they were going to open the gates!*

'NO!' screamed Alice. 'NO. NO!' Drawing her revolver from where it had slipped down inside her cummerbund, she ran after them down the steps. She saw that some of the soldiers were attempting to lift the heavy bar of timber that lay across the door. She clawed at the sepoy nearest her at the back of the crowd, but he pushed her away violently. The bar was being raised. What to do?

Alice immediately thought of the wounded. She had heard of the cruelty of the Pathans and how they would mutilate whoever of their opponents survived. She therefore ran to the cookhouse. The two orderlies had abandoned their post, so Alice slammed the door and fumbled around for a key, but there was none. Biting her lip and trembling, she therefore stood beside the nearest wounded man, one hand on his bandaged chest, the other levelling her revolver at the door. Waiting . . .

She could tell by the howling from outside that the gates to the fort had been opened and she heard the pounding of hundreds of feet across the square of the fort. There was a splintering of wood as doors leading to the barracks were smashed open and then, with a crash, that to the makeshift hospital was thrust aside.

Alice raised her revolver and shouted, 'Stop, or I shoot.'

She realised how pathetic she sounded for her voice could hardly be heard above the din, but the sight of this bloodstained woman levelling her revolver at them was enough to freeze the three Pathans who were jammed in the entrance. They looked at her with jaws dropped and Alice had a momentary impression of wild, exultant, black faces and eyes that regarded her with amazement, and then, puzzled amusement. Slowly, they looked her up and down and then, equally slowly, raised their curved swords.

Alice pulled the trigger of the Webley but nothing

happened. The revolver had jammed. She closed her eyes and prepared to die.

A voice suddenly screamed a command in what Alice presumed must be Pushtu and she opened her eyes. The men jamming the doorway were being pulled back and a tall figure, dressed in white robes that were of a quality and richness that emphasised his difference in rank to those surrounding him, pushed through. He carried a bloodstained sword.

His black eyes looked directly into those of Alice and then he said, in impeccable English, 'Good heavens. And who might you be, pray?'

With that, overwhelmed with hunger, exhaustion and shock, Alice fainted.

CHAPTER SEVEN

Alice had no idea how long she lay unconscious but it was a pungent smell of burning that first penetrated her senses and then a great noise, of people shouting, timber crackling and crashing and rifles being fired. She opened her eyes and looked up at the blue, Punjabi sky, now streaked with smoke. Ah, so she was not dead!

She tried to sit up but found that she was roughly bound and seemed to be tied to some sort of litter that was lying on the ground. She craned her neck and realised that she had been deposited high on the hillside and that she was looking down on Fort Landi Kotal, now well ablaze. Tribesmen were milling all around her and drums were still beating, obviously in triumph.

And yet, she could see that the fighting was not yet over and not all of the sepoys had capitulated to the tribesmen.

Down below, a group of the soldiers had somehow formed a square and fought their way through the gates and, still in a rough square formation, were marching along the road towards Peshawar, under the command of what appeared to Alice to be a *subedar* – so there was at least one left! – and occasionally firing at a few of the Pathans who still accosted them. It seemed that they had been allowed to escape, for the tribesmen were far more interested in looting and then destroying the fort.

Alice frowned and let her head fall back. It throbbed and her mouth and tongue seemed to be made of sandpaper. She tried to marshal her thoughts and make sense of it all but the hard work and anxieties of the previous day and night brought back her exhaustion and she allowed herself to slip back into an uneasy slumber.

She awoke to find herself being carried by two men, one at her feet and the other at her head, so that she looked up past his considerable stomach into the underside of his beard. As best she could see, they were typical Pathan tribesmen. The man ahead was wearing a skull cap and a loose *angarka*. He had a bandolier crossing his breast and back and Alice realised that the weight she could feel on her feet were those of the two men's rifles. Feeling her move, the man at her head looked down and gave her a broken-toothed grin. He was wearing a loosely wound turban and she recognised her revolver pushed into his belt. Fat lot of good it would do him, she reflected sourly. The bloody thing didn't fire when it was needed!

The man grunted to the other bearer and she was lowered to the ground. Then a rough arm was thrust under her head to tilt it forwards and a leather gourd put to her mouth. The water was lukewarm but it tasted sweet to Alice and she gulped greedily. The turbaned bearer produced a scrap of cloth and, with surprising gentleness, wiped away the water that ran down her chin. Then he stood upright and the journey began again.

Alice mouthed 'thank you' and then, more loudly, 'Do you speak English?'

The turbaned one gave her some reply in dialect then shook his head. Alice noticed that his face was pockmarked and his face bore a vivid scar across the left cheek. She tried to look around her but all she could see were one or two other tribesmen loping along and the inevitable rocks and scree. They seemed to be walking along an established track because the litter was tilting neither to left or right.

She tried again to think rationally. The fort had obviously been virtually overrun and, perhaps, some sort of deal done with some, at least, of the defenders: the tribesmen – probably related, like the lamented *subedar major*, to the soldiers in the fort – promising to spare their lives if they opened the gates. Then, she recalled, with a start, the apparition that had appeared at the doorway of the cookhouse, just when she was about to be butchered. Did she imagine it, or did he speak to her in perfect English?

Alice shook her head. She must have imagined that – working throughout the day and the night in the heat, amongst the blood and cries of the wounded, amidst constant noise, and with no rest and little to eat or drink – her mind must have tipped for a moment. She was at her wits' end and expecting a brutal death. The man must obviously have been some sort of leader and spoke to her in Pushtu or even Hindi. She must have fantasised his appearance and voice.

So . . . she had been captured and her life spared. Why? The Pathans usually killed and mutilated their prisoners. Her thoughts turned to the wounded in the cookhouse. Had they been spared too? Highly unlikely. Tears trickled down her face as she recalled the brown eyes of the sepoys she had tended and their smiles of thanks. Ah, but this was a harsh, cruel country!

But why was she still alive – and obviously being cared for in some way? Was she to be a hostage, a bargaining pawn in some further negotiations? Her eyes closed again and she was suddenly back in the fort, amongst the flames and then, through the door, appeared Simon, dressed in fine Persian robes. He swept her up, carried her outside and then, very tenderly lowered her down.

She awoke to find that, indeed, the litter was being lowered to the ground but, alas, not by Simon. She realised that it was nearly dusk and she was in some sort of encampment, though still in the hills, for they could be seen rising beyond a row of tents. Then the litter was raised again – this time roughly – and she was carried into one of the tents. There she was left and she struggled to break free from the bonds that bound her to the makeshift stretcher.

She had managed to free one of her wrists when Scarface reappeared. He was carrying some sort of tray containing a dish heaped high with rice and studded with what appeared to be some sort of meat. Alongside were two oranges and a beaker full of milk. The man bent down and picked up the ends of the cords that had bound her wrists, waved them about disapprovingly under her nose, shaking his head. Speaking to her in dialect, he untied the rest of the cords and helped her to sit up. Then he pointed to the tray and made eating gestures with his fingers, before indicating the entry to the tent and shaking his head again negatively, taking out a knife and drawing it across his throat. Clearly, she was not to venture outside.

Alice nodded her head. 'I won't run,' she said, 'even if I bloody well could.' She summoned up the ghost of a smile, picked up the milk and raised it to him in thanks. He nodded, repeated the gesture with the knife and then left the tent, returning quickly with an oil lantern that he deposited on the floor.

Looking around her, Alice realised that the tent had what looked like a comfortable divan in one corner, piled high with cushions, and a low table in the other. The milk halfway to her lips, she paused. Oh God! Was she about to be raped? Was this what it was all about – taking her from the fort, giving her sustenance and now laying her down by a lush bed? And was the milk drugged?

She took a cautious sip. It tasted delicious. Quite creamy and slightly warm. Probably fresh from a goat. Was she now, then, in the headquarters or even the tent of the fabled mullah, what was his name? Sayyid something, or something Sayyid?

Cautiously, Alice dipped her fingers into the rice. Warm and also delicious. The meat was probably goat but it was tender and succulent. If she was in the mullah's lair, then he obviously travelled with a good cook. And, she reflected, if she was about to be defiled then better that it happened after she had eaten well. If rape was to be on the menu, she certainly would not be acquiescent. And a good meal would give her strength for the fight!

She put her hands to her face in a moment of despair. Had it come to this? No. She took a deep breath. She certainly *would* fight! Then she looked down at herself. Her fingernails were edged with black – whatever would Miss Nightingale think? – and her hands were bloodstained, as were her jodhpurs and blouse. She was not, she reflected, exactly rape material.

Alice forced a grin and ate the rice and meat and then the oranges hungrily and drank the remnants of the milk. Then, a little unsteadily, she rose from where she sat cross-legged on the litter and walked to the door of the tent. Gingerly, she drew apart the folds of the entry and looked out. The darkness outside was broken by a series of fires that had been lit before other tents and they must have climbed into the hills for the air was cold. Tribesmen could be seen tending to pots hung above the fires but no guards seemed to have been posted outside her door.

Alice took a deep breath of the air, so keen and cold that it made her eyes water, then she withdrew back into the tent. She stood indecisively for a moment. Could she just walk away? Yes, but walk to where – and how could she slip through the village without being detected?

She felt herself stagger for a moment and perched on

the edge of the little table. She had been asking herself just too many questions over the last thirty-six hours and providing no answers. She attempted to take stock. Where was she? No idea, but wait . . . She had been looking down at the fort from quite high on the hills on its northern side and it would have been unlikely that her captors would have taken her down to the road again and carried her up the other side. Ergo: if she could escape now and hide amongst the rocks until the morning, she could gauge the south by the position of the sun when it came up and then walk down to the Pass and follow the road to the east towards Peshawar until she reached one of the other forts.

She smiled at her naïvety. Barton had said that the other two forts were sited less well, defensively, than Landi Kotal. If the latter could fall, how could the other two survive? And how the hell could she walk undetected through miles of mountainous country teeming with rebellious Pathans?

Alice looked around the tent. Apart from the roughly made stretcher that had brought her here there was only the bed with its . . . ah – blankets!

She pulled away the top one and wound it around her. The scarf which she had tied around her head as protection from the sun hours ago had long since slipped down to her neck, so she untied it and rearranged it as some kind of head cover. God knows if she looked like a Pathan woman – or even if the camp housed any women – but she was damned if she was going to stay in this tent and wait for . . . for whatever fate lay in store for her. She must make a bid for liberty.

Tucking the blanket round her, she shuffled to the tent opening and pulled back the flap.

'Ah, good evening, Mrs Fonthill,' said the tall, bearded, richly caparisoned man who stood there, a drinking vessel in each hand. 'I'm so glad you have recovered. But this night air is much too cold for a walk. Look. I've brought you a brandy. I thought it might . . . oh dash it, what is the English expression? Ah yes, I thought it might perk you up a bit.'

Alice felt her jaw drop. 'So you're not a figment of my . . . my . . . my imagination?' she gasped, involuntarily.

'Well, do you know, no one has ever accused me of being that before. Shall we go back inside and take a nightcap?' She saw white teeth gleam behind the beard. 'And frankly, my dear, you look vaguely ridiculous in that blanket. You might pass as the wife of an impecunious blanket weaver but not as a native of these parts.'

Alice took three steps backwards. 'Who are you and how do you know my name?'

'All in good time. Now, do sit . . . Ah. No chairs. Just one moment.' He held out the goblets. 'Do you mind holding these for a moment or two? Thank you.'

Then he disappeared back into the night and left Alice holding the brandy, feeling distinctly stupid as the blanket slipped from her shoulders and hung from her arms, making her look like some kind of waitress in a country alehouse.

He was back, carrying two large, soft cushions under each arm. 'Now, he said, 'let's try and be as comfortable as we can in these . . . ah . . . rather spartan surroundings.' He threw the cushions onto the floor and relieved her of the brandy, placing the cups on the table. 'Do sit down. Ah, good. You have eaten. I hope it was to your taste. Alas, I couldn't join you, for there was much for me to do after the capture of the fort.'

Slowly, Alice lowered herself onto the cushion and felt a ridiculous desire for some powder to dab onto her cheeks.

'I think you had better tell me who you are and how you know my name,' she said.

'Certainly. But do take a sip of this cognac first. It is French, you see, it cost me a fortune and I think it will do you the world of good after the, ah, miseries you have been through. Pick you up, as it were.'

Alice stayed silent and unmoving, watching him intently.

'Ah yes,' he said. 'I see. You suspect me of some dastardly plot to drug or murder you. Not so, look.' He picked up one of the cups and sipped from it before handing it to her. 'There, you see. No harm done. In fact,' he chuckled, 'it's doing me no end of good. Now, do come along. Here we go. Cheerio.' And he raised a cup to her in salute.

Slowly, keeping her eyes on his, Alice picked the cup up and took a sip. Immediately, she shuddered as the fiery liquid burnt through her, leaving a warm glow behind. The taste and the words that this man – this Pathan? – were using reminded her of her favourite and very English, old-world uncle, when he had first introduced her to a very fiery *digestif*, one Christmas, aeons ago.

She gulped, caught her breath and nodded. 'Thank you. Now, who are you? You are not the mullah something or other, are you?'

The teeth flashed again and he shook his head. 'No. As

a good Muslim, he doesn't touch these . . . ah . . . better things in life. No. My name is . . . No. If you don't mind I won't tell you that. It may turn to my disadvantage later.'

'But you are not English, surely?'

'No. In fact, I am from Rajasthan, in India, a good way south of here. So, you see, I am very much an Indian – although not Red, as you can see.'

'But . . . but . . . your English is impeccable. You could pass as an Englishman anywhere.'

'How kind of you. But I don't think I could pass as one of your fellow countrymen. I am . . . what shall we say . . . a little too sunburnt for that.' He smiled again and Alice realised that he was an incredibly handsome man, with high cheekbones, smooth, brown skin behind his beard, very white teeth and eyes of soft brown. Rather like Simon's, she thought for a brief moment. But the Indian was still speaking.

'In fact, I think I would be called a nigger, wouldn't you say, or more like niggah, if it was a well-educated English chap describing me.' Alice realised that the smile that lingered around his lips had not reached his eyes.

'Oh, certainly not,' she said immediately. 'That would be incredibly rude.'

He lowered his head in acknowledgement and took another sip of the brandy. 'Well, my dear Mrs Fonthill, that is what I *was* called many times at Winchester – such an old-fashioned English school, you know – and by the hearties at Cambridge.'

'You were educated at Winchester and Cambridge?' Alice's jaw dropped again.

'Oh yes, as well as at school here in India.'

'But what are you doing here, in this . . . this wilderness, with these tribemen – and fighting with them, against us, the British?'

'Yes, perhaps it is time to reveal all, as they say in the best plays in London. But only if you drink your cognac. I do insist.'

She took another sip and he nodded in approval.

'I know your name because when we were . . . er . . . I think the word is *sacking* the fort, we found your belongings in a room by the ramparts and your bag was brought to me. And I must say, Mrs Fonthill, that you do travel light for an English memsahib. Oh, I must reassure you. I have the bag in my own tent and I couldn't carry it *and* the brandy, you see. I will fetch it presently, so that you can change and retire here for the night, without molestation, I assure you. Oh, and some water and soap, etcetera, so that you can wash. But in the circumstances, you see, I felt the brandy took priority.'

He smiled again and Alice could not refrain from returning it. As he was speaking, her eye was taking in every detail of his appearance. He had been forced to duck very low to enter the tent so he must, she estimated, be very tall, perhaps six feet two inches, certainly tall for an Indian, yet he was obviously not a Sikh. The coat he wore was of calf length and seemed to be a mixture of cotton and silk, for gold threads lined the edges so that it glittered in the lamplight. He wore high boots of some soft leather, worked into a pattern along the calf, and a high-buttoned, collarless jacket reached to his neck. A cummerbund circled his waist and from a belt hung a long, curved dagger that seemed to have jewels in the hilt. She seemed to remember a coloured turban when he came through the cookhouse door but he was not wearing it now and his hair was black and long, curling up over his collar at the back. Two large rings glittered from his fingers. He was a man, Alice decided, of some standing and with more than one or two rupees to his name.

'Well, thank you,' she said. 'I am now beginning to enjoy the cognac. And,' she gestured down at her bloodstained blouse and riding breeches, 'I would welcome the chance to wash and change.'

She checked herself. What on earth was she doing exchanging drawing room pleasantries with a man who had taken part in – maybe even led – a savage attack on British/Indian sepoys? She made her voice take on a colder, more disapproving tone.

'What happened to the wounded in the cookhouse?'

He shrugged. 'They were killed, I am afraid. It is the way here, you know, in these hills.'

'Yes. So it seems. But you are clearly a civilized man. What makes you take part in this . . . this . . . butchery? I saw your sword. You had taken part in the fighting.'

'Oh. It is very simple. I hate the English, you see.'

Alice stared at him, her mouth open.

Then the Indian stood and slightly bowed his head. 'Now,' he said, 'if you will excuse me for a moment, I will leave my brandy here and fetch your bag and ensure you have water and a washing bowl. Then I hope you will be more comfortable.'

She watched him stoop and slip through the tent flap. Who on earth was he, this articulate, well-mannered Indian, who looked like a maharajah, sounded like an English aristocrat and carried a sword like Genghis Khan? She shook her head, absent-mindedly raised her brandy glass and then, without drinking, threw the contents onto the earthen floor with a sudden gesture of disgust. To hell with this! She had to get out of this place.

Alice started for the tent flap and then sat down again abruptly. How stupid! She was still unsteady on her feet and, anyway, he –whoever 'he' was – would be back in a moment and, even if she was able to slip through the encampment unnoticed, he would raise the alarm. She took a deep breath. Better to wait until the camp was asleep and, anyway, she must find out more about this man who was her captor.

There was a flurry of movement at the tent flap and then Scarface bustled through carrying a pitcher of water, soap and a rough, loosely woven cloth to act as a towel. He was followed by an Indian carrying her bag.

'It was only opened,' he said, gesturing to the bag, 'to establish your identity. Ah, I see you have finished your cognac. Good. I took the opportunity of bringing in what was left.' He raised the bottle he was carrying. 'I thought we might as well finish the bottle together.' He gave her his disarming smile. 'I don't often have the opportunity of indulging in interesting conversation these days.'

Alice lifted up her hand to refuse the cognac but he refilled her glass anyway. He gestured around him. 'I have been living rather roughly, as you see, for some days.'

She gulped. 'What . . . what has happened to the other forts in the Pass?' she asked, trying to keep her voice level.

'Take a sip and I will tell you.' He gestured with his glass.

Reluctantly, she did so, beginning to feel that she was playing some exotic – erotic? – game, here in these savage hills with this smooth, educated barbarian.

'Well done. The forts? Oh, we took the other two quite easily in the end, although you will be glad to hear that I was instrumental in us allowing the garrison of Fort Maude to retreat to Jamrud, after they had surrendered the fort. Some of the garrison at Ali Masjid were allowed to get away too. So, you see, I am not quite the butcher that you seem to think I am.'

'Hmm. The wounded at Kotal – and your sword was bloodstained?'

For a moment, his voice lost its urbanity. 'I had to fight into the fort there with the Pathans. But I personally do not kill wounded men, madam. Now,' his words resumed their level tone, 'at last, the Pathans have regained control of the Khyber Pass, *their* Khyber Pass, after it has been in the hands of your countrymen for so long. The main road into Afghanistan, then, you see, is back in the hands of the people whose country it is. Right and proper, don't you think?'

Alice suddenly thought of Simon and her heart almost missed a beat. Would he hear of the Pathan victories here and find some other way back to Peshawar? Her brain offered up an unspoken prayer and then she went on: 'Yes, but why do you hate the English so? You were brought up, it seems, in our country?'

His mouth eased into his mirthless smile again and he gestured to Alice to drink her cognac. She lifted the glass to her lips but allowed only the smallest drop to enter her mouth. 'I suppose,' he said, 'that that is one of the reasons. Your country, madam, or at least your class, has the most distasteful attitude to what they call the coloured races, you know. Oh, they like young Ranji – that's Kumar Shri Ranjitsinhji, a distant relative of mine, by the way, who was at Cambridge with me – because he's good at cricket. But I hated the stupid game and . . .' he paused. 'Come to think of it, one MCC member called Ranji a "damned dirty nigger" last year, even though he had just scored a century against the Australians for England. So there you are. You see, madam, it is easy to hate someone who calls you that, don't you think?'

'Of course.' Somewhere a drum had begun to beat again. Did they never stop? Alice thought quickly. Although she shared the views of the Indian about the English upper classes' ethnic snobbery, she was damned if she was going to appear sycophantic by agreeing with him. 'But your own race, you know, is quite as bad,' she said. 'Your caste system is nothing more than snobbery, now, isn't it?'

'Ah. It is much more than that, but that is too complicated a matter really to go into now. And, anyway,' he took another sip of the cognac, 'my hatred of your people is more fundamental.' He leant forward. 'After fighting over India with the French, like two dogs over a bone, the English have occupied my country and subjected its people, using them to prop up your empirical economy, sending back to "the mother country",' he spat out the phrase, 'our cotton yarns, our cloths, our spices, our dyes, everything that can be squeezed from India at rock-bottom prices to be converted into high-priced merchandise at places like Manchester and London and then exported to the rest of the world.'

His eyes were now flashing and his lip curled with disgust. 'And, what is more, madam, you have put Indian against Indian. You push our poor people into your so-called "Army of the Raj" and make us police the country for you. And when they revolt – as they did in the fifties – you stamp out the insurrection with great cruelty.

'Now, you have acquired new territory in these hills by laying down some arbitrary line, established by some idiot from Calcutta, and telling the Amir of Afghanistan, a friendly ruler of a so-called independent nation, that he must like it or . . . or . . . limp it.'

'Lump it,' corrected Alice distantly.

'What?'

'I think the phrase is like it or lump it.'

'Ah yes. Well, the same thing. So, having learnt a little of your ways – and also of your military strategy at Sandhurst . . .'

'Good Lord! You were there, too?'

'Yes. But I never served in your imperial army. So having acquired your so-called wisdom, I came back to my country . . .'

'*Your* country, sir? Is this actually your country? Surely, you would argue that this is Afghanistan, in truth?'

She saw a flash of petulance in his face and realised that he was not used to being corrected. 'I came back to

176

my country, I said,' he continued, 'and decided to help the Pathans here by putting something of my acquired military skills to good use. These people, you see, are brave, fine fighters, but they lack strategic and tactical ability – attributes needed to overcome well-defended forts like these in the Pass.'

Alice nodded slowly. She remembered seeing how the tribesmen had spread up into the hills so that they could fire down on the defenders of Landi Kotal. Someone, she had noted, was in charge of this rabble.

A silence fell on the interior of the tent. It was as though the Indian had spent his passion in argument and, indeed, that Alice, who had long argued against the Raj's exploitation of cheap labour in India to fill the coffers of the merchants of London and the cotton spinners of Manchester, could find nothing to say in opposition.

Then she cleared her throat. 'I – and there are many others in England in the Liberal Party there – who agree with much of what you say, Mr . . . Oh, do come along. You know my name. I must know yours. What shall I call you?'

The Indian's expression softened slightly. 'Ah, so you are a Liberal. Good. Call me Ali. It will do.'

'Very well, Ali, I agree with much of your argument, certainly about exploitation of your poor people. But your accusation about putting Indian against Indian does not exactly hold water, you know. I know, for instance, that a *subedar* within the fort here had one son defending it and two outside attacking it.'

'Ah yes. *Subedar* Akbar Khan. A fine fighter. His sons

were sorry that he died. But I must remind you, Mrs Fonthill, that Pathans are not Indians. They are not truly of the Punjab. They are virtually an individual race of many tribes, but if one must be nationalist, then we should call them Afghans. These hills are more a part of Afghanistan than India.'

Alice frowned and, in exasperation, took a far larger sip at her brandy than she meant to and coughed. Damn it, she was being worsted in argument! If this man was used to getting his own way, so too was she, in debate.

Ali seemed not to notice and leant forward earnestly again. Was he trying to convert her, she wondered?

'But this is not a political revolt, you know,' he went on. 'This is as much about religion as it is about who owns what territory. The Pathans are dedicated Muslims, as am I, and—'

Alice immediately raised her eyebrows and leant forward to meet him, interrupting his discourse. She pointed at his cup. 'I thought Muslims did not touch alcohol.'

He immediately slumped back on the cushion and, for a moment, looked embarrassed. 'This,' he said, tapping the cup, 'is a very bad habit I learnt in England. I trust that Allah will take it into account when he comes to decide whether I should enter Paradise. But back to the Pathans, they not only hate the English for occupying their land, taxing them, and telling them how to live. They hate them for being infidels, unbelievers. It is a double disgrace, you see, for a militant race to allow such people to rule them.'

'Yes, I can see that. So it must be easy for the mullahs

to raise the individual tribes. Like putting a match to dry grass.'

'Of course. I am glad you understand.' He lifted the brandy bottle. 'Now, this is an interesting conversation and one of the things I learnt at Cambridge is that one can debate better with the help of a little alcohol. So you really must help me finish the bottle. Come along, now.'

Reluctantly, Alice leant forward and offered her glass. He upended the bottle into it. She took another sip. It really was excellent cognac. She felt it speed through her nervous system like the effect of the hashish she had once tried in the Sudan. But she really mustn't encourage him by asking its provenance – and she mustn't, she *really mustn't* get tipsy. Ali was continuing and she frowned in concentration.

'So, as you say, it wasn't so difficult for the mullahs – and some of them, like this one, Mullah Sayyid Akbar, are splendid preachers – to raise the flag of rebellion. What's more, my dear Mrs Fonthill, this is no petty little revolt.' He put down his glass and, leaning forward, clasped both of Alice's, brandy glass and all, in both of his, to emphasise his story. Alice found herself looking deeply into those brown eyes and made no attempt to withdraw either hand.

'Do you know,' Ali was now gripping her hands tightly and moving them to emphasise every other word so that the brandy slopped around in the glass, 'there are about a quarter of a million Afridis living in roughly one thousand square miles of hill country south and west of the Peshawar Valley in the Safed Koh range. The only one of the seven clans living there that has consistently rejected the British is the Zakka Khel. The British have never been able to recruit any of them to be sepoys. So,' he threw back his head and gave a silent guffaw of triumph, 'once we had the Zakka Khel in our bag, the other clans flocked to our flag immediately. It was, as you said, like putting a match to dry tinder.

'The result is that this is not just a revolt, Mrs Fonthill, it is a damned great revolution. We have twenty thousand or more with us. We have set the Border afire and all your troops and generals in the world will not put this out. You will see.'

He gripped her hands ever tightly in one more act of emphasis, then relaxed his grip. He raised his glass again. 'I cannot expect you, madam, to drink to that but please allow me to do so.' And he drained his glass.

They sat in silence regarding each other for a few seconds, then, absent mindedly, Alice raised her own glass to her lips and drank. The Indian slowly leant towards her and Alice found herself dreamily going to meet him before she jerked herself back and cleared her throat. 'Oh dear,' she said, 'that was very interesshi . . . interesting, Ali. But now, you really must excuse me. I musht retire. Thank you for the brandy. Very . . . er . . . shtimulating. Yesh.'

She handed him the glass and tried to regain her feet. He put her glass onto the table, put both of his hands in hers and raised her. He then lifted her hands to his lips, kissed her knuckles and smiled into her eyes. 'You are a most . . . a most . . . interesting woman, Mrs Fonthill.'

Then he took two paces backwards and bowed formally from the waist. 'You will be perfectly safe in here for the night,' he said. 'But do not attempt to leave the tent.' He frowned for a moment and lowered his gaze. 'There is a thingummijig, a what-do-you-call-it? Oh dash it, a potty, in that corner.' And with that he was gone.

Alice clutched at the central tent pole, smiled dazedly, swung around it once and collapsed fully clothed onto the divan. Within a minute, she was fast asleep.

CHAPTER EIGHT

It was the early hours of the morning before Alice awoke, her head pounding. The lantern was guttering but there was still enough flame to light up the interior of the tent and she looked down at her bloodstained garments with disgust. Unbuttoning her blouse and riding breeches, she threw them into a corner and removed her undergarments. She wrenched off her boots and stockings and then washed at the little bowl provided. Feeling considerably better, she crawled back into the bed intending to rest for just a moment before dressing and investigating the possibility of escaping in the darkness. But sleep immediately took over again.

She had no idea what time she awoke but shards of light were streaming in through the entry to the tent, although the flap was tied. Alice swung her legs to the floor and sat for a moment, composing her thoughts. Her head was now clear. At least she hadn't been drugged; the brandy had been pure and, undoubtedly, of a good quality. But equally undoubtedly, she *had* been drunk.

She put her head in her hands and felt ashamed as she recalled the events of the evening. It was not so much becoming tipsy, although that was bad enough. Alice was not unused to strong drink but the last time she had been undoubtedly drunk was as a teenager at school in Switzerland. These days, she was careful to drink only moderately. No – it was the memory of her dark and undoubtedly attractive captor that made her shudder. For God's sake, *she had almost kissed him!* She shook her head. This was not like her. Clearly, it was the effect of the brandy on a brain and body that had been weakened by fatigue and worry. *No more of that now!*

She stood and rummaged in her bag for a change of clothing. Ali was right, she was travelling light so there was little choice. She had packed an additional set of jodhpurs when they had left Marden, but, on reflection, she put them back and donned a long cotton dress. Dark blue, it was plain and might – just might – pass as Muslim wear if she could find something equally anodyne to wear over it. She attempted to clean the riding boots with her towel and stuffed them into her riding bag and put on a pair of nondescript slippers. Digging out a dark-coloured scarf to wrap around her head as a makeshift burkha, she contrived to hang the blanket around her as a top garment.

She had no mirror with which to judge the result but it would have to do. In the semi-darkness, hopefully she

183

might pass for a Pathan woman. There was, however, one more item she needed.

Alice plunged back into the bag and felt for a little side pocket near the bottom whose opening she had sewn up so that it would appear virtually invisible to a not-too-meticulous searcher. She tore away the light stitching and produced from the pocket a small, Belgian Francotte 6.33mm automatic pistol that she had bought in London before embarking. Checking that it was loaded with six cartridges, she tucked it away under the blanket in the pocket of her dress and felt better immediately.

While she slept, someone had brought a plate containing buttered black bread, two slices of cold meat and fresh fruit and left it on the table. A cup containing goat's milk stood by its side. Alice devoured it all with relish. Whatever was intended for her, she was being looked after. Fattening up the calf for slaughter? She shook her head. Hardly likely. She was needed for some purpose. But what?

Taking a deep breath, Alice unthreaded the flap covering the entrance to the tent and stepped outside. The air was fresh – obviously they were comparatively high in the hills – though the sun shone from a cloudless sky and she looked around her with interest.

The camp seemed to be quite large, for tents of various sizes stretched away in all directions. Equally, it was not a permanent base, for there was no building to be seen. This seemed to be, then, the staging post for an army on the move – on the move, but to where? If all the forts had been taken, then the Khyber Pass was clearly in the hands of the Pathans, as Ali had confirmed. Would the Pathans now continue eastwards to attack Jamrud, Peshawar and attempt to invade the Punjab? Alice wrinkled her nose. That would be a most ambitious undertaking, for surely the Viceroy would now be gathering considerable forces there. The Khyber Pass had become a totemic symbol to the British in India, as the gateway to Afghanistan. It most certainly would not be left under the control of the Pathan insurgents.

There were tribesmen milling about amongst the tents, fierce-looking men with hawk-like faces and eyes as black as their skins. They loped by with a loose, athletic gait and seemed to pay no attention to her – ah, was her cobbled-together disguise working?

The camp itself gave off a distinctive odour, despite the crispness of the air. It smelt of woodsmoke, of course, and spiced cooking. But also of something else, something less tangible behind those obvious aromas: perhaps just strangeness and even apprehension, the combination of the purity of the clear sky and the ferocity of the expressions of the tribesmen. Did they never smile?

Alice turned her head to look for Ali. There was unfinished business between them. She would demand to know what he intended to do with her, and also perhaps she could extract from him something more about his identity and, more importantly, of the next move of this rabble of a Pathan army. But she could see no sign of the tall, beautifully clothed Indian amongst the tribesmen milling around.

Then a blow to the small of her back sent her sprawling on the ground. She lay there, partly winded partly stunned by the unexpectedness of it, and looked up. A tribesman, dressed in the ubiquitous, dun-coloured clothing of the Pathan, with crossed bandoliers across his breast and an unstable turban on his head, stood over her, yelling imprecations and gesturing. His fury seemed to mount until he drew a curved dagger from its sheath in his waistcloth, bent down and pulled back her head so that her throat was exposed.

Alice grabbed his wrist but it was like seizing a piece of steel and she was unable to deter him from lifting it before its descent. Then, an arm appeared from behind the man and encircled his throat, lifting him so that his sandals dangled at least three inches above the ground. Words were shouted into his ear from very close quarters until, with a twist and a shrug of the shoulders, the man was hurled away, leaving Scarface to look down on Alice.

She had not realised how big and strong was her erstwhile stretcher-bearer and carer. But his anger seemed no less aroused than that of her attacker, for he stood above her and screamed at her in a native dialect, drawing his own knife and pulling the blade across his throat.

'Oh, for goodness' sake, man,' Alice screamed back, struggling onto all fours. 'I was only taking some fresh air. I wasn't launching an attack on the whole blasted Pathan race.' She hauled herself until her eyes were level with his chin and looked up at him. 'If you think I am staying in that bloody tent all day, Sinbad,' she shouted, 'then you are quite wrong.'

For a moment, the two stood glaring at each other. Then the grizzled features of Scarface lapsed into his broken-toothed grin. He shook his head, patted her head in an avuncular fashion and pointed to the entrance of the tent. His meaning was clear.

Alice allowed herself to give him an answering and conciliatory grin and nodded. 'All right,' she said. 'I'll go inside. But, my friend, I am not going to stay there, I promise.' She bent her head and moved back into the tent. Then she was aware that the flaps were being laced together behind her.

With a scowl she squatted on a cushion. It was obvious that Scarface was her jailer as well as her carer and, it seemed, her protector. When he drew his blade across his throat he was not only implying that *he* would cut it but that there were plenty of others in the camp who would be only too happy to kill her also if they had the chance. They obviously did not like British memsahibs. Obviously, it would be even more dangerous than she originally thought to try to steal away through the camp, even during the hours of darkness. This deserved further thought.

She put her hand under the blanket and fingered her small pistol. She sighed. That wouldn't be of much use against the whole Pathan army. Even if she could slip away from the tent – perhaps under that slight gap under the bottom of the canvas to the rear, there – and evade Scarface or whatever guard they had placed at the entrance, she still would have to find her way in the dark, leaving no tracks, and hiding by day and walking by night, what? – some twenty miles or so – to Jamrud, through country teeming with men who would, it seemed, as happily slit her throat as look at her or to . . .

Alice gulped as the thought of rape re-emerged. Somehow, it seemed as if Ali would be more likely to attempt a gentlemanly seduction, possibly with the aid of expensive cognac, than a sexual assault. Although what could be certain in this primitive wilderness? It was quite likely that, after she had collapsed in the cookhouse, he had himself taken part in the killing and ritual mutilation of the wounded there. The blade of that sword of his was covered in blood. A Cambridge accent and Winchester vocabulary was no guarantee of civilized behaviour in these benighted hills.

She shivered and gave a slight shake of the head. No. There would be no attempt at escaping, at least that night. Perhaps later, when her strength was fully recovered and she had hopefully lured her captors into a state of complacency. And, anyway, she wanted to question Ali more, for he would surely return.

But he did not do so during the remainder of the day and the evening. She sat all day, occasionally rising to peer through the gaps in the entry flap fastenings to learn a little more of her surroundings. Apart from the ever-present threat of danger, she became completely bored, for there was nothing to distract her, although she did manage to prise open a little more the gap at the rear of the tent wall. Yes, she felt she could just about squeeze through it when the opportunity occurred. Otherwise there was nothing for it but to attempt a few desultory sit-ups and other exercises to help her regain her strength.

More and more her thoughts turned to Simon. Surely, his country-wise Guides would have picked up the news that the Khyber had become closed to troops of the Raj.

And surely, he would find a way of reaching Peshawar by some alternative and less dangerous route?

That night she dreamt that her husband had arrived at the encampment, had defeated the tribesmen there, killing Scarface in single combat, and swept her up on his horse and carried her away to safety. On wakening, she curled her lip. This was no scenario from some Walter Scott novel. Both she and Simon were in real danger and she devoutly hoped that, even if he did discover what had happened to her and found where she was imprisoned, he would not attempt any foolhardy rescue.

Ali arrived shortly after Alice had finished her modest lunch. He paused at the tent flap, coughed and called, 'May I come in, Mrs Fonthill?'

She quickly pushed a comb through her hair, briefly felt ashamed of herself for feeling pleased that she had earlier applied a touch of face powder and rouge, and then called, 'Of course.'

He entered the tent, seeming to fill it, and gave her that flashing smile. 'Jolly difficult to knock on a tent flap, of course.'

She deliberately refrained from returning the smile and merely said, 'Quite.'

He lowered himself onto a cushion and arranged his face into an expression of concern. 'I was disturbed to hear that there was some . . . er . . . violence directed at you while I was away. I do apologise and hope that you were not seriously hurt.'

'No, thank you. I was merely knocked to the ground. No more than I expected in this place.'

'Oh dear. I am so sorry. Abdul – he is the scarfaced man who is my special retainer and, I suppose, bodyguard – had strict instructions to ensure that you were not interfered with in any way. The man who attacked you has been dealt with. He was a particular hater of the British, you see.'

'*Was?* Is he no longer alive?'

'Ah, please don't worry about that.' He hurried on. 'I am also sorry that I had to leave you but there was urgent work to be done further up the valley.'

Alice seized her chance. 'Work? Reconnaissance, I presume?'

'Well, something of the sort, perhaps. I hope that – despite that brief lapse – Abdul has been looking after you?'

'Yes, indeed. Tell me, Ali. Who guards your ... er ... body while he is otherwise engaged, keeping me imprisoned, for instance?'

His eyes hardened at the sneer implicit in the remark. 'I do not need a bodyguard every day, Mrs Fonthill. I assure you that I can well look after myself, most of the time. It is just that . . . ah well, better not go into that.'

She leant forward. 'What exactly do you intend to do with me, Ali? How long are you going to keep me a prisoner and what will be the end of it all?'

He stood up, walked towards the tent flap and hitched it back so that light and air came into the tent. 'Well, it all rather depends upon your husband, Mrs Fonthill.'

'My . . . husband? What on earth has he got to do with it?'

'Oh, everything, my dear. You see, my spies have told me about his mission to Kabul to persuade the Amir to take

190

no militaristic part in the Pathan revolt. We know that he is on his way back to Peshawar now . . .'

'What?' Alice sat bolt upright. 'Where is he now? Has any harm befallen him?'

Ali shook his head. 'As far as I know, he is in splendid health and he is probably approaching the Afghan-Punjab border at this very moment, or, at least, he will be very near to it.'

Alice sat back and tried to compose herself. 'Good. Then tell me, what do you want of him?'

'Very well. Now listen.' His voice had taken on an edge of steel. 'As I told you, we have many, many men and we will undoubtedly win this fight. But there is no doubt that the British army will throw troops and modern artillery at us. The Amir – whom I know well, of course . . .'

'Of course.'

He ignored the irony. 'The Amir will probably accede to the Viceroy's request that he sends no troops to our aid. But if he is openly insulted he could well lose his temper, because he, too, hates the British and all their works. As a result, he could well commit a considerable number of his well-equipped army to join us. After all, they would all almost certainly be delighted to do so. They are brothers to the Pathans.'

Alice frowned. 'The Viceroy – nor anybody else in a position of power in the Raj – would dream of openly insulting the Amir. You know that.'

'Of course. But it is perfectly simple to forge a letter from the Viceroy – marked with an open copy, of course, to the Russian commander-in-chief at Bukhara across the border in their territory. I have the Viceroy's writing paper here, a copy of his seal and plenty of samples of his signature. The letter would say something to the effect that news had reached Simla that the Amir had been instrumental in sending mullahs across the border into the Punjab to raise the tribes. Something, by the way,' Ali's voice dropped to a purr, 'that is perfectly true.

'As a result,' he went on, 'the Viceroy will call the Amir a dishonest and disroyal cur and inform him that a force was being prepared in the Punjab to invade Afghanistan immediately. As a result, my dear Mrs Fonthill, the Amir will erupt with rage and send his army across the damned Durand Line to join us as soon as you could say Queen Victoria.'

Alice sat for a moment digesting what had been said. Eventually she said: 'But the Amir would know that the Viceroy would never write that sort of letter. He would immediately suspect that it was a forgery.'

Ali nodded. 'Of course. But not if your husband personally delivered the letter, informing the Amir that he had been intercepted at the frontier, told to turn round and deliver it and that he assured the old boy that it was no forgery.'

Alice snorted. 'Oh, don't be ridiculous. My husband would never . . .' Her voice tailed away. Then she spoke in a low voice, little more than a murmur. 'Ah, you would threaten that something would happen to me if he did not carry out this mission. Is that it?'

'Exactly so.'

She spoke now in a voice quivering with fury. 'That is

a dastardly thing to do. You misunderstand my husband if you think that he would agree to such a course of action.'

'Oh, I think he would. If, that is, we proved our intent by forwarding to him some part of you to show that we were serious. Shall we say your index finger, one anyway containing a ring with which, of course, he would be very well acquainted.'

A silence fell. 'And you would do such a thing?' Alice asked quietly.

'Oh, I'm afraid so. Our cause is just, you see.'

'Then you are, what I first thought you to be, an uncivilized savage. A disgrace to the human race.'

He held up his hand, a faint sneer on his face. 'Ah, Mrs Fonthill, I should warn you that I never did respond to flattery – even from those pretty girls at Cambridge. Now, we must first ascertain exactly where your husband is and then, I am afraid, we shall have to carry out what I fear will be rather brutal surgery. Oh,' he held up one finger. 'There is one way of avoiding the . . . ah . . . amputation.'

Alice turned her head away and did not respond.

'That is,' he continued, 'if you wrote him a letter pleading with him to do what we wish, confirming, otherwise, that you will certainly be harmed.'

'I shall do no such thing. Do what you like with me.'

'Very well. I shall ask Abdul to take the finger. Probably tomorrow. I would find doing such a thing myself personally distasteful, you see – although I shall certainly watch. I do apologise, but I fear we have no anaesthetics with us. It will be quite painful. I leave the thought with you. Now, if you will excuse me.'

He gave his customary half bow and turned away through the tent opening, carefully threading the closing cords behind him.

Alice sat staring bleakly at the canvas and began to shiver. She sat like that for a while before removing the two rings that she wore on the third finger of her left hand. At least she could prevent them from taking them off. She rose and, at a spot near the centre pole of the tent, she knelt and clawed at the earth with her fingernails. Having dug a small hole she pulled at the rings and, with an effort, was able to slip them off her finger. She pushed them into the hole and covered them with earth, stamping down the loose soil with her foot until any sign of disturbance had disappeared.

She lay on her bed and began to concentrate. Ali the Damned seemed to have her whichever way her mind twisted. If she refused to sign any plea to Simon, then the finger would be amputated; she shuddered – would they use a hammer and chisel or, even more horrifying, saw it off? If she signed the letter, so avoiding the amputation, Simon would know she must be under great pressure to have done so, possibly torture. Either way, he would be likely to agree, knowing his love for her. Could he find a way out? Perhaps taking the letter to the Amir and then explaining the circumstances to him personally? Would the Amir believe him, having what must seem like a genuine letter from the Viceroy in his hand *and knowing that the Viceroy's charge about sending the mullahs to incite unrest was true?* This last point was the clever twist.

Alice felt tears run down her cheeks but they were caused

as much by frustration as fear. What on earth could she do?

She lay for a while as her brain whirled. Well, there were two alternatives, both of them acts of despair. She could make her escape attempt that very night and, if she was able to leave the camp, at least delay the sending of the letter to Simon while they searched for her. This might give him time to cross the border and be more difficult to find in the hills and valleys as he sought a different way back to Peshawar. But, of course, Ali would anticipate her escape attempt and he would probably increase the guards, maybe so that the tent itself would be circled by them.

Alternatively – and she reached under her blanket top and touched the reassuring cold steel of the little handgun in the pocket of her dress – she could wait for the arrival of Ali and Abdul in the morning and simply kill them. What would happen then? Well, she would be overpowered and then probably tortured to death. Or, more satisfyingly, she could use the last bullet on herself.

She put both hands to her face and let the tears pour until the pillow was soaked. Oh! Simon. Would she never see him again? Then, with a jerk, she sat up. *This would never do.* Her dear husband would be ashamed of her if he saw her now. The escape must be attempted before she fell back on that final solution. She sat for nearly an hour, minutely examining possible courses of action before she decided exactly what she would do. It was full of risks and quite unlikely to succeed but, what the hell – what had she got to lose?

That evening, she ate only a few morsels of her meal, carefully wrapping what was left in the washbag that had remained in her travel bag. Then she lay on the bed in an attempt to rest and store energy. She did not sleep, of course, but lay with her mind racing.

Alice was dreading another visit from Ali but it did not materialise. She peeped through the lacings of the tent flap and breathed a sigh of relief when she saw that night had fallen blackly, with no trace of the moon. She twisted her head to see who was on guard outside the tent but could see no one. She hoped it would not be Abdul, because he had been kind to her and had certainly saved her life.

This waiting was the worst part, for Alice had no watch and she wished to time her attempt for the deepest hours of darkness, when the whole camp should be asleep. Eventually, she stood, discarded her blanket and retrieved her rings from their hiding places and replaced them on her fingers. Then she pulled on her riding boots – there was no way she could walk across the scree and rocks of the hillside in her slippers – removed her brassiere and knickers so that her pubic area was shamelessly nude and pulled down her dress, smoothing it over her breasts so that they stood out provocatively. She combed her hair and quickly checked the handgun to ensure that it was loaded and, as far as she could see, fully operative. Then she took the scarf that had functioned briefly as a burkha and wound it tightly round her hand, with the gun clenched in the fist, making a small bundle.

Alice stood by the entry to the tent, listening again so intently that she could hear her heart thumping. Thank God the camp was never quiet. Even during the hours of darkness someone quite near was thumping a drum, a fire outside one of the nearby tents was guttering low but still crackling and, inevitably, a dog was barking. She took a deep breath and began gently unthreading the cords holding the tent flap in place.

Very cautiously, she looked outside. Yes, there was a guard and, thankfully, it was not Abdul. He was a stocky (good, similar in height to herself!) man and, as he turned, she could see that he looked quite young. His beard was not fully grown, merely a stubble. He frowned at her and she held her finger to her lips, in the universal request for silence, thrust out her breasts and smoothed them with her free hand, smiled, lifted her skirt quickly before beckoning him to come inside the tent.

The Pathan's jaw dropped and he stood uncertainly for a moment. She flounced her skirt again and jerked her head, pouting her lips. Alice's heart nearly missed a beat as the guard remained there. Then, he looked around him furtively and moved quickly towards the tent. She held open the tent flap so that he could enter, but he gestured her in first with his rifle.

She flounced in before him and, holding the bound pistol behind her back, gently slid her free arm around his neck, pulling his head towards her. Then she kissed his mouth, forcing it open with her tongue – God, he tasted foul! Then she knelt down on the bed and waved to him to join her.

This time he grinned and, laying aside the rifle, he slumped onto the divan beside her and began struggling to remove his bandolier. Alice closed her eyes, offered up a quick, silent prayer for the man, pulled him towards her, pushed her pistol, still heavily wrapped in her scarf, against where she judged his heart would be and under where his loose gown was now lying in folds, and pulled the trigger.

The report, muffled by the tightly bound scarf and the Pathan's clothing, emerged as only a sharp crack, and Alice quickly put her free hand to the man's mouth to stifle any sound he might make. As he fell away with a muffled groan, she sprang up, discarding the scarf, and pulled the tent flap across to close the opening and stood, gun poised, ready to sell her life dearly.

She remained there for all of a minute, hardly daring to breath. No sound came from outside the tent, except the continued beating of the drum, the crackle of the fire and the barking of the dog – enough familiar noises, thank God, to have muffled the sound of the shot. She thrust the gun back into her pocket and loosely threaded the cord to hold the flap in place.

Then, gritting her teeth, she knelt at the side of the man and felt for the neck artery. He lay, his mouth and eyes open, a look of complete astonishment on his face. But she could detect no pulse and she began tearing at his clothes before the blood that was seeping through his clothing at the chest could stain it too noticeably.

Alice awkwardly slipped her knickers on over the riding boots, fastened her bra and began pulling on the outer garments of the Pathan: his coarse cotton overshirt, his *poshteen*, his cummerbund and belt, through which an Indian army leather ammunition pouch was slipped – yes, he too would have killed to get that – and from which hung his two-foot-long knife. Thank God his turban was not unravelled and she gingerly put it on her own head, pushing her hair up underneath it, so serving the extra purpose of wedging it there firmly. She picked up her sparse provisions and tied the bag to the belt, grabbed the rifle and tiptoed to the tent exit.

There, on an afterthought, she put down the rifle and returned to the bed, pushing the Pathan roughly into the foetal position and draping the blanket over him. Then she pulled the strands of his long hair over the edge of the blanket and covered much of his head with the pillow. At first sight, in the gloom of the tent, it could, she felt, be herself, still asleep.

'Sorry, young man,' she whispered to him. 'But you will know that this is a violent, *very* violent country. He who lives by the sword . . . and so on. But I am sorry. Perhaps I shall soon join you.'

Then she gently pulled back the tent flap and stepped out into the night.

If there was another guard posted at her tent, she could not see him – perhaps he was at the rear. Carrying the rifle at the trail she began walking firmly, as though on some duty, although she had not the faintest idea of where she was going. She remembered Simon telling her that, although the Pathans were magnificent fighters, splendid shots and skilled at finding and using cover, they lacked the formal disciplines of professional soldiers. Did this mean, then, that they never posted guards in camp at night? She fervently hoped so.

Without looking to right or left, she strode purposefully on, being greeted by dogs but only once being hailed in slurred speech by a man who lay outside a tent – drugs, probably, because, of course, Muslims never took alcohol. She raised a languid hand in reply and hoped to God that her turban was not about to slide off as a result.

Eventually, she reached what was the end of the irregular line of tents and the beginning of the ever-present jumble of rocks and scree. She chose to pick her way down the slope, hopefully towards the road. But this time, she would not turn to the east, towards Jamrud and Peshawar, to where, hopefully, the Pathans would expect her to head. No. She would turn west, towards the Afghan border.

She was going to meet Simon, or die in the attempt.

CHAPTER NINE

Kabul was about an hour behind them, and they had been riding through pleasing country, much of it orchards, that was now beginning to rise into foothills. It had not been easy to regroup the column ready to ride out and Fonthill had become restive at the delay. He had used the time to send Inderjit Singh into the bazaars again to see if he could pick up news about the Pathans' attack on the Khyber forts but the Sikh had been unable to gather anything more than that the mullah had raised a vast army and was descending on the Pass.

It was enough to fuel Simon's anxiety about Alice and he had urged the column into a trot as it pulled out of Kabul, accompanied now by taunts from the citizens lining the narrow streets. The pace, however, had had to be slowed for the sake of the horses and he now sat the saddle in some disquiet.

It was not just the inevitable adjustment to the pace of the advance that disconcerted him but the fact that, for the last minute or so, he had sensed instinctively that something was wrong. Nothing seemed to have changed: the sun beat down from the bluest of skies and the landscape seemed empty of people, but something had alerted him to danger. So what the hell was it?

He stood tall in the stirrups and looked ahead again to where the ground began to fold into valleys and dark rises. Ah yes! There it was. A sudden flash of the sun reflecting from bright metal, just where the road began to wind between outcrops of rock. A likely place for ambush, of course.

It could perhaps be that the sun had caught some bright part of a farm implement, or was even reflecting from a sheet of water. But farm implements in Afghanistan were invariably made of wood and they had long since left the river behind and pools were rare in this barren country.

He called to Appleby-Smith. 'Clarence. Use your field glasses and scan ahead where the road starts to climb and disappear. See anything?'

The captain focused the glasses and then lowered them. 'No,' he said. 'Nothing at all. Why?'

'I thought I saw the sun reflecting from some bright piece of metal. Could be a sword or a spear.'

The captain immediately showed concern. 'Ah. I suggest we halt here and send a scouting party on ahead.'

'No. We can't spare the time. And, anyway, that would show them that they had been seen and they would either wait and ambush the scouts or simply retire and try to attack us at another place later. No, let us keep advancing as though we have seen nothing.'

Simon regarded the officer closely. 'May I suggest you study the terrain? There may be a way around what looks like that defile.'

Appleby-Smith nodded and pulled out of the column to gain a better view.

'No,' shouted Fonthill. 'Come back. Look from here. We don't want them to think that we have seen them. We must keep advancing in the normal way.'

The captain rejoined the column and studied the hills ahead. He put down the field glasses, turned to Simon and offered them to him. 'I think I caught a glimpse of something moving there, where the road disappears,' he said. 'But it's probably nothing. Take the glasses. I can't see an alternative way round. The hills start climbing there and it looks like rough ground. I still think we should stop here and investigate further.'

'Hmm.' Fonthill gazed steadily and then handed the binoculars to Jenkins. 'Here, 352, you take a look. You've got the sharpest eyes of anyone I know.'

The Welshman refocused and sniffed. 'There are definitely blokes skulkin' in them rocks where the road bends,' he grunted. 'An' there's what looks like a bit of a separate track curling up and round to the right there.'

Simon handed the field glasses back to Appleby-Smith. 'Yes,' he said, 'that's what I thought I saw. Strange you didn't see it, Clarence. Never mind. I suggest that what we do now is alert the column, but take no obvious action yet. We will continue to advance as though we have not seen any evidence of the ambush. Then, at the last minute, we split the column into two, with Buckingham's troop peeling off and then galloping up the track to the right, so taking these people from the rear, while we attack them from the front. Would you agree, Clarence?'

'What? Oh, I am not sure about that. A frontal attack would be very dangerous . . .'

Taking a deep breath to control himself, Fonthill murmured, 'Good. I am glad you agree.' He turned to Lieutenant Dawson, who had overheard the conversation and was attempting to hide a smile. 'Would you be kind enough to slip back to give the necessary orders, Mr Dawson? Don't make much of a fuss in doing so. We are probably now being watched quite closely. The rear troop should approach that path to the right at the gallop, climb it and then dismount and attack those fellows with their carbines. Understood?'

Dawson stole an anxious glance at his captain then nodded. 'Understood, sir.'

Simon turned back to Appleby-Smith. 'Just a suggestion, Clarence, but I am sure you agree?'

'Well, I'm not sure—'

'Splendid. Carry on, Mr Dawson.'

Dawson pulled on his reins and allowed himself to be subsumed into the main ranks of the column as it continued to walk forward. He gave detailed instructions to the *daffadars* of his own troop, and then to Buckingham riding in the rear. Immediately, there was an air of expectancy among all the troopers and Buckingham's troop began slowly, almost imperceptibly drawing away to the right.

'Too soon, damnit,' murmured Fonthill. He turned to Jenkins. 'Slip back and tell Buckingham to stay in column until I give the order. He should not break out until the last possible minute . . .'

'Very good, bach sir.'

As the column approached at walking pace, Simon pondered the situation. Appleby-Smith was right, of course, it *was* dangerous to make a frontal attack on an enemy esconced safely behind cover, but he gambled that the diversion made by Buckingham's gallop to the rear of them would create alarm and confusion and allow the other troop to attack without meeting too much resistance.

He wondered about the origins of these men lying in wait. He turned his head but the plain behind was clear so this was not some concerted pincer movement. Perhaps they were just brigands? Unlikely. They wouldn't take on a squadron of Guides in broad daylight. So perhaps the Amir had sent a unit of his army out ahead to lie in wait? They could present a more dangerous threat. But this, too, was unlikely. The Amir would not risk attacking a squadron of the British Indian army in his own country and so aggravate his delicate relations with the Viceroy.

Jenkins had now rejoined Fonthill at the head of the column. 'Everything ready, bach sir,' he murmured. Simon nodded and stole a glance at Appleby-Smith. The man was undoubtedly uneasy at the prospect of battle. Perspiration was now beginning to show on his face and he kept adjusting his position in the saddle. How on earth had this man survived in command of a squadron on the North-West Frontier?

The column was now some two hundred yards from where the road began to climb and bend around a cluster of boulders that jutted out from the left. The path to the right could now be clearly seen. It was probably no more than a goat's track and offered only passage for horsemen in single file. Never mind. It would have to do. At least it seemed as though it was completely unoccupied.

Fonthill loosened the sword in his scabbard and hoped that it had been forged to perform duties more demanding than merely ceremonial. He swallowed. This could be difficult work, fighting man-to-man among the rocks. Something for which Afghans and Pathans were better prepared than cavalry, who lacked bayonets.

He licked his lips and nodded to Jenkins, who almost imperceptibly inclined his head in encouragement. Simon realised that he would now have to drop the pretence that Appleby-Smith was in command and he raised his hand to halt the column.

Turning his head, he lifted his voice, making sure that every word was enunciated clearly, for, although he had spent months in Afghanistan years ago as a captain in the Guides, he had never been a cavalry man and was unfamiliar with the formal words of command. And no bugle call could convey the convoluted nature of the orders he wished to convey.

'Rear troop,' he shouted, 'will pull out and approach that path on the right at the gallop and climb it. Front troop will remain at the halt. Now – rear troop, CHARGE!'

Immediately, Buckingham, revolver in hand, pulled his mount out of the column, dug in his spurs and led his troop at the gallop. A scattered volley rang out from the rocks ahead but seemed to have little effect as the troop thundered by, scattering dust and stones.

Fonthill waited just long enough to see Buckingham and his men break into single file and climb the track, now slipping and sliding, before he raised his hand and addressed the remaining troop. 'Troop will gallop to the front and then halt at the order, take carbines and dismount,' he shouted. 'Handlers will take the horses to the rear. Troop will then attack the enemy behind the rocks on foot. Now – CHARGE!'

Vaguely aware that he was ordering a most difficult manoeuvre in the face of the enemy – charging, halting, dismounting and then advancing as infantry – Simon kicked his spurs into the flank of his mount, drew his sword and lowered his head as his horse took off.

He was a poor horseman, but he could not fail to be elated as he led the most exciting act in the cavalryman's repertoire: the charge. In fact, the elation almost led him too far and the last horseman in Buckingham's troop was just beginning to climb the path when Fonthill held up his hand and screamed HALT! He looked around in some consternation but Dawson and Jenkins close behind him were slipping from their saddles and, as though on the parade ground, the troopers were pulling their carbines from their saddle buckets, similarly slipping down the sides of their mounts, and the handlers were rushing forward, each man taking the reins of four horses.

The charge had taken the troop to the right, at the foot, indeed, of the path up which Buckingham and his men had disappeared. For the moment, no rifle fire was directed at them, although Fonthill could hear shouts and shots coming from the path above them. Dawson was giving orders for his men to form up in a loose formation and when that was completed he looked expectantly at Fonthill. Of Appleby-Smith there was no sign.

'Right,' shouted Simon. 'Take command, Mr Dawson. Climb these rocks and direct volleys at the enemy.'

He waved his sword and wished that the ceremonial dress – that he had not changed in his haste to leave Kabul – carried a revolver holster. He had no faith either in this fancy sword or in his skill as a swordsman. Nevertheless, he scrambled up the rocks before him and rounded the bend in the road. Immediately he saw that, more by luck than good judgement, they had taken about half of the waiting tribesmen from the side, in enfilade, for they were lined up behind the rocks skirting the side of the road in some confusion, under fire now from Buckingham's men above them and still waiting for the main column to appear before them. On the other side of the road, rifles could be seen protruding from the cover there.

Dawson had now overtaken Fonthill and he immediately took command of his troop, which was deploying up the slope. '*Daffadar* Kummul,' he shouted. 'Take your section onto the other side of the road and attack the enemy there. Climb above them. The remainder, at the enemy ahead, commence volley firing. FIRE! RELOAD! FIRE! RELOAD! FIRE!'

Fonthill lowered his sword and watched in admiration as the volleys rang out, thundering like artillery fire in the narrow defile. There was little response from the men waiting in ambush, for those on the opposite side of the road were attempting to crawl away to avoid being surrounded by Kummul's men and those on the near side were falling like ninepins under fire both from above and the side.

It was over very quickly. The tribesmen began slipping away, disappearing between the rocks in the manner for which they had become famous, leaving their dead and wounded behind.

Simon had a sudden thought. 'Dawson,' he shouted. 'See if your chaps can take a couple of prisoners. They could be valuable. Let the rest go.'

'Very good, sir.'

Jenkins materialised at his side. 'Now where d'yer think the captain 'as buggered off to?' he murmured. 'Gone to get reinforcements, d'yer think?'

Fonthill grinned. 'Probably from Peshawar, I should say. Are you all right?'

'Absolutely fine, thank you. 'Aven't fired a shot in anger, see. Didn't need to, really. Felt like a bloody dragoon. Except that I didn't 'ave a sword to wave like you.'

Fonthill examined his weapon and pushed the point against a rock. It bent like cardboard. He gulped. 'Thank God I didn't have to use it. Come on. Let's scramble up the lane to see how Buckingham's got on.'

They met Inderjit Singh scrambling down the path towards them. 'The lieutenant says that the enemy are retreating on foot, sir,' he said. 'He will find it difficult to pursue them on horseback among these rocks. Do you want us to risk chasing them on foot?'

'No, thank you, Inderjit. Tell Mr Buckingham to bring his men back to the horses below and report to me on his casualties.'

The Sikh grinned over his shoulder. 'Ah, very few, I think, sahib. We caught them with their . . . er . . . undertrousers down, I think.'

'Good.' Fonthill turned back to Jenkins. 'A pretty damned good cavalry action, if I do say so myself. Wouldn't you agree?'

The Welshman pulled a face. 'Amazin' you didn't fall off in that charge, bach sir. I was ridin' be'ind you, ready to push you back on all the way.'

'Rubbish. Let's go and count the losses.'

They were indeed few. No fatalities and only two men with superficial rifle wounds. Simon was congratulating the two lieutenants when a familiar figure came limping in on horseback.

'Damned horse threw me in the charge,' panted a dust-stained Captain Appleby-Smith. 'Sorry. Hurt my shoulder a bit. Couldn't remount in time to join you.'

'Oh, hard luck, Clarence,' said Fonthill, with a straight face. 'Let Jenkins here have a look at that shoulder. He's a good man at first aid, though a bit brutal.'

'Not necessary, thank you. Just twisted it a bit. Damned horse just can't be relied upon. Sorry to have . . . er . . . missed the fun.'

'Very well. We sustained very few casualties, I am glad to say, and Dawson's men have managed to bring in a couple of prisoners. I am anxious to interrogate them, but then we must be on our way. I doubt if we shall be attacked again this side of the frontier. Jenkins, would you please fetch Inderjit Singh, we shall need him to interpret.'

'Very good, bach sir.'

The two tribesmen were dishevelled and sullen, clearly expecting to be shot. They were left sitting on a rock, under guard, while Fonthill examined their rifles. They were Martini-Henry army issue, obviously captured.

Simon showed them to Jenkins and the three officers. 'How did Afghans get these?' he asked. 'They haven't been fighting us, have they?'

The Sikh, who had just joined them, interjected. 'They not Afghans, sahib. They Afridis, from across the border. So are rest of these men, from what I can see. They all from the Khyber.'

Fonthill frowned and pursed his lips. 'Pathans, eh? Most of the Afridis are supposed to be fighting their way up the Pass. Why have they crossed the Border? Could it be,' he looked up at the others, 'that they were sent over the Border to stop us returning with the Amir's letter?' His frown deepened. 'That would presuppose that someone in that mullah's rabble knew of our mission – and I don't like the sound of that at all.'

Appleby-Smith wiped his brow with a handkerchief. 'If that is so,' he said, 'then I suggest we make a wide detour, perhaps to the north, and cross the border well away from the western end of the Pass. There could be others lying in wait for us and we are not sufficiently strong to fight many of them, although we did . . . er . . . quite well here . . .'

His words tailed away as five pairs of eyes regarded him coldly.

'Let us see what questioning the prisoners brings us,' responded Fonthill. 'But I am not prepared to abandon the route back along the Pass, which is, of course, the quickest way to Peshawar, unless we hear that the forts have fallen.' It was his turn for his voice to drop away as he voiced his concern. He hated to think what might have happened to Alice if the unthinkable had occurred. But then he recalled Barton's assurance about the impregnability of Fort Landi Kotal and his manner became brisk again. 'We will question them separately to see if their stories match. Bring the first one here, Inderjit.'

The Pathan was perched on a rock while the five men surrounded him. He looked at them in turn with wide eyes.

'Right, Inderjit,' said Simon. 'Explain to him that we are going to ask him a few questions. If he answers the questions honestly then we shall let him go . . .'

'I do think that would be a mistake,' interjected Appleby-Smith. 'We should shoot him afterwards otherwise he could rejoin his friends and inform against us. He can see that we are not a strong unit.'

Fonthill sighed. 'I don't believe in shooting people out of hand – apart from which, Captain, we *are* a strong unit and our friend here can see that. Now, Inderjit, tell him that if he lies he will undoubtedly be shot. And we shall know if he is lying. Begin by asking him what he and his friends were doing on this side of the Afghan border.'

As the young Sikh began translating, the look of relief on the face of the Pathan was evident. The *daffadar* turned back. 'He says that he will tell truth and that he honours English because he was a former sepoy. He says the party was told to wait here to ambush a squadron of Guides who were returning to Peshawar from Kabul.'

'Damn!' murmured Simon. 'So the Afridis, at least, knew all about us. Ask him who gave the orders for this.'

'He thinks it was the Mullah Sayyid Akbar himself.'

'Ask him if the forts in the Pass are still holding out.'

Inderjit lowered his eyes as he translated the response. 'He say that all three forts – Landi Kotal, Ali Masjid and Maude – have fallen and that Sayyid Akbar and his men control the whole of the Khyber Pass now. Landi was last to fall.' There was a unanimous intake of breath from the four white men.

'He could be lying,' said Dawson.

'Test him,' said Fonthill in a low voice. 'Ask him for details.'

The two men conversed in dialect for some time before the Sikh turned back. 'He say that he was at Landi when Afridi sepoys opened gates. The white officer Barton was not there and *Subedar Major* Khan, who he knows from time in army, was in command and was killed. Some sepoys fought their way out of fort and were allowed to march back to Peshawar.'

'Was there . . . was there a white woman in the fort when it was taken?' Fonthill's voice was now almost a whisper.

'Yes, sahib.' Inderjit's voice was equally low. 'It sounds like Fonthill Memsahib. He say she was working with wounded in cookhouse when they broke through. She . . . er . . . collapsed. But was taken, on litter, up into encampment in hills. He don't know where.'

'Yes, but . . . was she hurt?'

'He think not. Just fainted.'

A silence fell on the little group. Then Fonthill spoke again. 'Does he know what they were going to do with her?'

'He don't know. But he think they not hurt her. They put her on litter carefully and two men carry her away from fort. Then they set fire to fort. I think he tell the truth.'

Simon nodded, his face drawn. 'Very well. But press him on the location of the encampment. He must know where the mullah and other leaders have their headquarters. Anything he can tell us will help.'

The *daffadar* eventually turned back. 'He don't know exactly where camp is because he not been there. But he hears it may be about two miles in hills directly north of Fort Landi. He say other man don't know as well. He only joined the attack two days ago.'

Fonthill nodded slowly. 'Thank you, Inderjit. And thank the man, too. Tell him he and his friend may go, but without their rifles. And tell him that if either of them is caught fighting against the British again they will be shot immediately.'

When this was translated to him, the Pathan's face immediately lit up. He bowed to Simon and the others, saluted them for good measure and, waving to his companion, began climbing up the path before disappearing out of sight.

Jenkins immediately led his old comrade away from the group and gripped his arm. 'She'll be all right, bach sir,' he said. 'I feel it in me waters, look you. Miss Alice is as tough as . . . well, as tough as me, though she's just a touch better looking. They won't 'arm a white woman. They'll probably keep 'er as some kind of 'ostage, see. An' she'll fight back at 'em, that she will.'

Fonthill nodded and then whispered through clenched teeth. 'They mustn't touch her. They mustn't touch her.'

'Course not. She won't let 'em. Let's go and find this place and get 'er out of there. We've got enough men to do that.'

'No.' Simon found and sat on a rock, his head in his hands. 'There are too many of us to march up to this camp and attack it,' he muttered. 'We could not hope to ride through hills swarming with Pathans without being noticed and we would be overwhelmed before we got near it. But . . .' He looked up. 'Maybe three of us – you, me, and Inderjit to translate if we are stopped. Maybe three of us, suitably disguised . . .'

He looked around at the dead Pathans. 'There are enough native clothes there for us to wear.' He wrinkled his nose. 'Not pleasant, but it's our only chance.' He grinned faintly up at his old friend. 'We've blacked up before and got away with it. We can do it again. If only we are in time . . . If only . . .' He stood. 'Come on.'

The two strode back to where the three officers and the Sikh were standing, silent in their embarrassment.

'Sorry to keep you, gentlemen,' said Simon. 'One thing is sure: it won't be possible for the squadron to ride back the way we came to Peshawar, or even Jamrud Fort, if it's not been taken, now that the Pathans are in command of the Khyber. So the squadron must find a different way back.'

He looked at Appleby-Smith, Dawson and Buckingham in turn. 'When the Second Afghan War broke out,' he said, 'we tried to invade Afghanistan by three routes. Sam Browne tried to force his way through the Khyber, the quickest way, but he was blocked. A second army tried to get through in the south, via Kohjak to Kandahar, but it took ages to win miles that way. It was left to Roberts, with the smallest force, to fight his way through to Kabul. He did it by beating the Afghans at a 9,000ft-high pass called Peiwar Kotal, the only way through the Safed Koh range, up to the right here. We came through to Kabul the same way after him. Do any of you know it?'

Buckingham nodded. 'Yes. I climbed it with my troop about a year ago, trying to collect taxes from a very difficult headman in a village, who had fought General Roberts in that action.'

'Could you lead the squadron back to Peshawar, south of the Khyber that way?'

'Yes, I think so, sir. We would have to climb an even higher pass first to get to it from here, wouldn't we?'

'Yes. It's high at about eleven thousand feet, but it's the last mountain range leading down to this valley where we are now. You should be able to pick up the road to the pass a little further along here and I doubt if you will meet anyone, except the odd goatherd along the way. That's where we will part company.'

Appleby-Smith looked up. 'What? Where will you be going?'

'Jenkins and I intend to go and find my wife.'

The captain's eyebrows shot up. 'Good God! Just the two of you?'

'Not quite. If you, Captain, and you, Duke, will allow –

and if he will agree to join us – we would like to borrow the *daffadar* here to act as our interpreter should we be accosted. We will all change into Pathan clothing, gathered from these dead chaps here, take three Martini-Henrys, and try to find that encampment due north of the Landi Kotal Fort. At least I have a compass.'

Dawson looked askance. 'But sir, however well disguised, it will be difficult for you to pass as Pathans. You will be unmasked for sure.'

'Not if luck goes with us.' He nodded to his two companions. 'Inderjit here will be what he is, a Sikh from the borders whom we have hired as guide and interpreter; Jenkins looks more like a Pathan than they do, given a turban and slippers, and particularly now he has been letting his beard grow; and I will be a Persian who has come here to join the Pathan cause and fight the British, whom he hates. I speak reasonable Pushtu, as long as I don't meet another bloody Persian. Jenkins and I are sunburnt enough not to have to black up and he will be my Pathan servant, who is a deaf mute. Which will be a pleasant change for all of us.'

This brought awkward smiles from the four of them. Simon turned to Inderjit. 'Will you volunteer for this, old chap?' he asked. 'I don't need to tell you it will be very dangerous work.'

Solemnly the Sikh bowed his head. 'It will be an honour to follow the sahib in the footsteps of my beloved father.'

'And an honour to have you.' Fonthill turned to the captain and Buckingham. 'Can you spare him? We couldn't do this without him because he knows the hills as well as the dialects.'

Buckingham nodded. 'Of course.'

Appleby-Smith frowned. 'This will deplete our force, you know,' he said. 'Buckingham has always told me that the feller is a good soldier. We could well run into more trouble before we get to Peshawar and we shall need good *daffadars*.' His tone had now become querulous.

'Oh, I think we can manage, Captain,' interjected Buckingham. 'And I think that Mr Fonthill's need is greater than ours.'

'Thank you,' Fonthill hurried on. He turned to Appleby-Smith. 'There is one more very important thing.' He felt inside his jacket and produced the Amir's letter to the Viceroy. 'This is self-explanatory and it is vital that it gets through to the commandant at Peshawar for onwards transmission to the Viceroy. I give this into your care, Clarence. It is vitally important that it does not fall into the hands of the Pathans.'

He gave it to the captain. 'Now,' he said, addressing the two subalterns, 'you two gentlemen must ensure that the captain here carries out his duties as postmaster general.' His tone was bantering but all three understood the underlying meaning: whatever decisions were taken by the captain, who was in nominal command, the letter must get through to Peshawar. 'If Jamrud has not been taken and the line is open, you may be able to flag down a train.' Dawson and Buckingham gave sly smiles and nodded their heads.

'Thank you all.' Fonthill gestured towards the Pathans lying among the rocks. 'Now, give the three of us time to rob the corpses and find something that gives us elegance and a touch of class, then we must all be off.'

While the superficial wounds of the three troopers were treated, Inderjit, Jenkins and Fonthill began the sordid task of stripping clothes from Pathans of roughly the same size as themselves and whose deaths had been caused by shots to the head, so removing the need to scrub bloodstains away. They selected reasonably full bandoliers and good rifles and changed into their disguises. Then the column moved away.

Some ten miles or so further a road climbed away to the right to where the mountains towered above them. Handshakes were exchanged and then the column began its climb and one Sikh, one Persian and one rather dishevelled Pathan plodded on foot towards the border.

CHAPTER TEN

Alice slid and stumbled down the scree in the darkness after leaving the Pathans' encampment. It was difficult going and her first disappointment came with the presumption that she had only to keep descending eventually to hit the road that ran through the Khyber Pass. In fact, the way seemed to undulate so that she was going upwards as much as down. The second disappointment was in realising that she still had not recovered from collapsing at the fort. That, and the stress induced by the threat of the amputation, meant that she quickly began to feel tired and short of breath. She also felt that the inability to see properly was making her crash and blunder through the landscape, creating enough noise to alert any pursuers.

After perhaps two hours of painful progress – or lack of it – she decided to find some sort of cover and wait until daylight, where the sun could give her some guidance at least on the direction to take. Accordingly, she curled up underneath what appeared to be an overhanging rock, ate some of her precious provisions and tried to sleep.

Slumber, however, evaded her. The darkness was far from silent. Alice had a fear of snakes and scorpions and every scrape and scratch from the uncomfortable bed of stones on which she lay made her imagine either that a pursuing party was hot on her heels or that she was about to be overrun by reptiles. The fact that she had only been able to bring from the dead Pathan a small leather bag in which to carry water, tied inefficiently at the top by cord, meant that she could do little to assuage her thirst. Finding a stream of water nearby must be a priority for the morning.

As the night wore on, she also realised that, in attempting to find Simon and his squadron of Guides in this virtually trackless wilderness, she had undertaken a ridiculously difficult task. If, as she hoped, he had realised that the return route through the Khyber was closed to him, then he would probably veer either far to the north to ride via Marden or climb one of the passes to the south. Finding him and his squadron would be like looking for just one solitary pebble in this rocky series of mountain ranges.

So she sat, miserable and occasionally nodding with fatigue, and waited for the dawn.

It came with that sudden flood of light that characterised the beginning of a new day on the Frontier. Another of those small rock movements nearby that indicated the presence of something else alive, prompted her to slip a round into the breech of her rifle and cling to the shelter of the overhang. The Martini-Henry had been painfully heavy and awkward to carry among the rocks in the darkness but she had resolved during the night that she would not be taken alive by the Pathans. The rifle, then, would enable her to fight far more effectively than the little handgun she had tucked into her sash.

She waited, breathing softly, but nothing else stirred in the warmth of the morning. Nothing, that is, except the things that were now moving over her flesh and causing her to itch maddeningly. Alice realised, with despair, that the garments she had appropriated from the dead tribesman had obviously been lousy. The thought filled her with disgust and, for the moment, replaced her fear of being found, tortured and killed. Alice had lived rough on campaigns for many years, but to house these crawling, biting parasites was a new experience and she shivered with horror.

All the more reason, then, to find a stream to relieve her thirst and wash the lice away.

Cautiously, Martini-Henry extended, she crept from her cover. The heat that bounced back at her from the white rocks almost took her breath away, but she seemed to have this rocky canyon all to herself – at least, to herself *and* her active little fellow travellers.

The sun was still hidden behind the mountain tops but, from the glow that backlit the peaks, she could define the east, so she immediately began climbing to the other side of the canyon to continue to move away to the west, towards the Afghan end of the Pass. She seemed to slip back as much as climb now, for the ground was a mass of shingle, but she topped the rise and saw a blessed fall in the ground away to her left.

Surely, this must bring her eventually down to the Pass and the road, along the edge of which she could make her way carefully under cover to ... to ... to where? Alice took a deep breath. Maybe to one of the markings delineating the Durand Line, of course, so that she could at least wait there for Simon to cross it. Then she shook her head. What a ridiculous hope! The Line stretched for more than a hundred miles. What made her think that her husband would cross it just where she sat waiting for him?

She licked her dry lips. Water. Find water. If she could do that she could drink and wash these disgusting clothes. Then she would feel better and think straighter.

Her tongue felt like a hot, dry sponge inside her mouth when, at last, she heard what could only be the trickle of running water. She stumbled towards the sound, not caring now of the noise she herself made and there it was: a little mountain stream, as clear as gin, gurgling and splashing down between the rocks.

Alice plunged her face into the stream and drank deeply. Then she lay back and splashed the precious liquid over her hair. The cool water brought back her sense of danger and she lifted her head and looked cautiously around. Nothing. Just the inevitable jumble of stones and boulders.

Laying the rifle within reach, she began removing her garments and laying them, one by one, in the flowing water, using stones to hold them down. Could lice swim? She summoned a wry grin and began running her fingernails along the seams of the roughly sewn clothing to help remove her lodgers. Then, still cautiously gazing around her, she removed her own undergarments and gave them the same treatment, until she was kneeling completely naked. One by one, she spread out the garments on the rocks to dry.

She realised that she was risking sunstroke but she luxuriated in the warmth for a couple of minutes before she began putting on the clothes, even though they were still wet. She was almost fully dressed before she heard distant voices. She froze, picked up the rifle and huddled behind a large boulder.

The voices were too far away to detect the language, but it seemed, by the slight differentiation in the origins of the voices, that the owners were climbing. Very slowly, her chin close to the ground, she put her face around the rock. Some two hundred yards away, the Sikh, Persian and Panthan were slowly climbing the mountainside. They had spread out and were looking around them, the muzzles of their rifles following their gaze.

It was clearly a search party.

Alice sucked in her breath and withdrew her head. She must have left tracks! How else could she have been followed? She clutched the rifle across her breast and silently drew three, then four, cartridges from the bandolier that lay on the ground beside her knees and laid them out on a flat stone. If she could reload quickly enough, maybe she could kill all three if she heard them stepping nearer.

But she did not. Eventually, the sound of their voices grew more distant until it disappeared completely. She risked taking another look. The men obviously were still climbing for she caught a glimpse of a red and green wound turban among the rocks, much higher now and at least three hundred yards away.

Alice bit her lip and thought quickly. Three of them. There would be others and they were obviously combing the mountain. She must be very careful, for if they were climbing they could look down on her. Better to wait until dark. She slipped the bandolier over her head, replaced her own turban and huddled close to the rock.

She was not sure how long she sat there for the heat and her aching joints made her drowsy, but she came to life as she realised that the sun had slipped behind the mountain tops and that familiar deep purple that so distinguished dusk in the hills was beginning to enfold her. Better to move again.

Cautiously, she raised herself and began to descend once more, looking carefully all around her as she went and working her way diagonally across the hillside towards the dull glow that marked the west. Soon, however, the nature of the terrain made it impossible to walk further, for she was continually gashing herself against the rocks in what was now virtual darkness. Sighing, Alice found another little clearing and settled down for another miserable night.

This time it was the cold that revealed itself as her greatest enemy. Her clothes still seemed damp and she began to shiver. She had long ago eaten the last of the bread and meat taken from the encampment and hunger began to gnaw. Pulling the *poshteen* tightly around her, she rolled into the foetal position and tried to assess her position.

Her thoughts raced. It was clearly stupid to trudge blindly towards some point where Simon and his squadron might cross the border. Apart from the obvious odds against them being at the same point at the same time, he was most likely to have taken a completely different route back to Peshawar to avoid the Pathans in the Pass. So . . . what to do? It seemed to her, as she lay cuddling her rifle and shivering, that she had two choices once she reached the western end of the Pass. She could either cross into Afghanistan and follow the road that led to Kabul – hadn't Simon said that it was comparatively easy-going across the plain to the capital? – or turn right and climb the hills again and head for Marden, the home of the Guides.

Alice found that tears were now beginning to trickle down her cheeks at the hopelessness of it all. Either way presented huge problems. Even if she was able to reach Kabul without being molested, could she hope to find succour with the Amir? Wouldn't he suspect her of being some strange spy and shoot her out of hand? The other alternative seemed worse. Without map or compass or knowledge of the language, she would almost certainly get lost in the mountains to the north. And hungry now, she would surely starve or die of thirst in those barren hills.

She licked her lips and lowered her throbbing head onto the cool muzzle of the rifle. Ah, the rifle! Perhaps tomorrow she might be able to sight a mountain goat and shoot it? She had caught a glimpse of one or two. Surely she had outdistanced her pursuers now, sufficiently at least to risk a shot? And she had taken matches from the tent and there was just about enough bone-dry kindling about to light a fire and cook something. The very thought activated her long-redundant taste buds and she licked the skin of her still damp but now empty water bag.

Another dawn and she cautiously stretched and slipped a hand underneath her *poshteen*. She was as stiff as an ungreased wagon spring but at least the lice were gone. Up above her, in the now bright-blue sky, two eagles wheeled, but they seemed to be the only living thing in view. But were they . . . ? Down below to the left, there, just *there*. A movement of some kind, where the rocks opened out a little.

Alice raised a hand above her eyes to shield from the glare. Yes, there it was again. Something brown was moving slowly. She concentrated. Glory be! A mountain goat!

She swivelled her head and studied the terrain carefully. Nothing else, just the unrelenting boulders and rough scree. She looked back again and the goat was now nonchalantly walking towards her. With great care she knelt and slowly raised the rifle. Resting it on a large rock, she raised the backsight to give herself a range of two hundred yards, squinted along the barrel to where the foresight rested just behind the creature's right shoulder and then slowly, very, very slowly, squeezed the trigger.

The subsequent report boomed like a canon, sending echoes bouncing back from the mountain tops and causing black crows to rise in a hysterical flutter. The unexpected savagery of the kickback sent Alice back on her haunches and the rifle clattering to the ground. But the goat now lay still, oozing blood.

Seizing the rifle and slipping another round into the breech – 'always reload first' had been Jenkins's mantra –

Alice looked around once again. Silence and inertia had settled back onto the mountain and she scrambled to her feet and began stumbling towards the inert body of the goat. Damn! It was still breathing. She had despatched dozens of foxes, pheasants and partridges back home in Norfolk, but giving the *coup de grâce* to this brown-eyed creature, with its fine horns and elegant legs, was far more daunting.

She withdrew the Pathan's long knife from its scabbard at her belt and felt the edge with her thumb. Razor-sharp. Then, in a quick, almost desperate movement, she pulled back the goat's head by the horns, exposing the throat, and slashed it with the knife. Blood gushed out and Alice fumbled to untie the water bag at her waist to retain some, at least, of it. Thirst once again was becoming a problem.

The liquid was warm and tasted of earth and goodness knows what else but she gulped it down, conscious that the blood had poured down her chin and onto her breast. Wiping her mouth with the back of her hand, Alice immediately felt nauseous, but sensed that, almost immediately, energy seemed to be flooding back into her body.

'Thank you, dear goat,' she muttered and immediately began hacking at the haunch of the foremost leg with the knife. Twisting the bone and sawing at the sinews with the knife she eventually broke it free and held it up for inspection. Despite her hunger, she could not bring herself to taste the raw meat. So she rested it on the still-warm coat of the goat, covered it from flies with what was left of her handkerchief, and began scavenging for kindling wood.

It was not easy to find given the infertile nature of the ground on the hillside but, after thirty minutes or so, she had gathered enough to lay the foundations of a small fire. Breaking some of the wood into a dry dust, she held a match to them and, eventually, a little flame spluttered into life and spread to the rest of the wood. Alice gingerly put the haunch of meat onto the fire and immediately began waving the smoke away to avoid it rising straight upwards. She realised that, if the search for her was still continuing, then the smoke would take her pursuers straight to her, but – what the hell, she was stomach-achingly hungry!

The meat was burnt, of course, but she wolfed it down. The fire had quickly burnt away but she cut another haunch from the goat, thrust it into the guttering ashes, and waited awhile until it had partly cooked. It could be some time before she ate again. Then she brushed away the ashes from the meat, tied the bone to her belt with the handkerchief, patted the carcase of the goat in a last gesture of thanks and began making her way towards the west again.

With every few yards, Alice kept looking around and behind her. The shot and the smoke could well have alerted anyone looking for her, yet it became clear, as the day wore on, that she was alone in this wilderness. As she topped one rise, she thought she caught a glimpse of the road beneath her to the left. But it was difficult in this broken country to gain a feel for distance and it did not reappear again.

Eventually, as the sun rose to its midday height, Alice grew weary and realised that it was impossible to make much progress in the heat. She sought and eventually found a friendly rock with enough overhang to allow her to crawl beneath it, folded her *poshteen* to make a pillow and fell blessedly asleep.

It seemed that she had only closed her eyes for a moment when a strong, abrupt pain in her stomach awoke her. Her gaze met a bearded, grinning face bending down close to hers and she doubled up again in pain as a boot caught her again in the stomach and then in the ribs. She heard voices laughing and the kicking continued.

She raised a hand and weakly called, 'Enough, you bastards.'

Immediately, a command rang out and the kicking ceased. A hand reached down and seized her rifle and she looked up into a ring of faces. They were all Pathans, darkly visaged and glaring at her with hatred in their eyes. A man with a grey beard, who seemed to be the leader, issued another order and she was dragged to her feet and pushed against the rock. Her arms were stretched out and rough hands searched her. They found the pistol in her cummerbund and it was tossed aside in contempt. The search was finished with a hand thrust between her legs and jerked upwards, so that she bent over with a howl.

Greybeard shouted what sounded like a reprimand, for the searcher growled, spat at her face but backed away.

Alice grimaced with pain and disgust at being defiled in this way, but also in shame at allowing the Pathans to steal up on her so easily. Then she looked around. There were about six of them, all pointing their rifles at her now – all, that is, except the leader who turned to one of the younger tribesmen and muttered something to him.

The young man stepped forward and said, in halting English, 'Who help you escape?'

Alice felt a sudden surge of anger. 'Tell him,' she said,

nodding towards the grey-bearded one, 'that I shall say nothing at all to you until that man who touched me is told never to lay a finger on me again. Go on. Tell him.'

With obvious reluctance, the man spoke to Greybeard, who remained expressionless but replied briefly in Pushtu.

'He say,' said the interpreter, 'unless you answer questions you will be beaten and everyone here will have their way with you.' The young man had the grace to drop his eyes as he spoke.

Alice's eyes widened as she looked at Greybeard, who remained expressionless. She thought quickly. Would Ali have given instructions for her to be raped and beaten? Not if she remained valuable to him. She took a deep breath.

'And you tell him,' she replied, 'that he and every one of you will be hanged if I am touched. I am the wife of the Viceroy's ambassador to the Amir. A British army is on its way to attack you. I will not speak to anyone unless that man,' she nodded, 'is rebuked.'

As her words were translated she watched Greybeard's face closely. She was taking a hell of a risk and she felt her legs begin to tremble at the thought of what would happen if the gamble failed. But as the translation was finished she saw the leader's eyes flicker. Eventually he spoke.

'He say, nobody touch you if you answer questions.'

Alice experienced an inward sigh of relief. At least she had set herself on some sort of moral high ground. 'Very well. No one helped me to escape. The guard whom I killed with that handgun,' she nodded to where her pistol had been thrown, 'had tried to molest me, so I shot him and took his clothes and rifle. I simply walked through the village and have been walking for two nights.'

'Hah! Where you go?'

'I was walking towards the Afghan border. I intended to walk to Kabul to see the Amir.'

'Why you go there?'

'My husband was there.'

Silence fell. The old man studied her with what might be just a glint of admiration in his eyes. Then he spoke.

'He say you kill one of us, brother of man who touched you. You deserve to die.'

Alice tossed her head. 'We all deserve to die – you all deserve to die because of the way you killed and mutilated the wounded men at Landi Kotal, many of them your brother Afridis. So kill me, if you wish. It is of no concern of mine. But I am certain that Ali would punish you if I was killed.'

The old man looked puzzled.

'Ali? Who is he?'

'He is the man in fine robes who kept me a prisoner. Your general.'

'Ah. We take you to him now. Turn. Put hands behind back.'

Alice sighed with relief, turned and offered her hands for binding. At least there would be no summary execution. She was sorry that she had slandered the man she had killed, but he was a soldier who had deserted his post and had been quite prepared to possess her. And, for goodness' sake – this was war!

There now began the march back to the encampment

that brought new agonies to Alice. The Pathans were all agile and used to climbing among the rocks quickly and with purpose. After the first hour, she began to stagger in trying to match their pace, with her hands bound behind her adversely affecting her balance and her whole body aching after walking and sleeping rough with so little nourishment.

She attempted to establish some sort of bond with the young interpreter, who marched beside her.

'Your English is very good,' she said. 'Where did you learn it?'

The young man looked around nervously before answering. 'In British army,' he said. 'I was sepoy for three years.'

'I see.' Alice found talking and trying to climb up through the scree added to her breathing problems but she persevered. 'Why, then, do you fight the English now, your former brothers?'

'My family not like me being sepoy . . . So I run away. I fight now because Mullah tells us time has come to fight for sake of Allah.'

'And you agree with him?'

'Of course. Mullah speak word of Allah. I talk no more to you now.'

'One last word. How far away is the camp? I am very tired.'

'We reach when sun goes. I say you are tired but we talk no more.'

He lifted his voice and spoke to Greybeard, who was climbing up ahead. The man replied angrily and waved his hand. Nevertheless, in ten minutes he called a halt and

Alice slumped to the ground gratefully. 'Is there water?' she called. A gourd was lifted to her mouth and she drank greedily, but no food was offered – and none, it seemed, was taken by the rest of the party. After what could only have been three minutes she was prodded to her feet and the climb began again.

Alice realised that these Pathans climbed like mountain goats and that led her to wondering how they had found her. She tried to discover how from the young ex-sepoy.

'How did you find me?' she asked.

He shook his head. 'No talk.'

'Oh, come along. I shall keep asking you until you answer. Then, I promise, I will be quiet. How did you find me?'

'We have good tracker. Man brother of man you killed. We see where you sleep two nights before. And then, in distance, we heard shot and see small smoke. It take us to you.'

Alice cursed inwardly. She was foolish to have shot that damned goat. And yet she could have not walked much farther without food and that tracker was presumably taking them nearer to her all the time. They would have come upon her surely by the time she reached the Afghan border. She sighed. Ah, Simon! Where, oh where was he?

Would she ever see him again?

The light was fading when they reached the camp. By this time, Alice was exhausted and walking so badly that the ex-sepoy had been forced to help her for the last hour. Her head pounding, she screwed up her eyes and looked at her surroundings as she was led through the camp. There were far fewer tribesmen about than the last time she had arrived, on the stretcher. Nevertheless, there were enough Pathans about to jeer her as she was led through the camp.

Eventually, she reached the tent she recognised so well. This time, she realised that it was more impressive than those around it, being bigger than them all – apart, that is, from one that was even larger, made of black fabric and had some kind of banner stuck into the earth outside its entrance. Was it Ali's? – or even the mullah's? She also noticed that her tent was pitched on what seemed to be the edge of the encampment near a clump of trees, and that some twenty horses were housed in a rough paddock nearby, their heads down and eating hay. Ah, she needn't have taken the risk of walking throughout the encampment two nights ago – perhaps she could have made her way through the wood and even stolen a horse! Too late now.

Then her head was forced down and she was pushed roughly inside the tent. She sighed with relief as the cord binding her wrists together was untied and she rubbed the red wheals as she was pushed down onto the divan. From somewhere a manacle was produced. It was attached to her ankle and the other end secured by a padlock to the centre pole of the tent.

Greybeard spoke to the translator and the young man said, 'He say you move from here and you will be shot. Men all around tent. Food will be brought soon.'

With that, her captors ducked through the entry, the flap was laced up again and she was back where she started. Alice lay on her back, her whole body aching, and continued to massage where her bonds had rubbed the skin raw. For the second time since she had stolen away through the encampment, depression set in. As the tears trickled down her cheeks she bit her lip. What more could she do? Who could help her? She seemed destined to stay in this filthy tent that now smelt of something foul – oh God! Was it the body of the dead man? She looked around her in terror, but she was alone.

Within minutes, the interpreter had brought her bread and what looked like goat's cheese, two peaches and a gourd of milk. She realised that she was starving and began devouring the bread and cheese. The boy was retreating when she called, 'Thank you. What is your name?'

Looking over his shoulder, the young man shook his head. 'I don't say,' he muttered.

'Well, Mr Don't Say, as you can see I am covered in blood. Can you bring me water, soap and a towel please?'

'I try.'

He returned within minutes with a wooden pail containing water, soap and a rag. He also pointed to the corner of the tent where the potty remained. He turned swiftly to go but Alice held up a peach.

'Won't you eat with me?' she asked.

He shook his head, but his eyes stayed fixed on the peach. He was obviously as hungry as she.

'Do stay for a minute and eat the peach,' said Alice, trying to sound beguiling. The thought occurred to her that she might be able to befriend him. God knew she needed a friend in this place. 'They are delicious.' And she sank her teeth into her own fruit to entice him. 'Come on. I am not going to shoot you.'

Cautiously, he approached and took the peach from her. He bit into it and the juice ran down his chin.

'Where does this fruit come from?'

'I think Afghanistan.'

'Ah yes, probably near Kabul. Yes?'

'I think.'

'Look,' Alice smiled up at him. 'I know that the British army is on its way to fight the mullah's army and it will certainly be here soon. When it arrives, I can help you. As you know, desertion from the British army is punishable by death, but if you help me a little I can stop them shooting you.'

He stood looking at her with wide eyes, the peach juice still dribbling down his chin.

Alice continued: 'I know I can't escape from here now, particularly with this thing chained to my ankle. So I will not expect you to help me escape. But I need to talk to someone occasionally. Will you do that . . . ?'

He remained silent.

'Just talk to me, now and then. Otherwise I shall go crazy.'

He stood with his mouth open for some moments and then said, 'What you want talk about?'

'Oh, nothing important. Are you an Afridi?'

'Yes, lady.'

'From nearby here?'

'No. In Zakka Khel. Mountains. Small village.'

'Ah yes.' Alice thought hard, trying desperately to

remember the map that Simon had shown her. 'The other side of the Khyber, I think to the south?'

'Yes lady.'

'Are you married?'

'No.'

'Too young, perhaps?'

'Yes, lady.'

'But you have a mother?'

'Ah, yes. And two sisters.'

'You are lucky. I have no brothers or sisters and my only child died when I was trying to give him birth.'

He stood silently for a moment, then, 'Ah. Sorry, lady.'

'It was a long time ago. Now, tell me. This man Ali – that is what he told me to call him, the man who had me brought here – who exactly is he? It seems he was educated in my country, in England. Do you know his full name?'

At this, the boy's eyes looked away. 'No, lady. I go now.' And he turned and scuttled through the tent opening.

Alice called after him, 'Well, goodbye and thank you.' She lay back on the bed exhausted with the cerebral effort of trying to draw information from the young Pathan. What had she learnt that was of use? Nothing really, but it was a start. Maybe next time . . .

She stirred and began to wash. She could feel that the goat's blood remained caked on her cheeks and chin and it had also dried and stiffened on the Pathan's shirt that she still wore. She scrubbed away. Was she doing this because Ali might come to see her? She snorted at the thought. To hell with him! She must maintain standards and keep her self-respect. She was no Pathan!

238

There was no lantern in the tent this time and, the interior being dark, she crawled between the blankets and composed herself to sleep. She expected that the events and disappointments of the day would keep her awake but, despite her mind racing for some moments wondering what would happen to her and what *had* happened to Simon, she then slipped away into what was, this time, a dreamless sleep.

Ali arrived the next morning, just after she had washed. This time, of course, he brought no fine cognac and the smile was not in evidence. In fact, he loomed menacingly and seemed even taller.

'Mrs Fonthill,' he said, as he stood looking down at her, 'you have been very foolish.'

'Forgive me if I don't get up,' she replied, blinking, 'but some barbarian has ordered that I be chained up like an animal.'

'That was for your own safety, madam. The man you killed was a very popular man in this camp and he has many brothers here. They would all like to throw you to their women for a very slow death. You certainly should not have killed and then tried to escape.'

Alice sat up. 'What did you expect me to do – allow myself to be ravished and then wait here until you arrived to cut pieces off me? Don't be ridiculous.'

The interior of the tent was dark, but she could see that his eyes now flashed in anger. 'I may be many things to many men,' he said in steely tones, 'but I am never ridiculous.'

'And, by the same token, you should never underestimate

an English woman. Now, what do you intend to do with me? Is it to be toes, this time, or perhaps a foot or an arm?'

He let her words rest in the air for a moment and then spoke with quiet fury. 'You are in no place, woman, to mock me. One word from me and the women of my warriors will stake you out over an open fire, stuff the penis of a ram into your mouth and leave you to burn slowly. Oh yes, the ways of the people of these hills are very cruel, you know.'

'So I have heard.' Damn! Alice realised that her voice had broken.

She cleared her throat. 'If I am to die, then let it be soon. I do not wish to remain here, one way or the other. I repeat: what do you intend to do with me? You must know that a British force will be here very soon.'

'Oh yes. I have heard that the great General Lockhart is at this very moment assembling troops in Peshawar. But I am not impressed. We shall overwhelm him, as we have all the soldiers that have opposed us so far.'

He paused for a moment, but Alice did not respond. What was the point? Then he continued, in emotionless, matter-of-fact terms.

'Your husband, by the way, is dead.'

'What!' Alice felt that a dagger had been thrust through her heart. She swallowed hard, then sat for a moment, breathing hard. 'You lie, of course. It would take more than a man sent down from Cambridge to kill my magnificent husband.'

The thrust had obviously gone home, for she saw him start for a moment. 'Oh, I assure you. It is quite true. I decided that it would be a waste of time attempting to get

240

him to persuade the Amir to help us – and, indeed, we do not need the troops of that feeble old man. We have more than enough men to send Lockhart scuttling back to Peshawar. No, my dear Mrs Fonthill, I sent a unit of my troops into Afghanistan to intercept him and cut him down. They were successful.'

Alice swallowed again. 'I don't believe you.'

'Whether you believe me or not does not concern me.' He moved for the first time and paced around the interior, a tall, dark, threatening figure, despite the whiteness of his robes.

'However,' he continued, 'you can still be useful to me. We are quite prepared to negotiate with General Lockhart, who, by the way, is well known and quite respected in these parts, on the question of relinquishing some territory that we have captured – *Pathan* territory, of course – back to the British if they are prepared to spare both sides much bloodshed and relinquish their plans to invade Tirah.'

He stopped his pacing and stared down at Alice again. 'Let me explain. The Tirah is about 900 square miles of territory shared by the Afridi and Orakzai tribes and is found about midway between the Khyber and Kurram valleys. It is cut off from Peshawar by the great Safed Koh range. No invader has ever penetrated this upland territory but our spies tell us that General Lockhart is assembling a great force to do just that.'

Ali smiled, so that his dark eyes lit up. 'He knows – and we know that he knows – that this invasion is going to be extremely difficult for him. This is mountainous country that is unmapped and he will have no safe lines of communication. What is more, we can put between forty and fifty thousand rifles in the field to stop him. As I say, there will be much bloodshed.'

Alice had listened with great care. She frowned. 'But where on earth do I come in?'

'You can stop this invasion. At the moment, it is our estimation that Lockhart will stop at nothing to avenge the loss of his precious forts in the Khyber. They seem to have an iconic value to the stupid people of England, fuelled by the jingoistic press of Fleet Street. To regain them would placate the great British public.'

Alice's frown deepened. 'So why should Lockhart invade this difficult territory that you describe. Why not just storm up the Khyber Pass and retake the forts?'

'Ah. Two reasons. Firstly, he knows that this will not be easy. The Afghans were able to hold up General Sir Sam Browne's invading force in the Pass two decades ago and we are rebuilding the forts and they will be difficult nuts to crack. The second reason, however, is the main one. Lockhart understands that this so-called Pathan Revolt is something more than just another local uprising. He and his government have decided to advance into the heart of Pathan territory, the Tirah, and cut that heart out of the Pathan nation, so to speak. A conclusive victory – not some local triumph, such as the recapture of the forts – is what they require. They want to stamp out any further uprisings in this way.'

'Under certain circumstances,' Ali went on, 'we might concede, say, the forts, back to the British Raj. But we know that Lockhart will never negotiate with what he regards as a wild bunch of Pathan savages.'

'I don't blame him.'

'You are being stupid, Mrs Fonthill. You are also being hypocritical. We are well aware that, in your writings for the . . . what is it? Ah yes, the famed *Morning Post*, you have been less than supportive of the British Raj with its occupation of the Frontier country after the establishment of the Durand Line.'

'Well . . . yes. But only moderately so.'

'Maybe, but we know that the *Post* is very much a Tory newspaper and jingoistic at that. It is read by,' he hesitated and his voice took on a sneering note, 'the great and the good of Great Britain. We want you to write a more opinionated piece, based on an interview you have secured with the Mullah Sayyid Akbar, the most influential leader of the Pathan so-called rebels—'

Alice interrupted. 'I would genuinely get to meet him?'

'It could be arranged. You would put the viewpoint of the Pathans, including – what is very important – our religious views. If we approved it, we could make arrangements for it to be cabled directly to your newspaper in London.'

Alice sighed. 'I am afraid that you are very naïve, Ali. My newspaper would see through this in an instant and recognise it as propaganda written under duress – even if I was prepared to write it. Which I definitely am not.'

The silence that followed hung over the interior of the tent, seeming somehow to increase the heat already present. Then Ali nodded. 'Very well,' he said. 'I anticipated that response. Our second request is more important and you will not refuse it.'

Alice drew in her breath. 'Oh?'

'You will write to General Lockhart, explaining that you are in our hands. You will explain the reasons against invading the Tirah, that I have already given to you. You will refer to our agreeing to begin negotiations. And, you will say that, if he does not agree to meeting with us, you will be executed by us.'

'He won't care.' Alice shook her head. 'What is the life of one woman against the strategy of the British government? He will say that if you go ahead with your threat, you will be hanged when your armies are defeated, as they undoubtedly will be, given the greater firepower of the British. He will do his duty. If you know the British, you will know that. And, in any case, he will want proof that "my" letter is genuine . . .'

Her voice tailed away as she realised that she had given Ali, perhaps literally, a hostage to fortune. The black eyes gleamed again. 'Ah that is no problem, Mrs Fonthill. We will sever your ringed finger and send it to the general as proof of the letter's origin. And if you still refuse to write the letter, then we shall cut off a finger a day, until you do. Remember, madam, there is no anaesthetic. And we shall saw. Not chop.

'However, if you agree to our request, you and the general will be informed that you will be released to the British at the site of the meeting. Now,' he paused for a moment. 'Perhaps you do not believe that we would carry through all of this. Well, I am afraid that you have already seen that this is a cruel country. And a determined one. Let me demonstrate.'

He shouted in Pushtu and immediately two large

tribesmen entered. As Alice retreated in horror, one seized her arm and held it down while the other pushed her down onto the bed by the throat. In almost the same moment, Ali drew a long knife from the scabbard at his belt, inserted the tip of the blade into the soft flesh below the bend of her arm and drew it down quickly for some six inches.

Alice cried out at the pain and the blood spurted out onto her bed.

Ali nodded and the two Pathans released her. 'Now,' he said, 'that is only a flesh wound. The pain of cutting through bone will be considerably greater. You have just two days to reflect on this, for I have to be away on urgent business. This time you will not escape because your tent is surrounded. Writing materials will be brought to you. Think about it, Mrs Fonthill, and begin writing your letter . . .'

He turned on his heel and left the tent with his attendants, leaving Alice weeping at the pain and in frustration and trying to staunch the flow of blood with the scrap of fabric that was her towel.

CHAPTER ELEVEN

Fonthill and his two companions crossed the Border without knowing it, until Inderjit, looking back over his shoulder to the right, pointed to one of the boundary posts that could just be seen in the distance behind them.

'Welcome back to the Pathan States,' muttered Simon, adjusting his unusually flamboyant red and green turban. He wiped his forehead and cursed. It undoubtedly had become hotter as, leaving behind them the fertile plain of Afghanistan, they began to climb up into the hills.

They were trudging now by compass bearing, for Fonthill was wagering that the tribesman's estimation of the Pathan encampment being some two miles due north of Fort Landi Kotal was roughly accurate. They had long since left behind the Kabul road, the extension of the Khyber Pass, whose towering sides they had glimpsed to their right, but dared not risk approaching the fort to gain a precise bearing. So Simon was now leading his little party on a north-easterly direction and, of course, upwards.

'What exactly is the plan, then, bach sir?' enquired Jenkins. Because of his thick thatch of black hair that stood, broom-like, vertically from his scalp, the Welshman had never been able to keep any sort of cover on his head for longer than ten minutes or so. Now, predictably, his turban had become unravelled and the end was trailing down his back.

'The first objective is to get you looking something like a pukka Pathan again,' hissed Fonthill. 'Here. Let me try and fix that damned turban.' He began rewinding it. 'You've got to have something on your head to avoid heatstroke, although I doubt if anything would penetrate that skull of yours.'

'Oh, thank you very much, I'm sure.' He stood submissively as Simon began trying to retie the turban and then handed the job over to the more skilled *daffadar*. 'If it was left to me, I'm sure I could lead us straight to the heart of these Patroons, or whatever you call 'em.'

'Humph. If it was left to you we would walk straight into the only bar in the whole of India. Now, as to a plan, I don't have one, except,' Simon nodded upwards, 'to keep climbing this mountain until we find some sort of trail. When we do – and Inderjit tells me that there are one or two villages somewhere about here, higher up, and villages need tracks for their livestock – we will follow the track to the right. We will either then meet a village and ask where the encampment is, explaining that we have come to join the army of the Mullah Sayyid Akbar, or come to the camp itself, because that many men will need a good-sized track.'

'Ah, yes,' Jenkins nodded thanks as the turban tying was finished, 'but what do we do then?'

Simon's eyes clouded for a moment as he gazed again up the hillside. 'We find Alice – if she's still alive – and rescue her. Exactly how, I don't know. We must just react to the circumstances. If Alice is still alive, we get her out. If she is not, I will find the man who killed her and you two can slip away in the general confusion. Come on. That's enough talking. We can't waste time.'

They trudged on, sometimes slipping backwards as the shale became more fragmented and the climb steeper. Once, they thought they heard a sound off to their right and immediately stopped, covering the ground with the muzzles of their rifles. But nothing appeared and they continued their wearying climb, until night fell and they were forced to lie where they had halted, wrapped in their *poshteens* to ward off the cold that set in as soon as the sun had disappeared.

With the dawn, they made tea over a tiny fire of brushwood and chewed on the provisions they had brought. As they prepared to continue the climb, Inderjit caught Fonthill's arm.

'I have been thinking, sahib,' he said.

'Blimey,' muttered Jenkins, 'personally, it's somethin' I try not to do. I find it makes your 'at fall off.'

Simon sighed. 'Go on, Inderjit.'

'If we are questioned by Pathan soldiers, I think it best we say we come from Persia by way of Kabul. Because we are wrong end of country now to have travelled here from Persia. Better we say we had some reason to be in Kabul. And why do we walk? People from Persia would have come by horse.'

'Hmmm. Yes. I should have thought this through.' He frowned. 'Been worried about Alice, I suppose, which doesn't help anyone. We had better think of a plausible story to explain why we are walking about the Hindu Kush in old clothes. Do you have any suggestions?'

'I am not sure. But I am Sikh and Sikhs are famous throughout Border country for being horse-traders. Some of best horses are from Persia. Two go together.'

Jenkins nodded his head. 'Good thinkin', Inja. I was just goin' to say that.'

Simon closed his eyes in thought. 'Yes.' He spoke, his eyes still closed. 'We bought horses from you in Persia and then, with you, travelled to Kabul to sell them, via contacts you had there. We were on our way back, hoping to go through the Khyber and buy more horses in Peshawar, when we were ambushed by Afghan brigands, of whom there are plenty. They took our clothes and money and they were going to kill us but we regained our guns and fought them off but not before they had taken our horses . . .'

'So,' asked Jenkins, 'what are we doin' ploddin' about up 'ere amongst these lovely rocks, instead of walkin' along that nice an' level Khyber Pass, then?'

'Well . . . we killed several of them and took their clothes. We heard that the forts were taken and, without horses or money and with only our guns, we decided that we would join the Mullah Sayyid Akbar and offer him our services in the fight against the British, hoping that there would be loot from his victories that we could share in. We are looking for his encampment which we had heard was up here in the hills.'

'Not bad, bach sir, not bad. It might just work.'

'Can you think of something better, Inderjit?'

'No, sahib. We all know there are plenty robbers in Afghanistan. It sound . . . er . . . .plossi . . . plussib . . .'

'I think,' said Jenkins with an all-embracing smile, 'that "plissible" is the word you're searchin' for, old chap.'

'Or even "plausible",' said Simon. 'Right, that's our story. If we are stopped, Inderjit will do the talking. Only call on me if you think you must and if you think my Pushtu will pass. But don't call me "sahib".'

'Sorry, sah— Ah, sorry.'

Fonthill kicked the ashes of their fire away and covered them with stones, then they picked up their rifles and continued their climb. They found no real trails, only goats' tracks, and they camped that night again amongst the rocks.

They had been climbing for perhaps two hours the following morning when they met the boys. There were two of them, about fifteen years of age, tending to a small herd of scraggy goats grazing on a level scrap of sparse, yellowish grass that was sustained by a stream. At first they looked frightened as the three emerged suddenly from below but their apprehension disappeared as Inderjit gave them a wave and addressed them.

Fonthill and Jenkins hung back and sat on a rock, looking uninterested and chewing on a piece of dried meat as the conversation ensued. Eventually the Sikh ruffled the hair of the larger of the two and gestured to his two companions to continue the climb to the right. Out of earshot, he explained.

'Boys say their village is up ahead,' he said, 'and we can buy food there and fill our water bags. The Mullah Sayyid's camp is only about an hour's march from the village, up ahead and to the east. We just need to follow the trail. Climb no more.'

'Anything more – about the camp, I mean?' Simon tried to keep the anxiety out of his voice.

'Ah yes, sah . . . Lord. Yes, most important of all. Older boy says it is common knowledge that white woman is kept captive in camp. Nobody knows why but villagers have delivered food for her.'

Fonthill closed his eyes in relief and let out a huge sigh. 'Thank God for that,' he exclaimed. 'If they are feeding her then she must be all right and they are not harming her . . .' He shot an anxious glance at both of his companions. 'Well, I can't think why they would be harming her, can you?'

'Certainly not,' said Inderjit.

'Course not,' chimed in Jenkins. 'I told you they wouldn't. Did they say, Inja, where she was bein' kept, like? In an 'ut or somethin'?'

'He thought it was a tent, at far end of village.'

'Good.' Simon nodded, his face now a picture of relief. 'A tent. Good. That gives us a chance.'

'Can't quite see why, though,' muttered Jenkins. 'What are we goin' to do? Stride up an' 'uff an' puff and blow it down?'

'If we know she's all right, we can afford now to wait until darkness. Perhaps cut our way into the tent . . .'

'Which is bound to be guarded,' sniffed Jenkins.

'Of course. But whatever we do, we will have to do it stealthily. And that means under cover of darkness. As I said, we will need to react to the circumstances. Let's get food and drink from this village because we will need it if we manage to get away with Alice. We will see also if our story goes down with the villagers. If it doesn't, we'll just have to think of something else. Inderjit, see if we can learn something more about the camp – how many men there, how well it is guarded, and that sort of thing. But whatever you do, don't arouse suspicion.'

The village was little more than a cluster of small dwellings, built of random stones and huddled together in the lee of the mountainside on a rare patch of level ground on either side of a wide trail that led east to west through the hamlet. It seemed that the young men had been swept up by the mullah when he had stormed down from the north and west through the valleys, a few days ago, swelling his army by the force of his rhetoric as he preached jihad against the British. It was clear as they approached the village that a multitude had come this way, for the ground was flattened with rocks pushed away and the scree stamped down by thousands of feet.

The elders were only too happy to sell eggs, meat and unleavened bread to the travellers and allow them to replenish their water from a well. As Inderjit talked to the adults, Fonthill and Jenkins played with the children, the

Welshman causing squeals of delight as he mutely produced coins from the ears and mouths of the little ones, crouching in the dust.

Then, on the Sikh's return they nodded their farewells and moved away to the south-east, following in the footsteps of the mullah and his men.

'They seemed to accept your story?' asked Simon.

'Yes. Without question. People are coming from far to serve under the mullah's flag.'

'What about the encampment?'

'Some of the mullah's army is down in the Pass, rebuilding the forts, with more marching to the west and south to face General Lockhart's force when it leaves Peshawar. Mullah has gone with them with his main followers and the camp is only lightly guarded, for there is no danger to it at the moment after the capture of the forts.'

'Splendid. Did you learn anything more about Alice?'

'A little bit. A rumour had reached village that lady had escaped and only been found this morning on hillside and taken back today to camp.'

'God bless her pluck,' cried Jenkins.

Fonthill produced a ragged handkerchief and blew his nose. 'I just hope they didn't punish her for that,' he muttered eventually. 'Come on. I don't want to waste time.'

The road to the camp was well marked, of course, and they reached its outskirts by mid afternoon. They paused as they saw a straggle of animal-skin tents, stretching out up and down the hillside on either side of the road and ending, distantly, in the beginning of a rare and bold cluster of birches, standing out like an artist's smudge from the pastels of the surrounding rocks. If it was an encampment, however, it had the air of a ghost town for very few men were to be seen. The mullah's army, it was clear, had left its base, leaving behind the barest minimum of guardians.

Two of them now approached the trio as they trudged into the encampment: tall Pathans, unusually dressed overall in black and carrying what appeared, equally unusually, to be modern Lee-Metford rifles, not the older, conventional Martini-Henrys. They held up their hands and two pairs of dark eyes ranged over the bedraggled appearance of the trio.

'*Allah Kerim . . .*' Simon and Inderjit spoke the greeting in unison and Jenkins nodded and mouthed something indecipherably but all three raised their hands in greeting.

The taller of the two Pathans grunted something in Pushtu and the Sikh hurriedly intervened, speaking fluently in the language with many a gesture to his companions. The big man listened impassively, running his eyes over the very second-hand garments the trio wore, then, to Simon's relief, an obvious air of disinterest came over him. He nodded curtly to Inderjit, spoke briefly to him and waved the three of them through to the interior of the camp.

'Did they accept our story?' asked Simon tersely, once out of earshot.

'Oh yes. It seems there are many stragglers with strange stories limping into the camp to join the mullah. We just another three. He confirm that the mullah has led his men to the east to face General Lockhart if he tries to advance along the Pass. We are to stay with the rest of the stragglers who have come in and camp here until the mullah returns.'

254

'He did not say anything, of course, about Alice?' Simon's voice was anxious.

'No. I do not ask.'

'Quite right. Where are we to camp?'

'He did not say. Just waved us into camp. I suppose we must find a level piece of ground.'

'Good. Let us go as far as possible to the far end of the camp, by that distant clump of birches. That's where I think Alice will be.'

Their heads down, they trudged on along the trail that led through the centre of the tented village until they saw, at the far end of the camp, three slightly larger tents set somewhat apart on the edge of the wood: one black and gaudily marked, and two others, still larger than the skin-dwellings but, like the black one, made of canvas. One of the canvas pair was guarded by a tall Pathan standing at its entrance and the shoulder of another could be glimpsed guarding the rear.

'Alice has to be in that tent,' whispered Simon. 'Let's camp reasonably near but not too near.'

'I wouldn't call it campin',' sniffed Jenkins. 'We 'aven't got a tent, look you.'

'Well, sleeping out of doors hasn't killed us so far. We can . . .' Then Fonthill's voice tailed away as, from the corner of his eye, he saw a compound near the wood. Turning his head, he counted six well-groomed horses within it, nuzzling bags of oats. He knew that the Pathans rarely owned horses and that they invariably attacked on foot. These, then, must surely belong to the mullah and, presumably, his senior lieutenants. Simon's eyes lit up.

'Look,' he said, indicated the compound with a slight movement of his head. 'That has solved one problem, anyway. I have been worried about getting away from here with Alice on foot. Now we have transport. Let's make a fire, over there, near that compound.'

They were able to find adequate kindling among the birches and they laid down their blankets surrounding the blaze and brewed tea, under the disinterested gaze of the man at the opening of what hopefully was Alice's tent. There Fonthill sat, covertly looking around him as he frowned, deep in thought. Then finally, putting down his cup, he gestured to the others.

'Listen,' he said. 'Getting Alice out of that tent and this camp isn't going to be easy. Thank God the place is pretty well empty but, even so, I should think that there are at least a hundred Pathans here, so we need a plan.

'Now, we need to establish that Alice is, indeed, inside that tent. This is what we do. I will go into the wood again on the pretence of getting more fuel for the fire. Inderjit, if you can engage those two guards in conversation somehow – and it is essential that you get the guard at the rear of the tent to come to the front – then I will steal up to the back of the tent and see if I can whisper a message to Alice. If she is inside, she will answer and I can prepare her for a quick exit later.'

Jenkins nodded. 'I know,' he said, 'take 'em each a cup of green tea. That'll be a kind thing to do before we 'ave to kill the buggers.'

The Sikh nodded.

'Good idea,' agreed Simon. 'Now, we shall make our

attempt in the early hours of the morning when, hopefully, most of the camp will be asleep. The tea idea is a splendid one. There is nothing a guard on duty during the night welcomes more than a bit of refreshment. So, make another brew at about three o'clock, ostensibly for us because we are sleeping out of doors and it will be damned cold. Make sure the guards see you doing this. Then make another couple of cups and you two take them over, one for each guard. Also make sure there is no one else about. If the coast is clear then use your knives to kill them.' His voice became a low growl. 'It's a rotten job, killing a man in cold blood, but it's the only way.'

Jenkins nodded. 'What are you goin' to do, then, bach sir?'

'While you are giving them the tea I shall creep back into the woods, ostensibly to get more firewood, and approach the tent from the rear. I shall then call to Alice and cut a hole in the rear of the tent and pull her out. There is one proviso, though.'

'What's that, then?'

Simon jerked his head in the direction of the horse compound. 'At the moment,' he said, 'there is no guard on the horses. But they might well place one there during the night. He could well be stationed in full view of Alice's tent and the guards, so he could see you attack them. If that is so, I will go to him, with a third cup of tea . . .'

Jenkins sniffed. 'Blimey, we might as well set up a canteen 'ere, then.'

'. . . and put him out of action. Then I will double back and extricate Alice.' Simon frowned. 'Obviously, none of this is going to be easy and, if there are tribesmen walking about at that time, then we must either wait until the coast is clear or think of another plan. But it is absolutely vital that whatever we do, we make no noise in doing it. The guards must all be killed quietly.'

'An' with great kindness, I suppose.'

'Now, listen. I haven't finished. When the guards have been . . . er . . . taken out, you must drag them out of sight – the woods is the obvious place – and cover them with branches or whatever. It must be done quickly. I will take the place of the guard at the front just in case someone notices his absence – we needn't bother with the chap at the rear, because he can't really be seen. You two are good horse handlers, so you then go to the horse compound, fix leading reins to them all – there are bound to be ropes about the place – and lead them into the woods.'

Jenkins pulled a face. 'What? All of 'em? We will only need four.'

'No. *All* of them. I don't want to leave any behind so that we can be pursued.'

Inderjit nodded. 'Do we stop to put on saddles and bridles? It will be difficult to ride quickly without them.'

Jenkins grinned. 'An' you, bach sir, will fall off, that's for sure.'

'No. No saddles or harness. There will be no time. We shall just have to ride bareback. And that includes me. Now, any more questions?'

The Welshman's face suddenly became grim behind his half-grown beard. 'What if Miss Alice isn't in that tent? What the 'ell do we do then?'

Fonthill shook his head slowly and sighed. 'I just don't know. But I am gambling that she will be. We have heard that a white woman is in the camp somewhere and this seems to be the only tent that is guarded. Please God I am right. Very well. Now, Inderjit, please be mother and make the tea and ingratiate yourself with the guards. If we have to make a change in the plan we will do so. Otherwise we stick to it. All right?'

The two nodded their heads. Simon threw another branch on the fire and Inderjit washed out their cups from their water bags and began making more tea. Surreptitiously, Jenkins began to sharpen the blade of his knife on a stone.

The hours before nightfall seemed to be the longest Fonthill had ever spent. The Sikh's services as tea-boy were gratefully received and the camp remained remarkably quiescent. Once, an old woman arrived carrying something covered with a cloth on what appeared to be a tray and was admitted to the tent. The three watchers exchanged glances. Food for Alice? It seemed so, for the woman immediately reappeared without the tray and shuffled away to disappear among the tents. That seemed to confirm it and Simon bit his lip. He was clearly within hailing distance of his wife! Yet he must remain patient.

He looked up, away to the north. Snow-capped peaks could just be seen in the far distance, sparkling like triangular diamonds on a pink setting in the late afternoon sun: the Hindu Kush, offering beauty and serenity far away from this brutal war – the mountains that had promised some gentle sport to them all not so long ago! He doubted if any of them would see them now.

He turned his gaze to the west, to where the sun was already starting to slip away behind a darkened hilltop. As far as he could see, the broad trail that ran through the camp did not dip down into the Pass. Inderjit had not known if it continued, clinging high up to the hillside, in a straight line to Peshawar. If it did, hopefully they could follow it all the way in comparative safety. If it led down to the Pathan-occupied Khyber, they would have to release the horses and revert to scrambling over rocks away from the road, so negating the advantage of having transport. They must wait and see.

Nervous with the waiting, Fonthill studied the camp. As the temperature began to dip with the approach of dusk, there were undoubtedly far fewer tribesmen to be seen between the tents. The two Pathans who had questioned them on arrival seemed to be the only guards to have been stationed and it looked as though they had remained at the far end of the camp. Could there be others posted on the trail at the far side of the wood? Simon gave an involuntary shrug of the shoulders. If there were, then there would be no question of killing them silently, unless they were asleep. Another case of wait and see.

Then, he suddenly realised that he had overlooked the possibility that the guards at the tent, who had been on duty all day, would be relieved for the night shift, so undoing Inderjit's good work in befriending them. Again, there was nothing to be done about that now and he sat watching anxiously as the night began to close in on them. Replacements, however, did not materialise. Nor, to his great relief, were guards placed on the horse compound.

They ate an evening meal and, as the temperature fell, Inderjit placed their battered kettle onto the embers of the fire and tea was made. As the Sikh took two cups towards the guards, Fonthill rose and tramped into the birches for more firewood, taking a slightly circuitous route. Treading cautiously, to avoid stepping on dead wood, he approached the rear of the tent. Yes, Inderjit was doing his job splendidly and was chatting affably with the two Pathans at the front of the tent.

Simon bent low and crawled to the rear of the tent. Luckily, there was a slight gap at the bottom. He lifted it but could not see inside. Instead, he called softly: 'Alice. Alice.'

He felt rather than heard a movement inside. And then a cracked voice – unrecognisable as that of his wife – whispered: 'Simon. Oh my God! Is that you, Simon? Tell me I am not dreaming.'

'Yes, but be quiet, darling. We will come for you in about four hours' time. Be dressed. Be very quiet.'

'They told me you were dead.'

'Not true. No more now. Be dressed and waiting.'

'I am chained. The guard at the flap has a key.'

'Good. Later.'

He was attempting to crawl back into the wood when he heard a voice raised at the tent entrance and then repeated from within the tent. Immediately, his heart in his mouth, he froze. Then he heard Alice's voice, still hoarse but lifted, obviously for his benefit, as she cried out in English, 'Oh, for goodness' sake, can't a girl have a pee in privacy?' And she banged on something – the equivalent of a chamber pot?

Still trembling, Simon gained the darkness of the wood, piled together several of the branches into his arms and re-emerged. He heaved a sigh of relief as he saw Inderjit still in conversation with one of the guards, while the second was rethreading the tent flap entrance, seemingly unperturbed.

Fonthill threw some of the branches onto the fire to make a reassuring blaze. His heart fell, however, as he saw a tribesman – elderly, for he sported a snow-white beard – shuffling towards the horse compound. Then he realised that the man was carrying a pile of horse blankets which, having entered the compound, he threw over the beasts, fastening them roughly with ropes. To his relief the old man did not stay but threw a loop over the gate to close it and marched away into the innards of the camp.

As Simon unrolled his *poshteen* and laid it on the ground near the fire, Inderjit rejoined them. All three exchanged glances and Fonthill nodded and whispered, 'She's there all right. She'll be ready when we come for her.' He looked up at the Sikh. 'Was there a problem there for a moment?'

'No. Man heard a noise inside but,' he grinned, 'lady was taking a pee, that's all.'

Simon returned the grin. 'Good old Alice. Did you promise them tea during the night?'

'Yes. They miserable because no one relieves them until morning. Glad of tea.'

'Good. Now let's try and get a bit of sleep. I will awake you in about three hours' time. If guards are to be relieved in the morning, better to start a bit earlier, I think.'

'No need to wake us, bach sir,' growled Jenkins. 'We'll be ready. Bloody cold will wake us up, anyway. An' better to 'ave a nice cup of tea, look you, before you kill anyone, I always say.'

Nodding, Simon threw another branch on the fire, lay down on his *poshteen* and wrapped a blanket around him. He found that, despite the warmth from the fire, he was shivering. Exuding affability and then, under its cover, killing two men in cold blood was not something to look forward to. Sleep eluded him and he stayed awake, recalling details of his wedding to Alice – pregnant then with their son – in their tiny little village church in Norfolk. He bit his lip again when he recalled the exhaustion in her voice a moment ago. God! – had they done anything to her? The worry added to his anxiety and he fumbled to extract his old silver Hunter from the depths of his disguise and lay with it near his face to ensure that he did not sleep on.

At 2.30 a.m. he looked up. Both Inderjit and Jenkins were awake and caught his eye. He nodded and the Sikh threw away his blanket, threw more kindling on the dying fire and waved to where the guard by the tent flap was flapping his hands together to keep warm. The man waved back in gratitude and called to his comrade at the rear of the tent.

The kettle was soon singing. Fonthill looked around him. It was a dark night and the mountains were only visible now as deeper shades of blackness. He focused his eyes. No one seemed to be stirring in the camp. And the horses, still unguarded, were standing quietly, huddled in a group at the far side of the compound. It was cold and Simon shivered. It must have been just such a night when Macbeth slew his king.

Inderjit poured tea into the two cups and handed one to Jenkins. Simon threw aside his blanket, pulled on his sandals and nodded to his two companions. Carrying the tea, they strolled towards the two guards, now standing together at the entrance to the tent. Kneeling, Fonthill watched what happened next as though transfixed.

The two handed over the cups into the outstretched hands of the guards, then half turned their backs and, in a flash of action, drew their daggers, whirled back and thrust the long blades into the sides of the Pathans as they stood, the cups raised to their mouths. Simon caught a glimpse of the look of surprise on their faces as, slowly, they crumpled to the ground. The whole action, from the assassins leaving the fireside to their victims collapsing, took less than twenty seconds. And not a sound was emitted.

Simon turned away in disgust mingled with relief and looked around. Nothing else stirred and the darkness remained all-pervading. He rose to his feet, picked up his rifle and ran to where his comrades were dragging the bodies of the dead men towards the edge of the woods.

'Stop,' he hissed. 'We need a key. Which was the guard at the entrance?'

Jenkins nodded to his man.

Fonthill knelt and fumbled with the man's clothing. Nothing was fixed to his belt except his sword and there seemed to be no pockets in his cloak or *poshteen*. Then he found the key tucked into the man's cummerbund. Nodding to Jenkins, he doubled round to the back of the tent.

He dropped onto his stomach and wriggled his head and

shoulders under the low opening at the rear. All was dark inside. 'Are you awake, Alice?'

'Yes, Simon. I've been waiting. But I am chained by the foot. Did you get the key?'

'Yes. I am trying to wriggle in. Hold on.'

Within seconds he was inside and, still kneeling, holding his wife in his arms. She put her head on his shoulder and sobbed uncontrollably.

He kissed her tear-stained cheek and whispered into her ear. 'You are all right now, my love. Jenkins and Inderjit are outside and we have horses – or will have. Now, we must be very quick and very quiet. Where's this blasted padlock?'

'On my right ankle. Here.' She lifted it, but couldn't control her sobs. 'Oh, darling. I thought you were dead. And I was going to join you tomorrow.'

'Well,' he tried to grin but tears were trickling down his cheeks now, too. 'You're joining me now. Hang on. There. Let's get rid of this damned chain. Now, can you wriggle out the way I came in?'

'Oh yes. I am sure.'

'Good. I will go first. You slip into the wood and wait a second or two. I must pretend to be the guard at the front. Be strong now.'

He kissed her again, this time on the mouth and felt how dry and cracked her lips were. Then he wriggled back through the opening and found Jenkins and Inderjit waiting for him.

'Is she all right, bach sir?' Jenkins's voice was anxious.

'Not too good. Get to the compound and get the horses

out. I will keep guard at the front of the tent. Have you hidden the . . . er . . . bodies?'

'Yes.'

'Take the horses into the woods.'

Holding his rifle to his shoulder, he strolled as nonchalantly as he could to the front of the tent. He sucked in his breath in relief and adopted the guard's posture. All seemed quiet and from the corner of his eye he saw his two companions open the compound gate and approach the horses. He could just hear Jenkins talking to the mounts in a low, sing-song voice and remembered that his comrade had been brought up on a farm, amongst livestock.

Then he saw the two freeze and drop to the ground among the horses as a Pathan emerged from out of the darkness and began to walk towards the compound. Then, the man caught sight of the two crouching among the horses, looked around in puzzlement and then turned and half ran, half stumbled towards Simon. Towards the rear Fonthill could hear low gasps as Alice was attempting to wriggle through the low opening.

Simon half turned his back to the man and slipped the rifle off his shoulder so that it was hanging, at the trail position, at his side. He heard, rather than saw the man approach him and turned at the last minute, effecting to be startled, and growled 'Allah Kerim.'

He recognised the man's long white beard and realised that he was the guardian of the horses. But the old man did not return his greeting. His mouth dropped as he looked into Simon's eyes and was about to shout a warning when Fontill swung the rifle round and crashed it into the side of his head. With a whimper the man collapsed onto the ground, only momentarily stunned, and Simon immediately fell onto him and cupped his hand over his mouth, feeling desperately for his knife as he did so. The two struggled for a moment before the edge of the blade slashed across the old man's throat. He died with a gurgle.

Fonthill felt momentarily sick and then saw Jenkins and Inderjit rise to their feet in the compound. He looked around. The struggle seemed to have gone unnoticed and the merciful blackness cloaked everything but the immediate surroundings. He beckoned to Inderjit and, leaving Jenkins to begin fixing the leading reins, the Sikh ran over.

'Drag this poor devil into the woods,' Fonthill mouthed. 'I must stand guard. Be careful. Alice will be there. Don't alarm her.'

'Very good, sahib.'

'Don't call me sahib.'

'Ah, sorry.'

Wiping blood from his *poshteen*, Simon walked quickly back to his post. Unless the old man lived alone, it would only be minutes before he was missed and he strained his eyes into the surrounding darkness to pick up any sign of movement. But three men had been killed within the space of five minutes, without, it seemed, disturbing anybody in the encampment. For a moment he felt the stirrings of nausea again as he thought of the killings. Then he recalled the weakness of Alice's voice and his resolve returned.

It seemed an eternity before the horses had been roped and led out of the compound. Simon walked back and looped shut its gate. It was important that, at first glance, everything should appear to be as it should. Then he followed the last horse into the wood.

Alice had her arms around the shoulders of both Jenkins and Inderjit as they attempted to lift her onto the back of the third horse in the line. Simon noticed with a gasp how frail she looked and that she had a piece of bloodstained cloth clumsily tied around her forearm.

He ran to her. 'What's that?'

She attempted to smile down at him. 'It's only a flesh wound,' she croaked. 'I will tell you all about it later. Let's leave this filthy place.'

'Can you sit the horse, darling? As you can see, we have no saddles or bridles.'

'I will be fine, now that you are here.'

'Good. Hold the horse's mane. We may have to gallop. Now, I will take the lead; Jenkins, you look after Alice and see she doesn't fall. Inderjit, stay in the rear, about a hundred paces back and gallop up if you hear anyone in pursuit. We can cut out and release the two spare horses once we are well out of the camp. Now, let's go. Oh, for God's sake, 352. Help me up on this bloody horse, will you?'

The strange procession wound its way through the wood, on the now narrowed trail to the west, until the track widened out again and they were out in open country, studded with rocks climbing to their left and falling to their right. There were no guards in sight and a pale moon had now risen fortuitously, sufficient for them to see the way ahead quite clearly.

Simon turned his head. 'We've got to put time and space between us and the camp and I think we can try to gallop for a bit now if we're careful,' he called back. 'Grip with your legs and heels, Alice.'

Predictably, it was Jenkins who replied: 'She's ridin' a damned sight better than I've ever seen you, saddle or no. But bless you, bach sir, I think we've done it. Well planned. We've got the lass back. Well done.'

A weak-voiced Alice joined in. 'Thank you all. I am proud of all of you.'

'We are not out yet,' said Simon. He raised his arm and gestured forward. Then, tightly winding a handful of his mount's mane into one hand, he kicked his heels into the horse's side and the little party broke into a ragged gallop.

CHAPTER TWELVE

It was possible for them to gallop for no more than ten minutes before the moon dipped behind a cloud and the road seemed to narrow, making it difficult to see more than a hundred yards or so ahead. Simon, whose seat on his unsaddled horse was uncertain, was glad enough of an excuse to slow the little cavalcade down to a walk. He turned to look behind him.

Inderjit had allowed his horse to fall behind and was now out of sight. Jenkins had somehow managed to ride at Alice's side, but she now looked white and drawn and was shivering under the horse blanket that had been thrown over her shoulders.

He allowed the two to catch up with him. 'Are you all right, darling?' he asked.

Alice nodded. 'A bit cold, that's all.' She seemed to be

looking at him with a strange intensity . . .

Simon turned to Jenkins. 'Cut out the two spare horses, 352. They're slowing us down. And take their blankets off them and put them round Alice, there's a good chap.'

'Simon.' Alice's voice sounded a touch stronger.

'Yes, my love.'

'That turban. The green and red colours. How long have you been wearing it?'

'Oh, since I took it off a dead tribesman when we were attacked in Afghanistan. I think I picked the wrong turban, though. These colours look like those taken from a sepoy. Makes me stand out. Not much of a Pathan, wearing the damned thing. Why do you ask?'

'When I escaped from the camp the first time – did I tell you about that?'

'No, but we heard about it. You did so well, my love.'

'No. No. When I was on my own, out in the rocks, oh, several days ago, I saw what I thought were three Pathans looking for me. One of them was wearing a green and red turban, tightly wound, just like yours. I was ready to shoot them but I hid and they went on climbing. Oh my goodness. It must have been you three. If only I had known . . .'

Simon grinned. 'My word. You could well have shot us and we would all then have been considerably worse off than we are now. We must be grateful for large mercies. Can you keep riding? We must press on.'

'Yes. I think so. I just keep feeling woozy, that's all.'

'I am not surprised . . .' He turned as he heard hoof beats, to see Inderjit rounding a bend and riding towards them.

'Are we being followed?' he called.

'No, sah . . . Lord. Everything is quiet.'

'Good.'

Jenkins rode up and carefully arranged two blankets around Alice's shoulders. She smiled her thanks.

Fonthill nodded to him. 'Stay close to her, 352. Now, fast walk, if we can.' He kicked in his heels and led the way.

They rode until well after the sun had risen. Turning, Simon realised that Alice was swaying now and being held in position only by Jenkins's arm. He allowed the two to catch up with him. To the right the land fell away into a vertiginous cliff face, affording them a glimpse of the Khyber Pass far below them. Tiny figures could be seen moving along the road to the west. Tribesmen returning to the mullah's encampment? Before the edge of the cliff cut off his view, he saw the road below curl sharply away to the south. To his left, up the hillside, a goat's track wound steeply and disappeared behind rocks.

He nodded to it. 'Alice. You need to rest. 352, dismount and see if you can lead Alice and your two horses up there. Find somewhere out of sight of this track where we can stop for a while. I will wait for Inderjit.'

Within minutes, Alice and Fonthill were squatting on the ground in a little clearing surrounded by boulders, while Inderjit was feeding the horses with a handful each of oats and Jenkins was treading warily back up the goats' track, carefully obscuring the hoof marks that had been left in patches of dust between the rocks.

'Let me look at that wound, Alice.' Simon carefully

unwound the towel that had been tied round the cut. 'Hmmm. I don't like the look of that.' He poured a little water onto the wound that was still oozing a dark-coloured liquid and dabbed it with what was left of Alice's handkerchief. 'Does it hurt?'

She nodded her head, her eyes closed. 'Throbs a bit.'

He put his hand to her brow. It was hot, very hot. He bit his lip. It seemed that she was mounting a fever. Better to keep her warm, even though the day was hot. He replaced the rough-and-ready bandage, gently splashed water onto her face and laid his wife down on her blankets in what little shade was offered. She immediately closed her eyes and was asleep.

Jenkins joined him. 'Even if there was a search party,' he said, 'I doubt if they'd see we'd gone off the track . . . Ah – 'ow is she?'

'Not good. I think she's developing a fever.' Fonthill turned an anxious face to Inderjit. 'Have you any idea if this track will take us to Peshawar and how long that could be?'

The Sikh brushed oat dust off his hands. 'I see Pass curl away to the right down below,' he said. 'That is a big bend in the Pass that I remember. It goes due south and takes road to Fort Maude and meets with Bozai river.' He nodded to the east. 'This track look as if it much used and it go straight on.' A slight smile brought a flash of his teeth behind the black beard. 'I think this track is good for us. It could go direct to Jamrud Fort, much nearer than Peshawar. Pathans told me this fort not taken then.'

Fonthill shot a quick glance at his wife. 'Please God you

are right. How long, then, do you think before we reach Jamrud?'

'Maybe one more day riding.'

Simon exchanged looks with Jenkins. 'I hope to God she can make it. How are we for water?'

'Enough, if we are careful.'

'Right. Then we must be careful. Alice must take precedence. Now.' He looked up at the sun. 'We will just have to risk staying here throughout the middle of the day, when it is hottest, so that Alice can rest. We will take it in turns to keep guard. Obviously, we don't fire on anyone, unless it becomes absolutely necessary. Will the horses be all right, Inderjit?'

'Ah yes. They used to sun. I have more oats.'

'Good. You two try and get some rest. I will take the first watch.'

They stayed huddled in the rock-bound clearing, while Alice slept, breathing heavily. It seemed that no one had followed them and by late afternoon Simon took the decision to wake his wife and ride on. She was heavy-eyed and damp with perspiration but she nodded and was helped back onto the horse. Inderjit went on ahead to ensure that the way was clear and Simon, leading his own horse, supported Alice as Jenkins led the way down the steep incline.

They rode on, meeting no one. 'I thought Inja said this was a busy road,' called Jenkins but Simon merely shrugged. His mind seethed with worry about Alice. She was still perspiring and only Jenkins's arm prevented her from falling from the horse. She clearly had a fever but perhaps that wound had produced blood poisoning? And

274

did pneumonia follow a fever? He had no idea but they must get her to a doctor as soon as possible. Would there be one in Fort Jamrud? And had the fort fallen to the Pathans by now?

They rode for as long as they could see the trail after the sun had set, and then they found cover off the track again, with each of the men standing guard through the darkness.

On Fonthill's watch, as he sat in bright moonlight behind a rock covering the track ahead of them towards the fort, he stiffened as he heard hoof beats off to the east and then felt the earth tremble as the horsemen neared. Quickly alerting the other two, he cocked his rifle and the three took cover facing the direction of the oncoming party.

'Don't fire until I do,' Simon hissed.

Around a bend in the road appeared a party of six horsemen, all Pathans and led by an imposing figure. Dressed in white robes and, like his men, fiercely bearded, he rode with his head down at a brisk pace, so that his cloak floated out behind him. A rifle was housed in a saddle bucket at his side and a long curved sword hung down from his belt. Without a look to left or right, he thundered on, leading his party at what seemed to Fonthill a dangerous pace in the moonlight, until he finally disappeared round a distant bend.

'Blimey,' called Jenkins. 'Who was that? Old Nick 'imself?'

'Quick,' said Simon. 'We must wake Alice and be on our way. They might come back.'

And so on they rode, sometimes cantering, sometimes as the light improved, galloping for a while, but mainly putting their mounts to a brisk walking pace. They stopped now only for moments, to eat what was left of their unappetising provisions and to give Alice sips of water. She rode now mainly with her head on Jenkins shoulder, slumped sideways, so that it became impossible to gallop or even canter.

In an attempt to keep Alice awake, Simon told her of the horsemen who had thundered by.

'Ah,' she said, nodding slowly. 'That would be Ali.'

'And who the hell would *he* be?'

She looked across to him with lacklustre eyes. 'I think he is the mullah's general, or something like that.' She held up her bandaged arm. 'It was he who did this,' she said.

Fonthill and Jenkins exchanged glances. 'I wish I had shot the bastard, then,' growled Simon.

'Best you didn't, though, bach sir. The others might 'ave bin a bit of an 'andful for just the three of us.'

Simon shook his head. 'The meeting is postponed, that's all. I'll catch up with him, even if he is Old Nick himself.'

'And I shall look forward to bein' there as well,' said Jenkins. 'You can leave a bit of 'im for me, so you can.'

Alice said nothing but her head slumped forward and it was time for Simon to ride next to her, her head on his shoulder.

So they rode on, now with Inderjit going well ahead. The road had been falling away in a steep incline for some time when the Sikh came galloping back, his hand held high, his teeth cutting a white swathe through his dark face.

'We go down to Fort Jamrud now,' he said. 'And sepoys are manning the battlements. It not taken by Pathans.'

'Are you sure?'

'Yes. Colours of splendid Sikh Regiment flying from flagpole and sepoys are patrolling outside. No sign of Pathans. Maybe railway running.'

'Thank goodness for that.' Fonthill gently nudged his wife. 'Did you hear that, darling? The fort has not been taken and it is just down the hill. You will be taken care of now.'

Alice tried to lift her head and, from somewhere, summon up a smile. But her head flopped back onto Simon's shoulder and her eyes stayed closed.

'Oh God!' exclaimed Fonthill. 'Better get on quickly. Inderjit, gallop on ahead and warn them we are coming. I don't want us to be shot on the last lap. And see if there is a doctor who can be summoned.'

Within fifteen minutes, Fonthill, Alice and Jenkins were escorted by a patrol of Sikhs on horseback through the great gate of the fort and onto the parade ground inside, where Alice was slowly lowered to the ground. An officer Simon recognised as Captain Barton, the former commander of Fort Landi Kotal, hurried to meet them and his face immediately lightened as he recognised Alice.

'Good Lord,' he said. 'Thank God she's alive.'

Fonthill scowled at him. 'No thanks to you,' he spat. 'Why didn't you take her with you when you evacuated the fort?'

Barton shook his head wearily. 'No. I didn't evacuate it. It wasn't taken when I was ordered to report back to Jamrud and then I was told to remain here. I have been on hot bricks hoping that your wife had survived, Fonthill. We have been in daily fear of an attack by the Pathans but it has never materialised. But enough of that, we must get her inside now.'

'Is there a doctor here?'

'I fear not. But we have a subaltern here who was once a medical student. He has been useful to us before. I have sent for him and we have prepared a bed for her.'

Alice was now completely unconscious and perspiring freely. Between them, Fonthill and Jenkins carried her into the fort's interior where Barton led them to a room containing a single bed – the fort's sickbay, he explained.

They were joined almost immediately by a middle-aged major, whom Barton introduced as the commander of the fort, and then by a young, heavily moustached lieutenant named Barnes, who immediately knelt beside Alice, put his hand to her forehead and took her pulse. He spoke over his shoulder to Fonthill.

'How long has she been like this?'

'About two days.'

Then Barnes noticed Alice's bandaged forearm and immediately began untying it. He wrinkled his nose when he inspected the wound. 'What the hell is this?' he demanded.

'It was cut with a knife or a sword. I don't know how or when. A Pathan did it.'

'Ah.' The young man shouted over his shoulder and a tall Sikh appeared. Without looking up, Barnes gave a string of orders to the man, who inclined his head and disappeared. Then the subaltern laid his hand on Alice's breast and immediately covered her to the chin with the bed sheet. He turned to Simon.

'I'm afraid I am not a doctor, sir,' he said. 'Only did two years at Edinburgh studying medicine before the family ran out of money and I had to join the Indian army.'

Simon summoned a smile. 'I understand,' he said. 'But this lady is my wife and is very, very . . .' His voice broke for a moment, then he recovered. 'She is dear to me. She was captured by the Pathans when Fort Landi Kotal fell and she has been under considerable stress before we,' he gestured to Jenkins and Inderjit, standing in the background, 'were able to rescue her. Please do all you can to save her.'

Barnes nodded. 'The nearest doctor is at Peshawar, of course. We are surrounded by tribesmen, although they don't seem to want to attack us, and we haven't been able to run a train for days, so we cannot risk taking her there yet. But I will do my best here.'

He put his hand back onto her brow then he continued. 'She has a high fever and my guess is that it is caused by septicaemia, or blood poisoning, which has resulted from this damned wound. I am afraid this is a dangerous condition, which I must warn you could adversely affect the vital organs such as the liver and the heart.' He cleared his throat. 'You must understand that I have no drugs here that could treat it and the condition could result in death.'

Fonthill shook his head. 'No. It could not. It *must not*.' He seized the young man's arm. 'What *can* you do, Lieutenant?'

'Yes, there *are* things I can do. I can drain the wound and hopefully get the poison out and, of course, work to reduce the fever, get her to take plenty of liquids and so on. The next twenty-four hours will be critical. We must hope that your wife, sir, has a strong constitution that will fight the poison in her body. Has she always been strong?'

'Yes, thank God. But she has been through a lot.'

'Very well.' He was interrupted by the arrival of the Sikh carrying a bowl of water, a sponge, compresses and a package containing what looked like a tube. 'Ah good, thank you, *havildar*. Can you get a punkah wallah to motivate this fan?' he nodded upwards to where a long piece of calico hung from the ceiling. 'Now, if you would all kindly leave the room I will do what I can.'

The next forty-eight hours were the most distraught of Fonthill's life. He sat for hours holding Alice's hand, occasionally mopping her brow and changing the compress on her head as the fan above them stirred the air in that tiny room. The subaltern came in regularly to check her progress – or rather lack of it, because the fever seemed to increase and Alice lay moaning and tossing her head as perspiration dripped down her face. Barnes produced a strange glass tube that he held under her tongue for some minutes.

Eventually, he removed it and held it up to the light to examine a gauge marked on its side. 'It's called a thermometer,' he told Simon. 'I'd forgotten I'd still got it. It's been around for years but it was refined in the 1860s. Measures the patient's temperature, when the heat pushes the mercury up the tube. You have to have it inside the mouth for at least five minutes but that's an improvement. I gather it used to take at least twenty minutes to record any movement.' He sighed. 'Doesn't help much, anyway, because I know she's got a high temperature and I don't need this thing to tell me that. Mind you, that wound looks a bit healthier now I've drained it and put ointment and a clean dressing on it. Keep your spirits up, sir. She's a fighter. I can tell that.'

Fonthill nodded wearily. 'Thank you for what you're doing,' he said and held his wife's hand even more tightly.

The turning point came by the evening of the second day. Simon had fallen fast asleep with his head on the sheet covering Alice, while still gripping her hand. Suddenly he awoke to find that she had stopped turning and was lying quite tranquilly with her eyes closed.

'Oh God!' he cried. 'Alice, Alice don't leave me. Don't—' He stopped as, lazily, she opened her eyes. 'Hello, darling,' she murmured. 'I've had such terrible dreams. Have you been here long?'

He burst into tears of relief and buried his head on her breast. She patted his hair. 'Goodness, Simon,' she said. 'Don't take on so. They were only dreams. Do you think I could have a cup of tea?'

Barnes was summoned and announced that the fever had broken but still needed care. Tea was brought and then Jenkins and Inderjit, followed by Barton and the major, gathered round her bed. Barnes then ushered them all out and managed to find a pili to help Alice to sleep.

Once outside, Simon pumped his hand. 'I don't care what sort of soldier you are, Barnes,' he said, 'but you're a bloody fine doctor. Anybody can be a soldier but it took a damned good doctor to bring my wife back from the dead. I can't thank you enough.'

The young man sucked in his moustache in embarrassment. 'She did it herself, actually sir,' he muttered. 'Damned fine constitution, I would say. But she still needs to rest and I'm afraid I need to get back to my platoon. Let her sleep and feed her with as much liquid as she needs. I will be back the day after tomorrow.'

Fonthill nodded. 'Does it look as though the Pathans still might attack?'

'Don't think so. That's what the patrolling is all about. We're trying to find out what's happened to them. We think that probably the Afridis have gone home with their loot from the forts to lick their wounds and the mullahs are still trying to raise their fellows in the south, the Orakzais, to come to their aid. That and the fact that General Lockhart in Peshawar is gathering a pretty formidable army to attack them. But the major will tell you more.'

'Thank you again, Barnes. Come back safely from that patrol. The army has plenty of subalterns but not many good doctors. Oh, and don't break your thermometer thing.'

Alice's condition improved considerably over the next few days and, for the first time, she was able to tell Fonthill and the others exactly what had happened to her since they had left her in Landi Kotal. An embarrassed Barton also insisted on explaining that, on reaching Jamrud in response to an order from his superior in Peshawar, Commissioner Sir Richard Udny, he had been instructed to remain there and, furthermore, his request for reinforcements to resist the coming attack on Landi Kotal had been ignored.

'I'll tell you, Fonthill,' he confessed, 'it was not much

fun staying here watching my chaps who had escaped from Kotal march in. They spat at the troops all waiting here, nice and safe behind their high walls. Not their fault, of course. We had been ordered to stay put here.'

'For God's sake, why?'

'Just don't know. Presumably Udny thought that it was too late to send troops out along the Pass because they would be exposed to attack there. Once at the fort, I am sure I could have stopped the surrender – particularly if the four companies of regular infantry and the two guns I had asked for had been sent to back up my Khyber Rifles in the fort. There were twelve thousand troops hanging about in Peshawar, so they could easily have been spared. Disgracefully bad show.'

Fonthill enquired if anyone had heard whether the Guides under Appleby-Smith had reached Peshawar but nothing had been reported to Jamrud. Within two days all the scouts sent out to scour the surrounding area had returned to report that the hills seemed clear of Pathans. The telegraph line to Peshawar had remained uncut and it was decided to run a train back up the line from the capital. Barnes agreed that Alice could make the journey and she, Simon, Jenkins and Inderjit departed five days after their arrival at Jamrud.

Peshawar had changed since the party had left it five weeks before. Now the rather sleepy town had become a vibrant army depot as troops flooded in to make up Lieutenant General Sir William Lockhart's Tirah Field Force. Khaki-clad soldiers thronged the streets as Fonthill and his companions made for the little hospital in the centre of the town. Simon noted some of the most famous cap badges in the Indian and British armies: from the Gordon Highlanders and King's Own Scottish Borderers to the 'bread and butter' shire regiments of England, such as the Derbys and the Northamptons; plus the elite units of the Raj, like the Bengal Lancers, Hodson's Horse, the Royal Corps and Guides and the Gurkhas. It was as if the whole of the Indian subcontinent had been scoured to find the best fighting troops to send to the Frontier. The Empire, it seemed, was on the march and out for revenge.

At the hospital, Alice, now recovered from the fever but still weak, was welcomed by an army doctor, who immediately put her to bed in a large, comparatively cool ward which she had virtually to herself.

There she held out her hand to her three companions. Tears were in her eyes as she said: 'You are my three knights – not in shining armour, but in filthy turbans – who came to my rescue. I can't thank you enough for getting me out of that camp and looking after me so well.' And she insisted on kissing Jenkins and Inderjit before they left her alone to say goodbye to her husband.

'I don't want to stay here long,' Alice told Simon, holding his hand. 'I intend to get on my feet as soon as I can.'

Fonthill shook his head. 'No, my love. You will stay here as long as the doctors tell you to. You have lost strength and you must recover it.'

'Nonsense. Give me three days and I will be out.'

'Then you will soon be back in again.' He frowned. 'Alice, don't you appreciate the narrow escape you had?

That man – Ali, was it? – would undoubtedly have killed you. Your whole system has been under great strain.' He smiled. 'You may still be beautiful but you are no longer young, my dear. You must stay here until you are better.'

'And what are you going to do?'

Simon's smile disappeared. 'I am going to see General Lockhart and offer him my services in his campaign. I now have a personal score to settle with this Pathan leader and his bloody mullah.'

Alice struggled to sit up. 'You will not go without me.'

'I most certainly will – if the general will have me.'

'But I have work to do. I must report on this campaign.'

'You will stay here until you are better. Now lie back and try to get some sleep. You need to build up your strength. I will return tomorrow.'

'One request then, my darling.'

'What's that?'

'I need a notepad and pen and ink.'

'What on earth for?'

'I have a story to write for the *Morning Post*. And it's an exclusive this time because it's my own story, something that happened to me. Can you let me have them by this afternoon please?'

'No. You must rest. But I will compromise and bring them tomorrow. Now lie back and think of the Queen and all who are fighting for her.'

He pushed her gently back onto the pillows, kissed her lightly, waved and walked away, her eyes following him all the way.

Fonthill and his companions had booked into the little

hotel where they had stayed before – chosen because it was not marked 'Europeans only', so that Inderjit was able to stay also. Then Simon visited the offices of Commissioner Udny, 'Udny the Unready' as he was now called in Peshawar as a result of his refusal to send troops to Fort Landi Kotal. Fonthill had no wish to see the commissioner, whom he blamed for Alice's fate, but enquired of his young assistant if anything had been heard of Appleby-Smith's squadron.

To his relief, he learnt that it had arrived in Peshawar – unhurt, it seemed by any further skirmishes – and had only yesterday journeyed on to the Guides' base in Marden. And yes, a most important letter had been deposited into the commissioner's care and been immediately couriered on to the Viceroy in Simla. But Simon learnt more.

General Blood's campaign in the north, it seemed, had been successful and he now completely controlled the Buner Valley. Nevertheless, the Revolt was still gathering force all along the North-West Frontier and fighting had broken out in the land of the Orakzais just a few miles south of Peshawar itself. General Lockhart had now arrived in the city and was pulling together the largest army raised in India since the Mutiny, so reflecting the British government's alarm at the threat posed to the greatest jewel in its Empire.

In all, Fonthill was told, 34,500 fighting men and 20,000 supporting non-combatants, plus 72,000 pack animals, were gathering in Peshawar to form the Tirah Field Force. The force consisted of two divisions, made up of six mountain batteries, two companies of sappers, four British and four native field hospitals, a machine gun detachment, three battalions of light infantry, one regiment of infantry, two cavalry units and an artillery battery. This force would be confronted by an estimated 50,000 Afridis and Orakzais, all of whom had now flocked to the banner of the redoubtable Mullah Sayyid Akbar, who had been extremely active in the Khyber and also to the south of the great Pass.

Fonthill took note, established where exactly Lockhart had made his headquarters and diverted there on his way back to the hotel. He had been able to change his Pathan clothing for anonymous khaki at Jamrud, although, even so, he was received at the general's HQ with some suspicion. He was, however, allowed to scribble a note for Lockhart, introducing himself and begging permission to call on him as soon as possible.

It was pleasing on returning to the hotel, then, to find a note already there and waiting for him from the general. It regretted that their paths had not crossed previously but congratulated him on his part in the defence of Malakand, his success in extracting a promise of non-involvement from the Amir of Afghanistan and also on his 'amazing achievement in penetrating the Pathan camp and extricating your wife'. It briefly described Lockhart's mission now and invited him to call within the day, if possible, to discuss matters that 'might be of mutual interest'.

Fonthill's senses were immediately aroused and his first thought was to summon Jenkins. Then he realised that the duo had, perforce, recently become a trio and that something had to be done about that. Inderjit was not his property and ought to return to his unit. He summoned the *daffadar*, who immediately handed him a telegram addressed to the Sikh. It ordered him to make his way to Marden as soon as possible to rejoin his troop.

Simon read it and immediately held out his hand to Inderjit. 'Of course you must go, old chap,' he said. 'We can't keep you away from your unit and your career. But I can't thank you enough for all you have done in helping Alice to escape. Jenkins and I could not have survived for more than a couple of hours in those hills without you.'

The Sikh bowed his head. 'It was a great privilege to be of service to you, sah . . . Can I call you sahib again now?'

'No. We are friends now. You must call me Simon.'

The tall man shook his head and gave a rueful smile. 'Ah no, sahib, it is not the form. Even Mr Jenkins does not call you that. But thank you for taking me with you. I now know why my mother always said how much my father respected you and Jenkins bach, as he called him. She said that my father always had . . . what was it she said, now? Ah yes. She said that he had fun, that was it, fun. Fun always with you. I now know what she meant.'

Simon returned the rueful grin. 'Well, if it was fun, it was pretty dangerous fun. But we shall meet again, Inderjit. I shall write to your colonel saying how resourceful you were in every way and strongly recommend you for promotion.'

'Thank you, sahib. Now I must go.'

The two shook hands and when the Sikh had departed Simon shouted for Jenkins. The Welshman, a dense bush of black hair sprouting from above his cotton vest, shuffled in, looking bleary-eyed.

Fonthill frowned and stepped forward, putting his head

close to Jenkins's. 'Oh dear,' he said. 'You've been drinking again, 352?'

Jenkins nodded. 'Abshlutely right, bach sir. But not 'eavily. Just a couple of bottles of this pale ale rubbish. Well, p'raps four or five. Doeshn't affect me, though.' And he hiccoughed.

'Well, take another four or five if you must but don't, whatever you do, *don't* hit anyone. Get it out of your system today. How would you feel about going on active service with General Lockhart?'

'Dosh it mean 'avin' a go at this Ali feller?'

'I would expect so.'

'Then count me in. Anyway,' a dreamy smile came over the Welshman's unshaven face, 'I go where you go. You know that. When do we report for duty? Ah . . .' A frown descended upon his face. 'It don't mean joinin' up again, doesh it? I wouldn't fancy that much, would you?'

'Not at all. Now go and sleep it off and then shave and generally smarten up, for God's sake. You look like a Pathan second-hand horse dealer. And you smell like one. I am off to see the general.'

Simon took the opportunity of showering before retracing his steps to General Lockhart's HQ. This time he presented the general's letter to the orderly and he was immediately summoned into the great man's office without further ado.

As he entered the room Fonthill immediately had the impression of order and tidiness. Maps were pinned in what appeared to be a sequence across the far wall and another lay on a table, held down precisely at the corners by four chess pieces. The desk contained papers, but they were stacked in impeccably neat piles and two pens were set precisely in their holders.

The man who rose from behind that desk and advanced towards Fonthill, hand extended, perpetuated the sense of order. His riding boots were polished so that they shone and, despite the warmth in the room, his jacket was buttoned to the neck. The inevitable moustache, now pepper-and-salt in colour, was firmly clipped to an unfashionable stubble and his hair parted exactly in the centre of his head. His spectacles were rimless and complemented the overall spartan appearance.

Simon regarded the man with interest. He knew that the man had risen from an unpretentious background – he was the son of a Lanarkshire clergyman – to become regarded as one of the safest pair of military hands in the whole of India. Indeed, it was said that only Robert Warburton matched him in his knowledge of the Pathans and the Frontier, in which he had served for many years. He had seen active service in Abyssinia and Burma and was reputed to be a brave fighting soldier as well as a supremely efficient staff officer. The Pathans called him '*Amir Sahib*.'

Now, Fonthill, whose relationships with senior British officers in the past had never always been exactly equable, felt a touch of diffidence as he took the hand offered to him. This was immediately dispelled by the general's warm greeting.

'Delighted to meet you at last, Fonthill,' said Lockart, pumping his hand. His voice contained more than a trace of his Scottish upbringing. 'I can't think why we haven't bumped into each other before in some part of the Empire or other. My word, you have had the most interesting and unusual career, my dear fellow.'

Simon returned the warm smile. 'Not as distinguished as yours, General, I fear,' he said. 'I'm afraid that I have never quite fitted into the army, since my days as a subaltern in Zululand.'

'Doesn't matter. You have served extremely well in your . . . er . . . irregular capacity. Now, come and sit down. It's early in the day, but would you care for a wee dram?'

'No thank you, sir. Too early for me.'

'Quite agree. I've been recalled from sick leave at home to take this job, so I have to take care. Now. Tell me exactly how you got involved in this damned trouble – particularly this remarkable tale of rescuing your wife. Don't spare the details. They could be important. I need to know everything you can tell me about the Amir and these Pathans.'

And so Fonthill went through his experience at Malakand, his meeting with the Amir in Kabul, his clash with the Pathans on the return journey, the story of Alice's capture, her imprisonment in the camp and their eventual escape down to Jamrud.

At the conclusion, Lockhart leant forward. 'This Ali chap in the camp, what did he look like?'

'Well, I only caught a glimpse of him but Alice described him pretty well. Very tall, brown more than black, good teeth, excellent English – he had been educated at Winchester and Cambridge and attended Sandhurst. Rather charismatic by the sound of it, but as cruel as hell, as it turned out.'

'Did she say that he was always dressed in white, in

rather fine garments, hemmed with gold trim?'

'Yes.' It was Fonthill's turn to evince interest. 'Do you know him?'

'Not really, but I met him once and heard him preach. The man, Fonthill, was not the mullah's general. Your wife, my dear fellow, was in the clutches of the Mullah Sayyid Akbar himself.'

'Good Lord!'

'And, of course, he was not an Indian, but an Afghan. Never been near an English public school in his life, nor to Sandhurst, although his English is impeccable. The man's a great liar and tells these stories to impress. But he's a wonderfully charismatic preacher and not a bad soldier for an amateur. Cruel? I'll say. The fellow kills without mercy and your wife is lucky to be alive.' The general sat back, frowning.

Fonthill nodded slowly. 'Damn! I wish I had shot him when I had the chance. It could have saved us all a lot of trouble.'

'Don't worry. He will hang once I've caught up with him. It would have been the Amir, by the way, who would have sent him over the Border. Virtually all of the mullahs who have been stirring up the tribes came from Afghanistan. The old man has certainly not sent troops, so he has kept his word to that extent, but he certainly exported these priests and I would gamble he is sitting back now, thoroughly enjoying the trouble he has caused.'

'Hmm. What exactly are your plans, General? I would like to join you, with my man Jenkins, if I can, though we would not seek regular army posts.'

'Hah, the great 352! Delighted to have you both.' He stood. 'Come over here and I will show you roughly what I intend to do.'

They moved to the large map on the table. There, Lockhart jabbed a finger to the north of the Khyber Pass. 'The mullah's camp was probably hereabouts, but it won't be there now. When you saw him, he was probably galloping back to move his camp to the south. I think this talk to your wife about negotiating with me was balderdash. He was playing with the lady, I fear. Just amusing himself. But he *would* have cut off her fingers, I think, before killing her. Cruel, you see.'

Silence fell on the stuffy room. It was only broken by the distant scream of an NCO and the rattle of harness as an artillery battery passed by outside.

Then Fonthill spoke softly. 'The swine!'

'Quite so. Now listen. Akbar and his army will have moved south of the Pass, while he still controls it, because his spies will have told him that I intend to attack the Afridis and the Orakzais in the south, here, in this vast area. And they will be right. You will note, Fonthill, that the map shows very little in terms of detail. That's because we have never mapped it. All the approaches to Tirah are encircled by the most formidable logistical obstacles. The routes bristle with physical barriers, from the heights of the passes to the steep defiles cut out by the rivers, making road construction the most time consuming and laborious task.'

Frowning, Fonthill looked up. 'Why attack here at all, then?'

'Blood has cleared up resistance in the north but we have

hardly touched the Afridis and the Orakzai clans yet. They are among the largest and most fierce haters of the British Raj. This is their heartland.' He spread his fingers. 'Here, the Afridis straddle the Khyber and stretch south almost as far as the Kurram valley, joining up with the territory of their brothers, the Orakzais, whom we have never fought, but whom Sayyid Akbar has been successful in rousing, by the sound of it. If I can cut out the Pathan revolt here in this wild and vast country, that will kill it in the rest of the country, like cutting out a cancer and, by the way, taking back the Khyber as a result.'

The general withdrew his widespread fingers and pointed to an area of the map south of Peshawar and ominously empty of geographical detail. 'I shall go in here, at the Samana Range, in Orakzais country at the very south of the Tirah. This is the easiest route. But I must move quickly because I want to have wrapped this up before winter comes and snow blocks the passes.'

He moved his finger on the map further to the east. 'I want to establish my forces here as soon as possible in the Tirah Maidan, in the very heart of the Orakzais' homeland.' The general looked up with a smile. 'Troops of the Raj have never been there, of course, and the tribes boast that the area is concealed like Muslim women in purdah behind a curtain which has never been drawn aside. Well, I intend to tear aside that veil.'

Fonthill nodded. 'I see. I am happy to help in any way, General, but I am not familiar with this territory. What do you see as my role?'

'Ah, quite.' Lockhart walked back to his seat and

gestured for Fonthill to sit down. 'Let's have some tea.' He reached across and tinkled a small bell that stood on his desk. 'How d'yer take it?'

'As it comes, but preferably with a little milk.'

The tea was ordered from an Indian orderly, wearing the largest turban that Fonthill had ever seen, and then the general began answering Simon's question.

'I have,' he said, 'intelligence officers – chaps who know, or who say they know, the Pathans – and I've got scouts and guides too, as well as thousands of troops, civilian support chaps, artillery and even scores of bloody vets. And I shall need them all, for this is going to be one of the most difficult campaigns in the history of the British army, as far as I can see.'

He sipped his tea and leant forward. 'Now, nobody knows this area at all so you are not alone in that respect. I do have native informers but I doubt if I can trust any of them. What I don't have is someone like you and your Welshman: completely loyal men who don't think in straight lines like my officers, particularly the senior ones; men who have earned their spurs already acting as completely irregular soldiers; and men who can adopt disguise if necessary and go out on their own, live in the hills – as you have done in the last week or so and as you did for Roberts all those years ago.'

'I see.' Fonthill sat back. 'I must warn you, Sir William, that my Pushtu is far from fluent and Jenkins possesses none at all. If it is spies you are after, I am not sure that we are your men.'

Lockhart waved a dismissive hand. 'I've got spies. They

did nothing to warn us that this conflagration was going to break out – damnit, Warburton and I were allowed to go on leave just before it happened! No. What I need is a mixture of soldiers, who can fight like tigers when they have to – as you did at Malakand and on that road on the way back from Kabul – intelligence officers who can interpret what they see; and scouts who can slip behind enemy lines and melt into the countryside.

'And there is one more thing.'

'Yes?'

'The Mullah Sayyid is not exactly a commanding officer, as it were. These are tribesmen who owe allegiance only to their local chiefs and often not even to them. But it is undoubtedly he who has stirred up these Afridis and Orakzais and led them into action. I want to find out where he lives – I think it's somewhere in this area – so that we can hunt him down. You might, perhaps, have a vested interest in helping us there . . . ?'

A slow smile spread itself across Fonthill's face. 'I think you've just found yourselves two irregular scouts, sir. When can we start?'

The two men shook hands. 'Not straight away. From what I hear you will need to look after your wife for a wee while, anyway. And you will also need to get into mufti – Pathan mufti. No need for army uniform. I intend to begin the invasion as early in October as I can. So come and see my quartermaster next week sometime – I will warn him – and draw dress and arms. We will also provide horses and written accreditation for you. Now, as to pay . . .'

Fonthill held up his hand. 'Not necessary, sir. I have

adequate private means to look after myself and Jenkins. And after all, we are supposed to be on holiday.'

Lockhart's spectacles sparkled as he tilted back his head and laughed. 'Damned fine holiday you've had!'

'But there is one other thing, sir. There is a *daffadar* in the Guides at Marden, a Sikh by the name of Inderjit Singh. He has been with us in the hills, which he knows well. He speaks native dialects fluently, has the courage of a lion and knows how to kill a man if he has to. He is also the son of a magnificent man who was killed with me during the Second Afghan War. I would like him to be with us on this mission, if he could be released from his duties with the Guides, to which he has returned only today.'

The general made a note. 'I will see to it.' He stood. 'You will be on my personal staff, Fonthill, from next week. I know where you are staying and I shall call when I need you. We shall meet again soon. Now, please give my best regards to your wife for her recovery.'

They shook hands again. 'Thank you, sir. I hope that we can be useful to you.'

'I know you can.'

CHAPTER THIRTEEN

Fonthill returned to the hotel and found Jenkins asleep on his bed, snoring loudly and surrounded by a pile of empty beer bottles. Luckily, he had not shaven, for the embryonic black beard that now mingled with his chest hair and bristled over his vest gave him the appearance of a typical Pathan – albeit a drunken one. Simon sighed, nevertheless, as he regarded his old comrade. Jenkins was a magnificent fighter, in and out of uniform. But alcohol was his abiding vice. Although his threshold to drunkenness was high, once past six or seven pints he became raucous, aggressive and completely lacking in discipline.

Collecting the bottles, Fonthill reflected that at least there would be few opportunities for Jenkins to drink once they began campaigning in the hills with Lockhart. He decided to let his much-loved sleeping dog lie for the moment and went back to the hospital to tell Alice about his meeting with the general.

He found her sitting up in bed scribbling furiously. Predictably, she had found pencil and paper from somewhere. 'Hello, darling,' she said, hardly looking up. 'I cabled The *Morning Post* in London and had an immediate reply.' She waved a cable. 'They will be delighted to have my own story and have accredited me to Lockhart and his Field Force as their correspondent.' She grinned. 'They want me to report on the campaign.'

Simon groaned and perched on the bed. 'Have they any idea,' he asked, 'what you have been through and how ill you have been? I hope you have not accepted. It's one thing writing from a hospital bed about your own terrible experience in those hills, but it's quite another going out into incredibly rough country and sharing the hardships of a serving soldier on campaign.' He shook his head. 'Alice, you cannot go. You are still too weak.'

His wife frowned and waved her hand dismissively. 'I'm a bit wobbly at the moment, but I am really feeling better with every minute. By the time old Lockhart gets his damned great army together and gets it rolling I shall be as fit as a fiddle. So of course I have accepted. If you can go off a-soldiering again, then so can I. Oh, sorry, darling . . .' She offered him an apologetic smile. 'Have you seen the general yet? How did you get on?'

Sighing, Simon told her of what had ensued with Lockhart. It then became Alice's turn to become dismayed. Her jaw dropped, however, when she learnt of the identity of her captor.

'The great Mullah Sayyid himself, you say! And he was a miserable Afghan and had never been to England in his life! My God. I was completely taken in.' She slumped back onto her pillow and closed her eyes for a moment. Then she sat up again with a jerk. 'Do you know, darling, there was a moment, back there in that blasted tent when I drank his cognac, that I began to find him almost attractive.'

She shook her head. 'And all the time he was playing with me and intending to kill me . . .' She shuddered. 'What kind of a beast is he, do you think?'

'Well, he is a religious fanatic, to start with, and you said yourself that he had told you he hated the English. But, if Lockhart is right – and he is supposed to know these people like the back of his hand – then the man was never mistreated by us because of his race or colour. He obviously has charisma, otherwise he would not have been able to persuade so many Pathans to join his jihad.'

Alice frowned. 'I don't like this idea of you and Jenkins becoming Pathans again, of disappearing into the hills and trying to track down the bloody man. You will be playing with the devil, my love. He is obviously as clever as hell as well as cruel. Why can't Lockhart just fight his troops and crush him in the field of battle?'

'We are not being asked to fight him man to man.' Simon scowled. 'Although I wouldn't mind doing that for a minute . . .'

'He's much younger than you, darling.'

'Thank you for that vote of confidence.'

'No. No. I didn't mean to disparage your ability or your courage. You and Jenkins are the bravest men I know.

Really. But you will be playing against him in his own backyard. He is cunning as well as cruel. Please don't try and track him down, my love.'

Fonthill grinned ruefully. 'Well, I shall have my own army with me – Jenkins, of course, and I have asked for Inderjit to be released again. We couldn't live for long behind the enemy lines in those hills without him.'

Alice threw down her pencil and paper. 'Well. Let me come with you. I can black up as well as, if not better than, you. It would help your disguise to have a woman with you. What spy would take his wife with him, eh?'

'Indeed. He would be mad to do so. Whoever heard of a Pathan woman with the most beautiful grey eyes in the whole world.'

'No, be serious, darling. I could be a help to you and it would give me a much better story than I'd find just plodding along with the biggest army to serve the Queen in India since the Mutiny. Please let me come.'

Fonthill stood. 'No, my love. And that is final. The three of us will need to be able to move quickly and unencumbered.'

'Unencumbered! Well, I like that. What about when I—'

'That's enough, Alice. Now you must excuse me. I have much to do.' He leant forward and kissed her cheek, which was most reluctantly offered.

'Very well, Simon,' she said. 'If you insist on playing the Master of the Household, then the least you can do is shop in the town and get me some decent clothes for the campaign. I shall need some blouses, a lightweight jacket, two pairs of jodhpurs, two pairs of riding boots and some underwear. You know my sizes. Now off you go. I have a story to write.'

He sighed and, despite himself, gave her a grin. As he left, her head was down and, once again, her pencil was flying across the paper.

Inderjit arrived back three days later, uncomplaining about having to turn around and make the return journey so quickly. Troops continued to arrive in the town, trebling its population, so that the streets were choked with horses, wagons and marching soldiers and causing dust to rise everywhere. Fonthill sought the aid of the wife of one of the senior officers in shopping for Alice and he and his two companions spent the rest of their time gathering equipment together.

Once again they became Pathans, loosely dressed in homespun garments, criss-crossed with bandoliers and under precariously wound turbans. They were issued with modern Lee-Metford rifles but Fonthill eschewed the offer of horses. Pathans rarely possessed them and although they were esteemed by the natives as symbols of wealth, in practice they were often a hindrance in the rough scree and rocks of the hills.

Lockhart included Fonthill in his briefing and planning meetings. There, Simon learnt that the Orakzais had now undoubtedly been roused from their torpor by the mullah and had moved forward in some strength in the lower reaches of Tirah – just the route by which the general proposed to begin his invasion. Isolated outposts on the Samana Ridge had been attacked already, producing acts of outstanding courage by sepoys, particularly Sikhs.

In one engagement at Saragarhi, on a 6,500ft-high ridge, a remote signalling tower defended by just twenty-one sepoys of the 36th Sikhs under a *havildar*, held out for seven hours against huge odds before being engulfed. The defenders were all killed and mutilated, one being burnt alive. Nearby, the little fort of Gulistan then became besieged and held out for forty-eight hours before rescue came just as the garrison was running out of ammunition. The fort was commanded by a Major Des Voeux, whose problems were compounded by the fact that his heavily pregnant wife and two children were within the fort. Mrs Des Voeux gave birth immediately after the fort was relieved.

The tale of both these heroic defences were eagerly seized on by the hardened veterans of Fleet Street who had now gathered in Peshawar to report on the Pathan Uprising and their stories were to form part of the rich pageant that always shrouded the history of India's North-West Frontier.

The prodigious efforts involved in sending relief forces to Fort Gulistan and other outposts under attack also provided Lockhart with proof, if any were needed, of the difficulties he must overcome in terms of providing his troops with provisions, particularly water, as they penetrated deeply into the barren wastelands of the Tirah.

Alice eventually left hospital and joined the ranks of the war correspondents gathering in Peshawar. Despite her absence from their ranks for several years, she was welcomed by the other veterans there – a welcome tinged with respectful suspicion, for her name had long been linked in the profession with a string of exclusive stories cabled back over the years from far outposts of the Empire.

That suspicion was also fuelled by the fact that she did not stay with the rest of them in the tented compound provided for the press just outside Peshawar, for she preferred to remain with her husband in their small hotel. 'What is that woman up to?' was a frequent question asked around the card tables and over the whisky in the compound. But nor was this an easy time for Simon, Alice and their two companions in the hotel.

'Why the hell doesn't the bloody man advance?' demanded Alice of her husband one morning at breakfast. 'If he waits much longer the mullah will die of old age.'

'And snow will have closed the passes.' Simon nodded. 'But it must be one hell of a job provisioning an army of this size for such an undertaking. For one thing, Lockhart can't get enough mules and for another he has to solve the problem of carrying water in this climate over broken terrain. He tells me that he has been attempting to round up more than forty-two thousand pack animals – mules, donkeys, horses, even camels – to carry all the provisions and equipment that his two divisions will need. You can't exactly get these sort of animals overnight. And I know that he is worried that some of troops from the plains are going to have difficulties in fighting in mountains with slopes as steep as the sides of a house.'

He stopped because Alice had begun scribbling quickly in her ever-present notebook. 'I'm not sure I should be telling you all this, Alice,' he said. 'You mustn't take advantage of me.'

'Oh stuff,' his wife muttered. 'How many animals did you say? Was it forty thousand?'

'Something like that. As you know, the general is concentrating his troops in the south at Kohat, which has the benefit of being served by a reasonable road from the east, although the nearest railhead is miles away at Khushalgarh. He has pushed his advance force further west, some forty miles or so to Shanawari on the Samana mountain range. It looks as though that is going to be the jumping-off point for the penetration into the Orakzai heartland. I don't think it will be long now before the invasion proper starts.'

Nor was it. Within days, Lockhart had moved his staff on to the Shanawari fort and it was there, on a late afternoon in early October, that he called on Fonthill to join him on the ramparts of the fort. He lifted his arm and pointed between the hardened mud battlements to the north, where the road wound upwards and disappeared into the hills, now coloured mauve as the sun began to sink.

'That's the way we will be going, Fonthill,' he said. 'I am hoping that road will lead us right over the Samana range and into the central Orakzai tribal lands at Maidan. So get out early in the morning, with your two chaps, and scout ahead as far as you can go within the next few days. I want to send the whole of my second division up there – and you know that that's a hell of a lot of troops to move along one road. The Pathans know we are here, of course, and they can probably guess which way I am going to move. So I need to know if the road can take us and the sort of strongholds they are likely to hold ahead. Use your soldier's eye and prospect for me. Be back within a week.'

He took off his spectacles and wiped them with a handkerchief and his pale-blue eyes now looked directly into those of Fonthill. 'But for God's sake,' he continued, 'be careful, my dear fellow. Those mountains are bristling with Pathans and I don't want to lose you just days before the advance. Set off well before sunrise so that you can get into the hills before you are seen leaving the fort.'

Fonthill looked up into the line of the hills, now rapidly turning from mauve into a deep blue as the sun dipped behind the distant high peaks of the Hindu Kush. Those hills seemed empty but, somehow, full of menace. Overhead a crow croaked.

There seemed nothing to say except, 'Very good, sir.'

That evening Simon left a note for Alice who was due that day to begin the move from Kohat to Shanawari with the rest of the correspondents, and then, shortly before 3.30 a.m., he, Jenkins and Inderjit slipped out of a little post gate at the rear of the fort and began walking up the road to the north. They carried with them their rifles, sleeping bags slung over their shoulders, water bottles filled to capacity and enough dried meat, biscuits and hard-skinned fruit to last a week.

As the sun came up, the road divided and, with no map to guide them, Fonthill mentally tossed a coin and decided to take the right fork. Very soon after, they left the road abruptly, took shelter by its side and ate breakfast. Mainly, however, they sat in silence and listened. No one, it seemed, was following them and nor did the road disgorge any travellers journeying the other way. The hills, indeed, did seem to be empty.

They trudged on, always climbing until, in the distance,

they saw an old man tending scraggy sheep grazing on the hillside.

''E's wastin' 'is time,' grunted Jenkins. 'There's not enough fodder in this place to feed three gnats an' a tortoise.'

Without breaking the rhythm of their steps, Fonthill turned to Inderjit and nodded ahead. 'Let's not alarm him, so keep walking towards him steadily. When we're abreast of him call up to him and tell him our old story – we've walked from Persia to join the Mullah Sayyid Akbar to fight the infidels. Ask him if he knows where his camp is.'

The Sikh nodded and they continued their plodding pace. The shepherd seemed completely unconcerned by their approach and grunted a greeting as Inderjit climbed up the few paces off the road towards him and offered fruit. They conversed for a few minutes with much gesticulation from the old man to the north, before the Sikh nodded, saluted and fell into step with the other two as they continued their march.

'He say,' said Inderjit once they were out of earshot, 'that big army is up ahead. Many of them come from the fighting at Fort Gulistan off to the right there, about five miles. We have big climb to do . . .'

'Oh, bloody 'ell,' interjected Jenkins.

'. . . over Chagru Kotal Pass, when we are in mountains proper. Once over Pass, road which forked to left behind us rejoins this one. So both forks go in same direction, like a loop. Soon after Pass there is big hill to the left, called Dargai. It overlooks road. He say that Pathans are massing there to stop British going by. From what he say, Dargai is strong position.'

'Very well. Where does this road take us? Did he know?'

'Oh yes. It go all the way to Maidan. But long way. After Dargai road crosses Khanki river, just past place called Karappa.'

'Is the river fordable?'

'If no great rains soon, yes. But difficult later in year.'

'Go on.'

'Then we go very high over Sampagha Pass, then cross another river, the Mastura, but it smaller. But then another pass, the Arhanga Pass, which will be blocked with snow before too long. Then road takes us down to Maidan. After that he don't know.'

'Well,' growled Jenkins, 'that sounds like a nice little stroll, look you. Just what my feet need just now.'

'What about the mullah?' asked Fonthill. 'Did he know where his camp is?'

'He think the Mullah Sayyid is with Pathan fighting men waiting for British at this place Dargai. They expect to fight British there.'

They trudged on in silence for a moment. Then Simon asked, 'Is there any way around Dargai without having to take it?'

Inderjit frowned. 'Shepherd not soldier, so could not give answer to military questions. Did not like to question hard on this in case he become suspicious of us.'

'Quite right. You did well. Thank you.'

'Right then,' puffed Jenkins. 'What next, bach sir? 'Ave we learnt enough, d'yer think?'

'Certainly not. One thing is for sure. Lockhart is going to need his sappers to work on this road if it is going to take a whole division. But we need to know more. On to this pass, over it and then we must assess the situation at Dargai. It sounds as though it will be the key to Lockhart's advance, or at least the early part of it. No. Onwards and upwards.'

'Oh, bugger it. I liked it when we were in the cavalry.'

They toiled on with the ever-present sun beating down on them from a canopy of blue and the heat of its rays reminding them of why Pathans wore such clumsy but effective head coverings. All around them the brown, jagged-topped hills towered above with not another living thing in sight, except for the occasional lizard that scuttled out of sight as they approached.

Eventually, the road steepened to form a narrow defile before it fell and curled away, revealing a vista of more jumbled hilltops stretching before them.

'Why the 'ell would the general want to bring 'is bloody army this way?' panted Jenkins. His turban had become unwound, of course, and one end trailed down his back. 'There's nobody livin' 'ere except earwigs an' snakes.'

Fonthill leant on his rifle and wiped his brow. 'This must be the Chagru Kotal Pass,' he said. 'We must be getting near to the top of the Samana Range.' He pointed far ahead and to the left, where a succession of rocky billows seemed to end in two peaks, one sharply pointed and nearest to the road, forming the near horizon and shimmering in the heat. 'That must be the Dargai Heights. From here they look completely deserted.'

Inderjit squinted into the distance. 'Too far to tell,' he said. 'But plenty of rocks everywhere. Could hide an army . . .'

Simon nodded. 'Hmm. But they are just about within range of artillery based on that hill ahead.' His gaze turned to Jenkins. 'Oh, for goodness sake, Inderjit. Would you please tidy up his bloody turban? No self-respecting Pathan would walk around looking like that.'

He had hardly finished speaking before a rifle cracked and a bullet sang past his head. Then another hit the top of a boulder by Jenkins's shoulder, sending splinters of rock spinning upwards, one of them cutting his cheek.

Fonthill spun round. 'Off the road,' he cried. 'Behind the rocks quickly.'

The three ducked and ran as two more shots rang out, their echoes dancing back from the rocky walls around them.

'Where the hell are they?' demanded Simon.

'There are four,' replied the Sikh. 'High up on the right, there.' He pointed to where two wisps of smoke could still be seen hanging to a patch of scrub about fifty feet above them on the steep hillside.

Jenkins wiped his cheek. 'The buggers don't bother to shout "Oo's there, friend or foe?", do they?' he growled. 'I could 'ave been Ali Barber comin' up with the beer ration.'

Inderjit gave his slow smile. 'They don't care who we are,' he murmured. 'They want our rifles. Perhaps wrong to bring these Lee-Metfords. They much prized in these hills.'

'Well, they're not goin' to get mine.' The Welshman took off his turban, bent on his hands and knees and crawled away to the left. Then he propped his turban just below the edge of a high rock, so that only its top showed. He levered a round into the breech of his rifle and knelt before carefully aiming his Lee-Metford round the side of the rock. Two reports sounded as one, as Jenkins and the Pathan both fired at the same time.

The turban jumped as a bullet caught its top but a cry rang out as the Welshman's round found its target. A figure slumped and crashed into the shrub before rolling down the hillside and coming to a stop just above them.

'Good shot, bach,' said Inderjit, the Welsh term sounding alien coming from his bearded lips. Then he stood, released a shot and crouched down again.

'Damned if I can see them,' grunted Fonthill. 'Are you sure there are only four of them?'

'Only three now,' replied the Sikh. 'Odds even now. But don't expose yourself, sahib. They good shots.'

'Not as good as old 352, here, though.' Simon gestured to his right. 'Look. You two get ready to shoot because I'm going to make a run across here to draw their fire. They will have to expose themselves to have a go at me.'

Jenkins sucked in his moustache. 'Not a good idea, bach sir. I don't want to 'ave to carry you all the way back to the fort, now do I?'

'Well, we can't stay here all day. I'll count to three and then I'll go. Ready? One, two, three.' And, head down, Fonthill scuttled away and was just able to reach the shelter of a rock barely large enough to shelter him when two bullets cracked into it, showering rock fragments everywhere.

Two other shots rang out from Jenkins and Inderjit at the same time, however, and cries showed that they had found their marks.

'Well done, lads,' cried Simon. 'Now, Inderjit, shout to

whoever is left to come out with his hands raised, holding his friends' rifles above his head. If he does that, we will spare his life. Otherwise, it will be only a matter of time before we get him.'

The Sikh nodded and raised his voice. There was no reply but moans could be heard coming from the rocks above them.

'Let's give him a volley to make up his mind,' said Fonthill. 'Right. Now – fire!'

The three stood and delivered six shots into the rocks fringing the shrub. The bullets cracked into the stone and then ricocheted away down the Pass, their echoes thundering back as though a company of troopers had fired them. 'Shout to him again,' said Simon. 'Repeat the offer, but tell him it's the last time.'

After a few seconds, a ragged figure emerged, holding three rifles above his head and shouting something in dialect.

'He say,' interpreted Inderjit, 'two others are wounded and cannot shoot. Fourth rifle is lying on body of man Jenkins bach killed.'

'Very well. Ask him to come down to us. But keep him covered. Jenkins and I will cover the other rocks.'

Slowy, the Pathan began slipping and sliding awkwardly down the scree covering the steep slope, his eyeballs showing white in his black face. He came to a stop before the three and threw the rifles onto the ground. He made a poor sight, for his clothes were ragged and torn and his cheeks sunken.

Fonthill lowered his voice to a whisper. 'Ask him how badly hurt are his friends.'

'He say one bullet took man in head and he is dying. Second man hit in shoulder. First man killed.'

'Right. 352, hand me the first-aid kit from my bag. I will climb up and see what I can do. You come with me. Inderjit, tell this chap we are going to help the wounded but then question him and ask why they shot at us and what they are doing here. Try to find out if there are any of the Pathan army around here.'

Simon had brought a very basic medical kit with him and he and Jenkins now scrambled upwards carrying it. They found one man now clearly dead, with a bullet hole in his cheekbone, and the other lying in the shale, clutching his shoulder and moaning softly. His eyes widened as Fonthill took out his knife and he flinched backwards as the knife cut into his clothes at the shoulder. Simon revealed the wound and found that the bullet had gone completely through the shoulder and out the man's back. It was an ugly but clean wound.

'Bloody shoulder is the worst part to try and bandage,' muttered Simon as he cut away scraps of cloth from the wounds. He bathed the ugly holes with water, applied antiseptic ointment to two cotton wads and, as Jenkins helped him, he began bandaging them in place. After several attempts he managed to tie the bandage around the shoulder, watched all the time by the wounded man, whose eyes never left Simon's face. They gave him water from Jenkins's flask and left him lying in the shade.

Back with Inderjit, Fonthill drew the Sikh to one side out of the Pathan's earshot, leaving Jenkins with the prisoner. 'What did you find out?' he asked.

'They from village near here,' he said. 'Not part of mullah's army, which is at Dargai Mountain waiting for British army. Shepherd I talk with from same village. He go back and tell them that three foreigners walking on road, so they come to shoot at us here on the Pass and kill us and rob us.'

'Humph. Friendly lot. Do they suspect we were spies from the British camp?'

'No. They think we come from Persia to fight the British. He very impressed with our shooting.'

'Ah. So was I. Well done, you two. Where did they get these Martini-Henry rifles?'

'From sepoys killed at Fort Gulistan.'

'Very well. Do you know how far their village is from here?'

'He say about two miles. Not many other villages near here. Nowhere to graze animals.'

Simon wrinkled his nose. 'I don't doubt it. Now. I have done what I can for the wounded man, who is more or less able to walk. The other is dead. Tell this fellow that he must cover the dead man with stones and then help his wounded friend to walk back to their village. Tell him that if we see him again we will put a bullet in his stomach and we will surely kill anyone else from his village who tries to ambush us. We are good fighters.'

The Sikh grinned and nodded. 'I think he know that.'

They waited long enough to see the tribesman and his wounded companion limp away back in the direction of Shanawari, then the trio continued to trudge down the road, now gently descending. They met no one else after the attempted ambush on the Pass, although they walked slowly – not only because they were tiring in the hot sun but also so that they could scan the close hills on either side. As the sun was setting, the peak and squat ridges of the Dargai Heights came into sharp relief and Fonthill felt that it would be prudent to camp off the road. If the Pathan army was, indeed, at Dargai, then it would not do to blunder into its outposts in the dusk.

They found a tiny stream springing from the rocks and they were able to fill their water bottles from it. They chose not to light a fire and, as the darkness fell all around them, causing them to shiver at the sudden change in temperature, Fonthill wound a blanket around him and sat, cradling his rifle, to stand the first watch of the night as the other two crawled under their own blankets.

The night proved uneventful and as the three huddled together in the predawn, their blankets around them, Fonthill gave his instructions.

'If we carry on along this road we will soon be able to get a good look at Dargai,' he said. 'That's really all I want to do, so, if possible, I want to avoid having to explain ourselves to the mullah or anyone from his army. And I certainly don't want to join it.'

Inderjit nodded slowly. 'So we change our story, yes?'

'We do indeed. Trouble is,' Simon wrinkled his brow, 'I'm damned if I can think of an alternative likely tale to tell.'

Silence fell. Then Jenkins grunted. 'Seems to me,' he said, 'that we should stick to our original story – about comin' from Persia, with me bein' deaf and dumb and the village idiot, see, but we change the bit about us coming to join this mullah's bloody army. Just say we've got business, or somethin', further down the line, so to speak.'

Inderjit nodded. 'Yes. Horse-traders from Kandahar who sold our horses in Kabul and then were attacked near Border on way to Peshawar. We fought off bandits and took these rifles from them. We crossed border but lost our way.'

Simon pulled a face. 'It's a bit far-fetched but it will have to do. We met villagers who told us that there were horses to buy in Maidan and that's where we are heading. Yes, that will give us an excuse for marching on. It will have to do. Come on, let's go. If we are stopped, you will have to do the talking, as always, Inderjit. We must try and keep the rifles – or at least the magazines – covered so as not to invite envy.'

The Sikh nodded and they collected their meagre belongings, refilled their water bottles and made their way back to the road. As they walked they had their first close-up view of the Dargai Heights, looming to their left some 2,000 yards away. They could clearly see, at the top of the nearest ridge, hundreds of men moving like ants among the rocks.

At its nearest point, the road passed within about 1,500 yards of the base of the rocky hill and Fonthill could see that it would be almost impossible for Lockhart's force to pass it without coming under very heavy fire from the Heights. They increased their pace to obtain a better view when suddenly a group of Pathans, obviously a guard post or picket, suddenly materialised from rocks beside the road and advanced towards them, rifles levelled.

''Ere we go,' muttered Jenkins beneath his breath and gripped the trigger of his rifle beneath the fold of his cloak, as the leader of the picket, a towering man with a beard almost reaching his waist, came towards him. Inderjit, however, stepped forward and gave the man a greeting. The two remained in conversation for two or three minutes, while the rest of the tribesmen stood leaning on their rifles in a bored manner, evincing no interest at all in the three strangers.

Eventually the big man gave a sullen nod and waved them on their way.

'Did our story hold?' asked Fonthill once they were out of earshot.

Inderjit nodded. 'He not very interested in us. He want to know if we see any sign of British army advancing. I tell him we walk by fort at Shanawari and many troops there, but none coming here. He warn us not to go near Dargai Hills but to walk on and get out of way of big battle that is to come.'

'Did he mention the mullah?'

'Oh yes. He say that the priest is on the top of Dargai itself and that while he is there Pathans can't be hurt by British guns. He say one other interesting thing.'

'Yes?'

'He say mullah has built very fine house for himself up ahead somewhere in valley to show that he stay with Pathan people.'

Simon's eyes lit up. 'Did he say where?'

'Not exactly, but he think it somewhere east of Maidan.'

Fonthill made a mental note. 'I will remember,' he said quietly.

Now, however, he had more immediate tasks to fulfil. As they trudged to the north he surreptitiously studied the Dargai position. The village of Dargai itself could plainly be seen perched atop a precipitous cliff, some 600 feet or more high. It was a formidable stronghold. Sangars, walls made of piled stones, had been erected along the crest that was studded in addition by huge rocks. These positions commanded the only track up the cliff, a narrow, very rough path which zigzagged diagonally up the face, although its beginning, at the foot of the cliff, was invisible from the top.

The base of the track, however, could only be reached by another path which ran from the Chagru Kotal Pass along a narrow ridge or spur for about 1,500 yards. The track ended in an open space or saddle that would have to be crossed under the rifles of the defenders before the upward climb could begin.

Although no strategist or tactician, Jenkins had the eye of a soldier. 'I wouldn't want to cross that place under gunfire,' he muttered.

Fonthill nodded. 'A frontal attack could only be a holding one,' he said. 'We must find a way round the back of the Heights.'

'What – now?' Jenkins's tone was almost indignant.

'No. We mustn't attract suspicion. We'll try on the way back. I want to see what's ahead for at least a few days.'

'Oh strewth.'

And so they continued their march, passing through groups of tribesmen walking south towards the great battle, but none of whom paid them the slightest attention.

That night, they carefully bypassed the little town of Karrapa and camped about a mile outside it on the banks of the River Khanki in a pleasant valley. The river was easily fordable at this point and, Fonthill felt, would present no great obstacle to Lockhart's division, once it had overcome the formidable obstacle of the Dargai Heights.

For the next two days the three trudged along the road to the north, climbing over the Sampagha Pass, much higher, noted Simon, than the Chagru Kotal and presenting another obstacle to an invading army. They crossed the smaller Mastura River and looked up to the Arhanga Pass, set above the city of Maidan, the central point of the Afridi and Orakzai heartland. There, Fonthill decided that they had come far enough and should turn back to Shinawari, for they would already have difficulty in getting back to the fort within the week set for them by Lockhart. And there was the exploring to be done to find a way round to the back of Dargai.

The two days walking back to Dargai was uneventful, even though they were accompanied at odd times by tribesmen marching to join the mullah's army. Just north of the stronghold, they found a path to the west which led, a traveller told them, to the little village of Narik Suk, from which a track led over the Samana Range south to Shinawari. They took it and found the village to be little more than a hamlet, now almost deserted for its young men had gone to fight.

There they bought some fresh meat and milk and trudged on, for Fonthill was anxious to see if there was a track leading off the road to the east, providing a 'back entry' to the cliff of Dargai. They found such a route, but it was narrow, predictably humpbacked as it climbed towards a peak that Fonthill could only surmise must be Dargai. He decided to go no further. The track would provide hard going for an attacking force – if, that is, it could be reached from the south and Shanawari fort. And this, too, had to be ascertained.

They eventually arrived back at the fort, footsore, short of food and one day over their deadline. But they had made it without further mishap, with a bundle of notes and sketches for the general, now itching to launch his great attack, for the days were already beginning to feel perceptibly cooler.

CHAPTER FOURTEEN

Alice, of course, was the first to greet them on their return. She had been keeping vigil on the ramparts for the last two days, peering up the track to the north into the blue hills. She was surprised, then, to see the weary trio tramping in from the west, following their detour to seek an alternative route to attack Dargai. With a light heart, she ran down the steps and through the gates of the fort to throw her arms around her dust-coated husband.

'You're late,' she cried. 'I've been worried sick. And you're filthy. Do you have to go so *completely* native on these occasions, Simon?'

'Sorry, darling.' Simon hugged his wife. 'Jenkins has stopped looking after me. As a batman, he's become useless.'

As they stood laughing underneath the fort's mud battlements, an orderly arrived, saluted smartly and said,

'General sends his compliments, sir, and would like to see you as soon as . . . er . . . you are free. He is in his office.'

Fonthill, gently thrust his wife aside and nodded. 'Of course. Alice, are you camped there?' He nodded to where hundreds of army tents seemed to march from underneath the walls of the fort to the eastern horizon. 'Where do I find you?'

'No, darling. The general has allowed me a tiny room in the fort. I will wait for you there.'

'Very well. Lead on, soldier.' Simon gestured to his companions. 'Come with me. I think we should all go in to see the general together.'

They found Lockhart sitting at his desk in a room that seemed hot and airless, despite the listless efforts of a punkah wallah, sitting in a corner. Fonthill was surprised to see how unwell the general appeared: his face was grey and sallow, his cheeks were sunken and his tunic was unbuttoned at the throat. He remembered that the man suffered from ill health and had been recalled to lead the campaign from sick leave in England.

Nevertheless, Lockhart's eyes lit up at the sight of the three and he shook hands vigorously enough with them all, Inderjit standing rigidly to attention for his first meeting with a general. 'Thank God you have returned,' he said, waving to them to pull up three chairs. 'I was beginning to feel I had sent you on a hopeless mission. Now,' he picked up his little bell from the table and shook it, 'let's have some tea and I want you to brief me as quickly and comprehensively as you can. Start now.'

Simon took out his notes and rough maps and put them on the old soldier's desk. Then he recounted their journey, particularly describing the narrow pass at Chagru Kotal, the second and probably more difficult defile at Sampagha Pass, but spending most time on the problem awaiting the general at Dargai.

'You can't get round it,' he explained, 'so you will have to take it. I believe it would be extremely difficult to attack it from the road here.' He described the cliff face, the plateau beneath it and the sangars lining the top by the village. 'However, there is a way you can approach Dargai from the west, although the approach is extremely difficult for a large force. If I may, I suggest that you split your command and attack the place from front and back, so to speak. The frontal attack, from the main road, though, will be extremely difficult, so it should just be a holding operation, to draw attention from the main thrust from the west, here. This is the way we have just returned.'

The general adjusted his spectacles and studied the rough sketch presented by Fonthill. 'Hmmm. What about the main north road, here? Does it go all the way to Maidan?'

'Yes, although we didn't have time to penetrate that far. It's rough all the way and it will be a difficult march for a division-sized force. The road splits just north of the fort and you could send part of your force round on this loop road, so avoiding the Chagru Kotal Pass. But mountain batteries should get up to the Pass and would just about be in range to shell Dargai from the top there.'

'Good. I have been sending sappers out to repair the

road but they've come under attack and I have had to put out units to protect them, so the work has been slow. But . . .' he looked at the rough map Simon had drawn, silent for a moment, his chin resting on his fist. Then he made a decision.

'Yes. I will adopt your plan, Fonthill.' His finger traced the way that Simon and his companions had returned to the fort. 'I will send Brigadier Kempster with his 3rd Brigade to mount the main attack on Dargai from the west and the rest of the division will put up a show at the front here.' He looked up, 'Any chance of sending a flanking force to come across the hills from Fort Gulistan, here, arriving at the Chagru Kotal from the east?'

'Don't know, sir. We didn't have time to explore that way, but there seemed to be several tracks entering the top of the Pass from the east.'

'Good. We must move quickly now, for winter is approaching. We shall march in three days' time. You will be in the van with me, going directly north, Fonthill, to lead the way.' He smiled. 'With your two-man army. Well done, gentlemen.'

'Thank you, sir.'

'Now go and get something to eat. Ah . . . one last thing. Did you see any sign of the mullah?'

'No. But we were told that he is at Dargai, ordering the defence. And we heard that he has built himself a large house to the east of Maidan.'

'Splendid. I want to nail this chap, if I can. Cut off the head and the body collapses, you know . . .'

'Quite so. I would welcome the chance of tracking him

down, sir. I have a personal score to settle with him.'

'Of course. I remember. But I wouldn't want the man assassinated and made a martyr. I want him brought back so that we can try and hang the blighter. Let's talk about it after Dargai. Now, go and get some food and put your heads down for a while. Thank you for all you have done.'

'Nice old stick,' said Jenkins, once outside the office. 'No mention of a VC or promotion to general, though, was there?'

That afternoon, to a background of thumping feet overhead and the distant barking of army commands, Simon made love to his wife for the first time since they had left the Guides' depot at Marden, weeks before. Afterwards, as they lay intertwined on Alice's single bed in her stuffy broom cupboard of a room, near the ramparts, she told him that the story of her capture and escape had appeared in The *Morning Post* and that she and he had become household names throughout Britain.

Simon eased her head off his shoulder with a grimace. 'I never wanted to become famous,' he grunted. 'And would you mind moving, you're making my arm numb.'

'Sorry. This bed wasn't made for two. And wouldn't it have been better if you had had a shower first before crashing into my room like that?'

'Certainly not. The general has rationed the water here, and anyway, it's time I was granted my conjugal rights.'

They giggled together and Simon kissed the scar on her forearm. 'We were told that the mullah is waiting at Dargai to lead the defence there,' he murmured. 'I think I have the general's permission to go after him. Mind you, I intend to get the bloody man with or without Lockhart's approval.'

Alice levered herself up from the pillow and looked down at him. There was no laughter in her eyes now. 'If you do,' she said, 'this time I am coming with you, whatever you say. You forget that I have a score to settle with the man, as well.'

'Certainly not. Women are not supposed to settle scores. That's what husbands are for. Now, can you move over a bit? I could do with just a few minutes of sleep if you will allow me.'

Jenkins and Inderjit were allocated a small tent together outside the walls of the fort but Fonthill slept with his wife in her tiny room for the next three nights. The encampment around the fort swelled by the day as more troops arrived from Kohat. Simon watched from the battlements as columns of sweating troops marched in from the east: Highlanders, swinging their kilts; Indian cavalry, their long lances protruding from the dust clouds they threw up; Sikhs, anxious to avenge their comrades killed at Saragarhi and Gulistan; jaunty little Gurkhas; and, marching more slowly, battalions of English regiments of the line.

Fonthill noted with approval that the 2nd Derbyshires had washed all the pipeclay out of their belts, straps and pouches and soaked their equipment in tea to stain it khaki. They had also discarded the shiny black covers of their mess tins and dulled them to prevent them reflecting the sun and so betraying their movements to the enemy.

This army meant business. Long lines of baggage

supported the marching men. Simon learnt that Lockhart – the seasoned veteran of many campaigns in all seasons on the Frontier – had ordered that each man should be provided with a waterproof sheet, three blankets, a cardigan, a knitted 'Balaclava' helmet or nightcap, his home service blue serge trousers, mitts, a spare flannel shirt, socks and boots, all carried for him in the supply train. The soldiers themselves carried a rifle, 100 rounds of ammunition, a haversack containing the day's rations and any personal items they could cram into it, their water bottle, mess tin and, strapped under the waistbelt, a rolled-up 'Guthrie' or khaki serge over-jacket. The general knew that the hot days of summer, demanding khaki cotton drill, sun helmets and puttees, would soon be behind them high up in the mountain passes that lay ahead.

On the third day, at 4 a.m., Brigadier Kempster's 3rd Brigade marched out of the fort and began their long and demanding march to launch the main attack on the Dargai stronghold from the west. At Fonthill's suggestion, Inderjit went with them as guide. Shortly afterwards, the larger column snaked out and took the partly widened road to the north, splitting into two as the track divided. Simon and Jenkins marched with the general's party in the van, their destination the Chagru Kotal Pass.

Mountain batteries had been sent on ahead beyond the Pass to a north-south ridge called Samana Suk, protected by units that had marched in over the hills from Forts Gulistan and Lockhart to the east. Their task was to 'soften up' the Pathans on Dargai Heights. On arrival, though, it was clear that, at this extreme range, the little 'screw guns' brought up in dismantled form on the backs of mules, were largely ineffective against the rocks and sangar defences that bristled on top of the Heights, some 3,500 yards away. They barked away, but to little obvious effect.

Lockhart and his staff had joined the guns at Samana Suk but had bequeathed command of the frontal attack down below to Brigadier Westmacott whose 4th Brigade were under strict orders not to attack until Kempster had arrived to launch the main attack from the west.

It was clear that, as Fonthill had reported, Westmacott's men, now poised on the spur below, would face a most formidable task in attempting to cross the open ground at the foot of the cliff and then climbing upwards along the narrow path that zigzagged diagonally along the cliff face.

'Damn it,' swore Lockhart, sweeping the top of the Heights with his field glasses, 'where the hell is Kempster?'

The Pathans at the top of the cliff could clearly be seen firing tokenly on Westmacott's men out of range below them and offering derisive gestures, inviting them to climb up the path. Fonthill, at Lockhart's side, suddenly felt Jenkins dig him in the ribs.

'Top of the bleedin' cliff, bach sir,' he whispered. 'Standin' on top of them rocks, look you.'

Simon shaded his eyes and peered across the divide. He could only see tiny figures atop the rocks, individually indistinct at that distance. He turned to one of the general's ADCs. 'May I borrow your binoculars for a moment?'

He focused along the ridge of the sangars. Nothing. Then he stiffened as into focus came a familiar figure:

tall, turbaned and clad immaculately in long white robes. He caught a flash of white teeth in the dark face as the man hurled abuse down at the soldiers below. The Mullah Sayyid Akbar in person!

The general turned to his staff. 'I'm not waiting any longer,' he said. 'We can't be caught up here in the dark without the Heights being taken.' He scribbled a note to a subaltern. 'Take this down to Brigadier Westmacott. He must attack at once.'

Fonthill sucked in his breath. For Westmacott to advance across that open plateau at the foot of the cliff and then climb upwards in the face of the fire from above seemed suicide. Then he focused on the white-clad figure again. The man's grin seemed to extend a personal invitation even at that distance.

He handed the glasses back and stepped forward to the general. 'May I have your permission, sir,' he said, 'to join Brigadier Westmacott in his advance? I may be able to give him some assistance on the spot.'

'Me too, General bach,' echoed Jenkins.

'What? Oh, very well. But take care, both of you. I don't want to lose you.'

Fonthill seized a rifle from a startled trooper standing near, as did Jenkins to the man's companion. 'Lungers too, sonny,' grinned the Welshman. 'No time to give you a chit, but we'll bring 'em back, see, I promise. Yes, the bayonets, as well. Two of 'em. General's orders, look you.'

There had been no opportunity at the fort for Fonthill and Jenkins to be issued with European clothes or uniforms and they still wore the Pathan clothing in which

329

they had travelled. So if it was unusual to see two bearded tribesmen standing in the general's circle and conversing easily with him, it was even more startling for the two soldiers to have their rifles seized and be spoken to in the thickest of Welsh accents. Fonthill and Jenkins had been issued with armbands marked with the emblem of a Union Jack, to mark them as 'friendly' should they become involved in the battle, but they did little to reveal their European identity.

Grabbing the rifles and fixing the long bayonets at their muzzles, the two ran to the rear and began descending, in leaps and bounds, the steep slope that wound down to where Westmacott and his officers were standing on the spur. His brigade were strung out behind him to the little village of Mamu Khan, out of rifle shot from the Pathan defenders, although a section of the 2nd King's Own Scottish Borderers were deployed where they could open volley fire at a distance of about 750 yards onto the cliff crest.

Panting, Fonthill and Jenkins joined the little group of officers just as Westmacott was reading the general's orders.

'Good day, Brigadier,' said Simon. 'Fonthill, sir. The two of us scouted this position for the general last week and we have his permission to join you on your advance. He thought that perhaps we may be able to help.'

The brigadier, a slim man sporting the conventional florid face and full moustache of an old India hand, looked up from the note and gazed in surprise at the articulate Pathan standing breathing heavily before him.

'Brigadier Kempster's brigade has not arrived from the

west,' continued Simon. 'The general knows that a frontal attack will be difficult but he can't afford to wait for Kempster any longer in case he is caught out here when night falls.' He pointed ahead. 'You can't see from here, but when this track turns up ahead you will come out onto an open space, plateau-like, which will expose you to open fire from the defenders on the cliff top.'

The brigadier turned to the young subaltern who had delivered the order from the general and raised a quizzical eyebrow.

'True, sir,' said the young man. 'Mr Fonthill is on the general's staff and has been with him on the march.'

Westmacott nodded. 'Very well, Fonthill. Glad to have your help. Yes, I've seen that damned open space from up above. Is there any other way around?'

'No. Your men will have to double across. But once across, at the bottom of the cliff, the overhang will protect you from fire from the top. So you should be able to regroup there before starting the climb. But I'm afraid you will come under fire again about a third of the way up. Then, it will be a case of head up and go. The general will continue to direct fire from the screw guns at the top. We can lead, if you wish.'

'What? Very well. At least you have reconnoitred this infernal place.' The brigadier turned to his officers who had hung back a little to allow him to read the message.

'Gentlemen,' he said. 'Kempster has failed to arrive so we are ordered to launch a frontal attack on the Heights immediately. As planned, the first battalion of the 3rd Gurkhas will lead, followed by the 2nd Kings Own Scottish

Borderers, with the Northamptons in reserve.' He nodded to Fonthill and Jenkins. 'These . . . ah . . . chaps are the general's army scouts and they will show the way and lead up the hill.'

He turned to a young Gurkha lieutenant. 'Benyon. There is a section of the Northamptons back down the spur. Kindly instruct them to begin blazing away at those heathen on the top in . . .' he checked his watch '. . . exactly four minutes. The mountain guns will also give us covering fire. Any questions? No? Very well. Join your men, gentlemen, and good luck.'

Within less than a minute, the little brown men of the Gurkhas, in their tightly buttoned lightweight jackets and pillbox hats, began moving forward along the spur. Their rifles remained slung behind their backs but they had all drawn the wickedly curved kukris, with which Fonthill had heard they could sever the head of a buffalo from its body with one stroke.

He and Jenkins shouldered their way to the front, where the Gurkha colonel was waiting with his second-in-command and the lead company commander. They were formed up on a ledge that marked the beginning of the open space but in dead ground from the crest.

'I suggest, Colonel,' said Simon, 'that we charge across this space in companies, not all together, and form under that overhang at the cliff bottom. That will give impetus and unity to the attack.'

The colonel gave him a sharp glance. 'Very well. Pass the word back, Major. We will go one minute after the covering fire begins.'

Fonthill slipped the bolt on his rifle to put a round up the breach. He could see the beginning of the path up the cliff and it looked a fearsome climb. He felt hot breath down his neck.

'Excuse me, bach sir,' said Jenkins. 'But you know I can't stand 'eights, like. I'm goin' to be terrified up there. When we climb that bloody path, would you mind if I go on the inside, see? It would be better for me.'

'Good idea. Stay with me.'

'Mind you, I think these little buggers are goin' to be sprintin' up past us by the look of 'em. Bit younger than us, look you, an' faster.'

Simon turned to Lieutenant Benyon, who had returned to command the lead company. 'When we reach the top, old chap,' he said, 'I've been given instructions to capture the Mullah Sayyid Akbar – tall fellow, in white flowing robes – who is supposed to be leading the defence. If you get up before me, don't let your men kill the bastard. I am supposed to be bringing him back alive.'

Benyon grinned. 'I'll do my best, old boy, but it might be a bit hectic . . .' His words were cut short by a whistle blown from high above. Immediately, the mountain guns opened up, quickly joined by a succession of rifle volleys from the Northumberlands back along the ridge. Then a second whistle sounded, much nearer this time, and Fonthill shouted 'Let's go!'

In later years, looking back on that fearsome charge across the open ground, Simon's abiding memory of it was the noise. The whistles alerted the Pathans in their fastness, just as they signalled the advance to the attackers, and so to the cacophony of the screw guns firing across the open divide and the volleys of the Northumberlands on the ridge were added the cracks of the tribesmen's rifles firing down and the whine and ping of their bullets as they thudded around Simon and Jenkins and the lead Gurkhas. This spur, or saddle, was only some two hundred yards long and thirty yards wide so that it was impossible for the attackers to spread far to minimise the target. Even so, only one man fell as the company raced across the open ground to huddle with Fonthill and Jenkins at the foot of the cliff.

Simon waited until they all had regained their breath and then he yelled 'Up now', and the order was repeated in Gurkhali. The ascent was steep, narrow and dusty, but enough rocks showed through the surface dust to give the climbers grip. Despite the narrowness of the track, Fonthill was soon overtaken by a clutch of grinning Gurkhas, who seemed to be in competition to be first to the top. Then a panting Lieutenant Benyon, revolver in one hand, alpenstock in the other, also passed him, attempting to keep pace with his men.

Simon looked around and reached a hand out to Jenkins, who, ashen-faced, had flattened himself against the cliff wall as the little men bounced by. 'Come on, 352,' he yelled. 'Don't look down. Last one up is a sissy. Take my hand.'

His outstretched hand was grabbed by the Welshman and somehow the two climbed on up, now in the midst of the agile little Nepalese, whose kukris glistened in the sun as they swung on by. 'Keep going, old chap,' called

Fonthill. 'We've got to get there before that mullah gets away.'

Soon they were out again in full view of the riflemen behind the sangars at the top and the noise of their bullets as they bounced off the rocks and sped off into infinity was even more deafening than the crack of the rifles themselves. The mention of the mullah seemed to give Jenkins some kind of impetus, because his short, stout legs began to move with power and he now easily matched Simon as the two moved on up the cliff path.

It soon became obvious, however, that the fire from the Pathans had slackened considerably. Looking up, Simon could see now hardly any rifles protruding downwards from the line of the sangars as the first of the Gurkhas broke out onto the crest. He heard their yell of triumph. Had the defenders broken and run?

Soon, he and the sweating Jenkins crawled over the top and saw nothing but tribesmen in full retreat, dodging between the houses of the village and being sent on their way by a handful of kneeling Gurkhas firing at their retreating backs.

'Can you see the mullah?' yelled Simon at Jenkins.

'Can 'ardly breathe, let alone see anybody. But it looks as if 'e's well and truly 'opped it.'

Fonthill scrambled up to the top of a large boulder and directed his gaze at the retreating figures, most of them now well in the distance. There was no sign of anyone in white, flowing robes.

'Damn,' he swore. 'If only we had cavalry.'

'Look, bach sir.' Jenkins, swaying perilously on top of a

335

sangar, was pointing away to the west. 'That's why they've all 'opped it, look you.'

Simon swung round and shielded his eyes. Far away – perhaps a mile – he could just make out the flashes from the kukris of Kempster's Gurkha scouts leading in his brigade. Despite their formidable defensive position, it was obvious that the Pathans had become unnerved by the bombardment from below, the sight of the Gurkhas bounding up the cliff path and, then, the prospect of being attacked from the west as well.

Fonthill caught the eye of Benyon. 'Congratulations,' he called. 'I don't suppose you saw any sign of my mullah when you reached the top, did you?'

The officer slid his revolver back into its holster. 'As a matter of fact,' he said, 'I think I did, white robes 'n' all. But couldn't get near him. As soon as we came over the crest, he was off like a shot on his fine stallion, leading the retreat, of course. Sorry I couldn't nab him for you.'

Simon gave a rueful smile. 'Not your fault. I shall just have to stay on his tail – and I will. But you and your chaps did well.'

Benyon shook his head. 'Not really. If these fellers up here had kept their discipline and continued firing down on us, we would never have made it. They were Orakzais, though, that's why they left so sharply. They are not fighters, really. If they had been Afridis, we would have had a real scrap on our hands.'

The Gurkha colonel then appeared over the edge and shook hands with Benyon and Fonthill and then, after a brief hesitation, with Jenkins, whose turban was now completely unwound and hanging down his back. 'Well done, all round,' he said. 'Phew. I wouldn't want to have to do that climb again.'

'What does the general plan now, sir?' asked Benyon.

The colonel sat down on a rock and wiped his brow. 'Well, now that these heights are taken, this means that he can advance over the Chagru Kotal to Karappa and establish both his divisions in the Khanki Valley before forcing the Sampagha and Arhanga Passes further north. Trouble is that his 1st Division is still marching up from Hangu in the east, so I suppose he will have to leave both brigades here to hold this place until it comes up before he can advance.'

The Gurkhas had now arrived in Dargai in force and soon Kempster rode in with his brigade, Inderjit sitting his horse in the van in some embarrassment.

'Not my fault we are late,' he confided to Fonthill. 'Road so bad that we had to return mountain battery and hospital carried on mules to fort at Shinawari, with escort. Column too bloody big in first place, bach sir. Should not have been sent out so bloody big, you know. Guides would have been here hours ago.'

The Sikh's obvious disgust and unaccustomed use of bad language – and the adoption of Jenkins's method of addressing him – forced a grin from Fonthill. He put an arm round Inderjit's shoulder. 'Not your fault, old chap,' he said. 'Your arrival seems to have frightened off the Orakzais, anyway.'

It was now well past noon and the Scottish Borderers and Northamptonshires too had now climbed the cliff face so that the Dargai Heights were completely occupied by the two brigades. It was, then, a complete surprise when a signal arrived from Lockhart ordering that the position was to be abandoned immediately, with both brigades descending as soon as possible.

Throughout that hot afternoon the retreat went on, delayed to some extent by the need for the wounded – seven of the attackers had been killed and thirty-five wounded – to be carried laboriously by *dhoolies*. Fonthill and Jenkins delayed their own descent for they were anxious to gain information about the mullah from the few Orakzais that had been detained.

With the help of Benyon, who spoke the native dialect fluently, they learnt that the priest had, indeed, fled quickly as soon as the defenders at the cliff top had broken. But to where? Few could be certain, except to offer the opinion that he had gone to rally support from the Afridis in the north, where he now lived. They were still questioning when shots were heard from that direction, where the ground sloped away through the village.

'New attack coming,' shouted an officer of Kempster's staff. 'You had better get down the cliff quickly.'

'Bloody 'ell,' swore Jenkins. 'I can't get down that bloody path quickly, to save me life.'

'Yes you can.' Simon grabbed his arm. 'We can't stay here to be caught in another battle.'

Clutching hands, they followed Benyon, who soon left them behind, down the winding path to the sound of heavy gunfire echoing behind them over and round the top of Dargai. It was clear that, heartened by the sight of the retreating British, the Pathans had returned – perhaps strengthened by the warlike Afridis – and that what was at first seen as a leisurely, unimpeded retirement from the Heights had been converted into a fighting withdrawal against heavy odds on ground favouring the enemy.

Somehow, through the late afternoon and fast approaching dusk, Kempster managed to remove his brigade down the cliff face and across the saddle as Lockhart's mountain guns maintained their covering fire at the tribesmen now thronging the Heights. Then began the exhausting march back in darkness to Shinawari. It was 11 a.m. before the rearguard – Fonthill, Jenkins and Inderjit among them – reached the safety of the fort.

'Why the 'ell did we 'ave to run up that bloody cliff and then bugger off down it again, all in one day?' asked Jenkins, predictably. The answer came the next day, when the reason for the general's decision was passed on by Alice, who had attended a press briefing.

'It seemed that Lockhart felt that once the Heights were taken the Orakzais would not return,' she said. 'With his 1st Division still on the march, he could not hold Dargai *and* maintain a long line of communication back to Shinawar with just the 2nd Division, which was provisioned only for a one-day operation. In addition, there was little water en route. What he didn't bank on was the Heights being retaken. I gather they are being held in force now, not by the Orakzais but by the the Afridis – a much tougher proposition.'

'What does he intend to do now?'

Alice sighed. 'Well, I'm afraid that he is going to receive

much criticism back home for this, but, you know, he is now quite a sick man. So he has put General Yeatman-Biggs in command of the advance and is moving to Fort Gulistan to exercise overall command from there. It's higher and should be better for his health. Yeaman-Briggs feels that he cannot go forward without taking Dargai – as you have always contended.'

'What? Do you mean that the hilltop will have to be taken all over again?'

'Precisely. The advance begins tomorrow. And I am going with it, as part of the press contingent.'

A silence fell on the little room. It was broken by Jenkins. 'Well, bach sir,' he said, 'I'll fight this mullah bloke meself with me bare 'ands if I 'ave to, but, with great respect, I'm not goin' up that cliff path again, even if the good Lord was to give me wings, see.'

Fonthill looked at his wife. 'Well, if you are going with the advance then we will, too. But unless God is going to make an angel of Jenkins, I think we will sit out this second assault on Dargai. Now, however, if you will excuse me, I am going to see the general before he leaves.'

The force which set out for Dargai the next morning marched imbued with a grim air of determination. Fonthill noted with approval that the same troops were not being asked to repeat their climb of two days before and Brigadier Kempster's brigade, which had formed the rearguard on the retreat down the cliff, was assigned to make the assault. On arrival, Kempster scanned the cliff top with his binoculars. 'As I thought,' he muttered, 'Afridis. This is not going to be easy.'

The press corps remained with the commanding general, now Yeatman-Biggs, observing the action from the hilltop of Samana Suk – much to Fonthill's relief – but he and Jenkins were asked by Kempster to guide the attacking force once again along the spur to the edge of the saddle, although they were not requested to take part in the climb. This time it was the 3rd Ghurka Scouts who were given the honour of leading the attack, backed by the 1/2nd Goorkhas, with the Dorsets and Derbys under cover behind and the formidable 1st Gordon Highlanders still further back, among the rocks, in reserve.

Once again Fonthill and Jenkins crouched with the Ghurkas on the edge of the open space of the saddle, on the ledge away from the rifles of the Afridis above, as the protecting barrage opened up. Then the whistle blew and the little brown men surged over the edge. They were met with an immediate hail of bullets from above and men fell but most of the Scouts were able to reach the momentary safety of the cliff overhang. The second rush of men, however, drew even more intensive fire onto them, and Simon, watching with Jenkins from behind a rock, winced as men fell screaming.

A Major Judge led the next charge and was immediately shot in the eye. He continued to stagger forward, however, to be shot dead in the centre of the killing field. Lieutenant Colonel Travers, the CO of the 1/2nd Goorkhas had somehow managed to reach the cliff face and yelled back orders to stop further runs across the saddle but, in the din, he was not heard. Within ten minutes the Scouts and the 1/2nd Goorkhas had sustained seventy-one casualties and attempts to bring in the wounded were being thwarted by the sharpshooters up above.

'This is murder,' growled Jenkins. But there were insufficient men at the foot of the cliff path for an ascent to be begun. The Goorkhas had shot their bolt so now it was the turn of the Dorsets. These were not hillmen, like the Gurkhas or the Afridis themselves and they had only recently marched to the Border from the peaceful pastures of regimental cantonment life in southern India. Back along the spur, they had been attempting vainly to direct fire up to the cliff top to help their comrades. Now, without pausing they jumped down from the ledge and into the overhead fire.

They ran in company sections and they fell as they ran, the officers picked off first by the Afridis up above, many of whom had served as sepoys and knew how to distinguish the leaders from the men. Tears came to Fonthill's eyes as he witnessed many individual acts of bravery as men attempted to bring back the wounded and were themselves brought down. Some were able to find poor shelter at an outbreak of rock halfway along the spur but once there they were trapped, as were the men crouching at the bottom of the cliff path.

Of the Dorsets, only two officers and a handful of men dashed right across or reached the halfway rocks. There was now a crush of men huddled with Fonthill and Jenkins on the ledge of the spur, either wounded or waiting for some opportunity to run the gauntlet. A second attempt by the Derbys was made and it, too, failed. Their commander, Lieutenant Colonel Dowse, suggested to the Dorsets' colonel, Piercy, that he should move his men back so that the other Derby companies could try a rush across in mass. To this Piercy would not agree, nor would he allow his remaining four companies to run into the hail of bullets. It was now 2 p.m., four hours after the attack had begun. It was also stalemate on the spur.

'What the 'ell are we goin' to do?' hissed Jenkins, forced, like Fonthill, to watch the butchery without being able to do anything to alleviate the cries of the wounded. To move away from the ledge onto that open ground was to invite death or a fearful wound.

Simon shook his head. 'God knows.'

But Brigadier Kempster had one last card to play. From behind the men crouching along the ridge came the skirl of bagpipes and cries of 'Step back, step back, make way for the Gordons'. These were the men who had marched in two days before from the west with Kempster. All Highlanders and therefore hillmen and possessing the dubious advantage of having formed the rearguard on the retreat two days before, and so knowing the ground, they were veterans of many years fighting the Pathans along the Border. They came now, pushing their way through, kilts swinging, men with stern, set faces, for they knew what lay before them.

Fonthill and Jenkins exchanged glances.

Somehow, the Scotsmen formed up along the edge of the saddle as the English soldiers fell back along the ridge to make way. Their CO, a white-haired colonel with a comfortable paunch showing above his kilt, thrust his way to the front and surveyed the scene. He then gestured for his men to close up. Not for Lieutenant Colonel Mathias of the Gordon Highlanders the failed rushes by sections or companies. His men were going to charge across that body-strewn space in full battalion order.

Then, the batteries began firing up above, all twenty-four guns firing in unison to rain shells on the peak. Mathias stood, tugging at his moustache, until the barrage ended. Then he held up his hand and cried, 'Highlanders. The general says that the position must be taken at all cost. The Gordons will take it.' A bugle blew, the pipers struck up 'Cock o' the North' and the colonel, with Major Macbean on his right and the appropriately named Lieutenant Gordon on his left quit the safety of the spur and led the charge across the saddle.

Once again all hell broke loose and Fonthill and Jenkins watched in awe as the full battalion doubled en masse across the open space through the hailstorm of bullets. Piper Findlater immediately went down, shot through both ankles. He hauled himself to a rock, however, wedged his back against it and continued to play throughout the attack, urging the Highlanders onwards. Major Macbean fell, shot through the shoulder, five more officers were killed at once and many more men collapsed and fell. So thick were the numbers running across the open ground that it seemed impossible for the Afridis to miss.

And yet, whether it was because they were running out of ammunition or aghast at the impetus of the full battalion charge, the defenders' fire began to lessen. The sound of the pipes, the cheering of the men and the sight of the Gurkhas now running up the cliff path with the Gordons close behind them, were too much for the mixed bag of English infantrymen still pressed back on the ridge. They, too, now cheered and began running across behind the Gordons, skipping between the wounded and the inert bodies.

'Can't stay here, 352,' cried Simon. 'Come on. Up that damned cliff.'

''Ang on. Don't go without me. I'm right be'ind you.'

Just before the summit, the two comrades came up behind Colonel Mathias, now puffing and being pushed up the climb by an NCO. The colonel turned, nodded at Fonthill with a grin and observed to his colour sergeant – in words which would go down in Border lore – 'Stiff climb, eh, Mackie? Not so young as . . . I . . . was . . . yer know.'

To which the NCO slapped his commanding officer on the back in comradely fashion and replied, 'Never mind, sir. Ye're gaun vera strong for an auld man!'

To Simon and his old comrade, the sight at the top of the cliff was reminiscent of that of two days before. In the distance could just be seen the backs of the tribesmen – now, it was confirmed later, a mixture of Afridis and Orakzais – being fired at triumphantly by the victorious Indian and British soldiers.

'Ah damnit, no sign of the mullah,' panted Fonthill.

'Well, we know 'e's not the type to 'ang around, now, is 'e? I doubt if we'll ever see the bugger again, look you.'

Simon narrowed his eyes and looked after the retreating tribesmen. 'Oh yes we will,' he muttered. 'I'm going to sort it out with Lockhart. We're going after him.'

The Welshman's face gradually broke into a weary grin. 'Well, that's good news, that is. No more climbin' bloody cliffs. I'll sign up for that, bach sir. I'll sign up for that all right, look you . . .'

CHAPTER FIFTEEN

This time there was to be no vacating of Dargai, so expensively captured, and the Goorkhas and the Dorsets were posted on the Heights and the remaining battalions around Chagru Kotal. The cost of the second attack had been high. In all, 197 casualties had been sustained by the units taking part, more than three times more than those received during the first attack.

The journalists, including Alice, set themselves to singing the praises of the regiments involved, particularly the Gordons – always a favourite of the public back home – and there was some criticism of Lockhart's decision to abandon the Heights after the first success. Even so, when General Lockhart rode into Chagru Kotal the next day, looking refreshed after his brief sojourn in the fresh air of Fort Gulistan – or was it merely relief after the success of the second attack on Dargai? – he shook Simon's hand warmly.

'You would have been up for a decoration for your part in leading the attack on the first day, my dear fellow,' he said, 'but in the eyes of the army you are a civilian, I'm afraid, so that's ruled out. But I will see what I can do in some non-military area.'

'No thank you, General.' Simon shook his head firmly. 'I seem to have gained enough notoriety already. Jenkins and I were just happy to do what we could. But there is one way in which you can help me, sir.'

'And what is that?'

'I want your permission to go after Mullah Sayyid Akbar. I caught a glimpse of him on the cliff top and I am sure that he was responsible for riding off to rally support to the Orakzais and bring up the Afridis—'

Lockhart raised a hand to interrupt him. 'You are quite right. Our intelligence, such as it is,' and he turned his eyes to heaven, 'confirms this. The feller has escaped somewhere to the north. This revolt will never be put down completely, Fonthill, until he is in custody or hanging from the gallows.'

'Quite. So you will release me to go after him?'

'Yes and no. We have just had a success here, albeit an expensive one, but impetus is important, so we must get on to take the two passes up ahead, the Sampagha and Arhanga. They are the gateways to the Tirah itself and, of course, to Maidan, the heartland of the Zakka Khel Afridis, the toughest nuts on the whole of the Frontier. I expect to be harried all the way, with perhaps another battle at the Sampagha Pass. You will be needed to go ahead and guide us until at least there.'

'And then?'

'The word is that the mullah is headed for the Waran Valley. There is a river of that name that runs east from Maidan.'

'Where he has built a grand house?'

'Exactly. When we are nearing Maidan I shall unleash you, but not until then. But Fonthill . . .'

'Sir?'

'I shall want you to find the damned chap and then come back and tell me where he is. No heroics. I understand that he travels with a fairly large bodyguard so don't tangle with him. Once we know his whereabouts we can go in to get him. This will not be a personal vendetta. Understand?'

Fonthill closed his eyes for a second. There was no way he was going to offer promises at this stage about what would happen if he came within shooting distance of Sayyid Akbar. But that could wait, so he nodded obediently and said, 'Very good, sir.'

As soon as provisions had come up from Shinawari and the line of communication back to the fort had been consolidated, Lockhart's great caravanserai continued its march to the north, passing Karappa and climbing now continuously but meeting only sniping, particularly at night when camps had been established.

Ranging far ahead of the van, Fonthill, Jenkins and Inderjit were able to confirm that the Pathans had gathered at the 7,000ft-high Sampagha, approached by a valley three-quarters of a mile wide and guarded on either flank by spurs running down from the main ridges. These spurs had been occupied by the tribesmen, who had built stone sangars along their sides, so dominating the approaches to the Pass.

It was, reported Fonthill, a task for the guns.

Lockhart sent them forward in a meticulously planned operation during the hours of darkness, so that the batteries could open fire at a range of 1,850 yards as soon as the first rays of the sun streaked down from the mountain tops. As the barrage exploded onto the loosely stacked stones, the Pathans withstood it for twenty minutes before breaking and running. Under cover of the guns, the 2nd Brigade advanced and the barrage was lifted to attack the higher sangars around the summit of the Pass. Within minutes, all of the enemy – who turned out to be the Orakzais – had fled and the first of the gateways into the Tirah heartland had been forced, with the loss of only twenty-four casualties.

Anxious to exploit the success, Lockhart descended down into the fertile little Mastura Valley, and then pushed on again to the north. towards the second 'gateway', the Arhanga Pass. Once again hardly any opposition was met and the Pass was taken, with only two men wounded. By the next evening, the Tirah Field Force was camped at Maidan. The 'purdha curtain' had been torn aside. Would the Orakzais and Afridis now submit?

It was a question discussed by Fonthill, Jenkins, Inderjit and Alice, who joined the trio in their tent late that night for warming cups of tea. Simon had seen little of his wife during the advance, for she had been esconced with the Fleet Street contingent, moving with the general's staff, and he, with his companions, had been out from morning until dusk, scouting ahead of the main army.

'Does the general feel the job is virtually done, Alice?' asked Simon.

Alice sipped her tea and shook her head firmly. 'I understand that there are signs,' she said, 'that the Orakzais, whose territory has been completely traversed by our march from the south, are beginning to think of submission. But my old friend the mullah is said to be doing his stirring up to the east, in the land of the Zakka Khel Afridis.'

'Ah.' Fonthill's eyes lit up. 'Will they oppose the general, full on?'

'He thinks not. The thinking is that it is now going to mean constant harassment as the winter comes on. A guerrilla war, in fact, which indicates a long slog while the army scours the whole Tirah region.'

Alice looked around her as they huddled together by the light of the solitary oil lamp in the little tent. She grinned involuntarily at the three men, all sitting cross-legged, steam rising from their mugs of tea. She could, she reflected, be deep in the heart of the Afridi camp.

The beards of all three were now fully grown so that they reached down to their chests and their eyes glowed in faces burnt almost black by the sun and winds that had scourged the passes. In their loosely wound, dun-coloured clothes, 'pile-of-washing' turbans sitting atop high-cheekboned faces and with bare toes protruding from their sandals, they looked every inch tribesmen of the North-West Frontier.

'You know,' she said, 'I hardly recognise any of you. You have really *become* Pathans.' She turned to Simon. 'So now, husband of the hills, what do you propose to do now? Will there be any role for you three in this guerrilla warfare?'

'Oh yes. Now that we are at Maidan, I intend to keep the general to his word and allow us go out and find the mullah.'

The smile disappeared from Alice's face. 'What? Just the three of you?'

'If he will let us go alone, yes. You said yourself that we now make good Pathans and my dialect has improved considerably under Inderjit's tuition. We can now move in these hills without creating much suspicion. Why, we were even fired upon the other day by a British patrol up in the Arhanga.'

'But it will be terribly dangerous, Simon.' A quick shudder ran through her. 'That man is a monster and he is not to be taken lightly. He is no coward. He stormed through the defences of the Khyber fort leading his men. His sword was bloodstained . . .' Her words died away. 'Please don't go. This could be one mission too far.'

Fonthill exchanged glances with his two companions. Jenkins sniffed. 'Oh, 'e's determined to go, Miss Alice,' he said. 'And so are we two. This moollah bloke seems to 'ave an 'abit of escapin' from big armies, see. We think it's goin' to take us three,' he grinned, 'the finest Pataaanis in the 'ole British an' Indian armies, to nab 'im. But we'll do it, you'll see.'

Alice turned her glance back to her husband. 'All right, then. If you go, you really must take me with you.' As her husband drew in his breath to speak, she leant forward and put a hand on his knee. 'Look, the *Post* has sent someone out to help in reporting on the campaign. It's stupid having two of us attached to the general's staff. I am not needed.

But, Simon, I could be really useful to you. No one will suspect you if you have a woman with you who looks as native as you three.'

Simon scowled. 'You have made that point before. There is absolutely no question of you coming, Alice,' he said. 'Don't pursue the matter, darling. That's the last word on it.'

Silence descended on the tent. Outside somewhere a campfire spluttered and a horse stamped his foot and snorted. 'Very well,' said Alice. 'I shall apply for a widow's pension from the general straight away.'

Three days later, Fonthill was summoned to the command tent of General Lockhart, who was sitting with an old acquaintance, Colonel Fortescue of the Queen's Own Corps of Guides. The colonel's jaw dropped when a ragged-robed Pathan loped through the tent opening.

'Good Lord, Fonthill,' he gasped. 'Have you joined the enemy?'

'Thought about it a few times, Colonel, in the last few weeks. You get better food than in the British army.'

The two shook hands and then Lockhart outlined the task ahead of Fonthill. He was to ride out east, along the Waran river, but with a squadron of Guides Cavalry – whose regiment had just ridden in to join the field force – and ascertain the whereabouts of the mullah. Then they must return as quickly as possible, without engaging with the enemy, to lead in a larger force to capture him.

'I suggest,' said Fortescue, 'that you ride with Appleby-Smith's squadron. You did good work with them in going out to Kabul and back and at least this means that *Daffadar* Singh can be reunited with his troop.'

Simon's heart sank. He had no wish to join forces again with that pompous, hesitant soldier. If he was to go out into the Waran Valley to flush out the mullah with a protective force, then a squadron of Guides would be the optimum unit to accompany him: not too large and cumbersome, but big enough to fight off any force that did not outnumber them hugely. Most of all, it would be nimble and mobile enough to get out of trouble quickly. And he had never fancied combing the valley for the mullah on foot.

But Appleby-Smith . . . !

He realised that his silence was proving awkward. He cleared his throat. 'Very well, sir,' he said. 'I presume and hope that young Buckingham and his troop are still part of the squadron?'

Fortescue seemed not to have noticed his hesitation. 'Oh indeed,' he said. '*Daffadar* Singh can slip right back into his unit.'

'Good. Now, General, do you have any intelligence about the exact whereabouts of Sayyid Akbar?'

'I'm afraid not. He's out there to the east, somewhere. You tell me he's built a house somewhere in the valley. I suggest you slip away from the squadron and see what you can pick up from the villages. But, take care, Fonthill. Take care.'

'Very well, sir. We will leave as soon as the squadron is ready.'

That evening, Alice joined the three of them again in

their tent. Inderjit seemed less than joyous at the news that he would be returning to Appleby-Smith's unit.

'I can say, bach sir' – he had taken now always to emulate Jenkins when addressing Fonthill – 'that this sahib not the most popular officer in the Guides. He not sure of himself in action, which is bad for us all. You know what you do, although you no longer a regular soldier. This man does not know.'

Alice frowned. 'Ah, I can see, Inderjit, that this must be the last thing you would want.' She turned to Simon. 'Can't you ask to ride with another squadron, darling – put some excuse forward? If you are riding into the lion's mouth, you need to be with a good lion-tamer, I would have thought. Oh goodness, I shall worry even more now.'

'Oh don't fret, Alice. Appleby-Smith's number two, Dawson, is a sound enough fellow and Buckingham is first rate. We shall get along.'

Alice's gaze rested on Inderjit. The Sikh had a habit of melting somehow into the background in discussion. He rarely offered an opinion unless directly asked. She realised that she had no idea about his personal situation.

On impulse, she asked, 'Are you married, Inderjit?'

The Sikh's grin immediately seemed to light up the interior of the tent. 'Oh yes, memsahib. Two children. Boy and girl. Boy already good cricketer like his grandfather. They live in Marden.'

Simon immediately looked disconcerted. 'Good Lord, Inderjit. I had no idea. We have taken you away from your family. Does your wife complain about that?'

The grin disappeared. 'Wife died two years ago. Of the

cholera. But regiment is very good. Children are looked after while I am away.'

It was Jenkins who broke the resultant, awkward silence. 'You obviously like goin' a-soldierin', Inja. What about the killin' bits? Does that worry you?'

The Sikh looked thoughtful for a moment. 'In battle, it does not matter. It is you or them. But I did not like killing that man in the Pathan camp. You call it "in cold blood", I think. It seemed unfair.'

Simon was about to interupt, but Inderjit continued, 'But then I think that they were threatening,' he cast a shy glance at Alice, 'to kill the memsahib. So it had to be done. And I am a soldier, after all.'

Simon exchanged glances with his wife. The tall Sikh was clearly a man of some sensitivity as well as ability, even though he said little. But the reflective turn that the conversation had taken now was enough to cast a touch of gloom over the company and, shortly afterwards, Alice exchanged a goodnight kiss with her husband and the little party broke up.

Early the next morning, Appleby-Smith brought his officers to report to Fonthill. The captain, erect but seemingly a little more portly now, looked askance at the native dress of Simon and his companions.

'Good gracious,' he muttered. 'Is it necessary for you to look like that, Mr Fonthill? You will be riding with us, after all.'

Simon exchanged a surreptitious grin with Buckingham. 'Sorry to shock you, Clarence. But it may be necessary for the three of us to leave you from time to time to see if we can pick up information. Either that, or we may decide to join the mullah.'

The jest passed by Appleby-Smith, although it brought obedient chuckles from the officers. 'When do you wish us to leave, sir?' he asked. 'We are at your disposal.'

'Not until after dark. This camp will have many eyes on it, passing information on about the comings and goings from it. We will slip away as soon as night falls. We will follow the river to the east and pull away from it to camp. It will be necessary to post double picquets, Captain.'

For nearly two days the squadron rode out east, following the line of the Waran river along the Waran Valley. Fonthill was less than happy with the outdated Martini-Henry short-barrelled carbines and sabres with which the men were armed, but the Guides were a native regiment and that was the issue, so there was no choice there.

Nevertheless, the 160 men of the squadron were well mounted and they looked a fine sight as they trotted along the riverbank in their smart, lightweight khaki tunics and riding breeches, set in place by tightly wound puttees. Their turbans were equally tightly wound and were of dark blue and cream cloth.

'Smart lot, this,' confided Jenkins. 'And bloody marvellous to be back in the cavalry, after walkin' all over this bloody country.' Simon nodded. The valley of the Waran was, as Lockhart had predicted, less mountainous than the country of the south, but he was becoming a little surprised and slightly anxious that they had met no inhabitants on their ride so far. He looked up quickly, then, towards the end of the second day, when Inderjit, who had been riding with the rearguard, came galloping up.

'I think, bach sir,' he reported, 'that we are being followed.'

'How many?'

'Just one tribesman, on horse, which is unusual. He keeps well back from us but he is following for some time now. He seems to be alone.'

'Inform the captain and ask that the man be brought in for questioning.'

Within the hour, the squadron had halted and a trap set for the tribesman, who had put up no resistance, and was brought in and told to dismount. He was a man of small stature, riding a good horse but wearing the anodyne dress of a typical Pathan. Yet he stood defiantly before Fonthill, albeit with downcast eyes of the greyest hue.

'Oh, for God's sake, Alice,' sighed Simon. 'What the hell do you think you are doing?'

'I am following you, husband,' responded his wife. 'And I could do with a cup of tea or something. And I have been very cold sleeping out at night and rather frightened. So I am glad that you have discovered me – and too far out for you to send me back, so there!'

'Don't be too sure of that. Where on earth did you get those clothes, and the horse, too?'

'Clothes in the street market and I begged the nag from the horsemaster. I have to return it in good order. He thought I was only going for an afternoon hack with one of the correspondents. But I have bought a solid Webley revolver, strictly illegally.'

'Oh Lord! Jenkins get her some tea and see if we can

rustle up a little bivouac tent from somewhere. Now, we must ride on and find a campsite before dark. Alice, you are going to be an infernal nuisance and I shall sue for divorce when we get back.'

'And I shall grant it. On the grounds of you deserting me back there in Maidan.'

That night brought sniper firing onto the camp for the first time, forcing Appleby-Smith to give orders for the dousing of all fires and making Simon thank God that Alice had been discovered and brought in when she had. 'Did you see any sign of anyone spying on us when you were out there?' he asked her the next morning.

'No. But I was too scared to fall back too far from the column.'

'Hmmm. I can't think we have got this far undetected. I sense an attack coming.'

And so it proved. The river had curled away a little to the south to meet the Mastura and the squadron had pulled, on Simon's instinct, to the north and was riding towards a narrow defile, when shots were heard from it. The forward outriders came galloping back, one of them riding closely beside his comrade, supporting him in the saddle.

'We should retreat,' cried Appleby-Smith, riding to Fonthill's side. 'Bugler! Sound the—'

'No! Take the scout's report first. 352, ride at Alice's side.'

The trooper reported that shots had been fired down on them from high up on the right of the gulley. One of their number had been killed outright and another wounded. They had been unable to ascertain how many men were hidden behind the rocks.

Dawson joined Appleby-Smith and Fonthill. 'It sounds like a trap,' said the captain. 'They want us to ride in and then ambush us. We should retreat.'

'No.' Fonthill spoke firmly. 'I agree it might be a trap. But we cannot leave one of our men and allow his body to be defiled. And, besides, I am tired of riding without seeing anyone. We need to take a prisoner to gain information. Take the squadron back, Clarence – not too far, mind you – and form a defensive position. Give me Buckingham and ten men and we will dismount under cover of that overhang there and try to go in on foot above them and take them from the rear. 352!'

'Bach sir!'

'Hand Alice over to Inderjit and come with me and Buckingham.'

Appleby-Smith, of course, was nominally in command of the squadron and Fonthill sensed that, just for a moment, the captain was considering countermanding his orders. But then the man obviously thought better of it and turned away.

'Simon, be careful.' Alice was watching with wide eyes.

'Stay with Inderjit and try your best to be quiet.' Simon grinned at his wife to offset the harshness of his words. The squadron trotted back and then, as the track curved and the overhang approached, Fonthill and his little party pulled away, dismounted and left their horses in the care of two troopers.

'I knew we'd soon be back hoofing it,' growled Jenkins.

'Come on. Up this rock here. There's plenty of footholds.'

The thirteen-man party began to climb and Fonthill

cursed inwardly for not instructing the troopers to leave their sabres behind. The long swords hung down from their owners' waistbands and clattered on the rock face. 'Be quiet,' he hissed.

They climbed upwards quickly until they found a narrow goats' path leading them directly towards the defile at a height of about sixty feet above the track. Fonthill led the party in single file along the path, his Lee-Metford rifle carried at the trail. Jenkins was close behind him, attempting not to look down, and the others trailed back, perspiration dripping down everyone's face.

At last, the path turned a corner and Simon held up his hand as, on hands and knees, he looked around the bend. Immediately, he turned back and put his mouth close to Jenkins's ear. 'They're down below,' he said. 'Pass the word to crawl forward.'

They found themselves looking down on a party of about thirty or more Pathans, all spread out among the rocks, their rifles aimed down at the track some forty feet below. They seemed quite unaware of the men above them.

'Seems a shame to pick 'em off from here,' whispered the lieutenant.

'No, it isn't. All's fair in this bloody war. 352, when I say the word, put a bullet through the shoulder of that chap there, the nearest one to us. Tell your men, Duke, to shoot to kill at the rest of them, as soon as Jenkins fires. I want to take that wounded man prisoner, if we can, and send the others packing.'

As soon as the word was passed, Fonthill nodded to Jenkins, who snuggled the butt of his rifle into his shoulder, took careful aim and pulled the trigger. Immediately, the man clutched at his shoulder and rolled over and the hillside broke into flame as the troopers began firing systematically.

It was impossible to miss at that range and, if the Guides had possessed the Lee-Metford magazine rifles instead of the single-shot Martinis, then few of the Pathans could have survived. As it was, some eight or more of them managed to disappear as if by magic into the rock-strewn terrain as the troopers paused to reload, leaving at least twenty bodies behind them.

'Send two men to get that wounded man to bring back with us,' Fonthill ordered Buckingham. 'Get another two to retrieve the body of our own chap lying down there on the track. Then we'd better get the hell out of here. We'll just have to leave their wounded. I am sure that there are more of the enemy about. They wouldn't attack us with just thirty men.'

Within twelve anxious minutes the little party was back under the overhang and were reunited with their horses. To Simon's fury, there was no sight of the squadron. 'The bloody man would have heard the shooting,' cursed Fonthill. 'The least he could do would be to send a section back in case we needed help.'

Buckingham made a face and shrugged his shoulders. It was clear that nothing about Appleby-Smith could now disappoint him. In fact, the captain had halted the squadron about a mile away and had dispersed his men among the rocks. The prisoner, his eyes wide with fear as well as pain, was brought before the officers, one of whose number began tending to the wound, while Inderjit translated.

'Tell him,' said Fonthill, 'that we will dress his wound and not kill him. We will, however, shoot him here and now if he does not help us. I want to know where the Mullah Sayyid Akbar is. I know he is near here. Where is he and how big a force does he have? We will know if he lies.'

The man's reply shocked them all.

'He say,' translated Inderjit, 'that mullah is in his big house over next hill directly ahead and very near. He has several hundred men with him. He has been following our progress along river and is about to attack us. Ambush was attempt to weaken us while he gathers more men.'

'Ah!' Appleby-Smith's ejaculation was one of great relief, mingled with alarm. 'Good. Now we have what we have come for and we can ride back to Maidan.'

'Certainly not!' Fonthill's tone was crisp. 'I intend to attack the mullah as soon as possible. If we cannot capture him then we must kill him. We need five good scouts out ahead immediately to reconnoitre the way to the house and to spy out the Pathans' encampment. When this man has been treated release him when we ride out. Tell him, Inderjit, that if we see him again with the mullah's men he will be shot immediately. Now, we have little time before those chaps in the defile reach the mullah. So we must move quickly. I fancy this is going to be some fight.'

'Mr Fonthill,' Appleby-Smith's face had turned a shade of puce. 'I am in command of this squadron and I must protest. Our orders were clear: we should locate the mullah and return to Maidan so that a proper attack can be mounted on him.'

'So giving him time to slip away again. Your protest

has been noted and no doubt you will repeat it to the general when we return. In the meantime, gentlemen,' he looked around at the officers, 'I am in command. Is that understood?'

There were muted growls of assent. 'Very well. Go about your duties. Dawson. Get those scouts out ahead, NOW.'

'Very good, sir.'

In fact, the scouts were back within the hour, revealing how close the column was to the mullah's house. It was situated, they said, in a little valley over the hill. It was whitewashed and surrounded by a low wall. There seemed only one entrance. The Pathans were camped irregularly all around the house and numbered perhaps about three hundred. The camp bustled, but cooking fires were still lit and there seemed to be no formal guards posted.

Fonthill commended the scouts and called the officers forward. Alice, unbidden, stayed at the edge, notepad at the ready. 'Now,' said Simon, 'the object of this exercise is to capture or kill the mullah – not to have a stand-up fight with his bodyguard. We must presume that Sayyid Akbar is in the house. He is easily recognisable because he always wears long white robes. We will clearly have to fight our way through the encampment to get to him, which will not be easy.'

The circle was silent and Appleby-Smith's face was as white as a sheet. 'So,' continued Simon, 'we will create a diversion to draw away as many of the tribesmen from the house as possible. Mr Dawson, you will take half a troop and ride to the west. At exactly,' Fonthill drew out his watch and consulted it, 'half past noon, you will create great noise and fuss and attack the encampment from the west. Kill as many men as possible, and then retreat, drawing away as many tribesmen as you can.

'Then the main party, led by me, will gallop through the encampment to the house. We will line the wall outside to deter attacks, while I and a small party go inside the house and . . . er . . . extract the mullah. We will then mount up and cut our way out of the encampment. If you detect that our party is in trouble, Mr Dawson, I would be grateful if you would come to our assistance. If that is not necessary, we will meet up on the western end of the defile where we were attacked and ride like hell back to Maidan. The Pathans lack cavalry so we should not be followed closely. Any questions?'

'What,' asked Buckingham, 'if the mullah is not in the house?'

'Then we find the bastard – and quickly. Is that all? Good. I would be grateful, Mr Buckingham, if you would pick twenty of your best men and join myself, Mr Jenkins and *Daffadar* Singh in the party to go into the house.'

'Honoured, sir.'

Fonthill turned to Appleby-Smith. 'I would be grateful, Captain, if you would command the men manning the wall to keep the Pathans at bay, while we enter the house to take the mullah.'

'Humph!'

The squadron rode out within minutes and once reaching the point where the path parted, bade farwell to Dawson who rode away to the left. Then Fonthill threw aside his turban and, with great caution, led the rest of the party at walking pace ahead to where, the scouts had told him, a patch of trees looked down on the encampment. There, under their cover, the squadron halted and Simon looked up to his left to a hill where he could now begin to see a small party of horsemen gathering. Good, Dawson was in position. He pulled out his watch. 12.25. No sign of movement behind the low wall surrounding the house. But it was clear that the Pathans were preparing to leave, for fires were being doused and there was great movement between the tents.

Simon moved his horse towards where Alice was sitting on her mount at the rear of the group, two troopers posted one either side of her.

'Alice,' he said, 'do not charge with us. Stay here with these men who have been instructed to look after you. As soon as we have gone in, ride back to the defile and wait for us. If we are not back within the hour, ride back to Maidan.'

His wife showed no sign of dissent. 'Very well, Simon. Good luck.'

Fonthill nodded. Then, 'The men should draw sabres,' he instructed Appleby-Smith. He looked at the man sharply. The captain was perspiring under his pith helmet, but that was to be expected in the heat.

Suddenly, there was an outbreak of firing from the hill on the left. Immediately, all was confusion down in the encampment. Drums began to beat and tribesmen could be seen hurrying back to their tents for rifles and then running up towards the firing.

'Ah!' Fonthill suddenly rose in the stirrups. From the

door of the house, a familiar figure clad in white robes appeared, stared towards the hill and then pointed and shouted to the men by the wall. They, too, began running up towards the hill. The mullah paused for a moment and then disappeared back into the house.

'Now is our moment,' shouted Simon, drawing his pistol. 'At the trot, forward!' The horsemen broke cover from the coppice and trotted down the incline towards the encampment. Immediately, some of the Pathans running up towards the hill knelt and fired towards them. One trooper fell from his horse. 'Canter,' shouted Fonthill, and then, as the squadron gathered momentum, 'CHARGE!'

Once again and for the third time in his life, Fonthill experienced the supreme thrill of leading a cavalry charge against an enemy. He was conscious of Jenkins now riding at his side and of how hot the air was as he sucked it into his lungs, then he was among the tribesmen, riding with his head down, gripping hard with his knees and marvelling at the path he was carving among the Pathans.

One man lunged at him with a spear and he fired at him but he was past him before he was aware if the bullet had gone home. He was aware of Jenkins also firing and of bullets singing past his head before the gateway in the low wall suddenly appeared before him.

Damn! He was going too fast to rein in – he would have to jump it! Waiting until the last moment, he thrust down in the stirrups and hauled back on the reins, leaning forward as the horse rose and then back as it plunged over the gate. Miraculously, he stayed in the saddle and pulled the beast's head round to halt it. He half fell from the saddle and fired at a Pathan who swung at him with a sword, bringing the man down. A pistol shot at his side told him that Jenkins had arrived and, suddenly, the men of the squadron were dismounting at the other side of the wall and running through the gate.

Fonthill glimpsed Inderjit helping the handlers to pull the horses away behind the wall and Buckingham directing men into position along the wall – where the hell was Appleby-Smith? Jenkins, limping from a sword cut high on the thigh, was at his side again.

'Inside,' he shouted and pushed aside the door to the house. A bullet immediately cracked into the wall by his cheek and another whistled away over his shoulder. He fell to this knee and fired blindly into the interior, dark after the harsh sunlight outside. Suddenly, he was pushed to one side and he became aware of Buckingham, revolver in hand, leading a party of sabre-wielding troopers into the room and immediately engaging in hand-to-hand fighting with Pathans who seemed to spill into the room. Simon caught a flash of white robes from behind the fighting as a door was opened and shut.

'352,' he called, 'are you hurt?' It was still difficult to adjust to the gloom of the interior.

'Perfectly all right, bach sir, and right beside you. Just a scratch near the arse, that's all.'

'I think the mullah has gone through a door at the back there. We must get through this mob and after him.'

'Let me go first.' The Welshman, his eyes now ablaze and completely oblivious to the blood running down his thigh, picked up a chair and charged straight into the combatants ahead, hurling friend and foe alike aside as he whirled it from side to side. Close behind him, Simon blazed away with his pistol and, suddenly, the two were facing a door at the rear.

Flinging it open, Fonthill ducked through, pistol raised, and fired as a huge man with a scar down his cheek lunged at him with a sword. The bullet took Alice's old jailer squarely in the chest and, as he fell, Simon glimpsed a white-robed man pulling himself through a window at the far end of the room. He fired quickly, hitting the wall as the mullah slipped through and the hammer of the revolver then fell on an empty chamber.

Cursing, Fonthill tossed aside the gun, picked up the sword and ran to the window. He heard Jenkins's despairing cry, 'Don't go there, he'll kill you . . .' as he pulled himself up and then fell headfirst through the open window, and sprawled onto grass on the other side. But the sword spun away from him and, as he scrambled to his knees, he looked up into the black eyes of the Mullah Sayyid Akbar.

The toe of the Afghan's boot caught him under the chin and sent him spinning down again and he rolled away as the mullah's sword thudded into the ground by his shoulder. The force of the blow, however, embedded the blade momentarily into the thick loam that lay beneath the well-watered grass of the garden and gained Simon several seconds of precious respite, enabling him to pick up his sword and stagger to his feet.

For a moment, the two adversaries regarded each other.

Akbar's teeth flashed as he grinned. 'You must be Fonthill,' he said. 'I must say, your wife screams delightfully when she is hurt. I am sorry she didn't stay with me long enough for me to cut off those delicate fingers . . .' As he spoke he sprang forward, bringing his curved sword down in a glittering arc.

Fonthill was no swordsman. Now, as he jumped aside awkwardly to avoid the blade, he shot a quick glance up at the window. The glass had slammed shut, explaining the absence of his old comrade. He sucked in his breath. Well, he reflected grimly, this is one battle he would rather wage alone. He had a personal score to pay.

The mullah now circled him, his blade held low. Simon forced himself to think. Both swords were of the Pathan type, long, curved and slightly weighted at the end. If the Afghan was going to fight in the Pathan manner, swinging his blade in a cutting motion, then that might provide just a split second of opportunity if Simon used the point to thrust, European style . . . It was, after all, the most direct path to the target.

Then Akbar was on the attack again, skipping forward – he was obviously fit and, of course, the younger man – in a series of scything blows. But Simon's weeks of campaigning and of living roughly had toughened his own frame and he found no difficulty in avoiding these advances. Until, that is, his foot slipped on the wet grass and the mullah's blade caught him on the left upper arm, causing him to fall to one knee.

'You are dead, Englishman,' shouted the Afghan. He lifted his sword to strike again and then a shot rang out. It missed the mullah, but whistled by his ear, causing him to pause.

'Get up, Simon,' screamed Alice, her head protruding above the wall as she sat her horse on the other side, 'that was my last shot.'

Her shot and her voice distracted Akbar and as he turned to look at her, Simon sprang forward, thrusting low and catching the Afghan in the chest. The sword was no rapier so the point did not penetrate far enough to kill, but it gave Fonthill the chance to pull the blade back and swing it up and then down, two-handedly, cleaving the mullah's head in two.

CHAPTER SIXTEEN

Dawson and his little party had ridden down from the hill to help disperse what were left of the tribesmen around the house and the mansion itself was then torched, with the bodies of the dead Pathans inside it. Fonthill did consider taking the mullah's body back to Maidan but thought better of it. So he, too, was committed to the flames, although his white robes were hung on a tree nearby to indicate his fate.

The squadron had lost only twelve troopers, with four wounded. The biggest loss, by far, however, came when the dead at the wall were counted. Inderjit lay there, one bullet through his chest, another through his head. He, together with the other bodies, were tied to their horses for the ride back.

The death of the Sikh overshadowed any jubilation at the victory – or any chastising of Alice by Simon for disobeying his orders. She confessed that she had no problem convincing her escort that they should join in at the rear of the charge. Seeing Simon and Jenkins disappear into the house she had, on instinct, ridden round it to the rear until she heard the mullah's voice.

'I'm sorry I didn't actually kill him,' she whispered. 'I had my own revenge to take on that terrible man.'

As they set off for the return journey, with the blackened timbers of the mullah's house as a backdrop, it suddenly occurred to Fonthill that no one had seen anything of Appleby-Smith since the beginning of the action. The mystery was solved, however, as they rode through the thicket and, on the other side, found his horse, standing above his body. He had been shot through the back and then hacked to pieces.

What was left of him was tied to his horse and Fonthill gathered the officers together. 'Gentlemen,' he said, 'I propose to tell the colonel, his brother-in-law, that the captain was killed bravely doing his duty in the face of the enemy. Let it rest there.' Everyone nodded, mutely.

Simon's wound proved to be superficial and Jenkins's to be a little deeper but not serious. It had been the loss of blood from his thigh that had prevented him jumping up and climbing through the window.

'I let you down, bach sir,' he said, gloomily on the ride back. 'It could 'ave cost you.'

'You have never, ever let me down, 352. And neither has my wonderful wife.' He reached out a hand to either side and, for a moment or two, they rode three abreast, holding hands.

Whether because of the death of the mullah or the presence of Lockhart's patrols ranging ever wider, the squadron was not harassed on their journey back to Maidan. There, Fonthill reported immediately to the general, who heard of the death of the mullah with equanimity.

'It was him or me, sir,' said Simon. 'There was no way we could bring him in.'

Lockhart nodded and, as he removed his glasses to clean them in that well-remembered action, Fonthill noticed how tired were his eyes.

'I'm glad he's gone,' he said. 'That will help hugely. This campaign is not quite over, because I expect further trouble from the Zakka Khel Afridis, particularly as we retire. But the Orakzais are coming in to surrender and the winter is coming on so the end is near. I think it safe to say that the Pathan Revolt is virtually over.

'My dear fellow, you have given yeoman service and I can't thank you enough. I shall report accordingly to the Viceroy and back to the Horse Guards. You are free to go – and perhaps get on with this holiday of yours.' He gave a weary smile. 'But is there anything I can do for you before you go?'

'Yes, there is, sir.' Fonthill leant forward and told of the death of Inderjit and of his two small children, now orphaned, back in the Guides' depot at Marden. 'I propose to bequeath a reasonable sum of money to the regiment,' he said. 'I would be grateful if you would ask Fortescue to see that it is used for the *daffadar*'s children's education and upbringing. That would be important to Alice, Jenkins and me.'

'Of course.'

That evening, as Simon sat quietly, allowing Alice to replace the dressing on his arm, he told her about his decision to help Inderjit's children. She nodded firmly in agreement. 'Do you feel guilty about his death?' she asked.

'Yes. I keep thinking of his orphaned children.'

'Well, he was a soldier and a brave and good one. If you are a soldier, you live with death. And I certainly don't feel guilty about killing the mullah.'

'No. Of course not. But, you know, he had a sort of point.'

'What point?'

'His argument about the British possessing his country. Our whole imperial concept.'

'Humph! Well, to start with, it isn't his country. He was an Afghan.'

'Yes, I know. But . . . oh, never mind.'

Alice worked on in silence for a moment, bathing the wound. Then Simon told her of what Lockhart had said about the campaign being virtually over. 'What do you think?' he asked. 'Shall we go on up to the Hindu Kush for that bit of gentle climbing?'

Alice winced. 'Do you know, darling, having been kidnapped, forced to kill a Pathan at close quarters and having nearly witnessed you being decapitated, I would value a bit of piece and quiet, however gentle the climbing. What about Norfolk?'

Fonthill sighed. 'I hoped you would say that.'

'And there's another thing. We never thought, in planning the climbing, about Jenkins.'

'What about him?'

'Remember? He hates heights. He would never have climbed.'

'Ah. I'd forgotten. That settles it, then. Wouldn't want to upset Jenkins. Back home it is, then.' He looked up in admiration at his wife, now as bronzed as him from the sun and wind of the Border. 'Could you spare a kiss, nurse?' he asked.

AUTHOR'S NOTE

As always, I must distinguish between what is fact and what is fiction in the book. Fonthill, Alice, Jenkins, Inderjit, Captain Appleby-Smith, 'Duke' Buckingham, Colonel Fortescue, Lieutenants Dawson, Barnes, Benyon and others of the minor characters are fictional, of course. But Viceroy Elgin, Generals Lockhart, Yeatman-Biggs and Blood, Brigadiers Westmacott and Kempster, Colonel Meiklejohn, Major des Voeux and his pregnant wife, Commissioner Udny, Captain Barton, the officers named in the dash across the nek under Dargai, Lieutenant Colonel Mathias, CO of the Gordons and his Colour Sergeant Mackie, who *did* push him up the cliff face there, Piper Findlater VC, who carried on playing while shot through both ankles and later made a fortune playing his pipes on the halls of Victorian Britain, the Amir of Afghanistan, the Mad Mullah who led the attack at Malakand and the Mullah Sayyid Akbar himself – they all very much existed.

I have, though, to make a confession about the Mullah Sayyid Akbar. He was certainly one of the most charismatic of the priests sent across the border from Afghanistan to rouse the Border tribes. And he did howl defiance at the British from the Dargai Heights and he also built a house that was later burnt by the British. Alas, I have not been able to discover his fate after the Revolt, nor to learn much about him personally. So I have reconstructed his character, throwing in, ahem, more than a touch of colour – his fantasising about Cambridge, Sandhurst and so on. I can only plead that any novel set against the romantic background of India's North-West Frontier deserves a villain who is robust, so I decided to manufacture one, or at least, to tweak the character of one who existed.

I have done my best to relate the main manoeuvres and battles of the Revolt as accurately as a reading of respected accounts of the time allowed. The Viceroy at the time, for instance, did send a letter to Kabul begging the Amir not to intervene in the Revolt. And the Swats at Malakand, *did* try to tempt their Afridis cousins to join them on the other side of the *abbatis* and were shot for their audacity.

Fonthill et al. had to leave Lockhart at Maidan, otherwise this book would never have been finished. But the general's apprehension about problems in 'tidying up' in the Tirah were well founded. The Afridis fought up until and into the winter, harassing the British as they tried to pull out as the snow began. Eventually, there was a conclusion of sorts. But it was virtually a truce only, for intermittent fighting continued until, until . . . well the present day.

On the very morning that I typed in the magic words 'The End', the news came through that three Scottish soldiers had been killed by Taleban insurgents in Helmund Province, not so far from where, 116 years before, their fellow Scots, the Gordons, had made their magnificent ascent of Dargai. In both cases, the soldiers were fighting jihadists. *Plus ça change* . . .

It's enough to make you weep, though, is it not?

ACKNOWLEDGEMENTS

Once again it is a pleasant duty to acknowledge the help of the staff at London Library in researching this book; the constant support and encouragement of my agent, Jane Conway-Gordon; the work of Susie Dunlop and her staff at my publishers Allison & Busby – surely the most willing and delightful bunch of girls in British publishing! – and, as ever, my wife Betty, research assistant, proofreader and loving and constant supplier of tea and coffee.

The Pathan Revolt is rather tucked away in the annals of the British Empire and I found comparatively few books of merit written about it. The following, however, were of great help:

The Frontier Ablaze, by Michael Barthorp, Windrow & Green, London, 1996 (particularly good on maps and geography).

The Savage Border, by Jules Stewart, Sutton Publishing, Stroud, 2007.

My Early Life, by Winston Churchill, published (paperback), Scribner, 1997.

The Colonial Wars Source Book by Phillip J. Hawthornthwaite, Arms and Armour Press, London, 1995.

ALSO BY JOHN WILCOX

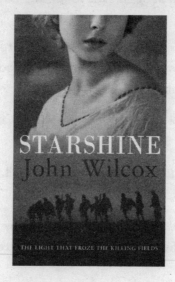

To discover more great books and to
place an order visit our website at
www.allisonandbusby.com

Don't forget to sign up to our free newsletter at
www.allisonandbusby.com/newsletter
for latest releases, events and exclusive offers

Allison & Busby Books
@AllisonandBusby

You can also call us on
020 7580 1080
for orders, queries
and reading recommendations